Claudia Carroll was born in Dublin, where ... ... nd now works as a full-time writer. Two of her previous books, *Remind Me Again Why I Need a Man* and *I Never Fancied Him Anyway* have been purchased for a TV series (Fox Television) and a film, respectively. Claudia isn't married and both titles come from phrases she finds herself using with alarming regularity, particularly after rubbish dates.

She is currently hassling producers for a walk-on part in the movie and isn't a bit fussy about what she plays, as long as they let her keep the clothes.

Do You Want to Know a Secret?

Claudia Carroll

TRANSWORLD IRELAND

TRANSWORLD IRELAND
an imprint of The Random House Group Limited
20 Vauxhall Bridge Road, London SW1V 2SA

www.rbooks.co.uk

First published in 2008 by Transworld Ireland

A CIP catalogue record for this book
is available from the British Library.

ISBN 9781848270220

Addresses for Random House Group Ltd companies outside the UK
can be found at: www.randomhouse.co.uk
The Random House Group Ltd Reg. No. 954009

The Random House Group Limited supports The Forest Stewardship
Council (FSC), the leading international forest-certification organization. All our
titles that are printed on Greenpeace-approved FSC-certified paper carry the FSC logo.
Our paper procurement policy can be found at
www.rbooks.co.uk/environment

Typeset in 12.5/15pt Bembo by
Falcon Oast Graphic Art Ltd.
Printed and bound in the UK by CPI Mackays, Chatham, ME5 8TD

2 4 6 8 10 9 7 5 3 1

Mixed Sources
Product group from well-managed
forests and other controlled sources
www.fsc.org   Cert no. TT-COC-2139
© 1996 Forest Stewardship Council
FSC

For Marianne. With love and thanks, always.

Acknowledgements

Huge thanks to the divine Francesca Liversidge; believe me, I know how lucky I am to have such an amazing editor. Thanks also to everyone else at Transworld, especially Larry Finlay, Madeline Toy, Joanne Williamson, Lucie Jordan, Gary Harley, Martin Higgins, Rebecca Jones and Vivien Garrett, for all their tireless hard work. I'm so grateful to you all.

Transworld Ireland is now officially launched, so a big hi to Eoin McHugh and Lauren Hadden; I'm really looking forward to working with you.

Huge thanks, as always, to the wonderful team at Gill Hess: Gill (the man himself), Simon, Declan Heeney and Helen Gleed O'Connor. You make life so easy for all of your authors!

Special thanks to Pat Lynch for everything and for being one of those people that you just don't know what you'd do without. And of course to the beyond-fabulous Vicki Satlow . . . please come to Ireland for a longer visit next time!

Thanks to Karen Glass in New York for all her wonderful vision. I'm so excited about *Remind Me Again Why I Need a Man* coming to the small screen and it's all down to you, Karen! While writing this book, my miracle-worker agent rang with the fabulous news that the movie rights to *I Never Fancied Him Anyway* have been bought in the US. So a huge hi to Wendy Finerman and Liza Zupan . . . this really is dream come true stuff!

Thanks so much also to all at HarperCollins in NYC, especially Carrie Ferron, Claire Wachtel, Julia Novitch and Tessa Woodward. See you all very soon, I hope.

On a personal note, thanks, as always, to Mum and Dad, Karen Nolan, Larry Finnegan, Susan McHugh, Sean Murphy, Clelia Murphy (and madam Clara!), Pat Kinevane, Marian O'Dwyer, Frank Mackey, Fiona Lalor, Alison McKenna, Sharon Hogan, Karen Hastings, Kevin Reynolds, Derick Mulvey and all the Gunn family. Old friends are the best!

Writing is a lonely, isolated gig, so I'm doubly grateful to have friends like Anita Notaro, Patricia Scanlan and Morag Prunty who've all been there before and know what it's like.

And just in case you think I've forgotten someone, this book is dedicated to Marianne Gunn O'Connor, who has become such a good friend . . . and who really can work miracles.

Chapter One

Right then, here goes.

Happy, positive things about turning, ahem . . . Well, let's just say about 'getting another year older' today.

1. I am finally able to handle my hairdresser.
2. I have learned to say 'NO', simply, clearly, emphatically and without any residue emotional guilt whatsoever. Unless it's a guy asking me out, that is, in which case, sorry, but at my age, as long as he's straight and has a job, then, hey, he passes the Vicky test.
3. I now understand the concept of Sky Plus and am able to work it. Sort of.
4. At long last, I accept each of the following, in no particular order.
- I will never carry off a pair of skinny jeans and may as well stop forking out for incredibly pricey gym membership, which invariably I only use the week before I go on holidays and am obliged to shoehorn myself into a bikini.

I am kidding no one, only myself.

- Nor will I ever become the effortless cook I once dreamed of, and I hereby vow to stop doing my usual trick of buying ready-made meals from Marks & Spencer, then artfully arranging them in oven-proof dishes, while disposing of the packaging, or hard evidence, if you will, in the outside bin so that none of my more devious friends (Barbara Fox, take a bow) will suspect that I'm a dirty big cheat. This, also, fools no one but me. Particularly as Barbara does most of her shopping in Marks & Spencer too.

5. I'm now scarily advanced into my thirties and still single. The time has come to accept that, unless I'm prepared to go down the grade-A-gay-sperm-and-a-spatula route, I will never have a child and will end up one of those sad old ladies in retirement homes who no one ever visits at Christmas, except kids from the local school and only then because it's part of their detention.

Ouch, ouch, *ouch*. That last one really hurt.

6. Furthermore, just while I'm doling out tough love, I will now stop believing that fortune-tellers, palm readers and psychics hold the key to my future. Every year I go to one, every year I'm promised that my future husband is out there for me, and every year he's a no-show.

Honest to God, if I ever do meet the poor idiot I'm destined to spend the rest of my life with, the first thing I'll do is smack him across the face and tell him it serves him right for being so bloody unpunctual.

7. And while we're on the subject of monumental let-downs, the time has come for me to come clean and finally accept that feng shui isn't all it's cracked up to be either. Embarrassment prevents me from recording on these pages how much I forked out for a self-styled 'lifestyle and home-design guru' (I am *NOT* making this up), to call out to my house, make me shift the TV out of the relationship corner, and then place pictures of lovey-dovey couples in my south-west corner with big lumps of rose quartz beside them. She then gave me a daily affirmation ('love does not conform to schedule'), and told me that I should really stop panic-dating, tell myself I'm a goddess and fully embrace my aloneness.

And there was me thinking you had to go to a hairdresser for that kind of deep, psychological insight.

Right, enough's enough. Decision made. At the grand old age of, ahem, never you mind, I hereby make this, my solemn vow. No more clairvoyants, psychics, mystics, cosmic ordering, on-line tarot readers or spending ages in the office pretending to be working when in actual fact I'm checking out my astro-logical compatibility with whatever guy I happen to be daydreaming about at the time. Time to act my age and leave my destiny in the very capable hands of the universe.

Yes, love it, brilliant plan.

Oh yeah, except that ... emm ... maybe I'll just start tomorrow.

Well, the Mind, Body, Spirit, Health and Healing Exhibition is on after work tonight, and I can't very well miss out on that, now can I?

Birthdays are so fabulous, the one day out of three hundred and sixty-five when you are allowed full emotional leverage over your best friend to drag her along to absolutely anything, against her will, with the promise of a lovely sushi meal afterwards plus as many margaritas as she can handle. My best friend, the aforementioned Barbara Fox, is just fabulous, you'd love her. When I grow up, I want to be her. We've been mates ever since primary school, all the way through college; and as Barbara always says, men may come and go, blue eyeliner and the bubble perm may come and go, but true friends are like the Manolo slingback or the Hermès Birkin bag . . . here to stay whether we like it or not. In all our years of friendship, we really have been through thick and thin together; thick mostly. And, in short, like I always joke with Barbara, my love for her is a bit like my appendix scar. Ugly and permanent.

So anyway, I drag her off to the exhibition, kicking and screaming. I'm not messing. Only my solemn promise that, come her birthday, I'll be her white slave for the day and will even go to one of her beloved rugby matches with her, should she so decree, shuts her up.

'This is what community service must feel like,' she whinges as we head into the packed hall, forking out twenty euro just for admission. 'Deliver us from drivel, that's all I ask, and if anyone comes near me with a crystal and threatens to cleanse my chakras, I'm so outta here.'

Barbara, I should point out, is absolutely cynical about anything remotely other-worldly and is probably the only woman I know who doesn't even bother reading her horoscope. I, on the other hand, will try anything once, and by that, I really do mean anything. I even did a novena to St Clare at one point, a few years back now, which, according to my mum, has never EVER been known to fail. Mum, the polar opposite of Barbara, is staunch Catholic, a daily Mass-goer and so deeply religious that she's still not over the death of Pope John Paul II.

'I can't take to that new German, Benedict or whatever he

calls himself,' she's always saying. 'The eyes are far too close together for my liking.' Then, with a heartfelt sigh, 'Ah sure, there'll only ever be the one Pope.'

Anyway, I was just so knickers in love with this particular emotionally unavailable guy (invariably the usual type I attract) that even if it meant going down on my hands and knees to Heaven for things to work out, then that's what I was prepared to do.

The novena itself was straightforward enough, all you had to do was say nine Hail Marys for nine days and it promised to deliver three favours for you, one personal: 'Dear St Clare, if he's the right man for me, then please let things work out with . . . well, let's just call him Mr X.' One professional: 'Please can Barbara get the part she's up for in that movie with whatshis-name, your man who used to be James Bond, she's a resting actress and hasn't worked in so long that she's actually starting to wonder if the profession is any different now, and this would be the big break she really needs, please, St Clare, ah go on, go on, go on.' And one impossible: 'Finally, please can I be happily married and pregnant within a year, St Clare . . . well, you did specify impossible, didn't you?'

You should have seen me. I was like Aladdin discovering the magic lantern and making my three wishes, but, wouldn't you know, the success-rate of that particular excursion into Catholicism was zero out of three. Although to be brutally honest, I didn't really expect it to work anyway, on the principle that life just isn't like that really, is it? Mum had the last word on the subject, wisely pointing out that God is not a bit impressed with people like me who don't attend church, don't do anything they're supposed to do, and then expect favours to be lavished on them, just because they bothered to ask. Ho hum. Back to the drawing-board.

The exhibition hall is jammers and when we eventually do

get inside, we're immediately approached by this hippy-dippy-looking guy wearing open-toed sandals, at a stand with a sign in front of it saying, 'Cosmic Orders Accepted Here!'

Well, actually it would be more correct to say that he approaches Barbara, who's just one of those women who guys seem to lose their reason over. We all have a Barbara in our lives, you know, those rare, lucky, lucky women who men just fall over themselves to go out with, begging them for dates. *Everyone* fancies her. Now, she is fabulous-looking, in a tall, lean, leggy, titian, curly-haired way, kind of like Nicole Kidman pre-Tom Cruise and most definitely pre-Botox, but for her part, she does absolutely nothing to encourage this reaction from guys. And I should know, over the years I've practically studied her modus operandi in action, on the off-chance that I could pick up any dating tips from her. Honestly, at this stage, I could probably write a thesis on her behaviour in bars alone. But Barbara really, truly, genuinely isn't looking for anyone special and just effortlessly flits from relationship to relationship leaving a trail of broken hearts behind her.

Theirs, I hasten to add, never, ever hers.

I don't know what her gift is, but the best way I can describe it is like this lethal, man-eating pheromone which she exudes from her pores that says: 'You can ask me out, or not, whatever, frankly I couldn't be bothered, I'd rather stay home and watch my DVD box set collection of *Lost*' . . . and men go *bananas* over her. The irony is that here's me dying for a fella I can call my own, and they run a mile from me, whereas all Barbara has to do is be her fabulous, non-committal, nonchalant self and they immediately turn into her slobbering lapdogs.

I swear, she was a 'Rules' girl before they'd even invented the term, but never with marriage as her end goal; she's just having a laugh and casting her dating net wide, as she calls it, all the while waiting for her big break in showbiz to come along. We often talk about this: I moan about how I'm turning into a human man-repeller and she jokes about how unemployable she feels, and how every single casting she now goes to, the parts invariably go to younger, perter, perkier twenty-some-things, so hungry they'd scratch your eyes out just for a walk-on part in something . . . *anything*.

Fab wing-woman that she is though, Barbara invariably points out that while I may be single and whinging, I am doing pretty much my dream job, which I do have to admit is true. I run my own PR company, by the way, and yes, I am very, very lucky. It's great crack, there's always loads of lovely invites to launches, and more freebies than I or my pals can sometimes handle. And business is booming so much that I've had to take on two extra staff, so no complaints there. In other words, while Barbara has a string of guys practically impaling themselves to ask her out, I, on the other hand, may be on my own, but at least I do have disposable income.

We're always telling each other, if we could just somehow trade life problems, we'd be grand.

Anyway, back to the exhibition.

'Peace be with you, ladies, would you care to place an order with the cosmos?' asks Sandal Man, and I'm not joking, the combined whiff of garlic, incense and stale BO from him is making my tummy churn a bit. Talk about taking a holiday from hygiene . . .

'*What* did you just ask me?' Barbara practically snarls back at him, reacting as if he'd asked her for the loan of a kidney. I decide the best thing is to exercise extreme tact and diplomacy here, and gently steer her away.

'This way, honey, you're not ready for cosmic ordering,' I say firmly. 'But it was worth the admission price alone just to see the look on your face.'

'Cosmic *ordering*? Explain please, in words of one syllable.'

'Well, the theory is, instead of asking the universe for what you want, you order it, with a set delivery date and all, then you relax and forget about it and just wait for it to happen.'

'So, let me get this straight, it's a bit like the way you used to write into *Jim'll Fix It* when you were ten.'

'Sort of, yeah.'

'And has this cosmic whaddya call it ever actually worked for you?'

'Emm . . . well, you see . . .'

'Yes or no?'

'OK, not really, no, but then I worried and stressed about things NOT happening fast enough for me, and that just delays delivery, apparently. When you order something and let it go, it acts like an express order on the universe. At least that's what the book says.'

'God, you sound like such a prescription-pad job. Lucky for you I'm your friend and therefore non-judgemental at the amount of money you waste on this crap.'

'It is NOT crap, and what's more, I'm going to prove it to you.'

I take a glance around at the aura consultants (no, Barbara would run a mile), channellers (ditto), and face-readers (let's not even go there), before I hit on something.

'Right, come on then, whether you like it or not you are having your tarot cards read. You have no choice, it's my birthday.'

'OK then, but I'm telling you now, you're only allowed to use that once today.'

'And it goes without saying, as a trade-off, I'll do anything you want come your birthday. Anything.'

'Oh birthdays, *please*. What's to celebrate? My bum dropping another inch?'

There's a fortune-teller sitting behind a very official-looking desk, so I steer Barbara over. She's doesn't look anything like those Mystic Meg types you see in magazines, you know, all dressed in black with beaded headscarves, beads hanging out of them and with three teeth in their head, saying, 'Cross my palm with silver, lovie.'

No, this one almost looks like she might work in the passport office; she's even wearing a suit, which I feel might appeal to Barbara's, ahem, no-nonsense nature. I plonk her down, fork out fifty euro for the reading and tell her I'll be back in ten minutes and that on no account is she to make a bolt for the exit when I'm not looking.

Then I spot another fortune-teller just across the hall, oooh, yes . . . *now* we're talking. This woman looks right up my alley, she has a crystal ball in front of her and a sign that says SHARON, SPIRITUALIST, SHAMAN AND SAGE TO THE STARS. There's even a photo of her standing beside Oprah Winfrey, so that proves she must *really* be good, mustn't it? I mean, everyone knows Oprah is like this total entrepreneurial genius on top of everything else, so she'd hardly waste her time with a complete messer/chancer/con-artist, now would she?

All excited, I sit down, hand over another fifty euro, shuffle the tarot cards that Sharon the Shaman hands me, then give her back ten, exactly like she asks. There's a long pause as she looks at the layout in front of her, but I'm supremely confident, full-sure that she'll predict that a soul mate will enter my life any day now, whisk me off my feet, and plonk an engagement ring on my finger quicker than you can say 'Boodle me, Baby'.

Oh yes, and then, I'll ask Barbara to be my bridesmaid and my friend Laura to be matron of honour, and I'll definitely have to try on a few of those empire-line dresses that you see in all the Jane Austen adaptations, and I might even get a wedding planner because I've just waited so bloody long for this that I want it to be bigger, longer and costlier than all of Liz Hurley's put together . . .

'Mmmm, all right then, love,' says Sharon the Shaman, 'just by looking at your cards here, I can tell that you're a nurse.'

'Emm, no.'

'A doctor?'

'Nope.'

'But you definitely work around hospitals, love.'

'Sorry.'

'But you've . . . *been* in a hospital. No doubt about it. Recently, too.'

'Well . . . only to visit my dad when he had his cataracts done, but that was, like, over two years ago.'

'Yeah, yeah, that's it, that's what I'm seeing here. Hundred per cent. The cards never lie, lovie. Oh, here we go, *now* I see what you do for a living, you're a teacher, then. Primary school.'

'I'm afraid not.'

'But there's no doubt you work with small children. I see you mopping up a lot of pee.'

Bloody hell. I wonder if Barbara's getting on a bit better than this.

And if the fifty euro is refundable.

'For the love of God, can we please leave now?' Barbara says, when we meet up, precisely ten minutes later. (Considering these people work in an esoteric field, the length of time they dole out to you is incredibly precise.) 'I need a margarita and a cigarette, in that order.'

'What did your one tell you?'

'Oh please, don't even go there. Apparently, I'm going to be pregnant by next Christmas and give birth to a girl that's my great-great-granny's reincarnated spirit. Pathetic. For the love of God, can we go now? This place pushes the parameters of sanity.'

Right, that's it, I officially give up. I'm just about to admit defeat and steer her towards first the exit and then the nearest bar, in that order, when something catches my attention.

'Anything you want in life is yours, if you just *ask, believe and receive*. It's as simple and as profound as that,' a woman with long, red hair, the palest skin I've ever seen, and an American accent is saying. 'Some of the greatest minds throughout history knew this truth. It's in the oral traditions of some cultures, it's in philosophies, in literature, and you'll even find it in religions right down through the centuries. There's nothing new in what I'm here to tell you.'

You should see her, she looks like an angel and is speaking soft and low, but with such absolute conviction, it stops me in my tracks. And Barbara too, I notice. She's standing on a sort of podium and almost looks like she's giving a seminar, with a microphone in one hand and a sheaf of notes in the other. But there's only one other person in the audience listening to her, a fair-haired girl about my own age.

'But I've been asking for the right man for years now,' this girl is saying, almost pleading. 'And all I meet are uninterested, unavailable morons. Now either my emotional sat-navigational system is waaaay off kilter or I'm doing something wrong. And believe me, I will pay good money to be told what that is, so that I can fix it, move on, and who knows? Maybe even find some tiny modicum of happiness in this life.'

Red-haired woman puts the microphone down and steps down from the podium to where the girl is standing. It flashes through my mind that this is actually a nice, sensitive thing to do. After all, there are some conversations you don't want any-one overhearing. Barbara and I are hovering close, not wanting to seem rude, but at the same time, dying to know what she'll say.

'The law of attraction is available to you at any time. It's working as often as you're thinking. The question you need to ask yourself is, *why* am I attracting the wrong kinds of men into my life? What is it that I need to learn here? What's the universe trying to teach me?'

OK, that's it, I can't contain myself any longer. Fair-haired girl doesn't exactly look impressed with this answer and moves off, so I'm in like Flynn.

'Excuse me,' I say in a voice I barely recognize as my own, 'but I couldn't help overhearing and . . . well, I can fully sympathize with that lady's dilemma. I hope you don't mind the interruption.'

'That's OK,' says red-haired woman, smiling kindly, 'that's why I'm here.'

'Ask, believe, receive? Is that true? Can you explain to me then how come I've been asking to meet my husband for what feels like decades now, and there's still no sign of him?'

'So, what have you learned?'

God, for a total stranger, this one really has that unflinching, direct eye-contact thing down pat.

'Ehh, don't calculate your Weight Watchers points in front of a guy on a first date, and don't keep asking him what he's thinking at regular two-minute intervals, or the chances are, he'll crack. There you go, all my unsuccessful dating years summarized in two concise bullet-points.'

I'm aware that I'm making light of it to cover up how defensive I really feel, plus I'm also conscious of Barbara standing close to me. I'm actually glad of that; I want her to hear this for herself.

'Then I can help you,' says red-haired woman, nodding sagely, like she's seen my type a thousand times before. Which, let's face it, she probably has. 'The law of attraction couldn't be simpler, really. Your thoughts determine your destiny. It's a well-proven scientific fact that like attracts like. When you talk about dating, all I can hear in your voice is negativity, a woman who is *expecting* to fail. If you expect failure, then that's all the universe is going to deliver. A simple mind-switch is all you need to change your entire life, and the choice, my dear, is yours.'

Her words hang there and for a minute I can't say anything. I'm too busy thinking, could this total stranger actually be right? Am I so busy focusing on how rubbish my love life is, that all I'm creating is even more of that?

Then Barbara's over, all businesslike with her 'you just watch me while I put manners on this one' face.

'May I just point out,' she thunders, 'that my friend here runs a highly successful business, so to make out that she's attracting negativity all around her . . .'

'Oh, do you? Tell me a bit about your business,' red-haired woman interrupts, shutting Barbara up.

'Oh, well, yes, it is doing very well,' I say, a bit wrong-footed.

'It's doing brilliantly, actually,' says Barbara defensively. 'Go on, tell her about the contract with the cosmetics company.'

'Well, you see, we're up for a huge contract and I won't know for another few weeks or so whether we have it or not, but I think it's pretty much in the bag.'

'You see?' smiles red-haired lady. 'Even your tone of voice changes when you're discussing an area of your life where you feel confident. You absolutely believe that success will come to you, so of course it will. How can it not? Your very thoughts are attracting it to you as we speak. That's the thing about the law of attraction, ladies, it's very obedient.'

'So how come I'm virtually unemployable as an actress then?' Barbara demands and I can instantly tell this one is *really* getting to her. 'Here I am trying to attract a decent gig for myself and . . . big, fat nada.'

'What are you doing to attract the right part to you?'

'Everything. I learn the lines, do my homework, turn up and pray very hard that the two-hundred-odd hot chicks in the casting queue ahead of me will all drop dead so the job will be mine. Simple.'

Red-haired woman just looks at her. Doesn't even raise her voice, nothing.

'You're attracting failure because clearly, that's what you expect. In fact, it sounds to me that you're so busy focusing on what you *don't* want to happen that, in actual fact, all you're doing is attracting jobs for other people.'

'Now hang on a minute here, I don't go into auditions trying to fail.'

'So what *do* you think when you're auditioning?'

'That here I am, classically trained and reading for the part of a life-sized cigarette in a Nicorette commercial, usually, that's what.'

'Can you hear how *negative* you sound? And all you're doing is attracting even more negativity towards you. Remember what I said: like attracts like. It's the most fundamental law of the universe. Now just take a moment to think. There must be some aspect of your life where everything's going your way, so you need to ask yourself . . . what is it that I'm doing right here, so effortlessly? Then I want you to take those same positive feelings and apply them to your work area.'

'She attracts fellas like flies to . . . emm . . . manure,' I blurt out.

Sorry, I can't help myself. God, I sound like the class swot ratting on my friend to the teacher. I just think this one could really be on to something here.

'There you go, then,' smiles red-haired woman. 'It sounds to me like you ladies need to learn from each other. *You* need to figure what your friend is doing to attract men so easily. Whereas *you*,' she says, turning to a very pole-axed-looking Barbara, 'need to be as confident and self-believing in your work area as you are in romance. If you walk into every casting with the attitude that everyone around you is far more suited to the part than you, what are you attracting? Unemployment, what else? There's a saying I often use to anyone who comes to me looking for help: if you want to fly, first of all, get the shit off your wings.'

Hours and hours and waaaay too many margaritas later, Barbara and I are still talking about her.

I mean, was she for real?

Or could there actually *be* something in what she'd said?

Chapter Two

In which our cunning plan is hatched, parenthesis, thunderclap, sinister laugh, ha, ha, ha, parenthesis . . .

Just one more friend to introduce you to and then we're done, I promise.

'HAPPY BIRTHDAY to the youngest-looking, hottest babe I know,' calls Laura, my oldest and dearest buddy, waving at me from across the swishy, Dublin 4 restaurant where we're having lunch with Barbara the following Saturday who . . . well, that might just be information overload, I'll come to what's she's up to in time.

Laura first.

'Look at you, not a line on your face, God bless your collagen levels, that's all I can say. Honestly, you're even more like Jennifer Aniston than Jennifer Aniston,' she says, as we and ooh and ahh, and generally squeal at each other like two dolphins on a nature programme having a dire emergency.

You know, all the normal ladies-who-lunch stuff.

Not that you could call either myself or Laura a lady who lunches, not by the longest of long shots. In fact, most days I'm doing well if I manage to wolf down a wrap at my desk in-between strategy meetings at the office. This is just the type of restaurant that seems to bring out the inner diva in all of us. Oh, you know the kind: where they bring fourteen types of bread to the table, when a plain old roll would do, and where they call gravy '*jus*', and when you ask for water they automatically bring the posh kind in blue bottles that immediately add another eighty euro on to the bill.

God, just listen to me. Age is definitely making me narkier. The only difference between me and my moany Auntie Maisie is a plaid shopping trolley and a tracheotomy.

'Either you're lying or else you're only saying that cos I straightened my hair especially for today, but bless you anyway,' I say, plonking down beside her and gratefully accepting the wine list she's thrusting at me.

I'm really delighted to see Laura, I never get to spend enough time with her. She . . . well, she leads this incredibly hectic, full-on life and is never able to come out on the razz at night-time with Barbara and me. (Childcare issues, don't even GO there.) So, anyway the three of us have this deal. The Saturday after any of us celebrates a birthday, said birthday girl is required to host lunch in the poshest restaurant that her budget will allow. This first commandment of our friendship dates back to when Laura had her first baby, not long after the three of us graduated from college together, and we've stuck to it through thick and thin, for richer for poorer, all the way from McDonalds, via Pizza Hut to the super-posh dining-room of Roly's Bistro which we're sitting in now.

On me. Ah sure, what the hell.

Plus I am so *bursting* to tell her about the exhibition we were at, and the law of attraction, and how it's finally, *finally* going to turn my love life around – and all the amazing wonders I've learned since I last saw her. Oh shit, does that make me sound like a Southern Baptist preacher that's trying to convert someone on the God channel? Better tread carefully, if so. If you thought that Barbara was a tad disbelieving, then I'm about to introduce you to the Dark Lady of cynicism. Like you wouldn't believe. I mean, back in college, Laura was even a founder member of the Sceptics Society.

Really, I am *not* kidding.

'So, another year older and wiser,' she says. 'How do you feel?'

'Honestly?'

'The whole truth and nothing but.'

'OK, put it this way. It's like Oscar Wilde said, the tragedy of ageing isn't that you're old, it's that you're *young*. I mean, look at me. I am now officially old enough to know that there's more to life than sex and shoes and boyfriends and partying, and yet still young enough to know that they are the best bits.'

And up until yesterday I might have added that, lately, I've been seeing damn all of any. But then I always feel a bit guilty for moaning in front of Laura, on the grounds that there's nothing worse than the failure stench from a lonely, single woman who desperately wishes that she wasn't. Besides, note to self: now that I'm a new convert to the awesome power and majesty of the law of attraction, I really shouldn't moan, sorry, sorry . . . ooops, I meant to say . . . attract negativity into my life.

Plus, further note to self: let's never forget that the second commandment of being a good friend is 'Thou Shalt not Bore'. So I opt for changing the subject instead.

'No, you first with the news, babe. So how are things on the home front?'

'Vicky. Today is your day. We're here to celebrate *your* birthday lunch. So by asking that question you've just confirmed that the vein in my forehead must now be pulsing like a thunderbolt. Like Harry Potter's proverbial scar, if you will.'

No kidding, this is actually the way that Laura talks. Sharp, clear and clipped. Witty, even without trying to be. She used to be a lawyer, which might go some of the way towards explaining.

'Tell me everything, honey. Omit no detail, however trivial,' I say in what I hope sounds like a sympathetic yet encouraging tone, which, trust me, always works best with her when she's . . . well, whenever she gets a bit overstressed like this.

'Ordinarily, I'd prefer to have some alcohol inside me to answer that question, but . . . all right then, seeing as you've asked,' she sighs, shoving her glasses into her hair and palming her tired, bloodshot eyes. 'Firstly, my dearest eldest son was caught shoplifting last night and at 4 a.m. I was still in the police station trying to troubleshoot. Secondly, my daughter, who's already behaving like a pre-teen, delivered me an ultimatum over breakfast. It seems the little madam now prefers living with Daddy and his new girlfriend, and that if I don't stop nagging her, then she's permanently moving in with them.'

'And I suppose by "nagging" you really mean trying to coax her to eat a little bit more than one packet of breath fresheners every day?'

I'm actually not messing here; this is a child whose main ambition in life is to out-skinny Nicole Ritchie or one of those 'sleb' types you read about in magazines. You know, the ones who all go around Beverley Hills looking like malnourished thirteen-year-olds, toting handbags that probably weigh more than them.

'Correct. Oh and speaking of my soon-to-be-ex husband, he is now almost four months behind on paying child maintenance. Which means I have to suffer the utter humili-ation of going cap in hand to my mother to pay this month's mortgage. Not to mention next term's school fees which are also due. Does my self-esteem need any of this, I ask you?'

Well, I did warn you. Laura's life makes mine seem like a Disneyland infomercial by comparison. I nod supportively, and do my best not to interrupt with insulting yet insightful comments about said soon-to-be-ex husband. With the balance tilted strongly in favour of insulting, on account of the fact that I can't abide the sight of him.

On she goes. 'Then for added entertainment value, my darling seven-year-old, who's still bed-wetting by the way, not only is taking the divorce worse than the whole useless lot of them put together, but I was reliably informed by his head-master yesterday that lately he's started mitching off class and, as of this morning, my baby girl . . .' she pauses here, just to catch her breath, 'now has a highly infectious case of head lice, picked up from a neighbour's child while I took my eye off the ball for all of two minutes. So, all in all, how great is it that I'm on Zanax?'

'Ooh, honey, not good,' I wince. 'Anything I can do to help?'

'Yes, dearest. You could do what you always do and make me laugh.'

'OK,' I say slowly, racking my brains for a decent gag. 'Ehh, well I could try and hire a full-time nanny on your behalf, you know, the sort who'll hopefully confuse child-rearing with criminal law enforcement.'

Bingo, I'm rewarded with a sly smile, just as Laura's mobile beep-beeps.

'Mary Poppins on a minimum wage, that's what I need,' she says, fishing around her overstuffed handbag for her mobile and dumping a tub of Sudocrem and a packet of Heinz banana biscuits on the table. It's a text from her mother, who's baby-sitting, to say that a Third Gulf War has erupted in the house over who had the remote control last.

'Shit, shit, shit,' says Laura. 'I'm really sorry about this, dearest, but do you mind if I just phone home and really give my babies something to cry about?'

'Course not, go ahead.'

'Serves me right for thinking that I could actually skive off for two niggardly hours and, who knows, maybe actually enjoy myself for once,' she says, furiously stabbing at the speed dial on her phone. 'This is your day, and look what I'm having to deal with. Just wait till I get home. I can tell you right now, they're in for a WORLD of pain. Yes, it's Mummy here, kindly roll your eyes BACK into the forward position,' she snaps crisply at whatever poor unfortunate child happens to answer. 'Now go and get Granny for me this instant. WHAT did you just say? Well I hate to disappoint you, but no, you are not a secret agent and you do NOT have a licence to kill your brother . . . hang on, is that the unmistakable sound of a Band-Aid wrapper that I hear being unpeeled?'

Oh dear. Right then, nothing for it but to order a bottle of champagne from the wine waiter (what the hell, when you're out, you're out), and let her get on with doing a major damage-limitation number on the home front.

Poor old Laura. Now don't get me wrong, it's not that she doesn't love and adore her kids, of course she does. It's just that, well, things haven't exactly been easy for her of late. In fact, not for a long, long time. Put it this way, if you'd met Laura when I first did, back in school, in a million years you would never have predicted this kind of life for her. No one's fault, no one to blame, it's just that things didn't quite work out for her the way you'd have foreseen.

Or for any of us, come to think of it, but let me tell you a bit about Laura.

OK. For starters, she comes from a very well-known and highly regarded political family, the Lennox-Coyninghams. Now we don't exactly have dynasties in this country, but believe me, Laura's family come pretty darn close. On pretty much every page of our recorded history, there's a Lennox-Coyningham in there somewhere: one of her illustrious ancestors had fought in the War of Independence, her granddad was Minister for Justice and her father served three terms as

Attorney General. I remember as a kid going to play in their huge mansion of a house and being completely intimidated by the fact that they would hold heated political discussions around the dinner table. Honest to God, it was like being pals with a Kennedy, minus the suntan and the toothiness. Especially as in our house, mealtimes revolved around whatever soap happened to be on TV at the time, and the only house rule was whoever got to the microwave first, got fed first. (We were a very microwave and freezer-dependent family.)

Anyway, from a very early age, great things were expected of Laura, a cherished eldest child, all of which were entirely justified by her perpetually stunning grades. She effortlessly graduated from college top of her year in law studies, and everyone – absolutely everyone, from her tutors and lecturers down – agreed that Laura Lennox-Coyningham had what it took to be a minister, an ambassador or maybe even (and I can still hear her father whispering this in suitably awed tones) . . . President.

It wasn't an impossible dream. She had everything going for her, the whole package. Brains, charisma, popularity, pedigree, wealthy political connections, great communication skills, the lot. She's even good-looking, photogenic in an Emma Thompson, dippy-quirky sort of way; but you'd have absolutely no difficulty at all picturing her smiling face on election posters hanging from lampposts far and wide with a caption under her saying: 'Vote Lennox-Coyningham No. 1'.

But it wasn't to be. That summer we graduated, when we were all aged twenty-one, in a long family tradition, Laura went off to King's Inns to become a hard-working, high-powered barrister, a necessary stop-off on her merry route to the presidental office in the Phoenix Park. And shocked all of us, not least her family, by falling madly in love with George Hastings, one of her senior professors.

Now, kinder people than me called George, a dusty academic
type, cuddly, if you didn't have a problem with either dandruff
or patterned cardigans. Put it this way, while the rest of us were
all drinking Malibu and thinking ourselves fierce posh,
slumming it around Europe on cheapie InterRail tickets and
debating as to whether Heaven 17 or MC Hammer would have
a longer shelf-life (no, *really*), George was escorting Laura to
cello recitals and violin concertos at his elitist, members-only,
old-man's club on Stephen's Green, that somehow always,
always smelt of boarding-school food, stinky cabbage and
watery rice pudding. And I wouldn't have minded, but he can't
have been any more than mid-thirties then; a young fogey
before they'd even invented the term.

Anyway, like him or loathe him, George and the lovely Laura
were married before she'd even reached the age of twenty-two.
By thirty she was a mother of three, still ambitious and still
practising as a barrister you understand, but well . . . It was just
so difficult, if not impossible, for her to put in all the networking hours and late-night drinking sessions in pubs near the
Four Courts that you practically *have* to, if you want to get on
in that profession. Her kids came first. Of course. Then she fell
pregnant again and was forced to take a career break just so all
her hard-earned cash wasn't entirely going towards childcare. I
often think she has the days counted until her youngest is in
'big' school, so she can get back to the workplace, knowing all
her kids are safely tied up in full-time education. She's aching
for it, itching to get back inside a courtroom, but right now
and for the next couple of years at least . . . she's a separated,
soon-to-be-divorced mother of four, while George is still
actively, you might even say aggressively, dating some of his
students right under her nose.

Like I say, not a destiny you might have foretold.

She finishes her call and apologizes profusely.

'Look at me, I'm calm, I'm cool and I'm keeping my peace, even with God. Even with George Hastings.'

Oh yeah, that's the other thing. She always, always, refers to her ex by his full name. I think, by doing so, she's imagining she's in court and about to send him down for arson or, you know, some grade A crime that carries a mandatory life-sentence and that his trial will end up on the *Six O'Clock News* with close-up shots of him looking miserable in handcuffs, with a raincoat over his head.

'Come on, then, Vicky, now that my heart-rate is back into double figures, please, for the love of God, can we have an adult conversation?'

'I've ordered champagne. And if Barbara is very much later, then too bad, we're drinking it without her.'

Barbara, by the way, is *always* late. In fact there are times when I'd nearly swear she's staged it just so she can swan in and make an entrance. Her being an actress might go some of the way towards explaining it, but unfortunately for her, I work in PR and know all the tricks. As it turns out, though, Barbara and the champagne arrive simultaneously.

'Hello, darlings,' she puffs, out of breath and air-kissing us both theatrically. 'Sorry I'm late. Audition ran over.'

'What was it for again?' I ask her as we hug. She'd told me and all I could remember was that it was for something so bizarre you couldn't possibly make it up if you tried.

'A *tableau vivant* for a detergent commercial.'

'Sounds pornographic,' says Laura drily. 'Is that what you wore?'

'Yeah, what's wrong with it?'

'OK, if I may just take a moment to mock here, do tell, Barbara, the history of that particular dress. Did it start out as furniture fabric? You know how I hate to criticize, but honestly, I wouldn't let you wear that on a desert island. Dearest, you're dressed like a homeless person.'

She isn't really. Barbara just looks the way she always does, like she fell out of bed and pulled on the first clean thing she picked up off the floor. Sexy, in a rumpled, crumpled, couldn't-be-arsed way that men just seem to lose their reason over. No make-up, and streaky fake tan like she put it on half of her body then got bored, gave up and found something more interesting to do. Unlike our Laura, who for some reason always manages to look neat. Scrubbed. Impeccable. All the Lennox-Coyninghams are the same: no matter how stressed their private lives are, like politicians, they're always 'on'. Always well-turned-out, always up for re-election.

'Ooh, look,' says Barbara in her 'acting the eejit' voice, as she and Laura pick up their menus together. 'Today's soup is crème de narky cow.'

'Ooh, look,' says Laura, well able for her. 'The only dish on my menu is dog's dinner.'

OK, so it may not actually sound like it, but trust me, this pair do love each other dearly. This is just the way they spark off each other, with the kind of intimacy you really only get with old, old friends. You know, the ones who never fail to remind you that you had a fringe in the eighties or that you used to work out to Milli Vanilli. And at this stage in our friendship, honestly, the three of us know each other more intimately than jailbirds sharing a cell. Besides, I think the main reason Laura gives her such a hard time about the way she looks is that, on the rare occasions when Barbara does pull out the stops, she can look traffic-stoppingly stunning. This is just Laura's way of exercising her mammy-gene. She'll be whipping tissues out of her bag, licking them and then wiping dirty smudges off Barbara's face next.

'Pay absolutely no attention to her, Barbara,' I say. 'You look fab. Any hotter and you'd set off the sprinkler system. And here's the proof . . . how many men have begged you for a date since you left your house today?'

'The casting director, who's a bit of a sleazeball so . . .'

'Curse your fatal allure,' I joke and they laugh. The champagne's started to kick in now and it's faaaab.

God, even the snooty wine waiter can't take his eyes off her, I can't help noticing. When we were all in college together, some wag nicknamed Barbara 'The Loin Tamer', and you can kind of see where they were coming from.

'Cheers,' she says, oblivious as usual to any fella eyeing her up, as she takes a big gulp and smacks her lips. 'Aaah, lovely. I've noticed I only ever have bad luck whenever I'm *not* drinking. Anyway, birthday gal, I bring you a gift. Now I don't want to over-exaggerate, but this could possibly be the most amazing pressie you'll ever get in your whole life. Prepare to be blown away, baby.'

She roots around in her bag on the floor and starts flinging the contents up on to the table, beginning with a copy of *Celebrity Heat* magazine, with a questionnaire half-filled-in.

'What's this?' says Laura, idly picking up the magazine at the page it has opened on. ' "Am I an Adult-escent?" '

'Oh yeah,' says Barbara. 'It's a quiz I started doing while I was waiting to do the audition. New cultural sub-group they've just discovered, which I think might include you and me, Vick. It's for, ahem, the thirty-somethings who still think they're teenagers. You know, who watch *The Office* and actually get it, and know all the characters on *The Simpsons*, and still shop in Top Shop and H & M and think they're cool.'

'God, I wish I was a teenager again,' I muse, swirling the champagne around the glass. 'I'm telling you, girlies, if I could go back, if I had my time over, I'd do things differently, and that's for sure. You know, reprioritize.'

'Explain,' says Laura, looking at me in that really focused, intent way that she has.

'Well, it's like this. Take, for instance, the two young girls I have working for me in the office. I'm not joking, their number-one priority in life is to get a nice, wealthy, eligible husband. Honestly, they're like this whole breed of neo-Victorians, and I wouldn't mind, but they're barely out of college. They're looking at my generation and thinking: "OK, so maybe you have a great career and money and a home of your own . . . but you're alone and that doesn't make you any role model for me." Ten years ago I'd have laughed at them, but now . . . today, it doesn't seem quite so funny.'

'Oh, come on,' Laura says, sounding a bit exasperated. 'I could be sitting here, blissfully happy, about to celebrate yet another wedding anniversary, but I'm not. This conversation is pointless. I mean, for God's sake, Hitler could have channelled all his energies into opening a nice chain of vegetarian restaurants, but guess what? That didn't happen, either. There is absolutely nothing to be gained either from beating yourself up over the choices you *didn't* make, or congratulating yourself on the ones that you *did*. Pretty much every decision you've ever made was half chance, same as the rest of us.'

'Or perhaps *not*,' says Barbara in a vaudevillian-baddie voice, producing a crumpled paper bag and spilling the contents out on to the table.

It's a hardback book, so dusty and old that you almost feel you should be wearing latex gloves just to touch it, like they do in those TV documentaries about museums, where they're handling bits of papyrus from Tutankhamen's tomb and the like. But that's not what's making me look at Barbara, gobsmacked. It's the book's title, almost faded but still legible.

Oh my God, I do not believe this.

The Law of Attraction.

'Barbara, you angel,' I say, a bit stunned. 'This is it; this is exactly what that amazing American woman was talking about only yesterday . . . where in God's name did you come across this?'

'Second-hand bookshop right beside where the audition was. I wanted to buy you something quirky slash unusual slash cheap for your birthday, and we all know how much you love self-help books, or anything with a title that promises you can change your life in seven days, and then I stumbled across this. So happy birthday, babe. Good, isn't it?'

'I can't believe it,' is all I can say, delicately fingering the book like it's a first-edition copy of the Bible, signed by all four apostles, who wrote it when they were on a book tour of, I dunno, Galilee or somewhere.

' "The law of attraction," ' says Laura, filching it from me and reading from a page at random in her best news-anchor voice, ' "clearly states that like attracts like, so by the very act of summoning a thought, you are attracting like thoughts to you." Oh I see, so now it seems I *attracted* an ex-husband with a girl-friend who makes him look like human Botox, i.e. twenty years younger.'

'No, no, this is amazing stuff,' Barbara and I chorus.

'I've actually been bursting to tell you about this ever since we got here,' I say, gulping down another big glug of champers. 'Right, Laura, just hear me out. Now, OK, I admit, I may not have consciously attracted ovaries with a sell-by date that, honest to God, at this stage might as well be carved in stone and written in Roman numerals, but maybe, just maybe, I've been so focused on what I *don't* want, that that's what the law of attraction is delivering, each and every time. If you're with me.'

'Just like me with work,' explains Barbara. 'I've spent years resigning myself to the fact that I'll never get offered anything other than Fakespeare and third-prostitute-from-the-left-type roles in crappy old cop operas; ergo, that's all I *do* get. It's almost like I'm attracting by default.'

'I'm sorry,' says Laura crisply, 'but the pair of you are sound-ing dangerously close to butterfly net territory.'

'Look, there's a bit here about quantum physics,' I say, shoving the book under her nose and hoping that this will appeal to her brainy nature.

' "Imagine yourself like a human transmission tower," ' Laura reads aloud in her best *Nine O'Clock News* voice, ' "transmitting a frequency with your thoughts. If you wish to change anything in your life, first you must change the frequency of your thoughts." OK, my biggest fear in life is that I'll end up pole-dancing to pay for my kids' braces. So this book is effectively telling me that I should just flick a mental switch, *think* that I've won the lottery and that should do the trick? *Please.* This conversation demeans all of us. If life was that easy, then why isn't everyone doing it?'

'It says here,' I say defensively, reading from another yellowy page that flipped open, ' "that for over two thousand years, five per cent of the world's population have controlled ninety-five per cent of the world's wealth. Now that is *not* a coincidence . . ." '

'And at fifteen ninety-nine for a copy, I'm not a bit surprised,' Laura says as her eagle eye spots the price tag still stuck to the back of the book.

'Well, girlies, it's like this,' I say, undeterred. 'We've tried just about everything else, so why not try using this to our advantage for a change? If you ask me, this law of attraction lark couldn't be more of a doddle, really. I mean, for God's sake, all we have to do is ask the universe very nicely for whatever we want, no matter how ridiculous it seems, believe that somehow it'll miraculously come to us, then sit back and wait for our dream lives to start. Come on, who wouldn't welcome that into their life?'

'To hear you talk about the universe,' says Laura drily, 'you'd think it was a giant mail-order catalogue in the sky – only free.'

'Which, when you think about it, is the perfect excuse to go out and buy that fab new Marni dress I've had my eye on for ages. Ooh, whaddya know, this law of attraction lark is fun.'

'Just listen to you,' says Laura, topping up our glasses. 'You sound like Pollyanna, except with a Magic Eight ball, a job, a mortgage, a healthcare plan and a *lot* of champagne.'

'No, I've just had enough stinking thinking,' I say a bit defensively. But then, sometimes this is just the way you have to handle our Laura. 'And I for one believe it's time we took matters into our own hands.'

'One of you better start making sense,' says Laura, 'or else I'm calling the Priory's bunny-boiler division. I'm sorry to pour cold water on this, but it seems to me that this new fad of yours is nothing more than a few grains of common sense dressed up as the Holy Grail. The great mystery of life, reincarnated as a House of Fraser catalogue. You'll forgive my bluntness, but I have a very finely tuned crap-ometer.'

Now Barbara rows in. 'OK, Laura, just shut up and listen. Now I may not believe in this stuff any more than you do, but here's the way I'm seeing it. Girlies, just take a look at us. Between the three of us there's a perfect life in here some-where. For my part, I've diligently pursued my dreams with acting, and the hard, cold fact is, that up until now, it hasn't worked.'

'But on the plus side, you have guys practically impaling themselves to date you,' I say. 'Look at me; I've been to hell and back so many times, with so many guys, I might as well have frequent flier miles.'

'Excuse me, if we're having a contest, then can I have a turn?' says Laura. 'So. I married my soul mate, then fast forward twelve years, to when he moves on and starts actively looking for his.'

'Laura, for all George's shortcomings, at least you *had* someone,' I insist. 'And, OK, I know half the time you feel like ringing social services, but you do have four healthy, wonderful kids. Take a look at me. I'm how you end up when you never find a soul mate in the first place. I mean, come on, is there any-thing more pathetic than a childless spinster who wishes that she wasn't?'

'A notion entirely peddled to you by Hollywood,' says Laura crisply. 'Every few years a movie will emerge targeted at women like you, which is calculated to scare you into marriage and motherhood. And to denigrate your self-esteem for being single. Fact.'

'Come on, Vicky, you do have a very successful career,' says Barbara. 'Your company's doing brilliantly, you've a home of your own, you've plenty of money, and you can afford to eat in fancy places like this. Look at my life. You know there's a high probability I'll end up a bag lady if I don't get work soon.'

Now it's like the floodgates have opened and there's a 'whose life is worst' contest raging between the three of us.

'George Hasting's last book,' says Laura, slowly and precisely, holding on to the edge of the table, like she's just warming up for a good old ding-dong, 'sold precisely ninety-one copies, thereby putting me into the acutely embarrassing position of having to beg my mother on bended knee for a hand-out.'

OK, so maybe she wins this round.

'What was the book called again?' Barbara asks.

'*A Brief Treatise on the Laws of Sewers, Including the Drainage Acts, 1980–2007.*'

'And you're telling me that wasn't snapped up and made into a movie?' says Barbara.

Laura gives her cute, slightly lop-sided smile. She knows she's been out-wisecracked.

'My go,' I say. 'The last DSM I dated, that merchant-banker guy, broke up with me via a message on my answering machine. Bastard said he felt he was seventy-five per cent compatible with me, but only twenty-five per cent compatible with himself. Now you can both laugh all you like, but that is without doubt the lamest excuse for being dumped *ever*, and I should know, I've certainly heard a few.' (A DSM, by the way, is our code for a decent, single man, something that eejit definitely wasn't.)

'Requiem for a relationship,' muses Laura, swirling her drink. 'I only hope you're keeping a diary.'

'But there are thousands of available guys out there,' says Barbara, while I look at her, thinking, yeah, easy for you to say. 'All you need to do is flex your dating muscles a bit, that's all.'

'Sorry, but when you say thousands of available guys, I hear, great, thousands more opportunities for me to be humiliated.'

'Oh, come on, you've got a dream home,' she goes on, 'or at least, it will be by the time the builders are finished, and —'

'A mother who thinks I can be cheered up with lovely new bedding plants and an order of guilt on the side?'

'I can top that,' says Laura.

'Oh come on, you're a wonderful mother and you know it.'

'Yes, you're probably both just waiting for the Disney bluebird to land on my shoulder. Anyway, during the course of my daily rummaging, I found a condom in my son's jeans pocket.'

'But isn't that an OK thing?' says Barbara, looking a tad confused. 'I mean, you know, he's being safe and . . . emm . . . responsible and all that?'

'Barbara, he's *twelve*.'

'Oh, right. Sorry.'

'My only fervent hope is that he doesn't know what it's for. Ladies, I just don't get it. I took a break from a hugely satisfying career at the Bar so I could be a full-time, stay-at-home mom, and I have the baby-vomit-stained T-shirt to prove it. I've invested all of this time and energy in my kids, so why couldn't I have reared the Waltons? Or the Railway Children?'

And then a eureka moment hits me more sharply than a chilli finger poked into my eye. 'I have it,' I say. 'It just came to me.'

'Top up her glass,' says Laura bossily. 'The girl looks as if she's having a road-to-Damascus moment. Come on, spit it out.'

'My birthday wish,' I say firmly. 'I know what it is.'

'Shoot.'

I pick up *The Law of Attraction* and shove it into the middle of the table.

'We're doing it,' I say. 'The three of us.'

'The three of us are doing what? Forming a jazz trio?'

'We, ladies, are going to project-manage each other's lives, according to the rules laid down in this book,' I announce, in what I hope is the same assertive tone of voice I use with my bank manager.

'Cool. Loving it. I'm in,' says Barbara, beaming.

'Project-manage?' Laura asks. 'Do you mean like Svengali? Or Henry Higgins in an all-girl *Pygmalion*, perhaps?'

'Ehh, well I was actually thinking more in terms of Simon Cowell on *The X Factor*. But same idea, yeah.'

'And exactly how much champagne have you had?'

Great, now she's looking at me like I'm only a few coupons short of a special offer.

'No, this time it's not the drink talking. Barbara, I'm putting you in charge of my love life, and I for my part will come up with as many ways as I can to turn you into a household name within . . . within . . .'

'Twelve months,' Barbara interrupts. 'Let's give ourselves till your birthday next year.'

'A good suitable bookend, I agree,' says Laura. 'Rest assured, I'll be observing how both of you progress from the sidelines, with great interest.'

'Sorry, Laura,' I say. 'You may not fully buy into all of this, but that's too bad. We need your particular no-nonsense approach here, so you're in. Welcome to the wonderful world of "got no choice". And if we happen to come up with a sure-fire way to make you a fortune into the bargain, so much the better.'

She tops up our glasses, doing her lop-sided smile. Which is always a good sign with her.

'I suggest we hold monthly, organized meetings in each other's houses,' I go on. 'Kind of like a book club, but without the homework, and with margaritas instead of tea and sandwiches.'

'Free booze. Always sounds good to me,' says Barbara.

'And we're really going to work on visualizing our perfect lives, too. You know, like they do on the space programme, Apollo Thirteen or one of them.'

'Well, maybe not thirteen,' says Laura quietly. 'Pick another Apollo. One that didn't almost kill everyone.'

'Girlies, I haven't a clue what the coming twelve months hold, but I can promise you this. If we just stick to the plan, by this time next year, our lives will be unrecognizable. Deal?'

I don't even know if what I'm saying is making any sense. I can't describe it, I just feel like I'm acting on inspired thought.

'Up until yesterday,' says Barbara, 'I'd have said it's useless to dream because nothing ever changes, but that American chick was pretty bloody convincing. So today, I'm prepared to give it a go. Right, I'm in.'

She clinks glasses with me and looks like she's really up for it, bless her.

'Against my better judgement,' says Laura slowly, 'and only because it'll mean I get to see more of you pair, then, OK, count me in, too. I don't particularly think it's going to work, but I am rooting for you. In short, you, my dears, have a deal.'

'Cheers.'

'Cheers.'

'Cheers.'

Chapter Three

The law of attraction in action. Well, at least that's the plan . . .

Now, if you're going to do a thing, you might as well do it properly, I always say. The only trouble is, my workload in the office has gone virtually stratospheric and I've had damn all time to sit down and actually organize my own project management task: turning our Barbara into a household name within twelve months.

Bloody hell.

Anyway, the following Friday after the birthday weekend, I'm still in the office late in the evening, working so hard it's almost like I'm stuck in a time warp. I have to come up with a pitch for a huge cosmetics contract I'm hoping to land, and pitching, let me tell you, is THE single most difficult part of my job. The idea is that I have to condense every single idea I'm simmering with for this product launch into a single sentence, then hopefully use it to bewitch a jaded advertising executive, who'll fall in love with my idea and pay me a fortune to make it happen. At least, that's the plan. The phone rings and I grab it, automatically answering, 'Hello, Harper PR?'

'Oh, listen to you, Cinderella, little Miss No-Date, still in the office at nine o'clock in the evening.'

Barbara, cutting to the chase as always. There's never any

preamble with her, never a: 'hi, how are you?' She's always just straight in, straight to the point.

'Shit, I didn't realize it was so late. I have to have a pitch done for a meeting on Monday morning and I'm not happy with what we've got so far.'

'And where's Paris Hilton and Nicole Ritchie then?'

That's Barbara's nickname for my two assistants, which actually really suits them as one is a tall blonde with long, swishy hair extensions hanging out of her, and the other's a skinny brunette. Anyway, they're both perky and pert and only about twenty-five. So, of course, working here for them is just the perfect excuse to go to a lot of parties and premieres, while they're waiting for Mr Right to show up.

Honest to God, there are times when I look at the pair of them and *really* think I got my life priorities all wrong. And even though I know to the penny exactly what I pay each of them, they're both always miles better dressed than me and always seem to have far more disposable income. Oh, and their real names, for the record, are actually Lucy and Kate, but somehow, behind their backs at least, the Paris and Nicole tag just stuck. Believe me, it just seems to suit their personalities an awful lot better.

'Left hours ago. Gone husband-hunting. Like single people are supposed to on a Friday night.'

'And why didn't you go with them?'

'Cos they've gone to one of those cool trendy bars where the only people you see over the age of thirty are there to collect their kids. Plus, I have to work.'

'Yeah, right, fine, way to go, Vicky, put work ahead of all else, that's what has you sitting in an empty, cold, dark office all alone on a Friday night while all the normal people have gone out to play.'

'Barbara, this isn't a Charles Dickens novel, you know. My

office does actually have light and heat, thanks very much. You make it sound like there should be hounds baying at the window under a full moon.'

'Just know that you'll end up at Paris and Nicole's five-star, fancy double wedding like some toothless maiden aunt, sitting in a corner hoping beyond hope that you'll catch the bouquet, and that the groom's seventy-year-old uncle, who's on a waiting list for hip replacement surgery, will ask you to bingo with him some Sunday afternoon. You keep this up and that's the road you're headed down, baby.'

You have to hand it to Barbara, she paints quite a picture.

'I know, I know, I should be out there, but it's just that this meeting on Monday is a big deal and I still haven't finalized the pitch,' I whinge, in an effort to get off this highly embarrassing subject. 'And on top of everything else, the clients are so bloody vague. All I can get out of them is that they want the product to evoke "the glamour of Hollywood during its golden era".'

'What's the product anyway?'

'Cosmetics. Oh, the usual, you know, face cream and foundation developed by scientists at NASA and so grossly overpriced, you'd swear they were personally hand-squeezed by the Queen from the hind leg of last year's Grand National winner.'

'What's it called?'

'Wait for it. "Original Sin".'

'Hmmm, biblical. Yeah, loving it. So what have you come up with for your pitch?'

'I'm thinking of a film noir theme for the launch. You know, the kind of party where just walking through the door will almost feel like stepping back into a black-and-white movie. Piano music, champagne cocktails, models floating around who look like Barbara Stanwyck, with the guys dressed like

Humphrey Bogart in white tuxes. Classy and sophisticated. Think Cole Porter. Think art deco. And of course the freebie bags will be stuffed with that pillar-box red nail varnish and the heavy lip-gloss all the great femme fatales used to wear.'

'God, you are *good*.'

'Piece of cake. The hard bit will be trying to talk the creatives into this. God alone knows what kind of ideas they have up their sleeve.'

'Just don't forget to wangle me an invite to the launch. You know me: I'm your girl for freebies. Well, freebies that other people end up paying for.'

'Consider it done.'

'And while you're at it, any chance you'd ask them to cast me in their ad – sez she cheekily, fully expecting the answer no?'

'Barbara, by the time I'm finished with you, you'll be such a household name, the cosmetic companies will be queuing up for you to front all their ad campaigns. You'll be like Keira Knightley on the Chanel ad.'

Now that's actually not such a bad idea, I'm thinking, if Barbara was only world-famous, she'd be a terrific brand representative, she's so gorgeous-looking and funny and charismatic. I mean look at Nicole Kidman or Catherine Zeta Jones or any of them: plugging perfume and night cream didn't exactly do their careers any harm, now did it? Or their bank balances, come to think of it . . . hmmm . . . I start absent-mindedly drumming a pen on my note pad thinking about just how in the hell I'm going to get her there . . .

'Excellent,' says Barbara. 'Glad to see you're on the case. Anyway, that's why I'm phoning you. I spoke to our lovely Laura and we've arranged to meet up tomorrow night to kickstart our cunning plan. I was calling our little gathering the "Maisonettes", you know, because we're there to help each other, like an all-girl freemasons, but Laura reckons it makes us sound like the Tiller Girls.'

'Yeah, it does put me in mind of the Rockettes at Radio City Music Hall, all right.'

Next thing I start doodling a picture of a butterfly . . . well, that's what the three of us are trying to do with our lives, aren't we? Change, just like butterflies . . .

'So, eight p.m. it is,' Barbara goes on. 'You provide the tequila and I'll bring the margarita mix. And I already know you're free and dateless, because that's what the whole point of to-morrow night is.'

'Thanks so much, why don't you just throw a toaster in my tub while you're at it?'

'Do you want to get sensitive or do you want to get a man, Miss Lonely Heart?'

'Point taken. You're right, I have to change my attitude a bit. OK, here goes. This is the start of the official countdown from Cape Harper to boyfriend-land. Right, there you go. Does that sound pathologically optimistic enough? Here I am, in the prime of life, ready for commitment.'

'Great, I'll sign the papers.'

'Commitment to a man, you big eejit.'

Barbara snorts down the phone. She never laughs in a girlie, tinkly, clinking-champagne-glass way like some women do, Paris and Nicole for instance; no, hers is a gutsy, bawdy, full-on belly laugh. When she laughs in bars or restaurants, people always stare over, and you can almost see the thought-balloons coming out of their heads: 'God, look at that table, they're having all the crack.' And usually they're right. Anyway, just the sound of Barbara's laugh is always enough to get me into giddy form as well. It's unladylike, as my mother would say, it's infectious but most important of all . . . fellas go mad over it. One bloke even told her he'd fallen in love with her purely on account of her laugh, which made me try impersonating her for a while, but I just ended up sounding like Dolores O'Riordan from The Cranberries. Only worse.

'That's the girl,' she says. 'You just wait and see, this time next year, you'll be living the life of a Danielle Steel heroine. I have great plans for you, baby. I've done homework on your behalf and everything.'

I'm just thinking, bless her for taking all this so seriously, she's so fab, when, out of nowhere, something strikes me.

'Barbara, hope you don't mind my asking but, how come you're home tonight? Not like you, hon. Friday night and all that.'

'I do have a date, I'm just running late, that's all. With the casting director from the commercial last week, remember? Can't even remember his name. It's something . . . somebody Vale . . . I remember thinking whatever he's called, it sounded like a housing estate out in the suburbs.'

'Are you seriously telling me you're going on a date with a guy whose name you don't know?'

'Honey, I've woken up with guys whose names I didn't know. Besides, I don't hold out much hope for him, he's taking me to Bang Café, and we all know that place is just full of knickerless Ukrainian executive-stress consultants and record-pluggers. You know, one of those kips that's like a rehearsal room for every lame pick-up line that doesn't work on match.com.'

Ladies and gentlemen, let me introduce you to . . . my relationship coach. The woman I'm pinning all my hopes and dreams on, of ever meeting a DSM by this time next year.

Oh God, even thinking about what I'm hoping to achieve in the space of twelve short months makes me break out in a flop sweat . . . right then. Only one thing for it. I reach over to my handbag and fish out *The Law of Attraction*, which, tonne weight and all as it is, I've been toting around with me all week, dipping in and out of it whenever the need arises. Like now.

'Before you go,' I say. 'I just opened the book you gave me, at random, and here's the perfect affirmation quote for me to leave you on. Are you ready for this?'

'Shoot.'

' "I choose today to give myself the best life ever." '

And she hangs up, pissing herself laughing.

Then a text message from Laura, which is never a good sign. It usually means there's a fresh crisis with one of the kids, such as the time her youngest threw the main house phone down the loo, and her oldest brother didn't realize and weed on it. Anyway, she asks if it's OK if we convene at my place the following night, that her mum has agreed to babysit, and that she badly needs a night off or there's a fair chance she'll strangle someone, so I text back, saying grand, no worries, my house it is. Well, house slash building site would probably be more accurate.

It WILL be lovely when it's finished, is my permanent mantra as every morning I sit gulping down cups of coffee at my washing machine, which is doubling up as a kitchen table for me at the moment. I'm not kidding, the house and renovations are costing me so much that I can't afford proper furniture.

Well, at least, not yet.

It's a dotey, tiny little doll's house Victorian railway cottage, which was waaaay over my budget when I bought it last year, in the face of a great deal of opposition from my nearest and dearest which I can neatly summarize thus:

DAD: 'It's nothing but a money pit, there's damp downstairs and I'd swear I see a bit of dry rot, and you know the maintenance on an old house is constant, a bit like the Golden Gate Bridge, you start work on one end and by the time you finish, it's time to go back and start all over again blah, blah, blah etc., etc. . . . .

Dad, I should tell you, fancies himself as a great handyman, on account of a power drill we got him one Christmas, and even though he spent ages swaggering around the house with a very authoritative-looking tool belt strapped to his waist, all he really ended up doing was putting a load of Swiss cheese holes in my mother's good IKEA occasional table. Poor Mum, every bank holiday weekend she has to put up with him strutting around, dismantling her hostess trolley and magazine stands to illustrate how badly they're made. ('Held together with glue, do you see? Total crap.') Then abandoning everything and leaving a big mess all over the living-room floor the minute a Cup Final match comes on.

I do not know how my parents haven't divorced, I really don't.

MIDDLE BROTHER: 'Should have gone for a cool penthouse somewhere in town instead, Vick, guys love that, plus you'll never get the old-lady smell out of that house. And is that actual stippling on the ceilings?'
MY INCREDIBLY CONDESCENDING SISTER-IN-LAW, A WOMAN WHO'D MAKE A STEPFORD WIFE LOOK LIKE WAYNETTA SLOB: 'It's so . . . what's the word? Oh I know, cosy.'

Which, by the way, we all know right well is code for 'small'. You know, just like when you say a guy is 'distinguished', it's actually a euphemism for 'really old and I wouldn't go near him in a sugar rush'. Then to add insult to injury, when I did eventually move in she said, 'I LOVE coming around to visit you, Vicky. It's just like camping out. And I can totally sympathize. When we had the builders in a few years ago, my masseuse said she never saw me retain such tension in my shoulders. Never get a conservatory, sweetheart, it's soooo not worth the hassle.'

Even Barbara had a go. She came to a viewing with me and grudgingly said, 'Buy it if you want, but you'll never get a man to move in here with you. For God's sake, the outside is painted pink. Pink, as a colour, is a very well-known man-repeller. That's a fact. Bit like a single woman with a cat. Guys tend to think you're a total weirdo.'

See what I mean? I ignored the lot of them and bought it anyway, all swept up in the romance of owning a house with beautiful period features, bay windows, a cast-iron fireplace in the bedroom, and a lovely, bright downstairs kitchen with actual coving on the ceiling. 'Listen to you, your trouble is you've seen too many Merchant Ivory movies and now you fancy yourself as Helena Bonham Carter in a tight corset, clutching your pearls, looking out the sash window,' Laura quips at me every time I enthuse about how lovely it WILL be in about two hundred years' time, when my builder, probably the single most useless individual in the northern hemisphere, eventually gets around to finishing the job. 'You'll end up selling, mark my words.'

I'm too bloody stubborn, and I've shelled out far too much cash at this point to swallow my pride and admit that she might actually be right. Instead, I've schooled myself to look on the whole renovation project as a lesson on the triumph of optimism over bitter experience – with such absolute force of will that if I could only apply the same attitude to my love life, sure I'd be laughing.

Honestly, every time I come home it's like there's a fresh disaster waiting for me with the builder, who is now a full six months behind schedule. He was to be finished at Christmas, it's now well after Easter, and I'm still living in a building site;

dust everywhere, all my stuff in boxes, and only a travel kettle in the kitchen to make the odd cuppa tea with, which I have to drink out of plastic cups because I've no way of washing anything.

I'm not making this up: the other night I came in to find my beautiful original wooden floor in what WILL be my elegant sitting room (trust me, even just saying it is an act of faith) completely and utterly destroyed. Builder-from-hell was supposed to sand it down for me, nice and evenly, then varnish it in a lovely dark, shiny teak; like the kind of floor you'd expect to see Fred Astaire swirling Ginger Rogers around on in a thirties black-and-white movie, at least that was my humble little vision. What I actually ended up with was the whole thing covered in lumps and bumps, not unlike the cellulite on my thighs, except all sealed in with varnish.

'Do you like it, love?' he asked me cheerily, seeing the 'slapped mullet' look on my face. 'It's all the go in these old houses. Gives a kind of "antique" effect. No extra charge for it now, don't worry.'

Anyway, for better or for worse, my house/building site it is. Barbara's flat is sadly out of the question as she shares with another 'resting' actress, so there's never any hope of peace or privacy. Now, I love her flat and I love going around there, it's kind of like a flashback to student days: pizza boxes and empty wine bottles everywhere, with Barbara usually wandering around the place still in her nightie at three in the afternoon watching *Oprah*. Great fun, but our Laura, hygiene fascist that she is, the woman who famously never goes anywhere without Parazone wipes in her bag, reckons she can only ever drink alcohol there, so it'll kill whatever germs are floating around the glasses. And it's not really fair for us to land on Laura either, mainly because, God love her, she'll always jump at any chance she can to escape for a night. It's rare, believe me, as she can never get babysitters, and, as she says herself, it's hardly surprising. Any child-minder in their right mind would demand payment in gold bullion to take responsibility for her precious angels. In fact, Laura reckons pretty much every seventeen-year-old in the area has her blacklisted by now.

Right then, deep breath, here we go.

Project 'let's all try to get what we want out of life for a change'.

No, hate it, too self-helpy. (Please understand I just love attaching names and titles to things; it kind of comes with my job.)

Oh, I know . . .

'The law of attraction in action.'

No, too rhymey.

Butterflies . . . something about butterflies . . .

Yes, got it.

For better or for worse, I'm calling us the Butterfly Club.

Now all we have to figure out is how in God's name we're going to completely and utterly do a three-sixty on each other's lives. Within one year.

Gulp.

Chapter Four

The Butterfly's first meeting. April.

Laura arrives bang on the dot of eight, and I'm not a bit surprised as this is a woman whose punctuality is the stuff of legend. For God's sake, even all four of her kids arrived promptly on their due dates – but as Barbara pointed out at the time, they were probably all too scared of her not to. (Unpunctuality is considered the ultimate war crime chez Laura, and the corresponding punishment is reserved only for the boldest of the bold: **NO TELLY**.)

Anyway, born mammy/candidate for canonization that she is, she arrives bringing a full bag of limes for the margaritas, plus a cocktail shaker, plus crisps and dips and other assorted yummy things. As usual, she's thought of everything. Honestly, if I were a fella, I'd marry her in the morning. No question.

'I knew you and Barbara wouldn't have bothered to eat today,' she says, as we air-kiss in my filthy, dusty hallway, which WILL be lovely when it's finished. (Trust me, the more I keep repeating this like a mantra, the more I actually start to believe it myself.)

'Angel from on high,' I say, leading her inside and down the bockity, narrow, uneven staircase to the kitchen, stepping over boxes of tiles and grouting as we go.

'Dearest, please understand I mean no rudeness by this

54

question,' she says. 'But what has your builder actually achieved since I was last here? If you don't mind me saying, the place, if possible, actually looks worse.'

'Well, emm . . . my new fridge arrived,' I say, a bit defensively, pointing to it, palm outstretched, a bit like a game-show hostess. 'And I do have electricity. And the loo now flushes properly and all.'

God, I sound just like my granny when she used to tell us about the happiest day of her life. It wasn't her wedding day, or even when her kids and grandkids were born, no: it was the day she got her first indoor toilet installed. In 1952.

Laura opens the fridge, sees that the builder has stuffed it full of his own things: Jaffa cakes, bagels, full fat butter and, for some bizarre reason, last Thursday's *Daily Star*, conveniently opened at the racing page.

She pulls out an ancient jar of peanut butter and shoots me one of her knowing glares. Put it this way, if you were a crime lord handcuffed in the dock and she looked at the court jury like that, you'd know instantly that you were a goner.

'Is there a section in *The Guinness Book of Records* for the longest time an unopened jar of peanut butter has been kept for no apparent reason?'

'I know, I know . . .'

'Vicky, only say the word and you can move in with me any time. Now my house may not exactly be the Ritz Carlton, but if you could endure my darling cherubs, we'd love to have you. At least it would be hygienic.'

'Honey, I really appreciate the offer, but at least this way I can keep an eye on Bob the Builder and . . .'

I'm saved from having to make further excuses by the doorbell and Laura's phone ringing simultaneously. Not that I don't appreciate her lovely offer, but I absolutely know that if I had to live under the same roof as her kids for a prolonged period of time, I'd end up either: a) an alcoholic; or b) on eight milligrams of Valium a day.

Note to self: never in my most drunken moment *ever* reveal to Laura that, while I love her kids and on a one-to-one basis am well able for them, the four together can be a bit . . . well, let's just say challenging.

I leave her to her call and race upstairs to let Barbara in.

'Hey, hon, how was your date?' I say as we hug, and I lead her inside. I'm really delighted she's here. Barbara's probably the one person I'm never ashamed of the state of my house in front of. Mainly because her flat is, if anything, worse.

'Eughh, not a keeper,' says Barbara, 'not by the longest of long shots. You should have seen him. The eyes were so cold and dead, it was like sharing a bowl of pasta with Nosferatu.'

'Sure as hell beats what I did last night, i.e., worked. Came home. Tried to figure out what the hell Useless Builder had done all day. Slept.'

'Exactly what I'm here to sort out. Where's Laura?'

'In my elegantly appointed kitchen, probably Parazone-wiping my borrowed patio furniture by now.'

'You got furniture? Way to go.'

'On loan from my mother. Has to be back tomorrow. God love her, she didn't want me to be entirely mortified at the state of the place in front of you pair.'

'Don't suppose by any chance Laura brought food?'

'Tonnes. Dips, crisps, the whole carb-heavy works.'

'Cool, I'm starving. Sex always makes me hungry.'

'Barbara, I thought you didn't even like him?'

'I didn't say I *liked* him, I just *fancy* him. Completely different thing. God, you've so much to learn from me in such a short space of time.'

We head into the kitchen where poor old Laura is deep in

mid-conversation/row with one of the kids, while (I was right) simultaneously Parazone-wiping down the patio table and neatly rearranging the chairs around it, as if you're *supposed* to have garden furniture indoors. Even though she's holding the phone at ear's-length, we can hear everything and it's not pretty.

'Emily, your brother is very sensitive and you are NOT to tell him that you can't heal animals, you just prefer to witness their suffering instead. You know perfectly well that he's very attached to that gerbil, and you're to go in there and apologize to him right now. Yes, well, when you're a mother, you can be mean too. No, that's not true, I *AM* glad you're alive. Right, that's it, I'm hanging up now, tell Granny she can referee the next row . . . ooops, sorry you had to overhear that, ladies,' she says, snapping her phone shut and looking very hassled, as she gives Barbara a big bear hug.

Poor old Laura, her kids really do come with two volumes: loud and deafening.

'Trouble at mill?' asks Barbara sympathetically.

'Oh, don't let's even go there, it could take all night. Barbara dearest, what in God's name are you wearing, did you really come out in public dressed like that?'

'Haven't been home since last night.'

'I thought you'd a date last night.'

'Well, what can I say? It was a good date. Apart from the eejit I was with, that is. In fact I've just done the walk of shame from his apartment . . .'

'And this is what you wore?'

Laura's now picking bits of stray fluff off Barbara's jacket, grooming her like female gorillas do when they've chosen a mate. I saw that on *National Geographic* once and made a silent vow never EVER to even attempt to 'tidy up' a bloke, just in case he runs a mile. At my stage of life, I'm taking no chances. Plus it's sort of evolved into a phrase Barbara and I use to describe the way really, scarily possessive women behave around their blokes: 'dust-fleckers'.

'Yeah, why, what's wrong with it?'

'Nothing, only just that it looks like the kind of fabric they use on the space shuttle to prevent it from burning up on re-entry.'

Now, granted, it might sound a bit stinging, but then that's our Laura for you. Always the barrister, ready with a rapier riposte.

'Mix me a margarita, and while you're at it, pour out a large saucer of milk for the dust-flecker here,' Barbara says to me, as I'm busy squirting lime juice into the cocktail shaker.

I keep my head down and wisely elect to stay well out of this one. Like I said, time and experience have taught me this is always the best course of action whenever this pair start having one of their legendary ding-dongs. The great thing about Barbara, though, is that she never takes offence and is virtually unembarrassable, so Laura's harping on at her tends to go right over her head. Besides, harping on is just a natural extension of Laura's innate mammy gene.

'Was I dust-flecking?' asks Laura, surprised.

'Most definitely.'

'Sorry, dearest, it's an involuntary action with me at this stage,' she says, putting crisps into neat little bowls that she's brought. 'It's just that you can look so lovely when you're dressed . . . how do I put this? A little more upscale and a little less flammable.'

'Right, just for that, we're starting with Vicky. Ladies, please set your bladders to "off".'

'Excuse me, did you say *starting* with me?' I say, peering over the top of the fridge and simultaneously trying to bash ice cubes out of a tray for the drinks.

'If I could jog your sieve-like memory, this caper was entirely your idea, Vicky, so yeah, you're up first,' says Barbara, fishing what looks like a shopping list, scribbled on the back of a gas bill, out of her handbag. 'No point in raising your eyebrow at me either, honey, I missed an entire repeat episode of *Oprah* doing this list out for you. I'm taking my project-management role here very seriously, so you might as well just shut up and listen.'

'Good girl,' says Laura, nodding at her, impressed. 'You not watching daytime television is always a step in the right direction.'

'Right then,' Barbara goes on, ignoring her and referring down to her gas bill, sorry, I mean notes. 'Here's the way I see it. Oh yeah, and you also have to remember that I'm saying all of this from the standpoint of love.'

'That an Oprah-ism too?' asks Laura, one eyebrow raised.

'Do you mind? As project manager, I'm officially telling you that if you interrupt once more, I'll make you go into what WILL be the state-of-the-art jacks, and grout tiles for the rest of the night. You'll get your turn later. Anyway, I think we all know how much you want to be with someone, Vicky . . .'

'The *right* person,' I correct her, slowly pouring the drinks out of the cocktail shaker and into three little picnic-sized plastic beakers. 'Please, dear God, no more emotionally unavailable messers, commitment-phobes, bores that I've nothing in common with and I'm only dating out of my pathological fear of being left alone, eejits, half-wits or, worst of all, most damaging of all, the nice guy, the DSM. You know, the one I actually think could be a runner, a keeper, who, after a few perfectly nice nights out, and a few nice kisses and some nice phone calls etc., drops me like a hot snot. Would you like me to back this up with examples, girls? You've only to ask, I've about two dozen at my fingertips.'

And if I sound like I'm ranting, you'll excuse me. It's only because this particular, painful subject is something of a well-worn hobby horse at this stage. The girls, thankfully, are well-used to me.

'I certainly do take your point about that lethal species, the *nice guy*,' says Laura, emphasizing her words. 'At least if you know in advance that a man is a complete bastard, then if nothing else, you're prepared for heartbreak when it inevitably comes. It's the *nice guys* that ought to come with a government health warning. Well, I married what I thought was a *nice, decent guy*, didn't I? And just look how that turned out for all concerned.'

'So if you can find me a life-partner that fits into the category "none of the above", I'd be eternally grateful,' I say. I'm not quite ignoring Laura, but, at the same time I am hoping to avoid getting into a slagging-off-her-soon-to-be-ex-husband marathon, which, let's face it, could easily go on into the wee small hours. I hate to sound selfish or anything, but we've all devoted so much airtime to that particular subject over the years, and it's most definitely NOT why we're gathered here tonight.

'OK, Vicky, I'm stopping you right there,' says Barbara, firmly. Or at least as firmly as it's possible to sound, given that she's also stuffing her face with tortilla chips and a dribbly blue-cheese dip. 'Just look at what you're attracting!'

'I'm not exactly attracting anyone, now am I? Can I just point out that it's Saturday night and here I am, at home, date-less, living in a building site and sitting on patio furniture borrowed from my mother.'

'At least you're working and earning and you know that you'll have the cash coming in to transform this place,' Laura butts in. 'Look at my life and feel free to gloat if you'd care to. Do you realize there's a very good chance I'll end up rotting in a debtor's prison?'

'As project manager, can I just say we're dealing with one issue at a time,' Barbara says to her, mouth still stuffed. 'You'll get your turn, don't worry, so just sit there quietly and drink your dinner.'

Then she turns her full attention back to me. 'Now, Vicky, I just want you to really listen to yourself: "I don't want this, I don't want that, he can't be like this, I'm so sick of guys who are like that . . ." Come on, what do you expect? You're putting out nothing but negativity, so of course that's what the universe is delivering right back at you. It's very obedient like that. At least that's what that American woman told us at the mind, body, spirit whaddya call it. Remember?'

OK, this actually shuts me up. She did say that and, what's more, so does *The Law of Attraction*. There's a quote in it from some Victorian philosopher saying that just like the law of gravity, the law of attraction never takes a day off. Or words to that effect. Suddenly I'm aware of how negative I do sound, and it's quite a sobering thought. Well, that and the fact that our Barbara, our wonderful, flaky, dippy, slightly off-the-wall Barbara has turned into a cross between Sir Alan Sugar and Donald Trump. You should see her, she's being *scarily* assertive.

'Oh, I'm sorry,' she says, clocking the bewildered look on my face. 'Am I being a bit hard on you?'

'No, but you just said all that with such authority, I bought it.'

Now Laura, who's genetically incapable of sitting quietly and letting other people get on with it, gets her two cents' worth in. 'Ladies, as you're no doubt aware, I have a tendency to tune out whenever you pair start talking about the universe; however, I do actually find myself in agreement here. What I mean is, I see it with the kids all the time,' she adds, taking in the blank expression on both our faces. 'Our brains just aren't programmed to understand negativity. If I say to the kids,

"Don't go outside, it's raining," all they hear are the words "outside" and "raining".' Therefore all I get is: But Mum, we really want to go out outside, that's all we want, you're ruining our lives, we hate you, all of our friends are allowed do what they want . . . etc., etc., etc.", repeat ad nauseam. However, if I rephrase and say, "It's horrible out, let's stay in and read," then they're all up for it.'

She takes in our vacant, non-parent, 'what-the-hell's-she-on-about' stares again. 'Sorry, but I'm only trying to keep this within my own particular frame of reference.'

'OK, OK, so maybe I do have a slight attitude problem when it comes to men,' I say, a bit grudgingly.

'So are you going to sit there whingeing, or are you going to listen to what I have to say?' says Barbara, in the all-new, business-like, assertive voice.

God, I'm thinking, looking at her and drifting off for just a sec, she'd be so fabulous in a soap opera, cast as the Joan Collins type, you know, looking stunning, with the long red hair tied up, wearing professional make-up and a tight little designer suit and a hat with a veil and saying lines like: 'Too bad, Dexter, I just bought ninety-nine per cent of your company, so actually *you're* the one who's fired. HA!'

Well, OK, so maybe with better dialogue than that, but you see what I mean. How come I never spotted this before?

'The way I see it, it doesn't matter how you got here,' she goes on. 'The big question is, what are you prepared to do about it? Which is what I'm here to tell you. And first up is: you're going to write out your dating cheat sheet.'

'Excuse me, my *what*?'

'Like a list. I want you to scribble down the absolute basic, minimum qualities that your future life-partner absolutely must have. Come on, you'd do it if you were buying a house, so why not a husband?'

'Well, maybe not this house,' says Laura, blithely.

'And I want you to be really specific, like, say, if you want him to have a hot body and do meals on wheels in his spare time, or . . . I dunno, be in Amnesty, whatever.'

'So you're saying it's not enough for a guy to be Mr Right any more, he has to be Bono as well,' I say.

'Just hear me out, will you?' says Barbara, referring back to the notes on the back of her gas bill. 'Now one of the more unpleasant sides to being project manager is that I have to get you to face up to the ugly truth. Namely, that for as long as I can remember, Vicky, it's like you've basically been dating any guy that'll ask you. I can't put my finger on it, but it's almost as if you're so bloody grateful that they've invited you out in the first place that you just say yes, regardless of whether you actually like them or not. Once they have a proper job and they don't have two heads you just slap your DSM label on them and away you go.'

Ouch.

There's a tiny, stunned silence from my corner while I'm thinking, could she actually be right?

'I'm afraid I have to agree,' says Laura, nodding like a Buddha. 'You are in fact suffering from indiscriminate affirmative syndrome.'

'Excuse me, I'm suffering from *what*?'

'You always say yes. To men, at least.'

'How *very* dare you,' I say, in a Catherine Tate voice, hands on hips, as though I'm messing, but I'm actually not.

That stung. And, as ever, when cornered, I get a bit defensive. That plus the fact that I'm beginning to feel a bit ganged-up-on by the two of them. God, this is starting to remind me a bit of school, when Laura was the one with all the brains and the great future ahead of her, and Barbara was the one who was never without a fella, and me . . .

Well, I just wisecracked my way through things, really. I'd launch into a comedy routine to cover up my shortcomings/ complete and utter failure with the male race.

And here I am, all these years later, *STILL* doing it.

'OK, so maybe I don't exactly run a screening programme on guys,' I say. 'But come on, I mean, all the dating manuals out there say you have to give every single potential boyfriend a decent chance. Besides, at my age, shouldn't I just gratefully take what I can get? The law of attraction book even says it: attitude is gratitude. So as long as he has a pulse, a job, can use a knife and fork and doesn't steal from my handbag, then I'm prepared to give any guy a whirl.'

Times like this, I wish I came with a canned laughter sound-track, like they have on sitcoms, but the two of them are just looking at me in stony silence.

'And now we're over to the opposition,' says Laura, as if she's hosting a debate on *Prime Time*, using a celery stick as a micro-phone, which she's now thrusting under Barbara's nose. 'I put it to you that Victoria feels her quest to find a life-partner is merely about having no standards at all, to which you reply . . . ?'

'Right then,' says Barbara, topping up our glasses from what's left in the cocktail shaker. 'Sorry to be the one to dole out tough love, Vic, but you've no choice. The longest relationship you've had so far this year was with . . .'

I sigh deeply. Christ alive, she already knows the answer to this one, but if she wants me to illustrate her point, then I may as well just get it over with.

She is, after all, only trying to help me, I keep having to remind myself.

'Lee Harrington. Architect. Met when he came to have a look at this place for me. Thanks so much for opening that particular box, Pandora.'

Although, in hindsight, the only thing I'm grateful for here is that I never actually gave Lee the job. His ideas were just way too 'out-there' for me. Put it like this, he wanted to rip out all the period features and turn my pretty little doll's cottage into a boy-toy heaven, all black granite walls, windows in the ceiling and a giant plasma screen TV built into the living-room wall.

Grand, if you happen to be a Formula One racing driver, but not for me.

'And, remind me again: why did you break up?'

'Barbara, you know perfectly well . . .'

'Say it aloud, dearest,' says Laura, doing her chairwoman thing. 'I think she's trying to establish a pattern here.'

'If you're asking me who dumped who, I can't give you a straight answer because I don't know. It was one of those weird awkward ones, where he went from calling me all the time to big fat nothing. Zero. Like turning off a tap. And of course, all my calls and very concerned texts went ignored. Absolute killer, cos if you both only knew the amount of time and energy that I wasted wondering whether it was something I said or did . . .'

'Now, I may not have been out there at the dating coalface for a very long time,' Laura interrupts, 'but is that the twenty-first century way of breaking up? A guy just stops calling, and somehow you're psychically expected to deduce that you've been dumped? No conversation, not even of the tired old "it's not you, it's me" variety?'

'Pretty much, yup.'

'How cowardly.'

'Cowardice is the least of my worries, the stupid bastard's office keep sending me bills for consultation fees.'

'The point I was actually trying to make,' says Barbara, mouth stuffed full of crisps, 'is that, at the time, you referred to him as, and I quote, "Mr Ah Sure He'll Do".'

'Well, in my defence, I've dated a lot worse.'

'Vicky, just listen to yourself. What I'm trying to get across to you is, if you set the bar low enough, only a louse can crawl underneath.'

'You're the one who just had a fling with a guy whose name you couldn't even remember.'

Told you, I have a very defensive streak. Particularly when I think the other person could actually be on to something.

'Yeah, but, unlike you, I'm not trying to get married. I don't particularly care if I never marry. Completely different set of life priorities going on here, babe. I just wanna be a star. Which is where you come in.'

'Oh yeah, now I had this great idea . . .'

'Stop changing the subject. We're not finished with you. So your homework is, do out your dating cheat sheet and then we need to discuss the way you act around men.'

'My behaviour around men? What, are you telling me now that I come over like some desperado cheap tart that's anyone's for a tin of beans?'

'Shhh, easy there,' says Laura. 'Remember we're here to nurture, not to torture.'

'Very well put, thank you,' says Barbara, wiping a dribbly bit of blue-cheese dip off her face.

'You're most welcome. I'll say this for you, dearest, when it comes to dating: you are something of a gold standard.'

They're 100 per cent right, of course they are. I should just shut up and listen and be grateful to have friends who are prepared to put themselves out and help me to this extent. And Barbara's not criticizing, I remind myself: all tonight's about is window-shopping each other's lives, then gratefully receiving the benefit from everyone else's particular field of expertise. And, to be fair to the girls, my love life could probably do with an industrial-strength, super duper power-hosing down, let's be honest.

'Sorry,' I say meekly, although I'm quite sure my face has gone the colour of gazpacho.

'Go on about the dating-behaviour bit.'

'OK, it's like this,' says Barbara. 'You know how sometimes you see stand-up comics, and it's almost like they have the begging bowl out, looking for laughs, and they're never, ever funny?'

'Ehh, yeah, I think so.'

'Same with fellas. If you try too hard, believe me, they'll know. It's like they come with a sixth sense, and if there's even the slightest whiff of a wedding seating-plan from you, they're out of there. I'm telling you, Vicky, it's a relationship weapon of mass destruction.'

'So what's the answer? Watch a lot of Grace Kelly movies and do my best to come across all cool and ice maideny?'

The two of them snort just at the thought of me trying to act like an ice maiden, and in fairness I can't really blame them.

'I think she's trying to say the solution is just to be yourself,' says Laura. 'Although, ladies, did we really need a book about the law of attraction to tell us that?'

'No, there's more to it than that,' Barbara answers. 'You've got to stop going into each and every relationship thinking: oh my God, this is him, this is the one. All you're doing is putting all your eggs into one basket, then when things don't work out, you're totally devo.'

'Devo?' says Laura.

'Devastated.'

Oh yeah, I forgot to mention that Barbara sometimes talks in kind of Bebo-style teenagery slang. Half the time, I don't really get it, but it makes me feel hip and young on the very rare occasions when I do.

'Right then,' I say. 'So my homework is: I've to do out my,

whatever you call it, dating cheat sheet and then . . . oh yes, have a complete personality change.'

'Be as touchy as you like, but if you want a fella, then hear me out. Before the three of us meet up again, I'm putting you on a two-date minimum. You've got to go out with at least two fellas . . .'

'TWO? Are you kidding me? This isn't Manhattan, you know. Where am I supposed to meet them?'

'Under bar stools if we have to. Hell on the liver, but quicker than speed dating.'

'Did you just say "we"?'

'Oh yeah, that's the other thing. I'm coming with you. I don't trust you not to end up with a complete eejit, if past experience is anything to go by. Plus, if anyone could do with a dating wing-woman, you could.'

'Thanks so much. Why don't you just drop a safe on my head while you're at it?'

'You're the one who wants to turn this year into an *annus mirabilis*, aren't you? So this is what's happening. Suck it up.'

'I agree with you,' says Laura. 'We should all have another margarita.'

'That's not what I said.'

'Well, it was implied. Any excuse to top up our drinks.'

I'm almost relieved when it's my go to have a crack at being project manager, special subject: transforming Miss Barbara Fox into a household name within twelve months. This isn't only relief that the heat's temporarily off me, you understand, it's that I really, really *REALLY* went to an awful lot of trouble on this particular task. Colouredy folders, the works. I was all day at it.

Anyway, while Laura's telling us the latest about her eldest son George Junior, who she calls ASBO boy (her nickname, not mine), I root around for my briefcase then remember that I left it perched on top of a bag of cement filler beside what *WILL* be my state-of-the-art utility room, oh, sometime in the next millennium probably.

'This is a child,' Laura's saying, 'who has no problem eating the dog's diarrhoea tablets, but who won't share a slice of pepperoni from the top of his pizza with his brother. He'll kiss the dog on the lips, but runs a mile when his granny asks for a hug, even though she pays him money for the privilege.'

Laura's always at her funniest, though without ever meaning to be, when she's giving out about her kids, and Barbara's still falling around the place with her big-man, meat and spuds laugh when eventually I find what I'm looking for.

'Da, da!' I sing, handing them each two identical, very official-looking presentation packs, neatly labelled 'project Barbara'. They both wolf-whistle and look dead impressed, and if I say so myself, it does really look fab, like a business plan, except I went a bit mad with the coloured stickers. Oh yeah, and the folders are shiny, see-through fluorescent pink plastic.

'You spent all this time and effort on little ol' me?' says Barbara, delighted. 'Way to go, Vicky, you'll be doing power-point presentations next.'

'If you'd both be good enough to turn to page one,' I say in the special voice I use for pitching meetings, when I want to come across as organized, efficient, you know, on top of things. Oh yeah, and available, just in case there's a single man present. And while we're on this subject, you should just see me in action. Not tooting my own trumpet or anything, but I am actually able to shake hands with a guy and, in a mere fraction of a millisecond, by the tiniest, barely discernible flicker of an eyelid, ascertain whether or not there's a wedding band there or not. God almighty, I should do it as a party piece. Just in case you think I've absolutely nothing at all to show for my decades of chronic singledom.

Anyway, back to our meeting.

'Point A,' I begin, 'is that you, Barbara, are a fabulous actress whose talents are at present criminally under-used. Agreed?'

'I second that,' says Laura.

'Now ladies, if you'll please turn to point B, this is possibly, in no small way, due to having the worst, most useless agent in the business . . .'

'I certainly won't challenge you on that,' Barbara interrupts. 'He's an out and out 'mare.'

'Mare?'

'Nightmare. Gobshite told me the other day that if he didn't get a job for one of his clients soon, he'd have to go full-time behind the checkouts in Tesco. Do you know he has a list of all his clients on his office wall, in descending order of how much commission he's made out of them? Then he's nice to you on the phone in direct proportion to how much cash he's earned out of you. And I'm fifty-third on the list. Out of fifty-four, and the last one is Daisy the pony who does all the pantos. Bastard.'

'So, to be brutally honest, you've attracted an agent into your life who doesn't exactly believe in you, to which I reply . . . let your useless agent just see my proposal and weep. Ladies, if you'll please turn to page one in your folder, clearly labelled "Shakespeare in the park".'

They both flip the folders open, whistling again at how impressive it all looks. But then, in my job, flash tends to win out over substance, it's kind of like the first rule of PR.

'Why Shakespeare?' Laura asks.

'Because he's dead. No copyright to pay. And I can't think of any writer that'll show off Barbara's talents more. You know what they say, if you can do classical theatre, you're able for any-thing. Even an aul soap, anything.'

'And why outdoors?'

'No set, thereby keeping costs to a minimum. Plus, we're coming into the summertime, and just look at how popular outdoor theatre is in New York. They get huge Hollywood stars earning buttons just to get a crack at the classical parts. Course we're going to have to really brainstorm to come up with the right director, but I've got a great pitch for him or her: Shakespeare meets *The Sopranos*.'

'Loving it,' says Barbara, eyes gleaming.

'I want this show to be contemporary and cutting edge and relevant, not like the held-together-with-Sellotape, crappy old productions of *Hamlet*, or the boring, boring history plays we had to yawn our way through in school. Oh, and I've got just the perfect venue in mind, the Iveagh Gardens. It's romantic, peaceful, central . . .'

'And there's a cool bar just around the corner,' says Barbara excitedly. 'What are you both looking at me like that for? The cast will want to go for a drink after the show, won't they?'

'You're going to be networking after,' I say to her firmly, 'like you've never networked before in your entire life. I'm taking personal responsibility to make sure every actor's agent in town will be there. I want this gig to be the hottest ticket since U2 did their homecoming tour. Therefore I suggest we do three performances only, a bit like the opera companies, to keep supply well below demand. Everyone except special invited guests pays full price. My personal vision is that we'll have ticket touts outside buying and selling tickets at twice their face value, like they did when Justin Timberlake played here. Remember? There were nearly fist fights.'

'What about funding?' Laura asks, flicking through the file on her lap.

'Ladies, if you'll kindly turn to your blue sticker, you'll see a list of companies and clients I already represent, who might just be willing to invest. It's a tax write-off for them too, you know. Now brace yourselves for this one, girls. My other idea is that any profit we do make is donated to charity.'

'What?' Laura nearly sprays the wall with margarita, she's spluttering so much, but then money is always a touchy subject with her.

'Because remember, this venture isn't about making money. It's about making Barbara a star.'

'LOVIN' it and LOVIN' you,' says Barbara, looking at me, stunned. 'Keep this up and I'll put you in my will.'

'Oh yes, and a big question for you,' I say to her. 'What is your absolute dream role? The one part that you'd knife someone in the back for?'

For once in her life, she doesn't have a smart answer to hand.

'Emm . . . oh . . . well, when you put it like that . . . jeez . . . can I think about it and get back to you? I just, well, I didn't expect you to be this . . . emm . . . *organized*.'

They both look at me, dead impressed, and I glow a bit.

Then they give me a round of applause, and although I act mortified, I'm actually thrilled. Then . . . oh *shit*.

I remember that I've gone to all this time and trouble over 'project Barbara', and I have sweet bugger-all for Laura . . . apart from one really tiny thing I thought of, but a) I don't know how she'll react, and b) I'm terrified of insulting her.

I mean, at aged thirteen when the rest of us were all squabbling over *Jackie* magazine and stuffing our training bras with tissues, Laura was a fully paid-up member of Mensa. Honestly. I mean, she's just so intelligent and brilliant, with first-class honours degrees hanging out of her, and what I'm about to propose is . . . well, it's not a million miles from asking Thomas Edison if he'd mind changing a light bulb for you. Or Einstein to give a hand with your four-year-old's sums.

Anyway, and I'm not just playing for time here, I get up, mix more margaritas and am just sitting back down again, when she says to me, 'So, Glenda the good witch of the East, don't suppose you've anything in your bag of tricks for this particular

Dorothy?' I look hopefully over to Barbara, but no joy. She's just looking back at me with an expression that might as well say, 'Go on then, you're the prime organizer here, you're the one with all the colouredy folders.'

Right, nothing for it, then.

'Right then, Laura, here's the thing. The way I see it is, of course you're dying to get back to the Bar the minute the baby is in proper, big school . . .'

'Which will be in approximately twenty-eight months' time,' she interrupts. 'But who's counting?'

'But until that happy day dawns, you need a way to generate cash while working from home.'

'You could become an escort,' says Barbara, crunching an ice cube between her teeth. 'You know, like in the film *Belle de Jour*. Pays in cash, too.'

A withering glare from Laura and it's back to me. I fish around in my briefcase, and after a lot of rummaging produce a copy of this month's glossy new *Tattle* magazine.

'What, you're suggesting I become a gossip columnist? Or an agony aunt?'

'Hear me out, honey. Have a look at this.' I hand over the magazine, with a page turned down. 'Now remember, it's only an amuse-bouche of a moneymaking idea, that's all.'

I threw that in casually-on-purpose, hoping the posh word would hook her.

'Amuse-bouche?' She shrugs. 'Fancy.'

'Thanks so much, please use it in a sentence by Monday.'

' "I was in love and then he dumped me like I was radio-active waste," ' she reads aloud from where I marked.

'No, not the problem page, beside it. There.'

'Blah, blah, blah short story contest, blahdy blah blah, theme is a brand-new take on modern motherhood blah blah blah three thousand words, blah blah blah, open to anyone over the age of eighteen, blah blah, closing date for submissions . . .'

Barbara's now stopped her ice-munching and is looking at me as if to say, 'You've certainly wiped the amuse off my bouche.'

'Take a look at the prize money,' I say, sticking to my guns.

'First prize, five thousand euro, second prize, two thousand, third prize, a grand . . . dearest, this is all very well and good, except for one minuscule detail you seem to have overlooked. I can't write. Treatises, yes, legal reports, yes, fiction, are you kidding me?'

'Laura, you are officially the funniest woman I know. Especially when it comes to stories about your kids.'

'Agreed,' says Barbara. 'Certainly the most unintentionally funny. I mean, you telling the story of how Emily is refusing to eat until you get cable is worthy of a slot on *The Late Late Show*.'

'Don't remind me. The little madam said I should change my name to mean.'

'You see? That's the kind of razor-sharp wit and humour they're looking for,' I say.

'And you honestly believe that anyone would want to read about my family life?'

'Come on, sweetie, if I can go on two dates, me the man repeller, and if Barbara can turn into a producer . . .'

'. . . And do bear in mind my last paid acting job was over a year ago, a stunning portrayal of a lump of cholesterol on a beach in the Benecol ad. Unforgettable, really. And the answer to your next question – "Why aren't you playing Broadway as a direct result?" – is "Beats the hell out of me".'

Laura's cornered and she knows it.

'Well, if nothing else, I've just thought of a title,' she eventually says.

'Tell us.'

'It's a sign I hung on the kids' bedroom doors. "Checkout Time is at Eighteen Years".'

Barbara cracks up, with her big he-man laugh, but this time Laura doesn't join in.

'You really think I can do this?' she asks me, looking a bit pole-axed.

'What's the worst that can happen? All you can do is try.'

'In my world, trying merely brings you one step closer to failure.'

'Christ alive, you think what you have to do is a challenge? In the next month I have to try and get two guys to date me.'

But I know exactly how she feels.

Chapter Five

Right then, might as well get this over with. It's Sunday morning, well, mid-morning would probably be a bit more accurate; myself and the girls having sat up till waaaaay late last night, giggling and messing and generally acting like three overgrown tequila tarts. Laura even got to stay out till well after 1 a.m., which for her is a new kind of record, but then she got so worried that her phone *hadn't* rung with updates on whatever row was going on at home, that she panicked herself into thinking that the house was probably on fire and that she should therefore leg it home post-haste.

A silent phone tends to have that effect on her.

Anyway, Barbara and I stayed up till all hours talking shite, taking the world apart and putting it back together again, and now here I am, still in bed, physically unable to budge, I'm that hungover. I'm in no mad rush to get up though, mainly because my bed is probably the most comfortable place to be in the whole house/building site, so I stretch over to my bedside table, grab a pen and pad and get cracking on my homework from last night.

My dating cheat sheet, by Vicky Harper.

Absolute minimum qualities my future life-partner (she sez

76

hopefully) MUST have, otherwise I hereby solemnly vow not to go within six feet of him, regardless of how fit, loaded and sexy he may be. Which neatly brings me to point 1.

1. He must be fit, loaded and sexy.
2. He must go out of his way to win over entire family including messer brothers, who, let's face it, will make it their life mission to reduce the poor fella to a gibbering idiot. And I needn't fool myself into thinking that they'll take pity on me and be nice: Vicky-boyfriend-baiting is something of a blood sport with them. Bastards.
3. He must survive said brothers re-enacting the 'hilarious' story of the time, aged nine, I shaved off the front of my hair in an effort to have that high-forehead look that Glenda Jackson had in *Elizabeth I* (at the time, my favourite TV show). Sadly I ended up looking more like my Uncle Jim, with a stupid look-ing comb-over that lasted for a full year while I waited for my hair to grow back. If asshole brothers are in particularly vicious form, they sometimes produce photos of me with said comb-over, to maximize mortification, then ask potential DSM whether or not I remind him of anyone? (Correct answer: Baldrick from *Blackadder*.)
4. He must find my complete inability to cook cutesy and endearing. Leading to . . .
5. He must love and adore take-out food and be prepared to live off nothing else. Well, until I eventually sign up for one of those cookery courses that celebrity chefs host from time to time, thereby becoming effortless hostess with reputation for holding glittering soirées and making all my own really complicated-looking cakes, like Martha Stewart. Well, Martha Stewart before all that unpleasantness . . . right, then, like Jane Asher.
6. He must on no account fancy Barbara, or Paris and Nicole

from the office. Eyes only for me at all times, regardless of how badly my roots need doing, how haggard I look after a night out with Barbara, or how much water am retaining.

7. He must not be a couch commando, and if I fancy watching *Desperate Housewives*, he'll be suitably quiet throughout and not keep talking through all the juicy bits. Nor will he fancy any of the women in it, either. I am fed up of listening to guys salivating over that Latino one that plays Gabrielle.

8. He must love that I live in a building site and be very handy with a power drill/bag of grout/good old-fashioned hammer and nails.

9. It's also a useful advantage if he knows his arse from his elbow, unlike Joe Egan (three . . . no, sorry, four boyfriends ago) who thought tsunami was an actual place somewhere. Laura had great crack altogether with this and wound him up that Nancy Pelosi was a 1960s folk singer in the Janis Joplin mode and how come he'd never bought any of her albums? Poor eejit, you'd nearly feel sorry for him.

Oh for God's sake, I think, crumpling up the list and flinging it on to the floor. Does such a man even exist?

Right, getting into dangerously negative territory here, I decide, so I hop out of bed, put on a pair of trainers that are lying on the floor, and head downstairs to get my law of attraction book, which I'm pretty sure I left lying on top of a pliers and wrench set strewn somewhere across the living-room floor.

As I'm racing downstairs, it strikes me that in this get-up I must look like that character from *Little Britain* that's escaped from a mental home and spends her time running around in her nightie and trainers going 'ah, ah AAAH'. Times like this, I'm almost glad I don't have a fella to see the state of me . . . *NO*, scrap that negative thought immediately on the grounds that your word is your wand.

When I do have a lovely, suitable DSM in my life, I will of course never wear the horrendous, ankle-length pink fleecy thing I'm in now. (Purely for warmth, you understand, I've no heating YET.) No, it'll be La Perla and fluffy slippers all the way, with spray tan done at *all* times, because everyone knows that makes your lumpy bumpy bits look a million times better and can take a full half stone off you, according to the beauty pages.

Anyway, I find the book lying beside some kind of wrench thing that almost looks like something they'd have used in medieval times to torture Catholics and get them to renounce their faith (don't waste your breath even ASKING, is my motto with Useless Builder), and I hop back upstairs and into my snug, toasty warm bed. I randomly flip open a page from the book, which was dog-eared to start with, but is practically falling apart by now, I've been dipping in and out of it so many times this week. Honest to God, there's whole chunks of it I almost know off-by-heart at this stage. Miracle I managed to get any actual work done.

Anyway, I come across an ancient quote from Robert Collier, dated 1925, which says,

See the things you want as already yours. Know in your heart of hearts that they will come to you, then simply let them come. Don't fret and worry about them, just think of them as absolutely belonging to you, as already in your possession.

Yes, love it, it's the perfect affirmation for me. And amazing that, although written so long ago, somehow it's still relevant today. Right then, time for a bit of unwavering faith. Belief in the unseen.

OK, fair enough.

Walk in the park really, I mean all I have to do is imagine my ideal life, or in my case, my *ideal* partner. The book says you're supposed to spend about ten minutes a day, morning and evening, meditating or channelling or whatever it is you want to call it, but basically it all pretty much involves the same thing: me lying in bed, staring at the ceiling, really, *really*, REALLY focusing on what I want out of life.

OK then. One simple, clear image that to me encapsulates what would make me happy, or as it says in the book, what would be my 'bliss'. There's also a quote from Einstein, of all people, about imagination being the highest kite you can fly, so with that in mind, I close my eyes and off I drift . . .

Yes, there I am. Still in bed with my wonderful partner stretched out beside me, except just not this bed as it's ancient and a bit creaky; no, what I'd love is one of those fabulous four-poster beds that really suit old houses, you know, you see them in posh hotels all the time. Oh, but then, how would it fit into the room? Oh I know, they'd have to dismantle it then re-assemble it . . .

Shit, shit, shit, this is not exactly what you might call focused concentration, now is it?

I start again, bearing in mind that the point of the exercise is to visualize my perfect life; soft furnishings are a detail that I can worry about later. Although, while we're on the subject, I definitely do want those stunning Frette sheets that cost a fortune, but that are just the sexiest thing against your skin, like satin only warm to the touch, and I'd nearly swear I saw that they were on sale in the House of Fraser . . .

Oh for f**k's sake, even Laura's seven-year-old has better concentration skills than me. Right, go again.

Yes, here I am all snuggled up in my yet-to-be-decided-what-it'll-end-up-looking-like-bed as my boyfriend/life-partner/future husband spoons into me from behind.

I chose that particular image on purpose, so I could *hear* what he sounds like but not actually *see* his face, because otherwise, knowing me, I'll only hold it in my mind's eye like some kind of Identikit picture and then measure any subsequent, future DSMs against the picture of perfection I'm about to conjure up. And, let's face it, how could any flesh and blood fella possibly compete? At this stage in my long and chequered dating career, the one thing I can say with absolute certainty is that it doesn't matter a shite what he looks like.

Although the voice is definitely . . . Johnny Depp's? No, no, I keep thinking of the way he sounded like one of the elderly Rolling Stones in *Pirates of the Caribbean* . . . James Mason's? No, too creepy . . .

Got it, George Clooney's. You know a gravelly, sexy, cigars and brandy voice . . . mmmm . . .

HIM: 'Darling, would you like me to bring you some breakfast in bed? You know how I trained to be a cordon bleu chef in my spare time, before I floated my company on the stock exchange and became a billionaire, and right after I won the Olympic silver medal for having such a hot bod?'

ME: 'Mmmm.'

HIM: 'But in spite of all my humble achievements, *Time* magazine Man of the Year, all of that, there's still nothing in this world that gives me more pleasure than to cook for you, my sweet, slumbering angel.'

ME: 'Fair enough, make it . . . ehh, two rashers, two sausages, scrambled eggs on wholemeal toast and a cappuccino, low fat. Thanks, love.'

HIM: 'It's my pleasure. Have I told you so far today how happy you've made me, darling?'

ME: (*Mock mortified, yet slightly raging that Laura and Barbara aren't around to overhear.*) 'Ah, you're embarrassing me now. But don't let that stop you, go on, keep going.'

HIM: 'I often think that until you came along, darling Vicky, my life was so empty and meaningless. I mean, all I ever did was flit around the world in my Lear jet, dating a string of vacuous supermodels, none of whom could hold a candle to you, even without your make-up, in that very fetching pink fleece thing you're wearing now. I would divide my time between all fifteen of my properties dotted around the globe and think, 'Where's the right person for me? When will the fates ever bring us together?' Little did I know that when I was invited to Dublin to accept the award for 'best and most generous humanitarian who ever lived, ever', that the woman of my dreams would be doing the PR for it. You, my darling, have made me the happiest man in the world. How long is it since I showered you with a token of my undying love?'

ME: 'Ehh . . . that would be . . . last Tuesday. The racehorse. No, hang on, that was the week before, oh, yeah, now I remember, this week it was the tickets to go first class on the Orient Express.'

HIM: 'Then how about we go jewellery shopping today, darling? And afterwards I absolutely insist that you go on the piss with Laura and Barbara while I play snooker with your delightful brothers. You know how I just can't get enough of their company and their hilarious pranks. Oh dear me, is that the door? It must be the people from *Architectural Digest* to photograph the house for their feature on 'the top ten most beautiful houses in the country'. No, you lie on, dearest, let me get it.' (*All of the above speech to be delivered in very sexy, non-doormat tones.*)

Well, if the secret to life is just ask, believe and receive, then I've already done two out of three. And the book is very clear that, just like ordering from a catalogue, once you've placed your actual order, then you only have to sit back, relax and wait for the miracle to happen, serene in the knowledge that it absolutely WILL. In fact, it's all sounding so scarily easy that I go back to my tatty book just to check I got it right.

Nope, there it is, in black and white:

As for receiving, all that's required is to feel absolutely positive that your bounty is on its way towards you. The more joyous you feel about the wonderful life that's just about to begin for you, the faster it will manifest, winging its way towards you with the speed of light.

How fab is this? I think, snuggling back under the duvet. All I need do is *feel* like I'm in love and Mr Wonderful, Mr Ah–Go–On–Let–Me–Cook–For–You should be here by the end of the week, by the sounds of it.

And this time, I'm not budging, compromising or settling for anything less.

Piece of cake, really.

Chapter Six

Monday morning and I'm just on my way into the big pitching meeting, when my phone rings. Laura. Sounding an awful lot more harassed and stressed than normal, which, God love her, is really saying something.

'I'm ringing to tell you never to have kids, do you hear me? If you feel an overriding need to reproduce, just borrow one of mine for a twenty-four-hour period, that'll cure you.'

'Oh, honey, what's up? Anything I can do to help?'

'Pure visual contraception, that's what they are,' she goes on, ignoring me and speaking in a scarily high-pitched voice. 'My God, why don't I just charge people?'

OK, now she sounds *really* upset, which immediately worries me. Laura never, ever gets upset or emotional, at any time, *ever*. She's the only person I know who even managed to sit through Princess Diana's funeral without a tear-streaked face. Honestly.

'What happened? Tell me everything.'

'Have you time for this?'

I don't really, I'm literally on the steps of Best Advertising agency. (No, I'm not messing, that really *is* the name, it's owned by someone called Best, which is kind of an advertiser's dream, when you think about it.) But of course I can't say that to her.

'All the time in the world, babe. Are you OK? Do you need me to do anything?'

'You could get a hit man after George Hastings, that'd be a start.'

'Oh dear. Something to do with last night, maybe? How did it go?'

From the back of my mind, I dimly remember her telling me something about Emily spending the night at her dad's. Emily is child number two, devoted to her dad and, at the tender age of ELEVEN, already acting and behaving like a pre-teen Lindsay Lohan, only worse, if you could imagine.

She's not quite a kid, not nearly an adult.

A kid-ult, if they've even invented such a term yet.

'Oh, your average night in hell. I went to collect her on my school run this morning, punctually on the dot of seven thirty and the hall door was opened by Miss Human Botox.'

Laura's nickname for George's live-in girlfriend. She's one of those permanent student types who goes round dressed like an eco warrior, has hair down to her bum, and who I don't think has ever been single once in her entire life.

'So what happened?'

'Human Botox tells me that she and Emily, who have now bonded in a frighteningly huge way, are taking a trip with George during the summer, all happy families together. So, I do my best to stay cool and I say, oh really, may I ask where to? Euro Disney, I'm casually told. Oh really, I say, deliberately keeping my tone measured, and who will be financing this little jaunt? Then she umms and aahs and calls George Hastings, who comes to the door still in his dressing gown, with the hair looking like he'd slept in a tree and I just *know* by his general laid-back demeanour that he'd been having early morning relations with that floozie.'

Laura, by the way, never says 'sex', always 'relations'. I think coming from a political dynasty must make you a bit prudish like that.

'So I calmly pointed out to Emily that Daddy really shouldn't make promises he can't keep, which only sets her off wailing, to the backing track of the other three screeching in the car. At which point I ask George Hastings how he can even suggest offering such a huge treat to one child, *nothing* for the others, and all the while being months behind on his child-maintenance payments? He says Miss Human Botox has kindly agreed to pay for half of the trip, I can only presume out of her student grant. In fact, I've a good mind to report her to the university authorities, that'd soften her cough.'

'But why do you think she's even doing this?'

'One of two possible motives. Either the misguided idiot is trying to parade her parenting skills in front of her boyfriend, or else in some warped way, she's trying to undermine me.'

'Either way, she's a stupid cow. May she fail every exam she ever sits and end up working behind a tea urn in the college canteen to finance her heroin habit,' I say loyally.

'Bless you for that delightfully charitable thought. Anyway, I flash her my falsest smile and say what wonderful news it is to hear that she has access to taxpayer's money. Then I remind George Hastings that school fees, mortgages and grocery bills are, in fact, not luxury items, and that if he doesn't find some way of coughing up, I have no difficulty hauling him into court and suing him for being in arrears. And that's not an idle threat, Vicky; I'd *kill* to get back inside a courtroom, even if it's only the family law court. He'd think he was hit by a stealth missile.'

'Good girl,' I say staunchly. 'Serve the bastard right.'

'So then, of course, back in the car I have to deal with Emily, who keeps up her wailing the whole way to school, telling me how mean I am, that I've ruined her summer holiday, and that she infinitely prefers Miss Human Botox to me. So, of course the boys want to know what's going on and Emily tells them all about how she was invited to Euro Disney and that I'm refusing to let her go. Then of course I get a full, disco-extended version from the boys of "why is she invited and we're not?" followed by a chorus of "you're so mean and we never get to do anything fun", and honestly, Vicky, by now I'm at boiling point. It's not even eight a.m. on a Monday morning, I still have a whole week to get through, and I really believe I could have a breakdown. I'm hanging on for dear life here, but every single passing day is just becoming more and more of a struggle. Listen to me and tell me the honest truth; do I sound like I'm having an anxiety attack?'

'No,' I say, as firmly as I can. 'You're wonderful and strong, and you're a fabulous parent, and when your kids are grown up they'll look at you in awe, because you managed to bring up *four*, pretty much single-handedly and with sod-all money to speak of. What you're doing is incredible. I couldn't admire you more, I mean that so sincerely.'

'No, Vicky, I'm doing all the things separated parents are never supposed to do, misdirecting all my anger at the kids when the person I really want to see dying a slow, painful death is George Hastings. I just hate this so much. I hate that I shouted back at them in the car. I hate that all their friends have fabulous things that mine will never have because I can't afford them. And most of all, I hate it that bloody George Hastings gets to play fun daddy all the time, while I have to be the tough disciplinarian.'

Her voice is cracking with emotion, and now I'm really worried. This is unheard-of. Laura's always the one who holds the rest of us together, she's never the one to break, ever.

'Where are you now? I'll drop everything and come over.'

What the hell, I can reschedule the pitch meeting if I have to.

They'll understand. They've no choice.

'Bless you for offering, but no thank you, dearest. I know it's a big day for you, and really, even just talking about this is helping me considerably. I can hardly ring Barbara, because she's probably still not home from wherever she was last night. Just tell me when you need to hang up.'

'I've ages yet,' I lie. 'Go on, keep talking.'

'So, anyway, the saga continues. I drop the three of them at the school gates, still screaming at me and at each other, and I can see all the yummy mummies in their Range Rovers with their immaculate blow-dries looking pityingly at me while they hand over packed lunches made by nannies to children who actually *hug them goodbye*. Mine just run out of the car and disappear into the throng, as if they can't get away from me fast enough. So I pull the car out, still furious and muttering phrases to myself about how much sharper than a serpent's tooth it is to have ungrateful children, and then it strikes me that Baby Julia's being quieter than normal. So I turn around and there she is, in her booster seat, the remains of her Coco Pops breakfast still congealed around the edge of her mouth, clinging to her teddy with silent tears rolling down her fat little cheeks. I ask her what's the matter, and even though she can't understand, her face lights up, just at the rowing and shouting being over and at my paying her some attention for a change. Then she gives me a smile so big I can see all five of her teeth, and in her little baby voice she says, "Mama."'

'Oh God.'

'I know. I pulled the car over, got in beside her and hugged the child so tightly, I thought she was going to break. And I howled, I howled to the four walls.'

'Oh, honey,' is all I can say. Poor Laura. I mean, every time she tells me a story like this, I silently vow never to moan EVER again.

'So my question is this,' she goes on, and I know by her voice she's struggling to sound composed. 'Are you honestly telling me that anyone could possibly want to read about this demented life?'

'Yes,' I say firmly, 'they would. And it's not a demented life, it's a real life.'

'This morning, a lifeline was thrown at me by an infant who can barely speak. And do you know what I said back to the child? I said, "I'm keeping you at home with me until you're forty, and up until then, every man you'll meet will be related to you." She's my little consolation prize sent from God, and I'm not having my angel growing up either resenting me like the others or, worse, throwing her life away at twenty-one on another bloody worthless George Hastings, like I did. Not exactly yummy mummy stuff, now is it?'

'Speaking purely from a PR perspective, I can tell you the yummy mummy has had her day. It's all about the slummy mummy now, babe.'

'Oh, thank God for that. I couldn't bear to read about another new mum, lovingly supported by her adoring husband, back in her size ten jeans two weeks after giving birth, and con-templating an affair with a sexy, single dad she meets on the school run. Could that be any more different from the life I'm living?'

'Just write the way you talk, and we're home and dry. Trust me on this.'

'Well, then, I suppose this is the final rung in my descent from noted young barrister to dancing bear,' she sighs. 'Right then. If only for reasons of catharsis, I'll write out something and send it to you from my new email address: "Laura at bottom of the barrel dot net".'

There's a tiny pause and I just know she's doing her lop-sided smile thing. This is a big improvement, this is great progress from the state she was in at the start of the call. She sounds cooler, calmer, more like herself. My God, she even went for a gag.

I make all the soothing, supportive, clucking noises I can, and just as we're saying our goodbyes and I'm heading in for my meeting, it flashes through my mind . . . is there anything in my dog-eared law of attraction book that might offer her a granule of comfort right now?

No. If I was to tell her that somehow, she *attracted* all this into her life, she'd probably never speak to me again, and I don't think I'd even blame her. Although I am pretty certain there's a reason for everything she's going through right now.

I just haven't a clue what it is.

At least, not yet.

Chapter Seven

Now, I've actually done some work with Best Advertising before and I *love* visiting their office. It's just the coolest place you could imagine; I honestly think if I worked here, I'd never throw a sickie, ever. It's an old malt house, completely refurbished but with a lot of the old, original features still intact. Exposed brick on the inside, frosted-glass brick staircases, you know, the sort of building architects must lie awake at night salivating over.

Anyway, two things you should know about Best's: a) I often think they must have a policy in their HR department that to work here you must be under thirty, hot and with a smokin' body, guys included, and b) the company motto seems to be 'at all costs, have a good time'. They often have these mad theme days going on, like champagne Thursday (I remember nearly falling out of here after one late meeting, but then two drinks on an empty tummy does that to me) and Fridays where everyone comes in wearing Hawaiian shirts and keeps saying 'aloha' to you down the phone, that kind of thing.

I'm half-afraid to ever bring Paris and Nicole here with me; they might start getting ideas.

'Vicky Harper here to see Amanda Smith, brand consultant,' I say to the very smiley, very blonde, cute-looking guy behind the desk.

'Take a seat and I'll let her know you're here,' he beams. I'm just about to plonk down on a very luxurious-looking leather sofa when he says, 'Hey, would you like a mocha kiss?'

'Excuse me?'

'It's just that today is Choca-Mocha Monday and I can highly recommend their kisses. They're a new account and they keep giving us freebies by the truckload. Here, you HAVE to try them. Utterly divine.' With that, he tosses me over a bright red, heart-shaped bag stuffed full with lovely, shiny, individually wrapped kisses.

Free chocolate handed to you first thing on a Monday morning? Bloody hell, I might apply for a job here myself.

A few minutes later, Amanda comes click-clacking down the glass brick staircase, waving a giant-sized, lipstick-shaped pack of mocha kisses at me. You'd love Amanda, she's bubbly and she's a howl and she's always full of hilarious stories about rubbish dates she's been on, and no kidding, every time I see her, the hair is a different colour. Today it's bright blonde, but with jet black streaks going through it, from front to back.

'Hey, gorgeous, I bring the best PMS treatment in the whole world,' she squeals at me as we air-kiss at reception.

'Freebies, loving it,' I say, gratefully taking the bag of kisses from her. 'And loving the hair too, by the way. Miles nicer than the time you had it purple.'

'You don't think it makes me look like a badger on NatureWatch, do you? The girls upstairs are giving me a rotten time. They say I look like an endangered species.'

'No, totally fab.'

I'm not just being nice; it's the God's honest truth. Plus she's got a stunning black-and-white Marni dress on, which I know cost a fortune because I looked at it in Harvey Nicks and nearly had to have a lie-down when I saw the price tag. She looks like a goddess in it, far better than I would have, but then Amanda's one of those people who, if they wore a bin liner, would make Kate Moss want to rip it off their back in a fit of jealousy.

I think it must be yet another Best company policy – at all times, staff are required to dress like they just stepped off a cat-walk in Milan – which makes me: a) doubly delighted I'm wearing my really good white linen trouser-suit from Zara today, and b) overwhelmingly grateful for the minor miracle that I actually remembered to pick it up from the dry cleaners. Actually, come to think of it, it's maybe the only disadvantage of working for a company like this: the sheer number of man-hours I'd lose worrying over what to wear the next day. It would probably kill me.

'Ooooh, Vicky, I love, love, *love* that you're pitching for this,' Amanda says, squeezing my arm as we both troop up the glass staircase.

'Well, I love, love, *love* hearing that.'

'No really, everyone here still raves about the fashionista launch you did for us. Most amazing night *ever*. Well, except the guy I ended up with at the after-show party turned out to be bisexual, but that was hardly your fault, and apart from that, it was just totally, like, *out there*.'

This was the last time we worked together, about a year ago, when Best's hired me to launch the new Peter O'Brien ready-to-wear collection for a big high street chain. Their suggestion was that we hold it in a trendy down-town champagne bar, but I had the strongest instinct that that would be just a bit too . . . obvious. So I rang the designer, the mighty Mr O'Brien himself, and asked him what his inspiration for the collection had been. Well, it was like striking gold: it turned out he'd based the overall concept for the entire collection on the portraits by Sir John Lavery hanging in the National Art Gallery. It was just the eureka moment I needed; I pitched that we host the launch there, had murder trying to win Best's around, but eventually wore them down, and the rest is history.

Honestly, if I say so myself, it was a glittering night. I'd arranged for models wearing exact copies of the Edwardian dresses in the portraits to pose in gilt-edged picture-frames, then step out and circulate. It was a gamble, but it worked a treat: the launch practically generated more column inches than the President's last state tour, and the stores that stocked Peter O'Brien's clothes sold out, literally in hours, leaving nothing but empty shelves and queues outside the doors, a bit like Stalinist Russia on Christmas Eve.

A few hardier shoppers even vowed that for his next collection, they'd camp in sleeping bags on the pavement outside the store the night before, like people do when U2 tickets go on sale, just to be on the safe side. And the icing on the cake: the whole story even ended up getting a novelty item feature on the *Six O'Clock News*, which in PR terms is kind of like the Holy Grail.

Which is kind of why I feel confident about coming back here this morning, with the new pitch I've worked so hard on for them.

Which is kind of why I feel, OK so it's not *technically* in the bag, but I think I might just be sending Paris and Nicole out to buy a lovely big bottle of pink champagne for us to celebrate with before the day is out.

Which is kind of why my heart sinks a bit when, just as we're about to go into the boardroom, Amanda turns to me and says, 'Oh, yeah, by the way, the boss is sitting in on this one. It's just that it's such a huge contract and this client is so important to us. You don't mind, do you?'

Shit.

Funny, this is normally the way the law of attraction works on my love life. Every time I feel confident about a bloke, I'm rewarded with a sharp smack in the gob from the universe.

I will seriously have to re-read that book when I get home.

Anyway, as you might expect from a company like Best's, the boardroom is more like somewhere you'd throw a party in; in fact I bet they use it for their staff Christmas party.

Note to self: do level best to get invited to their next Christmas do. I wouldn't be a bit surprised if they make it a condition of your Christmas bonus that you have to kiss the face off as many people as possible, therefore am bound to score. Yes, even me.

The room is huge and white and bright and fab, with a giant Louise Kennedy crystal chandelier, bright-blue swan chairs, and so many bowls of sweets dotted around that I almost feel like emptying one into my handbag for later. Don't worry, I don't, but when Amanda plonks down beside me and tosses me a mocha kiss I can't help myself. I'd no breakfast this morning due to having no kitchen, I just grabbed a Starbucks which I gulped back in the car, and am now half-afraid that the pitch I've put my heart and soul into will be drowned out by my tummy, which is now rumbling louder than a 747 cleared for landing at JFK. We're the first people here, there's no one to see, so within two seconds, I've stuffed two of them into my face in one go.

'Oh, God, Amanda, the only thing you got wrong with these is the name. Should have called them chocolate orgasms.'

'Mmmm, I mwah, merw mmmmmmmmm,' is what she comes out with, but I'm pretty sure she's agreeing with me.

Pretty soon, the room fills up and it's showtime. Amanda introduces me to about eight different people; more staff from Best's marketing department who I haven't met before, more design consultants, more brand consultants and then of course . . . drum roll for dramatic effect . . . the client herself, one Sophie Boyd. She's older than anyone else here, maybe fifties, and is dressed to kill in a stunning pale-blue pastel suit with a matching Hermès scarf. The hair is cut into the most perfectly executed blonde bob and I know just by looking it must take at least half an hour every morning with a GHD to get it sitting that poker-straight. She has a distant, bored look and kind of reminds me of Meryl Streep in that movie, *The Devil Wears Prada*. In fact, I'd safely say she's one of those frowningly important women who come with their icy stares all pre-graded, from class A to class C (the one that reduces her staff to whimpering wrecks), entirely depending on how narky a mood she's in.

Apart from her, there's two guys, the rest are all women, and needless to say, everyone's outrageously good-looking, fully in keeping with the company ethos. Amanda doesn't give me their actual job-titles though, and I'm frantically trying to put faces to names and names to titles, and even more critically, gulp, figure out who is this boss I'll have to try and impress the most, when suddenly a size-zero Posh Spice look-alike, wearing a suit just like mine only in black (thank you, universe), steers me away from everyone else and introduces herself as Best's senior creative adviser.

Oh, bugger. We shake hands coolly, and I swear I can practically see this one taking an instant dislike to me, which I probably should explain.

The relationship between creatives and PR people can pretty much be summarized thus: they hate the sight of me and I hate the sight of them. They tend to look on people in my game as jumped-up nobodies, outsourced and now trying to muscle in on their territory; whereas we look on them as behind the times for not accepting that launching any new product is a huge deal, and that PR people need to be involved in product development from day one, whether they like it or not. And, on a personal/slightly bitchy note, I have yet to hear any 'creative' come up with a concept that isn't a rehash of what's already out there, instead of being ahead of the game. Just like the fashion world: the real players there have already decided now what we'll all be wearing in about two years' time.

I don't have to pretend to be nice to her for too long. After a light bit of chit-chat, everyone just plonks down on the swan chairs and Amanda asks Posh Spice look-alike to kick-off. Which she does, giving me a sneaky few minutes to glance around the room, trying to figure out which one is the Don Corleone, so to speak.

'OK, well, in keeping with the Hollywood theme you envisage for Original Sin,' Posh Spice is saying, in her 'It' girl voice, holding up a storyboard, 'I'd like to suggest we go for a young, hip concept that will appeal to the broadest section of our target market. So, I've created Isabella to represent our ideal consumer. OK, so let me introduce you. Isabella is aged between twenty and thirty-five years old, OK? She lives in Malibu, California, she spends all her weekends at the beach, and she drives a Mercedes convertible, OK? She eats out at least three times a week, works out four times a week and is more likely to agree with the lifestyle statement: "It's more important to look good than to work hard."'

She keeps droning on and on about Isabella's favourite colours and movie stars and TV shows, and will probably be telling us what colour her knickers are in a minute, but I'm not fully concentrating, I'm too busy scanning the room for who could possibly be the head honcho around here . . . and having absolutely no joy whatsoever. I'm just wondering if maybe whoever it is couldn't show up at the last minute, for some multi-millionaire type reason such as the private jet ran out of Moët & Chandon or something, when the tag-line of Posh Spice's pitch suddenly pulls me back into the room.

'. . . so to conclude,' she's twittering, 'I would say our overall image could be summarized in a single phrase, Bel Air.'

What? Bel Air freshener, is what I'm thinking, as the rest of the room give her a small round of applause and, hypocritically, I have to join in. Oh my God, that is so NOT what I had envisaged for this product, I'm thinking, glancing down at my notes for the launch which so don't fit in with any of Posh Spice's pitch, not a bit of it . . .

'Great, fabulous,' Sophie says. 'Can you get preliminary budget figures to me ASAP?' There's a lot of relieved-looking faces around the table, and you can practically see them all thinking: great, now that that's out of the way, client's happy, let's all go to lunch. But Sophie clearly doesn't feel she's got her money's worth.

'It's not that I don't like it,' she says slowly, coolly looking out the window and clicking a pen, 'but I'd very much like to hear what else you've got?'

A few barely discernible panicky glances around the room followed by a cacophony of voices from everyone as the brainstorming instantly starts. Or maybe they're all improvising wildly; these people are all so bloody good, it's hard to tell the difference.

'What about a theme revolving around Hollywood musicals?' one cute guy in the corner throws in. 'Each commercial could tie in with a signature tune . . .'

'Yeah, like *Singing in the Rain* to plug . . .'

'Waterproof mascara!'

'The Hollywood epic . . .'

'Yeah, we could shoot in one of those swords-and-sandals locations and tie it in with . . .'

'The self-tanning products!'

'Or sunscreens!'

Sophie, I notice, stays very impassive, just jots things down and every now and then throws in, 'Hmmm. So what else?' And on they all go, one idea falling over another, till my head's almost swimming from listening to them all. Don't get me wrong, every idea they're throwing out is a gem. I mean, these are gifted, talented people clearly at the top of their game, it's just that . . .

None of their pitches ties in with what I've been working so hard on. Not a single one. Shit. Now instead of looking forward to throwing in my pitch, I'm actually beginning to dread it. They're going to hate what I have to say, and probably hate me too into the bargain . . .

As if she's picking up on my nervousness, on cue, Sophie slowly turns to me. 'We haven't heard from PR yet,' she says. 'So, can I have your pitch for the launch itself?' And whether I like it or not, I'm on. Right then, for better or for worse, there's nothing for it but to come clean and just admit that I've been working off a completely different hymn sheet to everyone else. Bugger it anyway. I wouldn't mind, but I'd have *killed* to have landed this gig . . .

'When I first heard the product was called Original Sin,' I begin, taking the floor and doing my best to sound loud, clear and confident, 'I thought the name was inspired. Yes, a Hollywood theme for this product is terrific . . . but . . . the thing is . . . my ideas were a little bit different. You see, I was thinking . . . how about we go back a little further? Back to Hollywood's golden era of glamour, to the age of film noir, to women like Barbara Stanwyck and Ingrid Bergman. Women who didn't have access to a fraction of the cosmetic wonders that we have now, but who never looked anything other than fabulous. I'm speaking, of course about the nineteen forties.'

Sophie raises a single eyebrow, à la Roger Moore, which I take to be a good sign. I include the rest of the room, but primarily address the pitch to her. What the hell, at this stage, I've nothing to lose.

'And the launch party itself?' she asks, impassive as you like.

'Should be like stepping back into an old film noir. Think

gentle, tinkling Cole Porter piano music, cocktails, models wearing pillbox hats with veils, Dior's New Look.'

'Hmmm,' she says, looking at me keenly. 'And do you have any thoughts about the commercials? As we're all here to brainstorm.'

OK, just at the mention of the word 'commercials', I'm dimly aware that some of the glances I'm getting around the table are starting to become a bit hostile, and I swear I can practically feel what they're all thinking. I'm an outsourced PR person, brought in to pitch for a product launch, who's now in danger of getting seriously out of my depth. But the thing is, I do have ideas about this and, well . . . she did ask . . . Figuring what the hell, I'm in this far, I take a deep breath and plunge deeper.

'Well, I would suggest,' I begin slowly, trying not to piss off the whole room. 'That is . . . I think it would be fabulous if all of your commercials were shot entirely in shadowy black and white, with one exception: the pillar-box red of our model's lipstick and nail varnish.'

Sophie just nods, so I plough on, getting into my stride a bit.

'One theme I would suggest is "the seven deadly sins": seven commercials, seven products, broadcast over seven months. The buzzwords would be elegance, old-world style and the cool sophistication of women who never have to try too hard. But, the way I see it, this wouldn't just be any commercial, it would be a mini-movie, and when it's broadcast, it'll be almost an event, just like when Chanel asked Nicole Kidman to advertise their No. 5 perfume, with Paris as the backdrop; except this will be more like a little piece of *Casablanca*. In fact, that movie has very much been a touchstone of mine for this project; I'd suggest Original Sin to evoke an era when femmes were fatale, just like Ingrid Bergman was in that iconic scene where she . . .'

'Hey, anyone here care to see me do Bogey?' asks a guy

from across the room, doing a pretty decent Humphrey Bogart impression actually, upper lip disappearing into his top teeth and all. Everyone giggles, and I give him a polite but firm 'I'm touting for work here and fighting for my professional reputation, so do you mind shutting up for a minute please?' look.

'Sorry,' he says, grinning cheekily at me. 'It's just that *Casablanca* is my desert island all-time favourite film.'

I smile politely and am about to get back to pitching when Sophie suddenly brightens and says, 'You know what? Mine too. Wasn't Ingrid Bergman just exquisite?'

Next thing this guy pipes up again, breaking into a full chorus of 'As Time Goes By'. Then he takes a mock bow as the whole room give him a polite ripple of applause, then stuffs a mocha kiss into his mouth and sits back, arms folded behind his head, grinning.

Oh, OK, I think I know what's going on here.

There's one in every company: the office messer. The comedian. You know, the one who reckons that all he need do is put on a one-man show at the Edinburgh Festival to be snapped up by the BBC, given his own sitcom and hailed as the next Ricky Gervais.

'Everyone thinks that's the only song in the movie,' Messer Man goes on, 'but it's not. Sam sings "Knock on Wood" too. Now the day will come when you'll all thank me for sharing that with you. Useless trivia like that comes in very handy at pub quizzes, I'll have you know.'

More polite laughter, which I barely wait to die down, before I get back to the pitch.

Don't get me wrong, this guy's cute: thick unruly dark curls, and black twinkly eyes. Imagine Heathcliff if he just fell out of bed and put on the first thing that came to hand. He's actually the only person in the room wearing jeans and trainers, and

101

seems so laid-back, he'll probably have his feet up on the boardroom table in a minute and start passing around a six-pack.

But I can't afford to let the messing get to me, whether Sophie loves or hates my ideas. I need the PR for this gig too badly.

I wrap up, then pass around the budget costings for the launch, along with some suggested venues I was all day yesterday working on, and mentally remind myself to make particular eye-contact with Sophie as I wrap up. She gives me a half-smile as she takes the presentation pack from me, which I interpret as a positive sign. 'We'll be in touch,' is all she says, as the meeting breaks up and everyone scatters to the four winds.

'Way to go, girl,' Amanda whispers to me, squeezing my arm encouragingly on her way to the door. 'That stuff about *Casablanca* . . . pure genius. I could tell the boss loved it. Oh, better escort this one downstairs,' she says, indicating Posh Spice, who's packing up her briefcase with a face on her like a bulldog sucking a wasp. 'Talk to you later, Vicky, and congratulations. Fab, as usual.'

'Great, thanks.'

The boardroom's almost completely cleared out by now, and I'm just packing up my stuff when Messer Man saunters back over, like he's all the time in the world. The only person in the room who's in absolutely no rush whatsoever to get back to work.

'So are you a black-and-white movie buff then?' he asks, arms folded, twinkling down at me, taller than I'd have guessed.

'Definitely,' I say, a helluva lot more relaxed now that it's all over bar the shouting, so to speak.

'Did you know *Casablanca* started out as a stage play?' he asks, plonking himself down on the boardroom table, one leg crossed over another. No kidding, if this guy was any more laid-back, he'd probably be dead.

'You're kidding, really?'

'Hand on heart. Called *Everybody Comes To Rick's*. "Now not a lot of people know that." '

'You do a great Humphrey Bogart.'

'Eh, thanks, but that was actually Michael Caine, that time. "You're only supposed to blow the bloody doors off." Go on, name that movie.'

'Ehh . . . oh hang on, I know this. Yes, got it, *The Italian Job*.'

'Well done, you know your stuff. I'm impressed.'

'Not really, I just have two brothers who make me watch that film every Christmas.'

'I'm told I do a mean Sean Connery as well, do you want to hear it?'

'Fire ahead.'

'It's better if you close your eyes.'

'What?'

'Trust me.' I do as I'm told, half-exasperated, half-grinning and half-wondering if anyone in Best's gets anything done with this messer around. Mind you, he does fit in beautifully with the company ethos: be good-looking, and at all times have a laugh.

' "Now, now, Moneypenny, I'd offer to take you to dinner, only I'd probably get court-marshalled for interfering with government property." '

'Fabulous. I'd have sworn there was a Scotsman in the room with us, and I'm only amazed you're not in a kilt.'

I give him a round of applause and he grins, then I half-glance at my watch. Not being rude or anything, but I really have to get back to my office.

'You're rushing?' he says.

Shit, I thought I looked at the watch subtly.

'Yeah, you know yourself. Mad morning ahead. I have to get back to work, sit by the phone and then pray very, very hard that somehow, miraculously, I land this contract.'

I badly want to ask him whether I overstepped the mark in the meeting, but my instinct tells me it's probably not a good idea to ask the office messer. Chances are he may not even have been awake for half of it. He nods and twinkles down at me.

'OK, well, here's my card. I'm sure we'll be in touch with you very soon. Great ideas, by the way.'

'Thanks for the encouragement, but I'll be starting a novena the minute I get into my car. Nothing like hedging your bets, is there?'

'Don't forget these,' he says, handing me my oversized bag of Choca-Mocha kisses as he walks me to the lift. Well, I stride and he ambles would be nearer the mark.

'Freebies and celebrities,' he says, pressing the lift button for me. 'The twin pillars of the advertising industry. Fond of chocolate, then, are you?'

'It's the single girl's best friend. Are you a betting man?'

'Only on monumentally important stuff. You know, like who'll be the first housemate evicted from *Big Brother*, or how long celebrity marriages will last, that kind of thing. What, are you suggesting that I'm some kind of timewaster?'

He grins and I notice he has the cutest dimple under his chin, like one of the Douglases, Michael maybe, or the dad who played Spartacus.

'Well, you see this pack?' I say, waving the bag of kisses under his nose, mock-threateningly. 'I can confidently bet you, that by the time I hear back about this contract, I'll have worked my way through the whole thing. A sugar high is the best recipe in the world for beating stress, in my book. If I do land this gig, I'll probably be four stone heavier next time you see me.'

He laughs. The lift doors open and I hop in and make a

'fingers crossed' gesture. Just as the door is gliding shut he says, 'It was lovely to meet you. I'm Daniel, by the way. In case you didn't catch my name.'

'Nice to meet you too, Daniel.'

The lift glides down and I roll my eyes, thinking, yes, he's sweet, yes he's a laugh and no, he's not married. (No ring, I checked; I *always* check.) But I know right well that if I worked with someone like that, I'd never get anything done. Fellas like that are just too much of a distraction.

I get back to the security of my car and check myself for dribbly mascara in the mirror and it's then that I make two horrifying discoveries: a) All around the edge of my mouth is the remains of the Choca-Mocha kiss I wolfed down before the meeting, so as I was pitching and doing my best to come over all business-like and assertive, I must have looked like the girl who ate all the pies, but that's nothing to point b).

It's only as I'm putting Messer Man's card into my wallet that I get a look at his full name and title.

There it is, in dirty big black-and-white italics.

DANIEL BEST
CHAIRMAN AND MANAGING DIRECTOR
BEST ADVERTISING AGENCY

Chapter Eight

God bless Google, that's all I can say. It really is the single girl's best friend. I mean, I just don't know what any self-respecting desperado like myself did before it came along, short of hiring private detectives to get the '911' on a guy. (Excuse the Americanism; I watch a lot of crime dramas in the *Law and Order* vein.)

OK, so it may not give the really vital information we all need about guys, you know, like star sign, annual income or marital status, but you'd really be amazed at some of the things you can pick up. The minute I get back into my office, I switch on my computer and look him up.

Yes, bingo, there he is in glorious Technicolor, and I'm not messing, there's only about forty entries.

DANIEL BEST, BEST ADVERTISING, CHANCERY ST.
Cutting edge advertising agency, founded in 1998, winner of the 2007 IMA creative award for excellence . . . company annual turnover well in excess of twenty-five million (WHAT!!!) . . . extensive client list including Guinness, blah, blah, blah . . .

My eye scrolls down the page, looking for, shall we say, information of a more personal nature. Can't help myself. I click on the Best website and it's so bloody good it makes me red-faced. I'm not messing, the Harper PR page looks so primitive and prehistoric by comparison, it might as well be carved in stone. Best's is just so cool and 'out there'. Every client they represent has a logo on the home page, and when you click on it, the advertising theme tune used in their campaign comes up, along with sound effects, the works. Randomly, I click on a big detergent company they represent and up pops the ad they shot for it on a tropical paradise island, palm trees, sound of crashing ocean waves, the whole shebang.

Right, that's it.

Note to self: I am seriously revamping my company's image next time I get a minute.

I'm absolutely dying to pick the whole morning over with Barbara in her official capacity as project manager with particular regard to relationships, but can't risk it until Paris and Nicole have gone out for lunch. Now, I do have my own office, but the partition is only frosted glass, and what can I say? There are certain conversations you don't want anyone overhearing. Particularly as I wouldn't put it past either of them to actually know Daniel Best socially. The two of them are both *unbelievably* well-connected and are always turning out to be boozing buddies or goddaughters or VBFs with all sorts of famous people, which, as you can imagine, comes in incredibly handy whenever I'm trying to get 'faces' to come to a launch.

In fact, on that subject, I'm still in bewildered awe of the time I was organizing a party to celebrate the twenty-fifth anniversary of the Film Festival and was like a madwoman, practically tearing my hair out going through my little black book of celebrity contacts. (Well, OK, so some of them are soap-opera actors, that you'd look at and know the face but not the name, but there are one or two you might just have heard of in there, honest.) Anyway, as bad luck would have it, the event coincided with the Cannes Film Festival, so any genuine A-listers I could have bagged were all out of town. Or washing their hair or getting their spray tans done or their bikinis waxed, well in advance of it. So there I was, having zero per cent success, working my way from the A-listers to the Z, on the verge of really scraping the barrel and just ringing up the local TV station's press office to beg/cajole/bribe with free booze (which *always* guarantees a few famous liggers) absolutely anyone, just to come along and show their face, in the hope we could garner some column inches. Honest to God, I was so desperate I'd have settled for a few weathergirls, a late-night DJ, the guy who does the Lottery numbers, *anyone*.

Next thing, just as I'm about to hit the gin bottle in my despair, Paris, who at that stage had barely started working for me, pipes up that her VBF's brother is only Colin bloody Farrell. Who she happened to know was in town. Who she also happened to miraculously know was at a bit of a loose end. Cut to the most over-publicized launch you ever came across, with pics of Colin falling out of the party with a brunette tucked under each arm, actually making the front pages.

Cut back to me giving Paris a pay rise and extending her contract, pretty much for as long as it suits her to stay.

Note to self: never, ever refer to Daniel Best in front of either of them, on the principle that loose lips cost ships.

I wait till they've both preened themselves to trot off for lunch then pick up the phone to Barbara. One o'clock, yup, she should definitely be well out of bed by now. She answers immediately.

'Well, prepare to relinquish your breath,' I say dramatically.

'Huh? Vick, that you?' God, she still sounds half-asleep. 'Hey, how'd your big pitch meeting go?'

I fill her in on the morning's events and it's like the more I talk about it aloud, the more I think I must have come across as being completely out of my depth in there, and that it'll be a minor miracle if I ever hear from Best's ever *ever* again.

'Your idea for the product sounds amazing,' says Barbara loyally. 'And if they don't like it, let them shag off. Their loss. That it? Can I roll over for my second sleep now?'

'And I wouldn't mind, but I met an attractive man when I was in there, too,' I say, not letting her off the phone. 'And before you even ask, no, there doesn't appear to be anything wrong with him, he doesn't have two heads or anything like that. No wedding ring either. But what's really going to shock you is . . . now, are you sitting down for this?'

'Yeah. Well, technically, lying down. Still in bed.'

'Oh, right. Anyway, I Googled him and he's like . . . founding director of the company and like a multi-millionaire into the bargain.'

'Ah, multi-millionaires. The forgotten minority.'

'Barbara, the point is, there's a very good chance I made a complete show of myself in front of him, not to mention all his creatives. Bet they're sticking darts into a photo of me right now.'

'It's beyond your control and you're only wasting energy in focusing on it. And as for this attractive guy, you are absolutely *not allowed* to do your usual trick and focus on him to the detriment of any other fella you might meet. I'm speaking now as your project manager, you understand. No more putting all your eggs in one basket.'

'As if,' I say, a bit too quickly.

God, it's amazing how fast Barbara can go from half-asleep mode to Donald Trump in . . . like . . . a nano-second.

'All I'm saying is, today I met an eligible, reasonably good-looking man who entertained me in light conversation for approximately three minutes and who wasn't married. Compared with last month, this is Mardi Gras.'

'Hey, don't get me wrong,' she yawns, 'it's all good, and moving in the right direction, baby. Just keep Thursday night free. And I don't give a shite how frazzled you are after that pitch meeting, you're coming out to man-hunt and that's an order.'

Right then. Here goes.

Pre-on-the-town check list for night out with Barbara.

1. Keep telling myself that if I can be successful in work then I can be successful with fellas.
2. On that subject, do not go on about work. This is my night off and must remember to relax and enjoy myself. Even though the pitch meeting was on Monday, it's now Thursday, three full days have passed and I still haven't heard anything back from Best Advertising yet about whether or not I got the contract. Which makes me think the worst: that I really did piss people off, and now they'll never use me again. And it's *really* driving me nuts. Especially because I can't very well ring them, and therefore have to sit back and behave like a model of patience and forbearance until I hear back from them with either good, bad, or terrible news. Jaysus.
3. As per my detailed instructions from Barbara, must constantly remind myself to avoid 'trying too hard' with guys tonight, on grounds that it's a major turn-off. This I find fair enough.
4. Well, no, actually, on second thoughts, maybe it is just the teeniest bit unfair. According to her, this even covers how I'm dressed: she's banned me from too much make-up on the grounds that men hate it and will never go near someone who looks 'like a drag queen'. (Her phrase, not

mine.) I think she meant well by this but . . . *ouch*. She can be very strict, Barbara, and has furthermore vetoed my bringing emergency touch-ups with me so I can 'do my usual' as she puts it. According to her, whenever we're out and I do get chatting to a DSM, this involves my alleged tendency to run to the Ladies and lather on a few extra layers of war paint, gloss, whatever you will, in order to maximize my chances, which she says all comes under the banner headline of 'trying too hard'. Personally I find this very tough to accept and suggested to her that she's talking through her bum. (Secretly don't believe the male population are ready for the sight of my bare face, so am limiting self to tinted moisturizer, concealer, nude eyeshadow, long-lash mascara and a juicy tube. Will smuggle these in my handbag and hope she'll be too plastered by the end of the night to even notice. Or care.)

5. Ditto, my clothes. Barbara has limited me to jeans and shirts, no work suits, flashy handbags/earrings/anything that says 'I earn a few quid'. Smashed broke, apparently, is less threatening to guys. Honest to God, the girl has more ludicrous rules than Blockbuster video.

6. No dust-flecking at any time on grounds that if it's irritating to a woman, just imagine how guys must feel. On this point, at least, we agree.

7. Right then. I give myself a very thorough up-and-down self-inspection check, just to make sure there's no grout stuck to any part of me. (Not as daft as it sounds, only last week, I found a gloopy bit of it stuck to the back of my good Karen Millen jacket. Very attractive.)

And if you think this is all obsessional detail, you should have heard Barbara on the subject of where we'd meet. Again, I had to bow to her on this one as no one knows the clubs and pubs of this city better than her. In fact, she could probably write a chapter in the *Lonely Planet* guide to Dublin.' Easy.

'It has to be somewhere MOR,' she said to me on the phone earlier.

'MOR?'

'Middle of the road, dopey. Can't be too posh or expensive. Put it this way, the Four Seasons is right out.'

'Ah, no why?' Shit, I was kinda looking forward to one of the amazing margaritas they do there.

'Because, oh socially challenged one, everyone knows that places like that attract married men on the pull like flies to shite. Known fact. Same goes for anywhere that charges more than eight euro for a bottle of fizz you'd buy in Tesco at half the price.'

'Oh, right,' I say, a bit worried we'll end up with a load of bikers in the Hard Rock Café.

'And I'm not taking you anywhere too rough and ready either, cos they only attract gangs over on stag nights from Liverpool.'

'Thank Christ for that.'

'The kind of place we're ideally looking for is . . . well, put it like this. If it was a singer, it would be . . . Frank Sinatra. Someone unobjectionable, someone that everyone likes. Or maybe at a push Norah Jones.'

This, I should tell you, is like a game we've been playing for years. 'If X was a country/cocktail/household detergent then it would be Y,' that kind of thing. Got a bit nasty one drunken night when Barbara said if I was a drink I'd be a milky cup of tea and if I was a car I'd be a second-hand Nissan Micra. To get her back, I told her if she was a TV presenter, she'd be Janet Street Porter WITH the teeth and the accent, and furthermore if she was an alcoholic drink, she'd be a flagon of cider, drunk under a park bench. A cruel game, you'll notice, but in public at least, it's a very handy language code that's come in useful on more than one occasion.

'Got it,' she says. 'We meet in Odessa for a quick margarita, then progress our way through Temple Bar. A strict one-drink minimum per establishment quota will apply, so get some soakage in first, baby, and you can tell Paris and Nicole you'll be late to work on Friday.'

'Oh God, but I can't, I've a meeting on Friday . . .'

'Then you cancel it and reschedule. Thursday it is. I've found I straggle home with approximately a fifty per cent higher hit-rate with fellas on a Thursday than any other night of the week. Don't ask me why, it's just a mystery.'

'Huh?'

'You know, there are certain things in this life we'll never fully understand. Why Kelly Osbourne has a career, for one. And another thing; if we have to stay out till six in the morning, we are *not* coming home till you've picked up three new phone numbers. As God is my witness, you'll never be single again,' she throws in, doing her Scarlett O'Hara voice.

I hang up, really touched at all the trouble she's taking on project me, bless her.

I could *hug* Barbara.

Chapter Nine

9.05 p.m.

I could *kill* Barbara.

I'll give her this much, she is on the money about her equation between Thursday night and single men, the place is crawling with them. (Something to do with it being pay day, perchance? Anyway, I digress.) These guys are bearing all the hallmarks of boom warriors: they're attractive, well-dressed, hot-to-trot, all in packs and all eyeing up women. That last one probably being the most important. There's just one bloody problem, every time a guy approaches us (or, approaches Barbara would probably be more accurate), she yanks me away and, on my behalf, is rejecting perfectly normal, ordinary fellas on the flimsiest pretexts you ever heard of.

Example one: 'Stay away from him, he has Red Bull breath,' she snapped as one poor fella walked/staggered away from us. Now, fair enough, the guy may, just possibly have been drinking since lunch time, there was a LOT of swaying going on and maybe, yes, I did have to keep asking him to repeat everything he was saying he slurred so much, but apart from that there was nothing wrong with him. Oh, yeah and he did burp really loudly into my ear at one stage. But hey, nobody's perfect.

114

Example two: 'Half of what that guy says is just plain stupid, and the rest of it is boring.' Right, well in fairness, Barbara mightn't be a million miles off the mark here. This was a guy who just plonked down at our table, asked us what we both did, then launched into his theory about why the computer will be dead in about five years' time. I think he meant to be entertaining in an ironic way, but then again, there's always the chance he was just as thick as the wall.

Example three: 'Eugh, I HATE that "too cool for school" type, he should be taken outside and sprayed down for Tarantinos,' she groaned about a fella who I thought was perfectly acceptable. To my eyes, anyway. Very little wrong with the guy.

That is, hardly anything. Yes, OK, admittedly he may have been wearing shades indoors, and admittedly, he did go on a bit about how pop culture influenced the beat poets in sixties Merseyside, and somehow, through a lot of rambling and free association, somehow got from that to telling us that he's the country's first professional blogger, but nothing I couldn't have put up with or sanded down over time.

Barbara gets rid of him with one of her level two contemptuous sneers then informs me we're leaving.

'But we have a table here. A TABLE! And chairs.'

'Listen to you, Grandma. Drink up, we're off. Zero per cent success here.'

'Thanks so much, but I don't want your pity. I'll just sit here and drink all night.'

'Vick, may I just remind you that, when it's my turn, I will gladly put my career in your hands, but when it comes to guys, you're in my house. Now grab your coat, we're out of here. Quick, gobshite, incoming, two o'clock.'

She yanks me out the door just as a text comes through from Laura, bless her.

ANY LUCK?

Barbara grabs the phone from me and texts her back immediately.

IN FINDING ARSEHOLES, YES.

Laura's straight back.

KEEP ME POSTED. COULD DO WITH THE DIVERSION. AM HOARSE FROM TRYING TO NAG MY WAY TO A PEACEFUL HOME.

10.15 p.m.
Things are looking up. Barbara is a great advocate of dating feng shui: change location, change luck. So now we're in Ron Blacks, a bar not so hip that it hurts, yet there don't seem to be a lot of wedding bands floating around (told you; I'm lightning quick at checking), so therefore for our purposes, it's a target-rich environment. Put it like this, like Barbara says, if this place was a singer it would probably be . . . Justin Timberlake. It's packed so she drags me right into the middle of the throng, muttering something about 'let the games begin'.

Right then. I grit my teeth the same way you see actors doing in submarine movies, and in I go.

11.15 p.m.
YES!!! SUCCESS!!! Can barely believe it myself, but brace yourself; I actually got chatting to a perfectly sweet guy who I honestly couldn't find anything wrong with. OK, maybe not

earth-shatteringly handsome, if he was a movie star, he would probably be . . . Philip Seymour Hoffmann. You know, that bit older, maybe early forties, slightly chubby, sandy-haired, at first glance not much to look at, but then slowly grows on you then you realize that he could actually be considered sexy. OK, so he mightn't ever get cast as Bond, but he's not going to scare small children away, either. Slight Scottish accent too, which only heightens his attractiveness quotient even further. He's wearing a cardigan, it has to be said, but in a Kurt Cobain way as opposed to the way my dad would. Now of course, the deal is he has to 'pass' Barbara and her unsubtle polite chit-chat/interrogation which goes along these lines.

'What did you say your name was?'

'Ehhh, Eddie.'

'Age?'

'Forty-one.'

'Single?'

'Yeah.'

'And not gay?'

'Definitely not.'

'Looking?'

'Aren't we all?'

'Proper job? I mean you're not a contortionist or anything?'

'Ehh, no, I mean yes, I have a permanent, pensionable job. Is that the right answer?'

You'd have to feel a bit sorry for him, the poor guy must either feel like he's in a Second World War movie about the Gestapo and should have a light shining into his eyes, or that he's on a game show and may be about to win a cash prize any minute.

Anyway, in the space of about three minutes, Barbara manages to find out more about him than I would have over the course of probably about three dates, namely that: a) he's an accountant who works for CarterSimpson, therefore he passes the 'must have a few quid' part of my dating cheat sheet; b) he owns his own home and let it slip that he's just had renovations done. Another box on the list of criteria successfully ticked. This means he's therefore unlikely to have issues around the fact that there's a plasterboard lifter in the bathroom chez moi. Oh yeah and no bath. c) Probably the most crucial of all, *he doesn't seem to fancy Barbara*, which, actually, is kind of unheard-of. The minute she's done giving him the third degree, instead of offering to buy her a drink, then slowly but subtly moving into her body space like any fella with a pulse normally does, the miracle happens. He turns back to me and continues the chat. We swap numbers and he says he'll call and, whaddya know, I actually believe him.

As Barbara drags me out of the bar, no kidding, I feel like breaking into the 'Hallelujah Chorus'.

Midnight
We had a bit of a row on the way to our next pit stop, on the grounds that I felt she'd severed me from the first interesting SINGLE guy who'd showed the slightest bit of interest in me since, like, Tony Blair left office, but she's adamant. We're on a one-drink maximum per establishment and that's it. Besides, she says, he has my number and if he's the type of bloke I'm now pursuing, i.e., one that actually wants to be with me, then he'll call, simple as that. She's quite right, of course, and this shuts me up. Plus, I remind myself, guys like to do all the running, at least that's what Miramax Films and just about any movie written by Nora Ephron has taught me. It's just that, up till Barbara took over 'project Vicky', I could never really relax unless I'd practically tattooed my number on to a guy's hand so he'd REMEMBER to call me and what can I say? Old habits die hard.

12.30 a.m.

Incredible, just incredible. Note to self: remember to send Barbara the biggest bunch of flowers tomorrow as a thank you. No, in fact, send two pizzas instead, timed to arrive just before *Oprah* comes on. She'd probably appreciate that gesture far, far more. We've barely walked in the door of Pravda, yet another packed, Thursday-night hangout for singles, when, with her trained eye, she spots a pair of likely lads over by these Las Vegas-style slot machines in a lovely, dark, thank God – no-one-will-be-able-to-see-all-my-wrinkles-in-this-dim-light corner. I go up to the bar and I'm not messing, by the time I come back with our drinks, she's already done her twenty questions thing and, with a significant nod, introduces me to both of them. Brilliant, this means they must have passed her stringent quality control tests and I didn't even have to be there to witness it.

Anyway, the slightly cuter one is called Peter, and if he was played by a Hollywood movie star, it would have to be . . . hmmmmm . . . Ralph Fiennes, definitely. Tall and lean, lovely deep-green eyes, and he looks right at me when we're shaking hands, always a good sign. The other one is more like an Edward Norton-type with a shaved head, who doesn't say very much and can't take his eyes off Barbara.

'*Peter* here was just telling me that he's never been to Pravda before,' Barbara says, palm outstretched as she's introducing him to me, which in girl-code means, 'He's the one I've earmarked for you, so whaddya think?'

'Really? Is that right, ehh, Peter, is it?' I say, nodding and smiling a bit over-enthusiastically, so what I'm actually communicating back to Barbara, also in girl-code is 'Yum, yum, yum. Me like.'

'In fact, Peter was just saying he's hardly been out at all since he broke up with his *girlfriend*, isn't that right?'

She obligingly points up the second half of this sentence, so again, in girl-code, what she's actually saying is, 'single, straight, available'.

'Yeah.' He nods. 'Towards the end, Clare and I hardly ever went out together, it was all staying in watching re-reruns of *Only Fools and Horses*, like you somehow end up doing when you're in a long-term relationship. I actually forgot places like this existed.'

Barbara and I exchange a fleeting but highly significant look, which in girl-code means: 'Did you hear that? He just used the phrase "long-term relationship" and he's *sober*.'

'Clare liked to stay in a lot then, did she?' Barbara asks, faux-sympathetically. But in girl-code she's actually communicating to me, 'Jesus, his ex must have bored the arse off him.'

'Yeah, but you know how it is,' he shrugs, in a not-at-all-feeling-sorry-for-himself way. 'You know you've safely arrived in staid-couple-land when you start looking forward to Saturday nights in front of the TV with a takeaway. That's the first of about ten signs. I should write a thesis, really.'

I laugh and say, 'So what's the second sign?'

'You mean you don't know? It's usually when you find yourself in IKEA on a bank holiday Monday looking for a tenner off towel rails, that's how you can be certain. Well, either that or when you're pricing decking in Homebase, then worrying that mice might nest underneath it in the winter.'

We all laugh and Barbara, grade A dating wing-woman that she is, steers the friend ever so slightly out of earshot, girl-code for: 'Right, do your thing and I'll keep muggins here occupied.'

Honest to God, I don't know how David Attenborough gets away with making documentaries about dolphins mating, and yet has managed to ignore the subtle yet highly effective workings of girl-code all these years.

It's noisy and packed but I do manage to have a light and

jokey, if brief, chat with Peter, and it turns out he's been single for over six months, which by my calculation is just the perfect length of time to lapse before you're really ready to move on and find someone else. Sez me, the girl who hasn't been in anything really serious since the last pope was alive. Anyway, it turns out he and the ex are in business, they run a language school, so they still do work together. But on the plus side, he seems really cool about this and not on the verge of a nervous breakdown as I would be if I had to keep working with an ex on a day-to-day basis after we broke up. The strain of trying to look fabulous in an 'I'm SO over you' manner, day in day out, would probably kill me. The fact that he's so easy with the whole situation I think bodes well; clearly this is a man of great inner strength and maturity. With a hot bod and lovely bulging pecs to boot.

1.30 a.m.
I'm having such a good time that I'm actually a bit disappointed when Barbara invokes our dating code-phrase, 'Come on, Vicky, we better call it a night, we both have those early meetings tomorrow.' Plus, I nearly splutter into my margarita at the thought of Barbara being out of bed before the crack of lunch.

Note to self: we need a new code-phrase that's a bit more appropriate, and a bit less of an outright lie. Anyway, Barbara's business here isn't quite done yet; as we're finishing up drinks she turns to Peter and says brightly, 'This was fun, we should do it again some time. Let's all swap numbers.'

1.45 a.m.
Me and Barbara are in a taxi now, and as the nippy night air hits me, I realize I'm drunkety-drunk-drunk, unlike her, but then she's famous for having hollow legs.

121

'You, you are my absholute and total, total heroine,' I slur, hugging her.

'Perfect time for us to get out of there,' she says. 'My guy was really starting to bore me. When he said he was a professional painter I thought he meant he was something cool, like an artist, but it turns out he meant apartment blocks. Two coats in one day, he was telling me.'

'But he has your number now, what'll you do if he calls?'

'What I normally do, you dopey innocent. Use him for sex, what else?'

I snort with laughter and tell her about fifty times how much I LOVE love love her and how cool and fab she is. 'I mean, why shidn't we do this *years* ago?' I slur a bit. 'Two attractive men in one night? Barbara my sharling, you should teach a dating master-class. You should give sheminars. You should be like this dating guru and you should be out there sphreading the word.'

'And you are completely twisted and I'm making you drink nothing but water at our next stop.'

3.00 a.m.
Krystal nightclub. You won't believe this and I can scarcely believe it myself. Me, the man-repeller, the one whose role in life it is to either get stuck at the bar or occupy myself by running to the Ladies to re-apply my make-up a lot while Barbara beats fellas off her with a stick, has just scored the hat trick, yes, you read that correctly, three in a row. Truly this momentous night will be spoken of in awe and wonderment for years to come. Anyhow, here's what I remember, although it's a bit vague and hazy, the natural effect of a night's boozing on me.

2.00 a.m.

We stagger, or rather, I stagger and Barbara just does her sexy, long-legged-glide-thing into Krystal with me still gushing on at her about how fab and sensational she is.

'Just tell me shis,' I say. 'Is tshis like a normal Thursday night out for you? Cos if it shis, I'm coming out with you every Thursday from now till they're wheeling us in here in bath chairs and we're both ordering old lady sdrinks, like . . . I dunno, sweet sherry. Harvey's Brishhtol Cream.'

'Oh, come on, Vick, you're fabulous, you're gorgeous, why wouldn't any guy want your number? Now cool down, you're overreacting.'

'You shthink *this* is an overreaction? Try being inside my head.'

'When it's your turn to be project manager, baby, I know you'll do the same for me and I make you this solemn vow. You'll be the first person I'll thank in my Oscar acceptance speech.'

She has my arm in a vice grip now and is steering me towards two empty bar stools.

'But shere's a sofa over there!' I have to shout over the DJ, but then I switch to an exaggerated stage whisper. 'I know, we'll just rob the reserved shign on it and just pretend we didn't know.'

'No, we're sitting here, you big lush. Chances are if I plonk you on a sofa, you'll only conk out, and I am *not* carrying you out the door. They *know* me in here.'

Bar stools it is. We plonk down and about two seconds later, the barman is over like a bullet, chatting up Barbara. It's only after she introduces me and keeps repeating, 'But Vicky, you must remember Nathaniel, I told you about him LOADS of times,' that I eventually cop on. This is not just the Barbara-goggle factor in action, that's not why he's all over her like a hot snot, I think she's slept with him and more than once, if memory serves. To cover my tracks I make a big show of saying, 'Oh, it's SO nice to meet you, you're THAT Nathaniel, of course, yeshh, hi!' As opposed to the other two hundred Nathaniels that we regularly hang around with. For good measure I think I even throw in, 'He'shh even miles cuter than you shaid, Barbara.'

'I'll have a margarita and can I get a large bottle of still water for my very sober friend here?' she says. This is girl-code for, 'You're making a show of both of us and now you need to sit quietly and drink about five gallons of water while I chat up the cutie barman.'

At least, I *think* she wants to chat him up. Barbara is some-times so cool and detached around guys, that it can be hard to tell the difference between someone she fancies and someone she doesn't. In fact, half the time I don't think they can tell, either. Anyway, I'm not in any state to argue with her as by now the room is kinda starting to spin a bit.

'Glass of water here and a margarita for the lady,' says Nathaniel, not taking his eyes off Barbara, not even for a split second.

'Ooh, still water, my, my, what *are* we celebrating?' says a guy on the bar stool beside me, who I've only just noticed. It's the voice that catches me first, deep and honeyed, very, very sexy. He's attractive too: older, maybe early fifties, slightly greying. If he was played by a hot Hollywood actor, it would have to be . . . Richard Gere. He's wearing a suit and drinking a large whiskey and it's all very rat pack and cool. In fact he looks like the type who might just break out into a chorus of 'My Way', any minute.

I try my best to think of something witty and sharp to answer back in a flirtatious coquette manner but all I can come out with is, 'Yeah, my brothers are always shhaying, drink as much as you like but a pint of water before you go to bed ish your only man, my friend. Reduces your hangover by approx-himantely fifty per cent. Fact.'

Oh God, I must be plastered. Did I really just say 'my friend' to a total stranger at a bar? I also think I may have burped a bit, but I'm actively trying to block that out.

'I love a woman who understands the delicate intricacies of the hangover cure. Although personally I think drinking still water in a late-night club is akin to drinking the devil's mouth-wash. So where were you two beautiful ladies earlier?'

'Meeting boys. Wisth great shuccess, I have to tell you.'

Now had Barbara not been so engrossed with flirty barman, and hadn't unofficially clocked off as my dating monitor for the night, chances are she'd have yanked me out of there on account of my having diarrhoea of the mouth, but no such luck, so I rabbit on, drunk and unsupervised.

'You shee . . . I haven't dated anyone sherioushly in waay too long and my friend here is just amazhing around guys so she's . . . sort of taking charge of my love life and we came out tonight on a bit of a mission and . . . what can I shay? Two lovely phone numbers in the can. Shanks to Barbara, in the space of a shingle night, I've gone from Mother Teresa to Mata Hari.'

Sober, I'd have crawled under the table and gouged out an eye rather than impart all that info, but honest to God, by now my head is actually lolling.

Anyway, handsome stranger seems to find all this hilarious.

'Go for it, lady, you *carpe* that *diem*.'

'Shritcly speaking, I shouldn't really be shpeakign to you until Barbara's vetted you. Just to make shure you're not some total arsehole, aka my usual type.'

'OK, well maybe you'd like to tell your friend Barbara that I'd like to take you out some time, if you don't mind adding my name to your list of conquests, that is. And please add that my intentions are entirely honourable.'

3.30 a.m.

The taxi ride of shame home. Me, Barbara and Nathaniel the barman, who's finished one shift and about to start another one, if you get my meaning. Oh yeah, and apparently he had to physically help me out the door of the nightclub, but that's yet another memory I'm trying to suppress. I get really giddy in the taxi and tell them all about rat-pack man who it turns out is called Tom, no, Tim, no, Tom.

Shit, I must be *plastered*. Plus I have this awful, nagging memory that when he asked me out, I demanded a pen from him and scribbled my number on the cuff of his shirt. In my defence I thought I was being very femme fatale, but more than likely came across as being anyone's for a bag of chips.

'Do you mean the older guy in the corner? Oh yeah, he's a regular,' says Nathaniel helpfully from the front seat of the car. 'Film director, or so he says. Great man for a few drinks. Good tipper, too.'

'I take my eye off you for two seconds,' Barbara hisses at me, 'and you blithely swap numbers with someone un-vetted. You should be ashamed of yourself.'

'Yeah, but curioushly, I'm not.'

'He was in a nightclub on his own, with no friends. Does that tell you anything?'

'Aloof, bit of a loner, all adding to his general sehxiness quotiensh,' I slur.

'Suppose it turns out that he used to be a woman?'

'All love ish a rishk, but a risk you have to take. Oh look, Barbara! That houshe looks exactly like mine! Skip outside the front door and everything.'

'It *is* your house. Now goodnight, you drunken lush. Drink another litre of water now and I'll ring you first thing in the morning. Well, first thing in the mid-afternoon.'

She helps me out of the taxi and on to the pavement and it's only by a miracle the taxi pulls off before I start shouting, 'Nathaniel, I hope you realishe you're a very, very lucky man!'

4.00 a.m.
In bed, fully dressed, pillow looking like the Turin Shroud with all the make-up that's mashed into it, room helicoptering around me. I'm just drifting off into a lovely deep sleep/stupor when the phone beside my bed beep beeps. Three unread text messages, all from some bloke called Eddie. I grab the phone, drop it, then have to haul myself out of bed to pick it up, all the while thinking, 'Eddie? Who's Eddie?'

First message was sent at midnight.

HEY VICKY, REALLY ENJOYED MEETING U TONIGHT. WILL CALL YOU TOMORROW. EDDIE X

Oh yeah, *now* I remember. Cutie Scottish guy, cardigan man, looked a bit like Philip Seymour Hoffmann, which as we all know is a polite way of saying chubby but attractive.

Anyway, there's a second message from him that came through at about 12.30.

MAYBE DINNER, THIS SAT? EDDIE X

And another one, that came through about 1am.

ARE YOU HOME YET VICKY? WILL I CALL YOU NOW? EDDIE X

God bless Barbara is all I can think as I stumble back into bed. Three fellas in one night? I mean, never mind the law of attraction, by the law of averages, unless I seriously bugger things up, one of them has to turn into a boyfriend.

Doesn't he?

Chapter Ten

Memories from last night that aren't just a nauseous blur.

Oh dear God, very, very few. I'm lying in bed, staring at the ceiling, still trying to piece the night together, when slowly I become aware of a thud-thudding noise all around the room. It flashes through my mind that maybe this is some new type of tortuous tequila-based hangover that I haven't experienced before, but then I realize it's actually Gerry, aka Useless Builder, who must have let himself in, and is now attacking some part of what WILL be my showroom-condition home with what sounds like a large lump hammer.

Or could it just be my head pounding?

No, definite lump-hammer action going on. Which has now stopped. Which means he's clocked off for one of his hour-long breakfast-roll breaks. (I wish I was kidding.)

Oh, shit and double shit. Which means that I'm late for work.

I pick up my phone and glance at the time on it.

Half nine. *Really* late. Bugger.

The only good thing is that I've no presentations today and, better still, I'm not expecting any clients to call into the office, which means I can skulk behind my desktop, quietly work away and not interact with or breathe stale alcohol fumes on or near any other human beings. Apart from Paris and Nicole, who with a bit of luck I can bag/cajole into keeping me in grande cappuccinos and lovely carb-heavy, hangover-friendly bagels or some such for the rest of the day. I've done it for the pair of them often enough, and now . . . it's payback time.

I'm just padding barefoot across the freezing concrete bedroom floor into what WILL one day be my stunning en suite bathroom when Gerry shouts up the stairs at me.

'Eh, Vicky, love, you weren't thinking of doing anything drastic up there now, were you?'

I open the bedroom door and try to shout back but it only comes out as a hoarse croak.

'Like what, for instance?'

'Like flush the loo. Or, God forbid, have a shower.'

'Oh, Gerry, are you really telling me I can't use the bathroom?'

'I had to cut the water off, love. There's a problem with your tank in the attic. Might need a whole new one. And sure, you know yourself, it's gonna cost you.' All this delivered in the tone of someone who actually *loves* imparting bad news; in fact, the worse the better. The bastard is wasted in the construction industry, he should have been a medical consultant.

I groan and slam the bedroom door shut, wince at how bloody *loud* the noise is, then throw on a suit and swab my face with a baby wipe. This physically hurts so much that I can't bring myself to go all the way and put myself through the torture of actually applying make-up, so I opt for the 'why bother?' option instead. Miles better idea.

I scrape my hair back, gargle with heavy-duty Listerine and off I go.

'Looking a bit rough there, love,' says Gerry as I stomp downstairs and into what WILL be my elegant yet homely kitchen, oh, I don't know, probably around the same time that hell freezes over.

There he is, sitting on the furniture I borrowed from Mum and forgot to give back, work abandoned, feet resting on a bag of grouting, fag in hand, reading the racing page of the *Daily Star* and eating a breakfast roll. You should just see him, there are Zen masters living in caves in Tibet less chilled-out and zoned. But then, why am I even surprised? After all, this is a man who considers three hours rolling a cigarette to be a morning well spent.

I take a deep breath, clench my teeth and remind myself, like it says in my *Law of Attraction* book, attitude is gratitude. A day that Useless Builder actually turns up for work is a good day.

'Overdo it last night, did you then, Vicky? I've seen healthier-looking ghosts.'

Now I don't know what's making me feel worse, the cigarette smoke, the smell of bacon, or just maybe the fact that I'm still a bit jarred from last night. All I know is that I have to get out of here NOW. If I don't, there's a good chance I'll a) have a fight with him, therefore have to get someone else in to finish the job, who'll probably charge me double, and that's if I'm lucky and I actually DO get someone. Option b) is that I throw up. And right now, I'm just not on form for either, really. Not to mention the fact that I'm stuck with a loo I can't even flush.

'Oh, just a quiet night out with the girls,' I snap. 'So, do you think I might have running water by the time I get home? Kind of difficult for me to function without it.'

I meant that to sound pissed-off and vaguely threatening, the way Laura would if she had to deal with this, but the rule of thumb with Gerry is, the more you try to assert yourself with him, the more his type B 'lazy-arse' personality asserts itself. In fact, times like this, I really, *really* wish I could be more like

Laura, who's capable of throwing a look so icy it could freeze an espresso.

'I'll do my best, love,' he says, managing not to lift his eyes from the racing page. 'But I can't guarantee you.'

'Gerry, can I just point out that you've now left me *without running water*. If I lived in Africa, people would be sending me money. Bob Geldof would probably have a fund up and running by now.'

'Would you relax? I've a great tip for you.'

'Oh, terrific. Is it perhaps to stand under garden sprinklers on my way to work and wash myself that way? Or maybe to invest in a few buckets, leave them out the back and pray for heavy rain?'

'Now, now, now, don't be taking your hangover out on me, love. Here's me only trying to do you a favour.'

I sigh deeply. Clearly better just to hear him out and then get out of here. I'm too tired and my head's thumping too badly for yet another fight with him.

'Yes, Gerry, what is it?'

'Little Dancer, in the four o'clock at Aintree. Worth fifty euro each way. The going is good and if you ask me, she can't lose.'

I grunt goodbye, fish my car keys out from under a packet of Jaffa Cakes on the patio table and mutter something about how I really want to see some work done by the time I get home.

'It's not up to me, love, it's up to the people at the builders' providers. I mean, if they *happen* to have a galvanized steel tank in the exact dimensions that'll fit your attic, with an access hatch and a ball-valve cover and all, then I'll have it done for you when you come home. Otherwise, sure you'll just have to wait.'

I glare at him, waiting for that catchphrase, which he always tags on to the end of every excuse, without fail: 'I mean, I'm not a miracle worker.'

If the law of attraction was instantaneous, I fume, stomping out the door and clambering into my car, then right now I would like to attract a ten-tonne anvil to land on Gerry's head, while I sat on the sidelines and laughed, like in a cartoon.

Laura calls me as I'm driving, instantly calming me down.

'I am slowly coming to the end of my rapidly fraying rope with Useless Builder,' I seethe in the direction of the hands-free cradle, where the phone's plonked. 'Do you think if I hired a hit-man to threaten him that might have some kind of motivational effect?'

'Ooh, you're sounding a tad under the weather, dearest,' she says soothingly.

'It's only because I'm a woman on my own, you know,' I fume. 'If there was a man about the house, Gerry wouldn't dare treat me like this. All I can say is, I must be paying off some hideous sins in a past life to have to put up with him and all his gobshitery carry-on.'

'Now, now,' she says in her best mammy voice. 'Would you care for me to put things into perspective for you? You're speaking to a woman who began her day at six a.m. this morning, by refereeing a screaming match between Jake and George Junior – who are capable of having a feud lasting both their lifetimes and well into the next generation over a box of Cheerios. So any delicious, distracting gossip you might have for me right now concerning last night would be like manna from heaven.'

'Fair point,' I say, suitably chastened. 'Are you OK, hon?'

'Vicky, I had four hours' sleep last night and that'll probably have to do me till mid-August. I won't be OK until the baby is eighteen. Back to last night. I take it by your *Exorcist* tone and the fact that you're only going to work at ten a.m. that it was a success? Full breakdown please: names, places, social security numbers, dish it out.'

'A roaring success. The bits I remember, that is. I mean, I *know* it was a good night, because I always feel rotten the next morning in inverse proportion to how good a time I've had. Oh Laura, I know this is the world's greatest lie, but I am never drinking again.'

'No, dearest, the world greatest lie is: 'You're my wife, of course I love you.' Trust me on this, I have personal experience. Anyway, at least you get to spend the rest of your day nursing your hangover in adult company. There's a lot to be said for it. When I hang up, I have to go and scour the inside of a gerbil's cage. Now don't let me down, I rang you for some grade A juicy news, please. My wounds could do with some balm.'

I fill her in and she sounds suitably impressed.

'I'd forgotten just how incredible Barbara really is when she's in action,' I say, beginning to feel a bit perkier now. 'You should have seen her, she's like some sort of man-whisperer. It's like they just roll over and obey her every command.'

'Do you think it might work with boys under the age of thirteen? I only ask because last night I caught George Junior trying to hold Jake's head under water.'

Just then my phone beep beeps as another call comes in. Shit, probably the office, wondering where the hell I am . . . if I've fallen down an open water main in my house or something.

'Laura, can I call you back?'

'No problem. Just know that I'm very proud of you. Three different eligible bachelors, all in one night? May I just say I expect you to become the subject of a trivia question very soon. Oh, I wrote my short story by the way, is it OK if I email it to you? I've a strong intuition that it's complete rubbish and that my writing style is the same staccato, brochure-cliché that you get in law reports, but I'd really value your editorial input.'

'Fire away, call you later! Hello?' I say, instantly clicking on to the call that's waiting.

'Ehh, hello, is that Vicky?'

Man's voice, Scottish accent, which is ringing a bell . . .

Oh my God, it's Cardigan Man, the first guy I met last night, in Ron Blacks bar. Shit, what's his real name, quick, quick, quick, what's his bloody name . . .

'It's Eddie here, I hope I'm not catching you at a bad time.'

'No, not at all, just on my way to a . . . ehh . . . meeting . . . emm . . . Eddie.'

'Ah great. I just wondered if you'd like to come to dinner tomorrow, Saturday, if you were free? After the grilling your friend gave me last night, I felt it would be downright churlish of me not to invite you out.'

Oh, isn't that sweet? I'm thinking, as I immediately accept. He seems genuinely delighted, and we chit-chat on for a bit, about last night mainly.

'You and your mate Barbara disappeared quite abruptly, did you both have early starts this morning, then?'

'Ehh, yeah, something like that,' I say, a bit guiltily. Anyway, we chat on and he tells me he's on his way to do an audit this morning but that he'll call tomorrow to confirm the restaurant, and for once in my sad dating life, I absolutely 100 per cent believe this guy. Three texts and a phone call within the critical twenty-four-hour period just after you first meet? Bloody right tomorrow will go ahead. In fact, this guy just sounds so enthusiastic, I might as well start calling him Eager Eddie. In a good way, of course. Hand on heart, this is making a lovely change for me.

I once read a quote that said that men are a bit like taxis: either their lights are on or they're off. And obviously, for my purposes, after all my years of dating emotionally unavailable cretins, a bright glaring 'I'm available' light is what I'm after, just like Eddie. This is all so *amazing*, I think, pulling into my parking space and nearly scraping the car on a pillar. (Shit, I must be

135

still a bit squiffy.) In fact, I'd almost forgotten what fun it can be in the early stages of, dare I say it, a courtship. You know, when everything is foreplay, even early-morning phone calls.

God, I cannot wait to pick the whole thing over with Barbara. I glance at the clock on the dashboard. Quarter past ten. Nope, nobody ever rings her before two in the afternoon, *nobody*. Even her agent knows just to leave a message, although Barbara did say he hasn't picked up a phone to her since around the time of the last Olympics.

Anyway, by the time I get into the office, Paris and Nicole are buzzing around with so much energy/enthusiasm/general sparkliness that I feel knackered just looking at the pair of them. They're getting goodie bags organized for a press launch that's scheduled for this morning, which in my muddy-minded haze had totally slipped my mind. In my defence, though, it's not really a major client. (It's for a new anti-stress spritz called 'Arctic Ice'.) I don't have to be there (thank you, God, I owe you one), and it's been more or less their baby from the word go.

They both do a bit of a double-take when they see how haggard I'm looking, but like the angels of discretion that they are, neither of them pass any comment. In fact, after I say my good mornings in an over-compensatorily bright way, Paris slips out to Starbucks across the road, gets a very large espresso and a Danish, and discreetly places it on my desk, without even saying a single word, nothing, not even a vague reference to the fact that I look like I slept the night in a tree, then gave about five litres of blood to a passing vampire on my way into work today. And this isn't done in an irritating bum-licker way either, just cos I'm her boss. Honestly, this is a girl so well-connected she could walk in anywhere and command any job in PR that she felt like. Her Rolodex is something that publicists lie awake at night dreaming about.

Note to self: give that girl another major pay rise, keep a close eye on her to make sure no one ever attempts to poach her from me. Rare diamonds like this one must at all costs be cherished and nurtured.

Anyway, pretty soon she and Nicole are heading off to set up for the launch, both looking fabulously glamorous, fresh-faced and so *young* that I feel like a granny just looking at them.

'Oh, Vicky, here's a product-sample bag for you,' Paris says, tossing over a fancy silver beaded bag full of anti-stress spritz. 'Have a try, they're fab.'

'Great, thanks so much, girls,' I say, trying my best to sound cheery and awake to keep up with their combined twenty-something perkiness. 'Get loads of coverage and I'll see you later!'

As they clickety-clack off, laden down with goodie bags, I revert back into full 'slump' mode, and with the minuscule bit of energy I have, fish the press release out from the freebie bag they gave me.

Introducing Arctic Ice, the latest cutting-edge development in unisex aromatherapy treatments! The Arctic Morning spritz invigorates both mind and body, Arctic Afternoon spritz balances out the chakras, while Arctic Night calms and soothes tired, frayed nerves at the end of a long day. Truly the coolest, most refreshing sensation this side of the polar ice-caps!

Oh, for God's sake, who wrote that shite? I think, stuffing it into the bin and switching on my computer. And then I realize. I did.

Anyway, I think I'd better do some work. The combination of a nice quiet office and lovely strong coffee is beginning to help considerably as I get cracking. Right then, today's agenda is as follows: on top of my normal day's work, I have to finish off reading a profile development and then come up with a launch strategy for a new jewellery designer brand. Now this is all very well and good, except that the manufacturing company involved have, up until now, been mainly noted for making cutlery. This is a big branch-out for them, so my one-line brief is, 'It's gotta be hot and it's gotta be good.'

No pressure or anything. Plus I have a ton of phone calls to make on behalf of 'project Barbara', all the more important now, seeing as she went to so much trouble for me last night. Anyhoo, I click on my inbox and bring up my emails before I get started.

My eye quickly scans down and . . . oooooh, yes, there it is, Laura's short story for the competition. I know I've a pile of work to get through before the weekend, but I can't resist. I click 'open' and up it comes.

From: lauralennox-coyningham@hotmail.com
To: vicky@harperpr.com
Subject: The things I will do for cash.
Dearest Vicky,
Now this is only a first attempt, so go easy on me. All comments gratefully appreciated, although am still unsure whether or not the world is quite ready for my particular take on yummy-mummy-hood. Have to dash, just got a call from Jake's school principal to say he weed on another boy's moccasin shoes, then accused the child of being gay when he cried, and is now being sent home as punishment for the rest of the day. Will have strong words with headmaster and try to explain that to an eight-year-old, being sent home is NOT punishment, it's a lottery win, as he will now spend rest of day with his feet up watching Nickelodeon.
Chat later, hopefully when my blood pressure is down to double figures,
Lx

I click on the attachment, absolutely dying to read it, and there it is.

Checkout Time is at Eighteen Years . . .
The Official Laura Lennox-Coyningham Guide
to Single Parenthood.
Or, why I'm absolutely not and never will be a
fully-fledged YM (yummy mummy).

Any reader expecting this to be about the jobs of motherhood, put this down right now and walk away. It is not, repeat, not for you. I fail all qualifications for yummy-mummy-hood and if you don't believe me, just ask any mother at the school gates who knows me, namely:

1. *I do not and have never owned a Juicy Couture tracksuit. (Which, for some reason, it seems to be de rigueur to wear with a highly visible G-string sticking out over the waistband, for all the world to see.)*
2. *Nor do I drive a four-wheel-drive jeep. This is not for any eco-friendly reason, it's purely because I can't afford one, so until the happy day dawns when my youngest is ready for school and I can pick up the frayed threads of my career and, God willing, start earning again, I'm stuck with a second-hand Toyota mammy-wagon which my children say embarrasses them outside the school gates. This is, in fact, the only thing they all agree on, so I suppose I should be grateful. Other than that, the only shared interest they have in common is a downstairs loo.*
3. *I did not effortlessly glide back into my size six jeans three weeks after giving birth by scheduled C-section as yummy mummies are wont to do.*
4. *I do not shop in heels, closing deals on my mobile phone like a*

true mom-preneur whilst waving finger puppets at my eighteen-month-old, to stimulate her growing cerebellum. (I did not make this one up, only yesterday I witnessed a YM doing this in Marks & Spencer. The worst kind of YM, too, i.e. one who recognizes that motherhood means making sacrifices, and so therefore reduces the 85mm heels on her Jimmy Choos to a highly unglamorous 65mm.)

5. During each of my pregnancies, I became more intimately acquainted with the inside of the toilet bowl than any human being rightfully should ever have to, whereas a true YM disguises her bleary eyes with Gucci sunglasses and tells all her friends that pregnancy is 'fabulous for detox, dahlings'.

6. A good day for me is when I get to put conditioner in my hair, whereas the YM's idea of low maintenance is going a full week without an aromatherapy massage, a facial and a spot of ashtanga yoga at an Elemis Spa.

7. Since becoming a full-time stay-at-home mom, I have effectively ditched make-up, cleansing, toning and moisturizing in favour of an extra ten minutes in bed. The YM, on the other hand, is so inspired by her post-baby 'glow' that she dreams up her own skincare range and actually pitches it to La Prairie.

You see what I mean, reader? The only two things I have in common with these women are kids and guilt. Four kids to be precise, and guilt about a marriage break-up in which I was the blameless party but somehow ended up taking full responsibility, at least in my children's eyes. And I don't quite know why, because my ex is the one who's adoring his kid-free, newly single existence, which of course makes me want to scream at him, 'I do know that you actually have a wedding ring. I KNOW. I was THERE.'

My two best friends have variously described this man as my emotional equivalent of Pearl Harbor and have jointly offered to *get a hit-man after him for my birthday present. If you're reading this, thanks so much, ladies, and I'll get back to you.*

Now the primary disadvantage to being a single mother is that, at the end of yet another tiring, exhausting day, I have no one to shout at apart from the TV. That, and of course the fact that the only man in the world who saw my stretch marks and sagging breasts in all their glory, and would still have normal marital relations with me, has now left home for good. Although, on reflection this could possibly be construed as a plus on the grounds that if I were still married and if my husband asked me what my ultimate sex-fantasy was, at this stage, I'd probably tell him it would be for him to run the Hoover round the living room a few times.

Another advantage is, given that Daddy isn't around on a regular basis, I do get to rule my household along authoritarian lines, like a little Fascist country in the thirties. As long they're under my roof, at least, my kids have no supreme court of second appeal: what Mummy says goes.

I'm just about to scroll down, totally engrossed, when the buzzer goes.

Shit. I'm not expecting anyone, am I? No, definitely not. A courier delivering something, most likely.

'Hello, Harper PR?' I say, about as chirpily as I can manage, into the intercom.

Ooh, bad idea. Even talking perkily is hurting my brain.

'Just dropping off something for Miss Vicky Harper, if she's there,' says a man's voice.

'Be right there.'

Poor delivery guy, whoever he is, I only hope the smell of stale alcohol fumes from me doesn't knock him over. I'll be lucky if he doesn't think he's delivering to a gin palace. I slip my shoes back on, head out the glass door that divides my office from Les Girls and open the main door that leads on to the corridor outside

Oh, sweet baby Jesus and the orphans, I do not believe this.

Standing right there, holding the biggest basket you ever saw, covered in cellophane and stuffed with Choca-Mocha kisses, is Daniel Best. On the worst, worst day he could possibly have called. I'm totally stunned, my jaw drops a bit, and all I can think is to stammer something about: how did he know where my office was? And he does that cute wide, dimply grin thing that he does. 'Sorry, I thought this was your place of work, I didn't think it was, like, classified information or anything. So, emm, can I come in? Carrying quite a load here.'

I usher him in, mortified a) at the state of the office. (Not that there's anything really wrong with it, OK, yes, there's a lot of pink going on, the company signature colour, but apart from that, it's on the small side and, well, comparing it to Best's is a bit like comparing a patch of greenery out the back garden to Wembley Arena.) This however is *nothing* compared with point b) the state that *I'm* in.

'Well, you did say you liked chocolate,' he says, dumping the basket on Nicole's desk and then sitting down on it himself, crossing one long leg over another in that lazy, 'I have all the time in the world' way that he has. You should just see him: Heathcliff in Gap chinos and a kind of rumpled denim shirt, the sort of work-look you have to be a true multi-millionaire to really carry off. In fact, I'd say Bill Gates could go round the place in shiny tracksuits and no one would ever dream of batting an eye.

'No, Daniel, I don't just *like* chocolate,' I say, grinning back at him. 'I LOVE chocolate. This is amazing, thank you so much, you couldn't have given this to a better home.'

'Now this isn't just any old selection of freebies, I'll have you know.'

'You're telling me, it's more like . . . a buffet of chocolate. Days like this I'm only too glad my assistants aren't here to share in this bounteous wonder. We have a strict division of spoils policy here, and what can I say? When it comes to chocolate, I'm greedy.'

I'm aware that I'm rabbiting on a bit, but then nervousness always has that effect on me and all I can think is . . . why am I so jittery around this guy?

And more importantly, why is he here?

'We have that policy at Best's too,' he nods, still grinning. 'All freebies to be divided equally. But for some reason, I always seem to end up getting women's fragrances and make-up. No kidding, there are drag queens out there who'd envy the array of cosmetics in my office.'

We both laugh and then he gets up, as if to go.

'Anyway, I just thought this would help you celebrate,' he says, a bit teasingly.

I look up at him wondering, could he mean . . . does he mean . . . ?

'Yes, you got the contract,' he says. 'My God, there should have been a drum roll there for dramatic effect. Sophie Boyd loved your ideas for the launch and for the campaign. She loved them so much that she pretty much wants you involved every step of the way.'

I can't help myself, I let a deafening squeal out of me, and without thinking, I instinctively hug him. He hugs me back and we're both laughing and then I remember that I must smell like a brewery so I pull back immediately and turn bright scarlet, mortified.

'Well, I should make a note to deliver good news in person more often,' he says.

'I am so THRILLED!!' I shriek, with my hand over my mouth to cover the fumey smell off me. 'I thought that I'd . . .

well, gone a bit overboard in there . . . I thought that . . . they all thought that I might have overstepped the mark a bit . . .'

'Why would they think that?'

'Because your people are all fabulous and all their ideas were winners . . .'

'Hey, yours were the ones she went for. Credit where credit's due.'

'You've no idea how much this means . . . you know, product development is a part of the business that I really want to grow . . .' I'm gibbering now. Can't help it.

'Well, here's your chance.'

Oh my God. He's just handed me the most incredible opportunity on a plate. This'll be like being on an amazing learning curve *and* getting paid for it. Bloody hell, I should be paying him.

'Daniel, I promise I will not let you down. This is going to be the biggest, hottest thing since . . .since . . .'

'Hey, you haven't heard the catch yet,' he twinkles.

'There's a catch?'

'I told Sophie that if we're shooting a *Casablanca* bar scene, then I want to be an extra. In a white tux or else a really sharp suit. But nothing that screams flight attendant. Just a little fantasy of mine.'

'Hey, Richard Branson did a walk-on part in *Friends*, so why not you?' I say, beaming. Although right now, if he told me he was going to appear in the ad naked, I'd probably tell him it was a stroke of genius. In fact, if he asked *me* to appear in the ad naked, I'd probably do it.

Then my mobile starts ringing.

'Right then, I'd better get going, you're busy and I've taken up enough of your time,' he says, making for the door.

'No, no you're fine,' I say, just as my landline goes.

'So, busy weekend ahead?' he kind of looks at me, sideways.

'Emm . . .'

'It's just that, if you were free, myself and a gang of friends are going to an outdoor screening of a Buster Keaton movie tomorrow, with a live pianist. I just though a fellow movie buff like yourself might have some fun.'

'Oh, that sounds fabulous,' I manage to say, all the while thinking, is he asking me out?

Could he be? No, he said 'a gang of friends', plural, so it's only a casual thing . . . *isn't* it?

Then my mobile goes again, as a text comes through.

'I'd absolutely love to,' I begin and then remember, shit . . . I can't.

I'm meeting Eager Eddie tomorrow night, for dinner.

'Only . . .?' he says, picking up my tone.

'I've something on tomorrow. I really am sorry, Daniel, the movie sounds like great fun.'

My mobile rings yet again and this time he takes it as his cue to go.

'Not to worry,' he smiles. 'Look, I'm in the States for the next few weeks, but I'll get Amanda at our office to get in touch with you, so we can get moving on this project right away. And just so you know, there'll be a separate clause in the contract signed in blood about my starring extra role. Just so you don't get any nasty surprises.'

I laugh as he opens the door. 'Enjoy your movie tomorrow, and thanks again for the chocolate mountain.'

' "You're welcome kid," ' he says, doing his Humphrey Bogart impression, then winking, and he's gone.

Still a bit shell-shocked, I slump down at my desk, trying to take it all in.

Oh, I do not believe this. Dateless for months and then two offers for the same night?

I have to take a moment to digest the irony.

I pick up my mobile: one missed call and two texts, all Eager Eddie.

The anti-stress spritz is still sitting on my desk so I open it and squirt it all over me.

No, it *definitely* doesn't work.

Chapter Eleven

It's only half seven the following night, Saturday, and by now Eager Eddie is really, *seriously* living up to his nickname. Honest to God, with his particular brand of doggedness, he's wasted in an accountant's office; the guy should be working on *Prime Time* as an investigative reporter. By ten o'clock last night, I counted eleven texts and five calls. (I answered approximately half of them and then just got too tired and gave up.) Then, today, on the actual DOD (day of the date . . . his phrase, not mine) he upped his game and has been either calling or texting at least once an hour, to remind me of venue/time/chef's special for tonight/parking tips.

He's booked Eden in Temple Bar, which is this well-known romantic restaurant, a bit like the Rainbow Room in New York. The kind of place that's always jam-packed on Valentine's night with guys who play rugby proposing to blonde women with caramel-coloured fake tan and pretty, perfect teeth. And yes, of course I know I should be grateful, and I also know that compared with the dating drought of a few months ago, this is party time, but, oh dear God, he's *really* starting to drive me scatty.

Then around lunchtime today, he started the 'no, I've a better idea, don't drive, why don't I collect you?' series of texts, all of which I strongly discouraged for two reasons, neither of which exactly bode well for the night ahead. a) Some inner nagging voice is telling me that if this guy knows where I live, there's a good chance he'll start camping out on my doorstep, and b) in the event that I might need to make a quick getaway, it's always handy to have the car on standby.

Barbara calls around before I head out this evening for a pep talk, or as she says, to play 'geek' chorus to the series of unfolding events.

'Your trouble is you don't know what you want, and I've absolutely no sympathy for you,' she says, sitting on a patio chair in my kitchen and chain smoking. 'OK, so maybe Eager Eddie is a bit on the over-keen side, but I thought that was what you were trying to attract into your life? Someone to lavish you with attention? Doesn't it make a pleasant change from all the guys who swear blind they'll call you and then don't?'

Before I even get a chance to answer her, my phone beep beeps as yet another text comes through.

'I know without even looking that it's him,' I say, picking up my phone from a bag of tiling adhesive which Useless Builder has thoughtfully dumped in the middle of the kitchen floor. And, whaddya know, I'm right.

HEY VICKY, WILL YOU KEEP TOMORROW AFTERNOON FREE, MY NIECE IS HAVING HER NINTH BIRTHDAY PARTY, BOUNCY CASTLE, THE WORKS, MIGHT BE GOOD TIME FOR YOU TO MEET MY FAMILY. I'VE TOLD THEM ALL ABOUT YOU. SEE YOU LATER, CAN'T WAIT EDDIE XXXX

I flash the text under Barbara's nose with a 'you see what I mean?' look. She doesn't even need to say anything, just finishes her cigarette in two drags.

'I have a feeling this guy hasn't dated in a long, long time,' I eventually say, neutrally.

'Well, now you see what a turn-off it is for guys,' she shrugs. 'You know, when women start behaving like wanna-brides. Oh, you know the type, the ones all the gossip mags call Muriels, you know like your one in *Muriel's Wedding*.'

'Yeah,' I say dully, making no attempt whatsoever to get moving, even though I'm meant to be meeting Eager Eddie in about half an hour. As he reminded me about twelve times today. Another beep beep as yet another text comes through.

No, make that thirteen times. This time I don't even bother reading the text, I just leave the phone sitting there.

'Vicky, what is up with you?' asks Barbara. 'Look at you, you're acting like you're going for root canal that's going to be performed by a trainee dentist aged about eleven, instead of a fun night out with a guy who, yes, OK, admittedly might just be a little over-eager, but otherwise there's *nothing wrong with him*. And I should know, I went to a lot of bloody trouble to screen him for you.'

'I know you did,' I smile at her ruefully, 'and I know you're right. Just wish I could get Daniel Best out of my head, that's all.'

'Oh please, not this again! As your man-ager I am officially telling you that by day-dreaming about him, all you're doing is getting back into your dirty old habits. Putting all your eggs into one basket and all the while, letting other perfectly good opportunities pass you by. And we all know where that road ends, with you fixating on someone totally unsuitable, bashing square pegs into round holes, and ultimately ending up calling a fella Mr Ah Sure He'll Do. No, Vicky, under my careful tutelage, you are going to become a skilled multi-dater with carefully screened men, and I guarantee you, within one year, you'll be happily partnered up.'

'Yeah, yeah, you're right,' I say, trying to motivate myself and not doing a very good job of it. Right now, I'd even give

Useless Builder a run for his money in the lethargy stakes.

'Vicky, dating is a numbers game, simple as that. You have to pump up the volume but with guys that are suitable, eligible, acceptable. I want you to be with someone that's good enough for you, one that really deserves you.'

'I know you do, hon.' I flash her a grateful smile. Bless her; she really has gone to an awful lot of trouble on my behalf.

'Plus, you hardly need me to remind you that you're on a strict two-date minimum, and you're not getting out of it.'

'Yup, got it.'

'So no more going on about Daniel Best.'

'I wasn't going on about him, was I?' *Was* I?

'You were thinking about him, I know by the look of you.'

I don't answer, mainly because she's right. God, I'm inclined to forget just how *good* Barbara is. That's the trouble with having friends who've known you for decades: they just see through you like you're a soggy bit of transparent cling-film.

'Furthermore,' she goes on, 'can I just point out that you were absolutely delighted with Eager Eddie, up until a billion-aire swanned into your office and threw a Snickers bar at you.'

'It wasn't a Snickers bar, as a matter of fact, it was a . . .'

'Vicky, we've discussed this, and as your project man-ager I'm telling you the guy is bad news. The Daniel Bests of this world just always are. Trust me.'

I should explain. Needless to say, I told Barbara everything that happened yesterday and her thoughts on the subject of Daniel can be summarized thus.

1. Whenever I come out with something like 'you should just see him, he's perfect,' Barbara immediately distrusts my humble opinion on the grounds that anyone that bloody perfect has very little potential for long-range likeability. 'You get to really know guys like that,' she said, 'and there's

always *something*. He'll turn out to be married or closet gay or else a Mormon. You mark my words. Wait till you see.'

2. Barbara has an innate dislike of seriously wealthy people on the grounds that she feels anyone with that amount of cash must have done some serious back-stabbing just to get to where they are. A mad theory, I know, but fortunately we don't get to test it out too often as none us know anyone really rich. Which is probably just as well.

3. She very forcefully pointed out that for the foreseeable future, Daniel and I are going to be working together, and everyone knows it's a recipe for disaster to fancy someone you work with, particularly if said guy also happens to be paying you for said job. On this at least we agree.

4. While Eager Eddie has left me in absolutely no doubt that tonight is a date, Daniel on the other hand was 'vague and offhand' (Barbara's phrase, not mine) about his 'let's catch a movie' night. And, when I actually come to think about it, he did make it sound like it was a group thing, a big gang, all pals. Nothing one-to-one about it at all, as Barbara has also pointed out to me. About ten times.

And deep down, she's right, I know she is.

His movie night just sounds like a million miles more fun than a coupley dinner with Eager Eddie, that's all.

'Right then, are you ready for your list of instructions for tonight?' she says, as we both grab our coats and get ready to go, me in absolutely no rush whatsoever.

'Fire away.'

'First of all, don't forget to ask loads of questions. Like you're interviewing him. Think of yourself as Larry King. Guys love that.'

'What kind of questions?'

'You know, like where do you see yourself in five years' time? That's always a good ice breaker.'

'And if his answer is "in prison" then am I allowed go home?'

'Listen to you, Vicky. If you expect the worst, then that's what the universe will deliver.'

'Sorry,' I say, smirking a bit at the way Barbara now freely refers to 'the universe'.

A few short weeks ago, she'd rather have choked.

'Oh yeah,' she says as I slam the hall door shut and we walk to my car, 'and don't forget to fake interest in all his answers even if you're bored. But whatever you do, don't come on too strong and turn it into an interrogation, guys hate that. Remember, keep it light, act like you're a Manhattan minx, not an NYPD homicide cop. Oh, and if you are bored, just make a mental list of all his pros and cons.'

'To help me attract what I want in a relationship?'

'No, it'll just pass the time quicker.'

I'm dropping Barbara off at a bar in town, where she's meeting Nathaniel, the barman from the other night, for as she puts it, a margarita, a pizza and another night of passion.

'Two dates with the same guy in less than a week?' I say in disbelief. 'Isn't this, like, going steady for you?'

'Either you can shut up, or I can poke my finger in your eye, your choice.' She smiles sweetly at me. 'He's my f★★k buddy and that's all there is to it. Suits both of us down to the ground. Now can we please change the subject? Hey, did you read Laura's short story? Wasn't it fab?'

We chat on about said story, which really is good, needs very little tweaking, and we both agree, our lovely Laura really has something . . . very different. Her story is just so witty and sharp, just like the lady herself, and as Barbara says, even her telling the story of how Emily got the neighbour's cat drunk would have you doubled over.

'And it'll be your turn next, you wait and see,' I say, pulling the car over to drop her off. 'Fame and fortune await.'

'One thing at a time,' she says, hopping out. 'Now just remember, you're any man's fantasy come true, and he's *lucky* to be spending a Saturday night with you. And keep in constant text contact with me all night. If things get really dire, just run to the Ladies and text me from there, he'll never know. Oh, and, worst-case scenario, even if he bores the arse off you and you run screaming out of the place, remember at least you're getting a free dinner out of it.'

'Where would I be without you, my cynical touchstone?'

By the time I park and get to the restaurant, Eager . . . sorry, I'll really have to start calling him just Eddie, is already at the bar waiting for me.

Right then. Just like Barbara is training me to do, my mind splits down the middle, like a computer screen.

Pro.

Just the mere sight of a guy standing waiting at a bar for me on a Saturday night is so heart-meltingly *amazing*, it almost brings a lump to my throat. Here I am, yes, me, Vicky Harper, dating on a Saturday night, like single people are supposed to, instead of sitting home alone, debating whether to watch *Tubridy Tonight* or *The X Factor*. And there he is, actually waiting for me.

Certainly makes a welcome change from the one particular guy I dated, who'd think nothing of leaving me sitting alone in a pub like Johnny no-mates for up to three-quarters of an hour before he turned up, plastered drunk because he'd been at a match and totally forgot he was even supposed to be meeting me. Then, and I really wish I were joking here, before we even ordered, he slagged off the menu (it was all French cuisine) at the top of his voice and, with the whole restaurant looking

153

at us, suggested we leave and go and get a kebab instead, which was really all he wanted.

And miles cheaper, as he pointed out.

Absolutely the last time I let my brothers match me up with one of their boozing buddies. They're all arseholes and the smartest thing I can do is avoid, avoid, avoid.

Another Pro.

OK, so Eag . . . sorry, I mean Eddie, might have gone a bit heavy on the aftershave, but he's ditched the cardigan, is wearing quite a sharp suit, and all in all I have to give him ten out of ten for making an effort. Meaner people than me might say he was middle-aged with a serious spare tyre going on, but I'm going with the 'life begins at forty' option.

Hand on heart, he does look really well.

Con.

That is, in the same way that Philip Seymour Hoffmann looked really quite well when he was in *Capote*. Or *The Talented Mr Ripley*. Nice, non-threatening and cuddly, but kind of reminds me of my dad, in a funny way.

Pro.

As we're shown to our table and we both order, the conversation flows easily, no awkward silences, and so far I haven't once had the temptation to run to the loo and text Barbara out of either boredom or despair.

Con.

OK, now we're about an hour in and I've just realized the reason *why* conversation is flowing. It's because he hasn't once shut up about himself. Honestly. It's almost like he's presenting me with his CV, everything, he's laying it all out, going right back to early childhood. Why his family moved back here from Scotland, where he went to school, why he thinks that particular school would be terrific for when he has a son and if he has a daughter, why he wouldn't go near the school his sister went to, that there's another convent school that his friend's little girl goes to which he feels is far more suitable.

Pro.

I give myself a sharp mental kick in the bum. Come on, this is good. Don't I want a man who plans for the future? And who actually wants children and isn't afraid to say so? Course I do. Anyway, he's just doing most of the talking because he's nervous, most likely, and I should give him the benefit of the doubt.

Con.

Oh, dear God, I don't believe this. He has his kids' names picked out, he just said it. Lily after his mother for a girl and Ed Junior after him for a boy. All he needs is an identikit wife to step in and complete the picture. The irony is that if a woman came out with something like that on a first date, any normal guy I know would run screaming.

Any normal guy *anyone* knows.

Another Con.

Right. Another hour's passed and he hasn't asked me one single thing about myself, not what my favourite movies/music/TV shows are, not even whether I preferred red or white wine (correct answer: neither, I'm more of a margarita gal), and yet he already seems to have me earmarked as his 'girlfriend'. Honestly, it's as if that's what's happening, in his head, whether I like it or not. We're on coffee now, and there's nothing I couldn't tell you about his life to date, right down to the view he looks out at from his office window and which football team he supports. And please don't think I feel guilty about sitting here making a mental list of the guy's pros and cons; I'm quite sure that he's doing exactly the same thing about me. And probably thinking that I'm about as interesting, witty and stimulating as a bottle of Heinz ketchup, given that I've barely opened my mouth all night.

No, for once I have to be practical and realistic. Nothing against the guy, I'm sure there's plenty of women out there who'd only love to have their whole lives mapped out for them, right down to what schools their kids will go to and what their names will be, but . . . not for me. Achingly lonely as my life has been, I prefer it to being with a guy who just doesn't melt the old butter. In fact, I think that's probably all that he and I have in common really: we're just two lonely souls prepared to try each other on for size, and it's a misfit, and now, whether I like it or not, it's back to the drawing board.

After what seems like one of the longest nights since the Normandy landings, eventually the bill arrives. I insist on splitting it fifty-fifty, remembering something Barbara said ages ago about how this is the fairest thing to do if you know you really, *really* don't want to see the guy again. Otherwise, he'll only think there'll be a second date, and it's just mean. He agrees and I think great, we understand each other, message received loud and clear. Then he insists on walking me to my car, which is parked miles away. Now it's late Saturday night by now, the city centre is hopping, people falling over drunk, throwing up, weeing in doorways and to be perfectly, selfishly honest, I'm kind of glad not to be walking through town this late at night and alone.

And then the alarm bells begin to ring.

It goes something along these lines.

EAGER EDDIE: 'So, busy week ahead.'

ME: 'Huh? Do you mean with work?'

EE: 'No, I meant you and I. Socially. We've a lot coming up. You and I.'

ME: (*Thinking fast.*) 'Em, sorry, Eddie, but I'm afraid you've lost me.'

EE: (*Patiently.*) 'Vicky, I did text you, several times, about my niece's birthday party tomorrow, and you didn't say that you *couldn't* make it, in fact you didn't get back to me at all, so the upshot is, I took that as a yes and told my family to expect you.'

ME: (*Thinking: 'WHAT?'*) 'Look, Eddie, I think that you might have the wrong idea here . . .'

EE: 'Then there's the work do I told you about, next Thursday in the Four Seasons, then there's the golf club dinner this day week. Vicky, were you listening to me?'

ME: (*Starting to get a bit impatient by now.*) 'Yes, Eddie, of course I was. You mentioned something about a work do and you told me all about the golf club as well; I just hadn't quite realized that I was involved in your plans.' (*I actually want to add, 'I apologize for not being able to read your mind', but I opt for being polite and dignified instead.*)

EE: (*Talking down to me a bit, as if I'm a simple-minded ditz.*) 'Well of course I want you there, I assumed you'd realize that it goes without saying you're part of my plans, honey . . .'

ME: (*Interrupting, starting to lose it now, to hell with politeness and dignity. In fact, I think it was the 'honey' that did it, and would you blame me?*) 'Eddie, how do I put this? You're a sweet, lovely guy and (*lying through my teeth*) I really enjoyed tonight, but I'm just not ready to jump into anything yet. I'm very sorry, but that's just the way it is, OK?'

EE: (*A bit downbeat.*) 'Oh. Right then. OK. Did I come on a bit too strong? Go on, you can tell me.'

ME: (*Thinking, well, this might give him a useful pointer for the future and if I were in his shoes, hey, I'd want to know.*) 'Honestly?'

EE: (*Smiling.*) 'Hey, I'm a big boy, I can take it.'

ME: 'Right, here goes. No offence now, girls love it when guys are attentive and call when they say they will, all of the above, but Eddie, I'm Irish. You have to tone it down a notch.'

HIM: (*Nodding gravely; if he's a bit stung, he's certainly not showing it.*) 'Yeah, yeah, OK, I've been told that before, and I certainly take your point.'

ME: 'What I'm trying to say is, sometimes it's no harm to let things take their own pace.'

HIM: (*Staring straight ahead.*) 'In what way?'

ME: (*Gently. I mean, if I were in his shoes, I'd appreciate the tip-off, wouldn't I?*) 'OK, it's like this. Apart from the night we met, we've had one date together and next thing you're talking about meeting your family, and your niece's birthday party and bouncy castles, and a big posh do in the Four Seasons, and golf club dos. It's just all a bit . . .'

HIM: 'It's OK, you needn't go on, I get it. I came on a bit too strong.'

We walk on in silence for a bit, with him dragging the pace down and me trying to speed it along, mind you the combination of my high heels and the cobblestones don't help. Still two more streets before we get to the bloody car park.

Then he speaks again.

'So I take it you don't want to come to my friends' wedding in July?'

'Eddie, I'm so sorry, this is just all happening a bit fast for me.'

'OK, OK, you need time, that's fine, hey! Cool. Not a problem,' he says, but in the same upbeat kind of tone that people use when they've discovered a way to solve a particularly annoying problem that's been at them for ages. Oh shit, he's just not giving up, I think. There was me politely asking him to back off a bit, under the misguided impression that I was doing his future girlfriends a favour, but now I'm beginning to realize he thinks I was referring to him and me and that I might just come round if he only slows it down a bit.

Oh bugger, I wish I could ring Barbara, she'd have this awful, icky, messy situation sorted in about ten seconds. Then I remind myself about the almighty law of attraction and how, just like my famous book says, it just doesn't come with a pause button. Somehow I attracted this guy into my life, for a reason yet to become clear to me, and now, guess what, here he is. And un-attracting him mightn't turn out to be as easy as it sounds.

On we walk, me willing us to go faster, like some kind of missile in slingbacks, him walking at a funereal pace. Suddenly, out of nowhere, the Saturday night crowds start to thicken considerably, and I can't figure out why, until we turn a corner and I realize.

Oh shit, I do not believe this.

Of course, it's the late-night outdoor movie that Daniel has talked about, and all these crowds are on their way home from it. Part of me is thinking, supposing we bumped into him? I'm half-attracting it and half-dreading it, given the situation I'm in, but as the book keeps on reminding me, the universe doesn't have a sense of humour. We're just turning a corner when we walk right into a gang of people, almost knocking each other over.

I look up, and wouldn't you know it?

Daniel Best, with a big gang of his friends.

Chapter Twelve

The Butterfly's next meeting. May.

It's Saturday, exactly a week later, and high time the three of us met up again to give each other progress reports. The bad news is that convening in my house is sadly out of the question, on account of Useless Builder, wait for it, actually accomplishing something, even if it is only scraping the stippling off all my ceilings and then plastering them. Don't get me wrong, I am of course thrilled that he managed to put down the racing pages for long enough to achieve this incredible feat, but the downside is that, apart from my bedroom, there's not a single square inch of the house that isn't at sub-zero temperatures, at least for a few days, until the plaster completely dries out.

'So,' I patiently explain to Laura and Barbara, 'unless you fancy contracting TB from the damp and spending the next week coughing and spluttering and sprawled out on a chaise longue like one of the Brontë sisters, maybe we should try to hook up somewhere else?'

Barbara's flat is sadly even less suitable than before, as her flatmate, Angie, is now in the throes of a mad, passionate affair with probably the only straight make-up artist in the entire acting profession, who has pretty much moved himself into their tiny flat for the duration of said affair. Now, as Barbara says, it's virtually impossible to get any kind of privacy, ever, in their flat and it's seriously beginning to drive her nuts.

'I mean, I can never even get into the bathroom any more, and when I do, he's used up all the hot water *and* the loo roll. He eats all our food, runs up our phone bill, then at night, the two of them are snuggled up on the sofa, all loved up watching *HIS* programmes on TV and there's me, sitting on the floor cos there's nowhere else to go, gooseberry of the millennium. I mean, for Christ's sake, Vicky, if I'd wanted to live with a guy I would have. In fact, this carry-on would almost drive me into moving in with the next fella that asks me, anything just to get out of there.'

Not for nothing have Laura and I nicknamed said flatmate Evil Angie, and not only because of this latest twist. We both have a long list of grievances against her, the main one being that, even though she's an actress too (so far this year, she's done two commercials, three voiceovers and a small part in one of those fringe shows where the cast dress in black and cluck around the stage pretending to be chickens), she never *ever* tells Barbara anything that's going on, and is for ever sneaking off to auditions then acting all surprised whenever she gets jobs. It's particularly unfair as poor Barbara always passes on information to her about castings and open auditions, but gets absolutely nothing back in return; and bear in mind that theirs is a profession that runs pretty much entirely on word of mouth.

Many, many margaritas have been knocked back while Laura and I patiently try to point out to Barbara the general horribleness of Evil Angie's behaviour, but Barbara, loyal soul that she is, will never have any of it. The two of them trained at drama school together and as far as Barbara is concerned, Evil Angie is her closest friend in the acting business. Friend, frenemy, Barbara won't hear a word said against her. She's just one of those people. Those she likes can do no wrong.

Anyway, I suggest we meet in a nice discreet restaurant where we can chat/de-brief each other freely and without interruption, but Laura vetoes it on the grounds that she's smashed broke and can't afford to eat out, so her house it is. We've no choice. Even our failsafe blanket excuse doesn't work: 'But don't you fancy a night off from the kids?' Her mother's out to dinner tonight and, as it's Saturday, she hasn't a snowball's chance in hell of getting a babysitter.

I drive Barbara there, and as ever, am amazed at how spotlessly spick and span Laura's house always looks given the stress that she's constantly under. Barbara and I shake our heads in wonderment as we park in her perfectly tidied front driveway, every shrub obediently blooming beside her freshly mowed patch of grass, and look at each other as much as to say, 'How does she *do* it?'

Her house is right at the end of a modern, suburban cul-de-sac and it all looks very flowery and very Wisteria Lane, that is until a gang of boys start circling around us on bikes as we clamber out of my car, shouting at Barbara: 'Hiya, sexy, great jugs, what are you doing later?' She's just about to shout something suitably obscene back at them (Barbara's well able to give as good as she gets and, no, before you ask, even being under age is no defence against her sharp tongue), when we realize that one of the be-helmeted yobbos is actually George Junior.

'This is your godmother you're talking to!' she splutters at him as I ring the doorbell. 'It's not that long ago I was changing your dirty nappies!'

Laura answers, Baby Julia crying in her arms, looking as tidy and scrubbed as she always does, just very, very tired, God love her. We all hug, and I simultaneously hand her a bottle of wine and take the baby from her as she marches down the driveway to deal with George Junior and his gang of thuggo friends. Now, I don't know what he says to her, all I can hear, clear as crystal, is her reply. 'If you speak to me in that tone once more, I will consider it strike one. I do not CARE where all your friends are off to, you're not going anywhere until you've finished all of your household chores. Now get off that bike, wash the car and this time, USE WATER.'

Baby Julia is squealing and trying to wriggle out of my in-experienced child-carrying arms when Laura's mother comes out of the kitchen.

Oh *shit* and double shit.

Barbara and I shoot a panicky look at each other, but there's no avoiding her, given that the hallway is about the same length and width as your average toilet cubicle. 'Oh, there you are, girls, well, three guesses why I was summoned here this evening,' she says, crisply putting her cheque book away and snapping her handbag shut. 'Honestly, there are times when I feel like some sort of cash-dispensing machine.'

'Hi, Mrs Lennox-Coyningham,' we both mutter, instantly reverting back to a pair of teenagers. I don't know why it is, but Laura's mother just has that effect on us. She's one of those women who, when you meet them, your accent automatically upgrades to several degrees posher and politer, and you almost feel you should be curtseying, as if they're minor royalty. She looks a bit like Princess Michael of Kent: tall and imperious, impeccable and be-suited, with a knuckle-duster ring on every finger and a permanent whiff of Chanel No. 5. In fact, no matter where I am – airports, theatres, any public place you can name – all I have to do is get the slightest sniff of that perfume for my 'fight or flight' hormones to immediately kick in, and I immediately start darting around looking for places to hide from Mrs Lennox-Coyningham. And I'm thirty-four years of age.

She also has the most intimidating way of looking down her nose at you that just makes me regress to the time, aged about nine, when I was sitting at their vast, scary dining-room table, too afraid not to eat the fish supper, even though I have a chronic allergy, while Mrs Lennox-Coyningham bragged on about how Laura got straight As in her exams, top of the class as usual, and how did I do? 'Two Cs and 4 Ds and an F,' I muttered in a tiny, frightened voice. To this day, I'll never forget the look on her face, it was as if I'd befouled her immaculately polished parquet floor. And I wouldn't mind, but for me, that was a particularly good result. In fact, my parents celebrated by taking me to McDonald's and generally acting like they had a Stephen Hawking in the house. Anyway, ever since then, as far as Mrs Lennox-Coyningham is concerned, I'm her daughter's thick, loser friend. And Barbara is her permanently un-employed, waster friend.

They're our labels and we're stuck with them, whether we like it or not.

'So, Barbara dear, when am I going to see you in something?' she asks, as usual sensing a weak spot and going in for the kill. 'Very soon, I hope. It's been quite some time now, what is it, two, no three years, since that production of *Lady Windermere's Fan* which you played the maid in?'

'Dunno, Mrs Lennox-Coyningham,' says Barbara, suddenly acting like she's chewing gum, even though I happen to know she's not. 'I'm doing a lot of hard-core porn these days. Tough gig, but it pays the rent, and at least my nights are free.'

Barbara, as you can see, is an awful lot better at handling Mrs L–C than I am.

We're saved from the misery of having to come up with any more small talk when Laura comes back inside and takes the baby from me.

'Well, we won't delay you, Mum,' she says, pale and stressed-looking. 'Thanks for . . . helping me out, and I hope you and Dad enjoy the law society dinner.'

'Oh yes, well we always enjoy an evening with Martha,' she beams, her mood changing like mercury. I'm not kidding, she's actually *smiling*. 'Her friends are such wonderful, stimulating company, all doing *so* well for themselves at the Bar, and somehow Martha always manages to get us the very best table at the Inns, you know.'

Martha, I should tell you, is Laura's sister, younger by a year, rising young barrister and general all-round pain in the face. In school, her nickname was 'Laura-lite' because every single thing Laura ever did or achieved, Martha copied. Never as successfully, though, she didn't have Laura's natural brilliance, and try as she might, couldn't live up to her promise; but now that Laura is a full-time mom, her parents have decided that, actually they'd been wrong all along, and that Martha was the horse they should have bet on to pursue a glittering political career and generally keep the Lennox-Coyningham tradition alive.

'Drippy, boring Martha,' as Barbara often says behind her back. 'I'm telling you, if that stupid cow ever ends up running the country, that's it, I'm emigrating.'

Mrs Lennox-Coyningham lets herself out, saying, 'Well, I'd better fly.' A cue to Barbara to mutter something under her breath about how brilliant it must be having a broomstick to get through the traffic that bit quicker. Laura bangs the door behind her, and the atmosphere lightens considerably now that she's safely out of the way.

'You know, I can physically see the thought-balloon coming out of my mother's head every time she mentions my beloved sister,' she says as we follow her into the kitchen. 'Martha, the daughter who *didn't* turn out to be such a sad disappointment, Martha, the daughter who *didn't* ruin her life by getting married to a worthless git when she was barely out of college.'

'Absolutely not true,' says Barbara, plonking down at the kitchen table and helping herself to some neatly sliced ciabatta bread. 'Although it does my heart good to hear you refer to George as a worthless git.'

'Oh come on,' I say, defensively. 'You're the one who gave your mother four beautiful, perfect, wonderful grandchildren.'

On cue, Emily strolls through the kitchen, with her iPod on, totally ignoring us as she wafts through one door and out another, only stopping to shout over whatever she's listening to, 'I don't want any dinner, Mum, I ate mints and now I feel fat.'

'I won't even attempt to dignify that comment with an answer,' says Laura, turning back to the cooker the minute Emily's out of the room. 'Nor will I embarrass you by initiating an argument/screaming match with the little madam and generally turning into Momzilla, but, by God, if I could only afford a decent boarding school, that would soon knock corners off her.'

Dinner is very Laura, that is to say, absolutely perfect. Wholesome, healthy, meat-and-two-veg mammy food, only slightly ruined by Emily picking at the corners of hers (and that only under extreme duress and a lot of grade two nagging from Laura), then telling all of us about her friend in school who cut out all wheat, refined sugar and dairy and managed to lose thirty pounds.

'Thirty pounds,' Barbara quips. 'Wow. That's like, half a Backstreet Boy.'

'Who are the Backstreet Boys? Never even heard of them,' sneers Emily, looking at Barbara like she's an old, old lady, in a way that only a true pre-teen can really pull off.

'Never you mind. I'll give you one tip though, Emily. Guys hate skinny girls. Known fact. They prefer curves. That's why Kate Moss only ever goes out with complete losers, you know, they're the only ones who'll put up with her having no flesh on her bones. So if I were you I'd do what your mother says and eat up. Mints are not a food group.'

Amazingly, this approach actually works, and Emily now grudgingly shovels a few morsels of lamb chop into her mouth, accompanied by a deeply grateful look from Laura. Then she starts going on about how much she wants a boob job for her sixteenth birthday: 'I mean, come on, Mom, all the other girls in my school are getting one.' But as Laura calmly and sensibly points out, we've a few years yet to pee on that particular fire.

Meanwhile George Junior and Jake manage the feat of wolfing back a full meal in approximately three minutes flat. This is followed by a heated discussion/row between Laura and George Junior, who wants to go back out biking with the thuggo friends. It goes along these lines.

'I told you I was going back out after dinner, Mom.'

'You most certainly did not.'

'I did. In body language.'

Laura sighs exhaustedly, in that way parents have when they recognize that the fight is actually futile. 'Right then. Back here by ten sharp, or else I'm ringing the police and then your father, in that order.'

Anyway, Jake is dispatched out the back to clean out his gerbil's cage, Emily wafts upstairs to go on her favourite internet chat room, and finally we have a bit of peace.

'Do you want to know what my secret dream is?' says Laura as we help her wash up. (Everything in this house has to be hand-washed *before* it's deemed clean enough for the dishwasher. Honestly.) 'To live in a house with a panic room,' she goes on. 'That way, I could either lock them into it or myself if I needed calm.' Meanwhile Baby Julia gurgles peacefully away, dozing off in her little Moses basket. 'Never learn to talk properly, my little cherub,' Laura coos down at her, wiping her hands in a dishcloth. 'Because the sooner you learn to speak, the sooner you'll speak back.'

The unusual peace (for this house) continues as the three of us move into the living room, uncork a bottle of wine, dim the lights and light all the little tea-lights dotted on the fireplace. We all sit in a kind of circle, with the baby miraculously dozing away in her little basket beside us.

God, we must look like some weird kind of coven, except with crèche facilities.

'You're the hostess, you go first,' Barbara says to Laura, gently, for her, sensing that she's had a rough day.

'Oh, ladies, where to begin,' she says, tiredly pouring out wine for the three of us. 'All right then, shameful admission number one, I had to ask my mother for yet another lend of money this evening. And it's a measure of how little pride I have left that I calmly took the cheque from her, listened to the accompanying lecture, and didn't even care. All I could think was, thank God, that's this term's school fees sorted, and at least I have another couple of months before I have to fret about September and all the usual back-to-school expenses.'

Truth to tell, I kind of copped on when I saw the old dragon with her cheque book earlier, but thought it best to say nothing.

'Shameful admission number two,' she goes on, taking a long deep mouthful of wine, 'the long summer holidays are around the corner and for once, I actually feel sorry for my kids. They have to listen to all their friends going on about trips to Spain and Portugal when they'll be doing well if I can bribe my parents to let us have their holiday cottage in Connemara for a week. Oh, ladies,' she says, running her fingers through her fine, neatly cut hair. 'I sometimes have these road-to-Damascus moments where I look at my life and wonder, how did I get into this *mess*? I just need cash so, so badly.'

'Your short story was brilliant,' I say encouragingly. And for once I'm not even exaggerating, it really, *really* was.

Barbara and I chipped in with a few, really very few,

comments and suggestions about the piece, which she took on board, then emailed off the finished product to *Tattle* magazine yesterday. So she's actually the only one of us with her Butterfly Club assignment all done and dusted. Which kind of gives me a brief, momentary flashback to our schooldays, when Laura was always Miss Perfect, Goody Two-Shoes, everything done on time, without any hassle or fuss. Always.

'Shameful admission number three,' she goes on, 'I actually *enjoyed* writing that story. I found it strangely cathartic. There I was, snatching what little time I could, and for some reason I kept thinking about J. K. Rowling.'

'J. K. Rowling?' says Barbara.

'Was a single mom and wrote the first Harry Potter in a café somewhere, to save on light and heating bills in her flat. What can I say? It's a tale I can relate to.'

'And look at her now; she's, like, richer than the Queen,' I chip in encouragingly.

'But, Laura, this is amazing,' says Barbara, flicking through my dog-eared law of attraction book and stopping at a page she's turned down. I lent it to her a few days ago and ever since, you should just hear her; it's all 'the universe this and the universe that'.

'Oh please, not that bloody book again. Honestly, you pair treat it like it's the I Ching,' Laura says, tiredly.

'No, hear me out. Yes, here it is. "Imagination is the preview of life's forthcoming attractions," she reads aloud, in the voice I happen to know she only saves for doing voiceovers. 'It's a quote from Einstein actually, so it must be the real deal. By thinking about J. K. Rowling and focusing on how she turned her life around, you, honey, are creatively visualizing a wealthy fab life for yourself and the kids. You just don't *know* that you are.'

'She's dead right,' I say, knocking back a big gulp of wine. 'We have to train ourselves to see the things we want as already ours. Act as if.'

'So are you both suggesting that I go to my friendly bank manager, demand a ten-grand overdraft and whisk my kids off to a villa in Barbados for the summer? And won't my justification just sound fabulous in bankruptcy court. 'Your honour, all I'm guilty of is acting as if, just as my head case friends advised me to.'

'You're missing the point,' says Barbara, in her assertive, Donald Trump voice. 'You have to focus absolutely on seeing yourself living your best life. In your dream home, with no financial worries, wondering whether or not you'll buy the new Lexus jeep or say to hell with the mammy wagon, and treat yourself to a flashy little Porsche.'

'Pre-paving,' the book calls it,' I butt in. 'It even has all these case studies about people who, when it came down to it, didn't really know what they wanted out of life. The point is: if you don't even know in the first place, then how can it ever manifest for you?'

'Is this some kind of cautionary tale?'

'Emm, no, I'm just saying, at least you're very clear about what it is that you do want. It's a start, isn't it?'

'Ladies,' says Laura slowly, 'it's not that I don't appreciate you trying to help me out, honestly. But when you both tell me that all I need do is think wealth and it'll just magically land in my lap, I have to say I think we're in serious danger of straying into men-in-white-coats territory here, and not for the first time either.'

'You're focusing on money worries, so all you're doing is attracting even more of them,' says Barbara firmly. 'Here's a good one,' she continues, opening the book at yet another well-thumbed-down page. 'This'll help. "Attitude is gratitude. Be grateful for what's already yours, and more of it will somehow find its way to you."'

Laura is looking intently at her, and I swear I can almost see some witty, cutting riposte formulating at the back of her sharp mind, so in I jump.

'Four healthy kids is a great start. Come on, I'd be over the moon if I had that.'

' "And when you begin to feel deep joy about what you *do* have," ' Barbara continues, reading aloud, ' "there is no speedier way to attract your true heart's desire into your life." '

There's a long, long pause as Laura swirls wine around the bottom of her stem glass.

'Yes,' she eventually agrees, palming her tired, bloodshot eyes. 'Of course I'm grateful for my family. And even on the very worst day, when I have to resort to grade one nagging, believe it or not, I love and adore the little monsters and I wouldn't have things any different. In fact at this stage, my nagging is like a reflex action, and I honestly don't know why I even bother doing it. It seems to have absolutely no effect on them whatsoever.'

'Can I just remind you, that if you were practising at the Bar and you'd never married or had kids, right now, you'd probably be the broodiest woman in the northern hemisphere,' Barbara adds, which is actually a terrific point and I only wish I'd thought of saying it first.

'And they are fundamentally great kids,' I offer.

'You think? You want one?'

'Stop messing.'

'All right, ladies, I'll admit you're quite right, and I suppose any kind of reality check does me no harm. Do you know, my neighbour down the road was in the A & E the other night with her little boy who has chronic asthma, and yes, I do hear stories like that and just want to hug mine. If they'd let me, that is. All I'm saying is, I would dearly love not to have to worry about money the whole, entire time. It's wearing me down.

And I'm tired, and I'm fed up, and I honestly don't know how much longer I can keep up the struggle. It's like I'm constantly moving from one worry to another, and I'm never, ever out of the woods.'

'Right, then,' says Barbara in her assertive voice. Clearly, she's the chairwoman and that's all there is to it. 'In that case, your assignment for next week couldn't be simpler. I want you to write out a list of everything you'd do if money was no object. Take the kids on a summer holiday, pay fees, move to a larger house, change the car, whatever. And then . . .'

'Staple it to George Hasting's head?'

'No, smart arse, then you're going to really work on visualizing it. In fact, I think we might all do a creative visualization exercise at the end of this session,' Barbara decrees. 'If no one has any objections?'

'Well, as long as the neighbours can't see in through the windows.'

'Just tell them we're doing yoga or t'ai chi or something cool, that'll shut them up.'

'Oh, and while we're giving Laura assignments, I have one to throw into the pot,' I venture.

'Yes, dearest?'

'Keep writing.' I don't even know why I'm saying this to her, selfish reasons most likely. I loved reading her short story, and it's not often I get a chance to read something in my office and crease myself laughing at the same time. 'Just keep writing,' I repeat. 'Offer it up to J. K. Rowling.'

'Right, then,' says Barbara, flicking *The Law of Attraction* open to the chapter on relationships. 'Moving on to you, Vicky.'

Oooh, great, I'm dying to talk about Daniel Best.

'Except you're vetoed from talking about Daniel Best.'

Shit.

There was me thinking I could re-analyse with the girls in

fine forensic detail the story of bumping into him on the street with Eager Eddie last week. For about the thousandth time. Not that there's actually that much to tell: he was his usual laid-back self, chatted affably about the movie they'd all seen, then politely asked where we'd been, whereupon Eager Eddie went on about Eden and how wonderfully romantic the whole meal was, the dirty big liar.

As for me, I can't be 100 per cent sure, but I think what I came out with might have been along the lines of, 'Well, err, umm . . . you see . . . yeah, we did have a quick casual bite to eat and now we're calling it a night. I'm absolutely dying to go home.' Then, with horror, I realized, as if Eager Eddie and I didn't already look coupley enough, that I was making it sound as if we were rushing off home together to rip each other's clothes off. So I back-pedalled, and added, 'Emm . . . home to my house, that is. Where I live . . . emm . . . on my own.'

Daniel did that slow, lazy smile he has which makes his eyes go all crinkly at the edges, then, as far as I can remember, he threw in something like, 'Well, I'd better catch up with my gang. Nice meeting you, and safe home, Vicky. To your house, where you live. On your own.'

Then, pretty much all last week, I was in touch with Best's about the ad campaign which I've started working on in earnest, but all I could glean from Amanda was that he'd gone to the States on business and that no one was really sure when to expect him back. Not that I'm bothered, really.

In fact, I don't even know why his name keeps slipping out.

The thing is, though, I just . . . well, I'd just hate him to get the wrong idea about me and Eager Eddie, that's all. And Barbara is dead right: I shouldn't keep going on about him. I should just sit here quietly, hear what she has to say and reap the benefits of her far superior man-agement skills.

Oh f**k it, I can't resist.

'Can I just ask you, oh wise dating guru, one teeny question about Daniel?'

'NO!'

'It'll take you ten seconds to answer it!'

'NO!'

'I don't want him to think that I'm seeing someone!' I blurt out anyway, what the hell.

'We've been over this and over it, and the fact is . . .'

'Oh, come on, what is your main objection to him?'

'For about the hundredth time: one, if you start fixating about him, then you know right well that you'll end up doing your usual trick of focusing entirely on him while ignoring other lovely guys all around you; and two, you're going to be working for his company. Bad idea to get involved with anyone you work with, trust me.'

'You're always getting involved with actors you work with.'

'I'm not looking for a life-partner, though, am I?'

She has me there, so I'd better just shut up. Honestly, half of me thinks, yeah, she's right, I shouldn't fall back into my sad old way of putting all my eggs into one basket, which let's face it, has a success rate of zero per cent; but the other half is screaming inside, But I really *like* this guy! And now he thinks I have a boyfriend, and I bloody well don't!

'Could you be ignoring the obvious possibility that maybe Daniel thought you were just out with a friend?' says Laura, kindly.

'I appreciate your lovely sentiment, but come on, it was a Saturday night, me and a guy, just the two of us, out for dinner in a restaurant like Eden, which everyone knows is a well-known couples' hangout . . . I'm sorry, but an intellectually challenged alien newly landed from Mars could have figured out we were out on a date.'

'Well, in that case, isn't it a good thing that Daniel realizes that other guys are after you? Shouldn't that, theoretically, make him keener?'

'If he was ever keen to begin with,' says Barbara firmly. 'Sorry, Vicky, but I'm afraid asking you to join him and a gang of his mates to see some open-air movie isn't a date. I think we can safely say we're in the friend-zone here.'

She's right, and deep down I know she's right. I just hate hearing it, that's all.

'You're still not off any hooks though, honey,' she goes on, stretching herself out on the sofa and kicking her shoes off. 'By the non-negotiable rules of this club, you were required to go on two dates before we met up again. So, technically, you still owe us a date. And then when you've done that, we'll pick another Thursday night and go out trawling the town for single, suitable guys again. Like I keep saying, it's a numbers game and nothing more.'

'God, Barbara, in moods like this, you make coffee nervous.'

'So what about Eager Eddie?' says Laura, topping up our wine glasses. 'Any word?'

'Got the hint. At least I think he did. It's hard to tell, as he keeps texting me to say thanks for a great night, which proves he's a filthy liar, as it most definitely was NOT a great night, not by any standards.'

'You said on the phone today you had other boy news,' says Barbara, looking at me keenly.

Ooh, yeah, I do. Good news, too, at least I think it's good news. In fact, I can't believe it almost slipped my mind. In fact, this probably should have been item one on the 'project Vicky' agenda.

'OK, remember the miraculous night of three guys?' I say, far more animated now. 'Well, hang on to your odour eaters, now . . . number two only called me yesterday! Peter. Remember?'

'Honey, I can barely remember where I was last night, never mind the week before last. Give me a visual.'

'We met in Pravda, there were two of them, the friend was chatting you up, my one looked a bit like Ralph Fiennes . . .'

'Oh yeah, yeah, now I have you, my one looked like a baldie Edward Norton. Yeah, gotcha. So, anyway, what happened?'

'Well, nothing, really,' I say, starting to hope that I didn't build this story up too much and now it'll be a let-down. 'But we really did have a lovely chat, no awkward silences or long pauses, none of that, and we said we'd meet for a coffee next week. Now, I know it's only a coffee, but it's something, isn't it?' I look at her hopefully.

'Right then, missy,' says Barbara, knees up as she's sprawled out on the sofa, staring at the ceiling with this really scary glint she gets in her eye when there's devilment afoot. 'Now maybe this is coming to me in a vision, or maybe it's a drunken haze, but boy oh boy do I have the scariest assignment for you. If you're man enough to take it on, that is.'

'Shoot,' I say, thinking, how bad can it be? Go skydiving with him? Introduce him to my messer brothers? Reveal my cellulite in all of its thundering glory?

'I want you to go on the coffee date with him . . .'

'Right, yes,' I say, thinking, easy peasy, so far so good.

'Then . . . you know your big PR dinner in a few weeks' time? You're going to invite him, as your date.'

I look at her, stunned.

'And, as a sweetener, I'll even come with you myself, with the baldie friend as my date. We'll go as a foursome. Now come on, can I say fairer than that?'

'You have to be kidding me.'

'Fine, be a bloody coward. Stay single, see if I care. And me and my teenage lover will come and visit you in your old folks' home when you're eighty.'

'Oh Barbara, I'm really not sure, I mean, if I ask him to the do, it might sound like I'm jumping in too fast, like a female Eager Eddie . . . it could end up being a complete disaster . . .'

'If it does, I'll be right there for you, with a big margarita in my hand.'

'And most people don't even bother bringing partners, I mean, they'd be bored stupid, it's a work night, it's a PR dinner for God's sake, full of advertisers, people are really just there to network . . .'

'Vicky, you are going, and I'm coming with you, and we're double-dating and that's final.'

Right then, nothing for it, but to do what I normally do, i.e., say yes now, then worry about it later. Much later. Like the night before it or something.

Anyway, in what seems like no time, it's Barbara's go and I get a little self-important glow as I take the floor. Not blowing my own trumpet or anything, but I really spent ages working on this, and I really think the girls will be blown away about how much progress we've made. Plus, in our little Butterfly gatherings, it's nice to actually be in control for a change, and not be permanently stuck in my usual 'manless loser' corner with a big 'serially single' label stuck to me.

I make a big show of opening my briefcase and producing a neatly labelled file for each of us.

'Bloody hell,' says Barbara, sitting up on the sofa, 'whenever I see the colouredy folders coming out, I know you mean business.'

'OK then, ladies, let's begin by opening the pink file labelled 'possible directors'.

They both ooh and aah and look suitably impressed, but what neither of them realizes is that I have a bit of a trump card up my sleeve. Barbara works her way down the list, with a pencil in her mouth, muttering under her breath, 'Slept with

him . . . dated him . . . told him get lost at a drunken wrap party
. . . I *think* I might have kissed him . . . he's definitely gay, had
some kind of civil ceremony on a beach a while back . . .'

'If you'd be good enough to flick to page two,' I say, 'and
check out the name with a star beside it . . .' I pause a bit here
for dramatic effect. OK, so I am milking it a bit, but it's just that
I cannot WAIT to see the look on Barbara's face when she sees
this. 'Serena Stroheim . . .' I say, trying to be as blithe and cool
and throwaway as possible.

'Serena Stroheim?' says Barbara, now sitting bolt upright.
'Not *THE* Serena Stroheim?'

'The very one.'

Oh my God, you should just see Barbara. It's hysterical, and
I only wish I had a camera; she has exactly the same glazed look
that big winners on the lottery get, or else people who've just
come out top in *Big Brother*.

'Sorry, ladies, can you fill me in?' says Laura. 'You'll forgive
me for being a little out of touch with the world of culture.'

'Serena Stroheim . . .' says Barbara, and I'm not kidding, she's
actually now beginning to stammer, 'is so, so hot, she's
practically volcanic. She's won . . . like, a Tony, a Critic's Circle,
an Olivier. You name it, the woman's sideboard is practically
gong central. Actors, and by actors, I mean real A-listers, practically queue up to work with her in the theatre, and by the
theatre I mean Broadway, baby. She directed, like, this break-
through production of *The Women of Troy* last year and, I'm not
joking, the standing-room-only tickets were selling on eBay
for, like, a hundred smackaroos.'

'Well, are you ready for this?' I ask, almost wishing I came
with a drum-roll effect. 'We, and by we I mean you and I, only
have a lunch date with her next Wednesday.'

Laura whoops, and then remembers there's a slumbering
baby in the room and instantly covers her mouth with her

hand, while Barbara clutches her chest and gulps for air, like some elderly dame in an Ealing comedy, circa 1950.

'Tell me . . . tell me . . . tell me everything . . .' she manages to splutter. You should just see her face, she's gone snow-white, and now there's wine actually dribbling on to her white blouse. Oh rats, I really wish I could bask in the credit for this, but, much as I'm enjoying my little moment of being the group miracle worker, I have to own up.

'OK, so during the week I got Paris and Nicole in the office to cold-call every single director's name on that list and pitch the idea at them. They were brilliant the pair of them, I made them rehearse first, and I earwigged on the calls, and hand on heart, they got everything note-perfect. Shakespeare in the park, three nights only, everyone gives their services for free, and it's all in aid of the Children's Hospital.'

'The Children's Hospital?' Laura asks.

'I heard on the grapevine that they had been doing the fundraising rounds and I thought, who better to be our beneficiary? Now pay attention, Bond, because that becomes critical to the plot in a minute.'

'Go on,' says Barbara, still looking at me with the ghostly face.

'So the girls are working their way down the list and keeping me posted on what response they're getting. A lot of the directors we targeted said they were "committed elsewhere", which we reckoned was code for: "Couldn't be arsed getting involved with a project that'll take up about eight weeks of my time and that's not even going to pay me." '

Laura shakes her head sadly and keeps topping up our glasses.

'So then Nicole bounces over to my desk, clutching the list and pointing madly at Serena Stroheim's name. It turns out, she's only a VBF of her mother's, apparently they both have holiday homes right next door to each other in the South of

France. Although, I think when Nicole says "holiday home" we would probably call it an eight-bedroomed mansion house with a pool and a tennis court and a view right over the Med.'

'Keep talking,' says Barbara, who's knocked back an entire glass of wine in the last couple of seconds alone.

'So next thing she's only whipped out the woman's ex-directory phone number, has actually got her on the phone and is chatting away to her goodo, while I'm sitting at my desk with a face like a slapped mullet. I'm not joking, at one point she actually calls her "Auntie Serena". Then Nicole hangs up with a big cheerie bye and I could be mistaken, but she may even have said something about seeing her at the Monaco Rose Ball and was it true Prince Albert was bringing a new date? She's so connected, that girl, I mean you wouldn't believe some of the names that she drops . . .'

'Never mind about Prince bleeding Albert,' hisses Barbara, bristling for me to come to the punch line. 'Go ON with the story.'

'Oh right, sorry. So anyhow, the upshot is: not only has the almighty Ms Stroheim got a gap in her schedule, before she goes off to, I dunno, direct Dame Judi Dench or someone like that, with, you know, BAFTAs and Oscars hanging out of them, at the National or somewhere, Nicole told me what she was doing for the autumn and it's totally slipped my mind . . .'

'Go ON!'

'Barbara, I am now pissed to the tune of two glasses of wine, so you'll just have to bear with me if I ramble a bit. Anyhoo, she loved, loved, loved the idea, said she'd always wanted to direct *A Midsummer Night's Dream* in the open air, but here's the clincher . . .'

'WHAT!' Barbara's on the edge of her seat now and Laura has to shush her a bit so she doesn't wake the baby.

'Turns out her granddaughter was a patient at the Children's

Hospital, she had to have major surgery, and apparently they took such amazing care of her, and the child is doing so brilliantly now that Serena said, and this is a direct quote, that she felt the least she could do was to give something back to them. So I do hope you can squeeze us both in for lunch this Wednesday, then, sweetie.' I sit back and wink at her, if I say so myself, *thrilled* with her reaction.

'But do you think she'll cast me?' says Barbara in a very small, insecure little voice. 'I mean, she's worked with the best of the best, and here's me, a total unknown. Now unless Joe Public studies the "background artistes" in cholesterol commercials very closely, no one has the first clue who I am or what I've done . . .'

'Honey, you're attracting panic now, so stop right there,' I say, holding my palm up to her face like someone on *The Jerry Springer Show*. Not a gesture I'd *ever* attempt sober. 'You, my future Broadway star, are part of this package, and that's all there is to it. We've got the meeting. It's happening. Suck it up.'

Barbara hauls herself off the sofa and gives me a bear hug so tight I think I might break. 'Vicky Harper, I will be thanking you till the day I die,' is all she says simply. And a bit tearily – unusual for her.

'Oh, come on, honey, you are gonna be fab and you're going to steal that show, and I'm going to make sure you get the hottest agent in the business; and in one short year, the sky will be the limit. A guest voice on *The Simpsons*, a movie role in a blockbuster, anything you can dream of, will be yours for the asking.'

'Oh, that reminds me,' Barbara says, the eyes still all sparkly. 'Come on, girls, a quick creative visualization exercise while this miraculous peace holds out.'

Laura and I just look at her, suddenly silenced, and don't move.

'A creative visualization exercise?' Laura eventually says.

'Old actor's trick. It's like you dress-rehearse what you really want out of life in your head, thereby when your moment comes, you're ready for it. Come on, if I can visualize myself sitting calmly over lunch with Serena Stroheim, like I meet with scary, hotshot directors every other day of the week, then anything's possible. Right, shoes off and lie down. This'll be a terrific way to turn our dreams into reality,' she says, stretching out and lying down on the floor. 'The book even says, as you visualize, so you materialize.'

Laura and I look at each other, shrug, then do as we're told.

'OK,' says Barbara, who's actually sounding remarkably sober. 'Just concentrate on your breathing, in and out, in and out, tune out all other sounds . . .'

It's particularly hard as my will to talk is just too over-whelming, but after a few moments of doing just that, concentrating only on breathing, it actually does start to work. In, out, in, out, in and out . . . A few breaths later and I find myself giving an involuntary yawn. As does Laura, I notice.

After all our chat and messing, eventually a long silence falls and now all you can hear is a clock on the fireplace ticking and the distant, muffled sound of Emily on the phone to one of her friends upstairs. It's lateish now, and the light's nearly gone, but the candles make the room seem serene and tranquil. Or maybe it's just the two . . . no, three glasses of wine I've just had. Oh well.

'Just so you know, I've been up since six a.m. and there's a good chance I might fall asleep,' mumbles Laura. I know exactly what she means. There's something about the quiet and the baby's peaceful gurgling in the corner that's making me a bit drowsy, too.

'Now, to help us, I want us all to say our worst fear out loud and then focus on the polar opposite,' Barbara eventually says, sounding exactly like a children's TV presenter talking to five-year-olds. The exact same soothing, dulcet tone.

'Easy,' says Laura. 'That one of the neighbours will look through the window right now and think I've turned lesbian.'

'You're not concentrating.'

'Why do we have to do this? I feel like a right gobshite,' I say, now that the mood's . . . slightly shattered. 'Can't we just keep drinking, like normal people do on a Saturday night?'

'Because, you said it yourself earlier, Vick. The trouble with most people is that they haven't the first clue what they really want. And the one thing we have going for us is that we each are really clear on what we're asking for. So we're each going to say our greatest fear out loud, face it head on, then let it go and concentrate on attracting the exact opposite and not worry about how it's going to come in. The book says something about not worrying about how your dreams will come to you – the universe will, sort of, re-arrange itself to make it all happen.'

OK, I'm getting a bit giddy now, not at what Barbara's saying, just at the way she's become such an expert on the law of attraction in such a sort space of time. I look over at Laura, whose head is nearest mine, and figure she must be thinking the same, because I can see her, eyes closed, but doing her slightly lop-sided smile.

'So come on, who's first up?' says Barbara, still in group-leader mode.

'OK then, my greatest fear is that I'll end up selling an organ to pay for next September's school fees,' says Laura, and I start tittering.

'Stop messing.'

'Miss? Miss? Is it my go yet?' I say, waving my hand in the air.

'You're only allowed to contribute if you're going to take this seriously,' says Barbara, but out of the corner of my eye, I can see her dying to have a good laugh as well.

'My greatest fear is that I'm only a step away from being one of those scary old ladies who live alone and scream at kids who ring on their doorbells and then run away.'

OK, now I can see Barbara starting to shake, and this suddenly reminds me of school, when she and I would sit beside each other and I could nearly sense when she was about to go, so I'd keep whispering funny things at her, needling at her weak point until she'd eventually crack up laughing.

'Oh no, hang on, I just thought of a better one,' I say. 'OK, my greatest fear is that I'll end up in the moratorium section of the lonely hearts' column.'

Right, now even Barbara is snorting, and it's too much, the whole mood is shattered as the two of us just roll around the floor, in fits of laughter, while Laura looks on, with her funny, sideways smile.

Not even the sound of a blazing row erupting from the back garden stops the giggles. Laura gets up and calmly goes to the window to see what's going on. It's George Junior and Jake bickering over something, God knows what, but the key words of the row are 'gerbil', 'thief', and 'stupid arsehole'. The good news is, though, instead of getting all stressed about it, like she normally would, Laura just waves her finger at them and says, 'Now, now, now boys. You are brothers and just remember that blood is thicker than diet cola.'

Then even she joins in the laughing, and I'm not kidding, just the sight of that alone does me more good than anything else this evening.

Chapter Thirteen

Shit, shit, shit, I'm going to be late, and Barbara will KILL me, and it's not even my fault. Well, not really. That is, not entirely. You see, I've been at the Best agency all morning, working side-by-side with Sophie, Amanda and the rest of the team on what will be the first cosmetics commercial to air. (Original Eyes, all very smoky and sultry. Trust me, in black and white, it'll look just stunning.) And, as often happens in brainstorming meetings, time just ran away with us. So now I'm standing on the street in the lashing rain, newspaper over my hair that I got specially blow-dried first thing this morning (for a particularly good reason, tell you later), trying to hail down a taxi like a demented lunatic.

On the plus side, I think, squinting through the rain and trying to make out whether the cab about to knock me down has its light on or off (curse my impressionist vision), we did do a great morning's work. AND, more importantly, my worries about the Best gang being annoyed at my not just sticking to the press-coverage end of things was completely groundless. Sophie couldn't have been sweeter to me, no graded scary looks thrown in my direction at all, and Posh Spice look-alike actually congratulated me on the seven deadly sins theme. Then there was a heated debate about whether a ten commandments theme might work better, but in the end we've opted for a combination of both. Commercial one will be themed around 'envy' and is roughly titled 'Thou Shalt Not Covet Thy Best Friend's Eyes'.

Then, the stroke of genius, which I'd love to claim credit for, but it was actually Amanda who came up with it. The voiceover tag-line will say (in suitably husky, femme fatale tones), 'Free, wickedly sinful gift with every purchase. For all you envious babes out there.'

I just love, love, *love* working with Amanda: she listens, she's up for absolutely anything ideas-wise and she's always full of chat about Daniel. (Still away apparently, but is holding fast to his demand to appear in one of the ads as an extra, watch this space.)

Anyway, miraculously, I grab a cab and head for the Unicorn, probably the coolest restaurant in town, where I've arranged to meet Barbara and, wait for it, THE Serena Stroheim, as she keeps referring to her. I arrive a couple of minutes late and Barbara's standing outside under a canopy, doing her trick of finishing a cigarette in two drags, which she only ever does at times of extreme stress.

This can officially be classified as a Very Bad Sign.

'Jesus, I thought you'd never get here,' is her snarled greeting as I pay the taxi driver and hop under the dry canopy beside her.

'Sorry, meeting at Best's ran over, not my fault. Honest.'

'You were at Best's?'

'Yeah, all morning, but the divine Daniel wasn't there, he's in the States . . .'

'OK, I need you to stop right there. I was only feigning interest about where you were out of politeness. And I'm just too bloody stressed to be polite right now.'

This might sound a bit rude, but I've known Barbara long enough to know that when under severe pressure, she reacts by getting unbelievable narky. I learned the hard way years ago never to even go near her just before of one of her theatre opening nights: there's a fair chance she might hurl a pointy object at you. So, instead I decide to go down the Kofi Annan softly, softly route.

'Never mind, hon, sure I'm here now, so will we go in? You're looking a million dollars, by the way.' Which is only the truth: she's in a tight-fitting short grey woollen dress, with a matching cashmere cardigan in the same beautifully soft shade of the palest grey. It sets off the long red curls to perfection, and I nearly fall over when I see that she's actually wearing tights and *heels*. I think it's the first time in about five years I've seen her not stomping around in either a) Reeboks or b) a particularly horrendous pair of bovver boots she's had ever since she left drama school.

'It's all Laura's, every stitch,' she says, stubbing out her fag as we head inside. 'It's her good going-to-court outfit. She made me call over to her this morning to get kitted-out. The deal is, I get one stain on any of this ludicrous politician's inauguration get-up, then I have to babysit for one entire week, God help me.'

'Well worth the gamble, you look sensational.'

'Oh piss off, I feel like a stupid, bloody, over-made-up tart. Laura forced me into this get-up, then said: "OK, now let's accessorize." I said, "With what? A lamppost and a pimp?" '

'No need to take the nerves out on me, my name's not Serena Stroheim.'

'Could you please stop saying her name? I'm close enough to throwing up as it is. All over the outfit.'

A smiley, bouncy waitress – with fingernails so long it's a wonder she hasn't lost the use of her hands – takes my soaked jacket from me and shows us to our table. We've arrived before our distinguished guest, thankfully, or else poor Barbara would probably have an anxiety stroke. It's a lovely, secluded table, too, tucked into a nice discreet corner of the restaurant, ideal for our purposes.

'May I get you something to drink?' beams fingernail girl.

'Still mineral water for me, please,' I say.

'And a paper bag for me to breathe into,' says Barbara.

Thankfully, the waitress assumes she's messing (although truth to tell she probably wasn't), and as she moves off, I fish around in the bottom of my bag for some rescue remedy. Bingo, I find my homeopathic 'dire emergency' bottle and hand it over to Barbara, who takes about five times more than the amount you're technically supposed to have.

'How can you be so, like, *chilled* and calm?' she gulps at me. 'Right now, I feel . . . I feel . . . like some kind of a prisoner of war. I feel . . . like you've traded me for tights and chocolate. In fact, come to think of it, I feel . . . oh shit, I feel I want to leave, Vicky, I want to get out of here RIGHT NOW. Would you be annoyed with me if I ran away? Would it mean the end of our friendship?'

I don't even have time to answer, as fingernail waitress is straight back, and by the gob-smacked look of recognition on her face at who she's leading to our table, I immediately guess that she must be an out-of-work actor. Has to be. Anyway, she's followed by the almighty Ms Stroheim herself, who politely introduces herself with a firm handshake and apologizes for being a bit late.

Now, I had of course Googled her in preparation for today, and kind of knew what to expect, but am still a bit taken aback at just how *young* she looks, and how energetically she comes across. She's maybe mid-sixties, tiny, with spiky grey hair and sharp grey eyes to match; she speaks in an East Coast American accent and kind of reminds me of Annie Leibovitz, in a funny way.

We all stand, then awkwardly sit back down again, then launch into a bit of chit-chat along the mundane lines of: 'So how are you enjoying the city?' and, 'Did you have trouble finding the restaurant?' Although it would probably be more correct to say that Serena and I chit-chat about inconsequential shite while Barbara, most unusually for her, goes completely mute. It's just the weirdest thing, I've never seen her so terror-struck before, ever. I'm not kidding; she's about as tightly coiled-up as a Walnut Whip. So anyway, in the absence of back-up, I make an executive decision to take the reins and off I go, steaming ahead into full-pitch mode. My reasoning is, business first, lunch after. I even produce a colouredy folder, which I had specially done for Serena, stuffed full of information, a list of sponsors that I'm targeting, photos of our venue, some advertisers that have already expressed interest in taking out ads in our programme; you name it, it's all in there.

'I gotta tell you, I greatly admire what you're doing,' the woman herself says, blithely flicking through her folder. 'And all for such a wonderful cause, too.' She speaks slowly, distinctly, and this slows my pace down a bit, too.

'Thank you so much. We're very honoured that someone of your stature is even considering this project.'

'Don't mention it.'

I look over at Barbara, who remains mute, so, just to be on the safe side, I thank her profusely enough for both of us.

Another pause, so I decide to fill it.

'And, as of early this morning,' I add, shooting a wait-till-you-hear-this-latest glance over at Barbara, 'we have full permission from the Parks Department to use the Iveagh Gardens for the show, plus, the dance studios in town have kindly agreed to let us use their largest studio for rehearsals, absolutely free of change.'

'Well, isn't that absolutely how it should be?' Serena asks

flatly, peering at me from over the glasses, and suddenly I realize why Barbara's so panic-stricken. This is a woman used to intimidating people, and for a split second I even find myself wondering if the specs are only for show. I decide it's best to say nothing, just nod and smile respectfully and let her get on with reading her colouredy folder.

Another silence, made all the more uncomfortable by: a) Barbara sitting there like human wallpaper, and b) the fact that the lunchtime gang are all here, the restaurant is buzzing and noisy and we're very obviously the only table where no one is speaking. And in Ireland, believe me, that just *doesn't happen*. Especially not with three women sitting together; normally, in this country at least, you'd practically have to invest in a talking stick and then bicker over it for airtime. A rank outsider looking at our table would think one of us had just been told she'd got two weeks to live.

Barbara, I can't help noticing, by now is starting to get very glowy (meaning: sweaty), but, to be honest, the protracted silence actually isn't bothering me nearly as much as I thought it would. In fact, I've done far scarier pitches, and some still inner voice is telling me to just stay very cool and calm and that all will be well.

Eventually, Serena puts the folder down, putting her glasses on top, very authoritatively.

'I gotta question,' she says.

'Of course. Please ask anything.'

But we're interrupted by fingernail waitress who bounces back over to us and launches into what I can only describe as a stand-up routine about the day's specials, I'm assuming solely for Serena's benefit. She certainly addresses her and only her, completely blanking Barbara and me. If the whole situation wasn't so surreal it would be comical: it's like the girl is doing an audition piece, except with dialogue like, 'pan-roasted chicken', and 'sautéed skate Grenobloise', her flashy long fingernails all over the place. Honest to God, by the time she's finished, I'm not sure whether to order or give her a round of applause.

Serena, however, is obviously well used to inspiring this kind of reaction, she just calmly orders the carbonara and calmly waits for fingernail girl to leave. Which she eventually does, but only after topping up Serena's glass with mineral water, beaming brightly and telling her for about the fifth time that if there's anything else she needs, absolutely ANYTHING, she'll be right here. Hovering about two feet away, to be precise.

Bloody hell, at a time like this, I'm so delighted *not* to be famous.

'There's something I need to clear up,' Serena says, when we eventually do get a bit of peace.

'Yes, of course, go ahead,' I say, noticing out of the corner of my eye that Barbara's hands are trembling, as she almost knocks over a glass and just saves it from spilling all over the colouredy folder.

'Ordinarily,' Serena goes on in her measured, even tones, 'I take approximately one year to mind-map a performance. I work slow. I like to experiment, improvise, use the text as a springboard, not as an end result. But if we want this to happen this summer, the pressure is already on. I'm gonna need to see the venue, speak to my costume and set designers, all of this takes time – and time, ladies, is not on our side. Most important of all, however . . .'

'Yes?' I say expectantly, although I've a fair idea of what's coming.

'. . . is casting. Getting that right is half my job.'

'I completely understand, and of course, you must have absolute control over that. But . . .' I shoot a do-you-want-to-jump-in-here imploring glance to Barbara, who just looks back at me ashen-faced. Right, nothing for it then but to go it alone. 'We had envisaged that the performance would be a showcase for my friend here, who is classically trained and we feel, perfect for the show. *A Midsummer Night's Dream* has so many terrific women's parts . . .'

'Oh, you're an actor? Where did you train?' Serena turns to Barbara, and puts the specs back on, I notice, heightening her scariness quota by about five levels.

I'm nearly on the edge of my seat, willing Barbara to blow her own trumpet a bit, how she won a scholarship to drama school and graduated with the gold medal, but God love her, she looks like a rabbit caught in the headlamps and just about manages to stammer a reply.

'Emm . . . well, you see . . . I haven't worked in a long time . . . and I'm such a big fan of yours . . .'

'What's the last job you did?'

'I trained at . . . emm . . . the Central School of Speech and Drama,' she eventually says, looking relieved that she is actually able to answer something, even if it is the wrong question.

'And what classical theatre roles have you played?'

'I was there from, emm . . . '93 to '97.'

'Who were your tutors?'

'Two radio plays in January and a Benecol ad last year,' she says. Then adds, 'Emm, that's, emm, this stuff you take for . . . ehh . . . lowering cholesterol.'

Oh my God, my bowels are withering up I'm so embarrassed for her; it's like watching the worst job interview in history. Note to self: next task on project Barbara is to work on her presentation skills for about, I dunno, the next ten years or so. I've no choice but to jump in. No kidding, this is what rescuing a drowning person must feel like.

'Barbara is very much a part of this project,' I say slowly and firmly. 'And I can guarantee you she will shine in whatever role you choose to cast her in.'

'Well, you got one thing going for you,' Serena eventually says, shrugging. 'You're not a star. I hate working with stars. Give me a passionate actor – with fire in their belly and willing to take any risk I can and *will* throw at them – any day, over a star.'

It's the first time that Barbara visibly relaxes.

'But of course,' Serena continues, taking the specs off again, 'you'll have to audition, same as everyone else.'

An hour later, we're saying goodbye to her under the canopy outside.

'So, we'll talk?' she says to me.

'Yes, of course, I'll be in touch,' I smile back.

'I'm in France for the next few weeks, but you can reach me on my cell.'

'Thank you so much for your time. We're so grateful,' I say, just as her taxi pulls up. Then a sudden bolt of inspiration. 'And I know the Children's Hospital will be, too.'

A tiny hint of a half-smile as she gets into her cab. Then whaddya know, fingernail waitress is hot on her heels, bounding out of the restaurant, still with her apron tied around her waist. 'Miss Stroheim? Miss Stroheim?' she calls out as Serena lowers down the passenger window. Oh shit, I'm thinking, please don't let this be what I think it is . . .

'Just to let you know, Miss Stroheim, I'm a huge fan of your work, and if you're going to be in town, I'm currently appearing in *The Threepenny Opera* at the moment, playing Polly Peachum, the lead role. Because as well as acting, I sing and dance, too, and, well, if you wanted to come along to see me, I'd be happy to organize complimentary tickets for you.' Then, and I really wish I were joking here, she produces a flier and shoves it through the car window. Serena says nothing, just takes the flier, rolls up the window and off she goes.

'The *Times* called my performance a tour de force!' is fingernail girl's parting shot, as the taxi disappears from view. Then she turns to Barbara and me and I swear you can practically see her weighing up whether or not we could be useful to her in her career.

'You're both very welcome to come along and see my show as well,' she beams, mistakenly thinking we're either producers or directors, too. 'Here, have a flier.'

I mutter thanks out of politeness more than anything else, and shove it in my handbag. Barbara and I are just about to head off when she calls after us, 'Excuse me, ladies? I don't suppose you happen to know where Serena Stroheim is staying when she's in town, do you?'

Chapter Fourteen

I have, ahem, another appointment not too far from here, so, as it's temporarily stopped raining, Barbara walks me there, so we can do a post-mortem. And it's not pleasant.

'OK, Vick, as my oldest, closest friend, I need you to tell me the truth and nothing but. Just exactly how bad was I in there?'

'Well . . .' I break off, not having the first clue how to be tactful here. And, to put it mildly, she's vulnerable right now. This could well turn out to be one of those instances where honesty *isn't* refreshing.

'Come on, Vicky, tell me. Because the whole time we were sitting there, it was like, I could almost feel myself fucking-up invisibly.'

I say nothing, just walk on in silence. Mainly because her self-assessment may sound critical, but it's not too far off the mark either.

'She kept asking me all those questions,' Barbara goes on, still torturing herself, God love her. 'You know, about where I'd trained and what I'd done, all of that. And on the inside, I just felt like that Edvard Munch painting, *The Scream.* There was so much on the tip of my tongue, and it just wouldn't come out. Story of my bloody life. Before an interview, I'm OK, after an interview, I'm OK, during the interview, I just fall apart. Please Vick, tell me honestly, how did I come across? If you were her, would you want to hire me? Come on, I'm a big girl and I can take it. Promise.'

I glance over at her, but it's hard to make out her expression because she's shoved her big, face-covering shades on. On probably one of the darkest, coldest days we've had in ages. She stops for a second to fish a cigarette out of the depths of her bag, and attempts to light up. Which is easier said than done as her hands are still shaking, and people keep bumping into her. And she doesn't even tell them to piss off like she normally would. Which is unlike her. Worryingly unlike her.

We walk on and I make a decision. In her shoes, I would want the feedback, wouldn't I? Course I would. It's absolutely no different from me with fellas, is my reasoning: until I figure out where I've been going wrong all this time, how can I ever hope to get it right?

'OK then, honey, it's like this,' I eventually say, picking my words carefully. 'You're a fabulous actress, no question about that. But . . .'

'I was waiting for the but.'

'. . . As they say in marketing, the product isn't the problem, we need to work on selling *you*. Barbara, I don't mean to rub salt in, but you walked into that restaurant with the job in the bag and you walked out without it. That waitress did a better job of selling herself. Yes, she was pushy, yes she was annoying, but you have to hand it to her, the girl saw an opportunity and went for it, acrylic fingernails and all.'

'But I have an audition! With Serena Stroheim!' she splutters at me in a cloud of smoke. 'An hour ago, she'd never heard of me, and I'm going to get to do a classical piece in front of her. I mean come on, that's some progress, isn't it?'

'Honey, my point is, you were a shoo-in for just about any part you wanted, and now you have to *audition*. God forbid and

I hope I'm not tempting fate here, but worst-case scenario, suppose . . . just supposing . . .'

A tough sentence to finish but Barbara does it for me.

'Supposing I flunk the audition?'

'Then . . .'

Shit and double shit, I can barely finish that sentence myself. Then all of this will have been for nothing. All of my hard work, all the hours I put in and will certainly be clocking up over the next few months, will count for naught. Like it or not, we're committed now. We have Serena Stroheim on board, we've the Children's Hospital on board, and the ice cold reality is that, with or without Barbara, the show must go on. The only thing I'll have succeeded in doing will be making stars of other actors, a gang of total strangers most likely, and if Barbara's audition goes anything like today did, she'll be doing well if Serena lets her hand out programmes or help with costume changes backstage. And that's if we're very lucky and she's feeling charitable.

We cross the street, and keep walking on, each of us wrapped in thought. Or in my case, that sickening sense of frustration you get when you've worked your arse off on something and then realize, in spite of all your blood-sweating efforts, the kite just won't fly. It's only when Barbara stops to stub out her cigarette that I realize why she has the shades on.

Oh sweet Jesus, she's actually crying. Barbara, the one who never cracks, at any time, EVER. In fact, I could be mistaken, but I think the last time I saw her shed a tear was when John Lennon was shot. And that was only because he was her favourite Beatle. And at the time, she was only about, like, six.

'Oh, now come on, it's not that bad,' I lie, slipping my arm around her waist.

'Yes, Vicky, it *is* that fucking bad,' she snaps, pulling away. 'In fact, I don't know how it could be much worse. You don't understand.'

'Now, that's not true, OK, so you were a bag of nerves in there, but . . .'

'No, Vicky, I mean you don't understand what it's like for *me*. I am so completely bloody sick and tired of being a failure. And make no mistake, that's what I am, a useless, bloody, washed-up failure.'

'Come on, honey . . .'

'Just hear me out, will you? No one knows more than me how you slaved over this, to get every tiny detail right. And I just went in there and buggered it all up on you. And you know what the worst thing is?'

'Shhh, shhh . . . here, love, have another ciggie.' But the tears are tumbling down now and there's no stopping her.

'Time was, I used to be a good actress. I *know* I was good. I was confident in myself. It was all out there for me. I could have gone the distance. But, right now, I have to face up to the fact that I have wasted the best years of my life on a pathetic career that didn't work out for me the way I wanted it to, the way it should have done. Look at me: I'm well into my thirties, the death years for any actress; I live in a rented flat which I share with a couple that are slowly driving me more and more mental every day; I'll never own my own home, I'll never be famous. Christ alive, I'll be doing well if I ever get another acting gig ever again. I'm somebody that could end up homeless, Vicky, sleeping rough. And what I don't get is . . .' She breaks off here, voice trembling, to suck on a fag. 'I followed my dreams. I mean, I thought that was what you were supposed to do in life? I look at you, with your booming business, and Laura who'll go back to the Bar in a couple of years and just pick up where she left off, and what have I got to show for myself? Nothing, absolutely big, fat nada, because

I'm worthless and hopeless and useless, useless, *useless.*'

'Hang on one second, you are NONE of those things,' I say firmly, stopping to fish a hanky from my bag, which she reluctantly takes from me, as if by doing so, she's acknowledging just how upset she is. 'And, let me tell you, "project Barbara" is going to work. You are going to do the best audition you've ever done in your life, and you're going to be cast in a leading role, and that's all there is to it. Yes, OK, so we had a setback today, but on the plus side, now we're clear about one thing: it's not your acting that's been the problem all this time . . .'

'It's me. Go on, you're thinking it, so you might as well say it.'

'I was going to say your presentation skills let you down, that's all. Come on babe, don't shoot the messenger.'

'The messenger had it coming,' she sniffs, but I notice the tears have stopped. Which, at least, is something.

'You've got to help me, Vicky. I watched you in there and thought, "God, I wonder if she ever realizes how amazing she's being?" You were so cool and articulate and unafraid. I need you to train me to be like you for this bloody audition. Cos the way I feel now, you're more likely to get a part in this than I am.'

'You can count on me, you know that,' I say, squeezing her arm. 'We're in this together, and I'll never let you down. We just . . . have our work cut out for us, that's all.'

Two cigarettes and a lot more walking later, Barbara's heart rate seems to be back into double figures. But as we slowly turn down street after street, all the while getting closer and closer to the scene of my, ahem, next appointment, guess what, now it's my turn to start getting antsy.

We turn a corner and now we're on the street where the Café en Seine is, scene of my scheduled rendezvous. With Peter. Handsome, funny Peter, guy number two from my miraculous night of the hat trick. And it's just the freakiest thing. It's like every shred of nervous tension that poor old Barbara had to deal with has, by some mysterious osmosis, left her and taken over my body, like in an *Alien* movie.

'Now remember, you're just trying him on for size, to see how he'll fit, that's all,' says Barbara, sounding an awful lot stronger and more assertive again, now that we've moved into her particular field of expertise; and nothing like the gibbering wreck she was only a few short minutes ago. 'Just think of this guy as the flesh-and-blood equivalent of a Donna Karan dress. You know it may not necessarily suit you, you probably won't end up buying it, but it's there, so you try it on anyway.'

'Right, yeah, OK,' I say, a bit short of breath, but otherwise no visible panic-attack symptoms. Well, not really. 'Right, here I go, once more into the fray. Check me for mascara gloop, will you?'

'You're perfect. Want me to stay with you till you've made a connection?'

'I'd love you to stay with me for the entire date, except it might look a bit like I'm clinging on to my security blanket.'

'OK, so here's your instructions. See how you bond in daylight hours, only stay for forty-five minutes and not a minute longer. I'll ring your mobile and you can pretend it's the office and that you've a crisis you have to go and troubleshoot.'

'Why the time limit?' I ask, a bit panicky, thinking, suppose, just suppose, we're getting on? Won't I look a bit aloof and snooty by just abruptly getting up and leaving?

'So he'll realize just how busy and important you are, dopey. Haven't you ever heard the old showbiz saying, "Leave them wanting more?" Oh, come on, don't tell me you've never cut a date short before.'

I'm too embarrassed to admit that I haven't. Even with Eager

Eddie, I stuck out an entire three-course meal. The triumph of optimism over experience, that's me. When it comes to fellas, I'll stick anything out, no matter how miserable, because there's always the hope that things might improve.

'Let him pay,' Barbara continues, 'then, when you're back at work, send him a short text message saying thanks for coffee, and see you soon. Nice and vague, so it's up to him to make another arrangement.'

'Right, got it.'

'Oh, and remember, don't talk about yourself too much, just keep asking loads of questions, like with Eager Eddie. Tell yourself you're Jonathan Ross and he's a reluctant guest that needs the answers coaxed out of him.'

'OK. Got it.'

'Remember your ultimate goal is to take him as your date to the PR do in a few weeks time.'

Shit, I was kind of hoping she'd forgotten about that.

'Don't forget, he's already survived my incredibly thorough screening process, so before you even go in there you know he's single, available, interested and straight.'

'Got it.'

'And like the law of attraction book says,' she goes on, 'just believe in your own fabulousness and you'll attract guys to you that think you're fabulous, too.'

'No, it doesn't.'

'Well, words to that effect. Piss off and leave me alone. I've had a rough day.'

'Nice to have you back to yourself. I always know you're feeling better when you start telling people to piss off.'

'If you're not careful, I'll march right in there and tell him that up until a few weeks ago, your nickname was The Dateless Wonder.'

If there's one thing I love about our Barbara, it's her ability to bounce back. From deep despair to wisecracking in the space of one short walk. She's amazing.

Anyway, one big hug later and in I go, with our watches synchronized, like in an espionage thriller. The lunchtime rush is well over and I immediately spot a lovely bright table in a corner so quiet and discreet, it might as well have a sign hanging over it saying 'suitable for first dates'. Right then, I text Peter, to say I'm here, as per our arrangement, then whip a colouredy folder out of my briefcase and pretend I'm studying it intently while I wait for him. Oh, and re-apply lip-gloss while I'm at it. Approximately four minutes later, the door opens as someone comes in, I look up and there he is.

Pro.
Oh my God, so much handsomer than I remembered. Dark hair, lovely piercing green eyes, and he's dressed in casual teacher gear: blue shirt and chinos. Put it this way, if I was a student in one of his classes, I would definitely have a crush on him. No question.

Another pro.
He's straight over, full of chat and how am I and how was my lunch meeting? It's all very easy and relaxed, then, as he goes up to order for both of us, Barbara's words come back to me. Shut up going on about myself and concentrate on him.

Slight con.
The minute I ask about how work is going for him, he starts talking about Clare. The ex-girlfriend. Turns out the school the two of them run together teaches those English as a foreign language TEFL courses, so this is probably the busiest time of the year for them. His conversation is peppered with 'Clare was just saying', and 'Clare had this terrific idea', and at one point we even had a: 'You just have to meet Clare. You both have lot in common.'

Definite pro.

Turns out they were together for seven years. SEVEN years. That beats the longest relationship I've ever had in my entire life. By about, ahem, six years to be exact. Anyway, isn't it a healthy, emotionally mature thing that they still run the business together and get on so amicably? Course it is.

After a bit more of Clare this and Clare that, I eventually pluck up the courage to ask the one question that's been burning me up. There's a slight lull in the chat so I go for it. 'So, Peter, if you don't mind me asking, why did you and Clare break up?'

'Oh, you know how it is, we just grew apart,' he replies, stirring the froth around his cappuccino. But he's smiling at me when he says it. And me like . . .

Biggest pro of all.

Barbara calls me precisely forty-five minutes later and, although I'm glad to see her back in messing mode again, I can only hope Peter doesn't overhear any of what she comes out with.

'Hi, Paris Hilton here,' she says in a faux-LA-valley-girl voice. 'There's an emergency and you have to come back to the office right NOW.'

'Oh, what kind of emergency?' I ask, acting all pretendy-concerned, purely for Peter's benefit, you understand.

'Well, I was photocopying my arse, and my G-string got stuck in the machine, and I'm having afternoon tea with my godmother, the Duchess of Cornwall in half an hour, so you'd better get back here with sharp scissors right now or else Auntie Camilla will set the corgis on you.'

'I'll be right there,' I say, snapping my mobile shut immediately, so Peter can't hear the raspberry she's now blowing down the phone.

Then, just as we're getting ready to go our separate ways, he lets slip, 'Actually, it's no harm to cut our date a bit short and leave now. I'd better get back to the school fairly pronto, or else I'm in for a right slagging.'

'Why's that?' I ask innocently.

'Because I told Clare I was meeting up with the first gorgeous woman I've met since we broke up – and if I'm gone any longer, she'll think I've run off with you.'

All this delivered with this cute, broad, slow smile he has.

Yummmmmm . . .

I wait till I'm safely back in a taxi before I ring Barbara.

'I don't want to jinx it,' I say excitedly, 'but I think we might just have a keeper on our hands. Now I ask you, when is the last time you heard me say that?'

Chapter Fifteen

The Butterfly's next meeting. June.

OK then. Our progress reports to date.

BARBARA. She is giving herself five out of ten, although personally I think she's being a bit harsh and deserves a minimum score of at least eight. On the plus side, she worked her ass off on polishing up an audition piece for Serena Stroheim; she did Hermia's forest speech from *A Midsummer Night's Dream* and was stunning. Absolutely the real deal. And I should know, I only saw her rehearsing it about fifty times. In fact, I could probably recite the lines along with her myself at this stage.

Anyhoo, her audition was held yesterday, at the dance studios, in front of the mighty Serena and her casting director. I met her both before and after and for the agonizing thirty minutes or so while she was in there, I paced the corridors outside, willing her luck, happy thoughts, huge success, you name it. No kidding, there were probably expectant fathers in maternity wards at around the same time yesterday, in a calmer and more relaxed state than I was. The upshot is, I can report that she went in a bag of nerves (grade one snappiness, never a good sign with her), and came out even worse. All I could get out of her was that if her audition had been a natural disaster it would have been comparable with either: a) Hurricane Wilma, or b) Britney Spears with the shaved head. Any more info I patiently tried to coax out of her was rewarded with getting the face chewed off me, so I quickly gave it up as a bad job.

Oh yes, and the reason I'm deducting two points from Barbara's overall score is because, in a moment of misguided generosity, or pure gobshitery if you ask me, she only went and told Evil Angie, flatmate from hell, about the whole Shakespeare in the park summer project. So of course, nothing would please said Evil Angie until she somehow managed to wangle an audition for herself.

I pointed out to Barbara that this was little more than an act of the most blatant user-ism on Evil Angie's part, but Barbara's having none of it. Plenty of parts for everyone and may the best girl win, is her incredibly generous and philanthropic answer. Now, the amount of work I've put into this, and the very real possibility that Evil Angie might get cast and Barbara won't, kind of makes me want to be sick. Shame we're not casting *Macbeth*, though, Evil Angie would be a natural for Lady M, albeit a bit typecast.

Anyway, the die is cast and there's nothing for us all to do now but sit patiently and wait for The Call. And try not to attract negative thoughts along the lines of how much I want to kill Evil Angie. Which is a bit like trying not to breathe. On the plus side, Serena did say that she hoped to have the show cast 'in a New York minute' (her phrase, not mine), with the result that every time either my phone or Barbara's rings, we both leap about six feet into the air, nearly giving ourselves full-blown panic-attacks just in case this could be The Call. I don't think I'll be able to eat properly until I know one way or another, while Barbara has upped her cigarette intake to I think about twenty. Every two hours, that is.

VICKY. OK, my progress can be neatly summarized thus. Number of phone calls from Peter since our coffee date, three; number of times I've actually seen him since said date, one; number of texts from Eager Eddie, twelve; number of phone calls from Eager Eddie, seven.

Oh, and number of sightings of Daniel Best on the two occasions I've been to his agency recently, big fat zero.

Let me elaborate.

Right then, Peter first.

Now, personally, I think the amount of contact I've had from him is quite respectable, actually, given that he's busy and I barely have time to wash my knickers these days, work has gone so crazy. However, Barbara, my personal PM and wise guru, claims his performance to date is classic borderline-interested, most likely to do with the fact that he's just come out of a long-term relationship. I mean, we all know what most guys are like about switching allegiances from one football team to another, so imagine how much harder it is for them when it comes to contemplating a new girlfriend. Slowly, slowly, softly, softly will win the day, is her logic.

The good news is, Peter did ask me out to lunch last week, which I thoroughly enjoyed, but the bad news is: a) he never made a move on me afterwards (OK, admittedly, it was broad daylight and we were both racing back to our desks, but not a peck on the cheek, nothing); b) he does talk a LOT about Clare. Honestly, until I actually meet her, I'm beginning to feel like I'm stuck in a Daphne du Maurier novel, you know, along the lines of *Rebecca*. The unseen rival can be excruciatingly boring and overdone in movies or plays, but in real life it's enough to make you start gnawing at the furniture with frustration. Is she thinner/younger/prettier/richer/funnier/just a better person than me – all the usual stuff is racing through my overactive imagination.

Barbara for her part, has nicknamed Peter 'Ex-Files' and says I should just visualize Clare, the ex, as being the kind of woman who goes through Marks & Spencer saying: 'Oh look at those lovely viscose slacks with the handy elasticated waistband, wouldn't they be great to wear to the highlight of my social calendar, Bingo on Sundays? Hmmm, wonder if they have them in my size, twenty-four. Oh, have to dash, time for my mid-afternoon snack of pizza and a tin of Bulmers.'

Bless her, I think she's trying to cheer me up.

I can't be entirely honest with Barbara, because she's so anti-Daniel Best and every time I as much as mention his name she instructs me to hold a mental picture in my head of him shagging models in the States, like billionaires are supposed to – at least in her vivid imagination. Although, personally, I think she's seen way too many TV programmes about Hugh Hefner and all his bunny girls in the Playboy mansion, and they're making her unfairly biased against wealthy unmarried men. Anyway, in Daniel's temporary absence, I've decided I do actually, really, seriously fancy Ex-Files, sorry, I mean Peter, on the principle that a bird in the hand is worth two in the bush. In addition, I'm exhibiting all the classic signs of Woman with a Crush: a) I'm waxed everywhere, therefore am fully match-fit and ready for action, if you get my drift; b) I went out and bought all new underwear; c) every time my phone rings I secretly want it to be him, and am always a bit sorry when it's not; and d) as well as reading my own horoscope every day, I now read his as well. Oh, and he's Pisces by the way, which scores a very promising eight out of ten for compatibility with my sign, Aquarius, according to the iVillage website anyway, which is bloody well good enough for me.

The *really* good news is that the PR dinner is coming up. So, I was very brave and grown-up and I asked him straight out, *and he said yes*, and best of all, Barbara is all set to double-date with his friend, fab wing-woman that she is. It'll be the first night-time excursion for Ex-Files, sorry I mean Peter, and me, so I'm expecting, ahem, a result of a physical nature, if you get my drift. Otherwise it'll be a total waste of a Brazilian wax, and I did NOT put myself through that agony and torture for nothing. The thing I'm most looking forward to, though, is having Barbara on hand, right by my side for the whole entire night, to monitor the whole situation. Oh, and prevent me from downing one too many margaritas, never, ever, a good plan. So it's all looking good, and the added bonus of having a chaperone on hand is helping my nerves considerably and making me feel a bit like a debutante in high society between the wars, circa 1937.

On a less positive note, however, I have to report that, as of about a week ago, Eager Eddie started calling and texting again. Now, in my defence and just so I can't be accused of leading him on, I only answered one call, and the minute I heard the Scottish accent, my heart sank. I thought we had pretty much agreed to leave things be and that was the end of that, but it turns out his rationale is, 'You said you wanted to take things slowly, so that's why I gave it a few weeks before calling again. You needed time, so that's what I gave you.'

Jaysus.

It so happened that I was in the office when he rang, so I had the ready-made excuse of phones ringing and the door buzzing to get off the phone as politely as possible. Then, that night, he calls again. So this time, I recognize the number and don't answer, so he leaves a message. Asking me out. To, wait for it, Glasgow. And this is the best part, to go and support his brother who's playing in the World Pipe Band Championships on Glasgow Green. Where he's playing the bagpipes. In public.

Now, nothing against bagpipe players, but I'd be a bit more of a Snow Patrol woman myself.

Needless to say Barbara howled laughing at this, and now whenever Eager Eddie's name comes up (which it usually does, but in sentences along the lines of 'can you believe that eejit still hasn't got the message, if I went on like that with a fella, he'd call me Glenn Close and have me arrested for being a bunny-boiling stalker . . . etc., etc.'), she launches straight into the chorus of 'Mull of Kintyre'. She even has a joke she made up specially. Q: why do bagpipers march while they play? A: to get away from the sound.

Ha, ha, very funny.

When she eventually stops laughing at my misfortunes, she does, however, remind me that, irritating as his persistent calls and texts are, I should just smile serenely at each one and tell myself that this is prima facie evidence that the law of attraction is actually working. And she's right. I may not be getting quite the result I want, but I have to remember that a only few short months ago, I used to wonder if my complete lack of success with guys was some Darwinian way of weeding me out so I wouldn't be able to propagate the species. At this moment in time, however, the sands are beginning to shift and that's good enough for me. Right then. End of my moaning. Onwards and upwards. Ex-Files . . . sorry, I mean Peter . . . here I come, baby.

LAURA. OK, so I admit, I was saving the 'best girl in the group' award till last. You just won't believe this, and I can barely believe it myself, but prepare to relinquish your breath. About a week ago, Laura got a phone call from the features editor at *Tattle* magazine to say that not only did they all roll around laughing at her short story but that she's actually been selected as a finalist in their competition! Cue massive whooping, punching fists in the air and screaming jubilantly at each other, and that's just me and the girls in the office. Even though I secretly had a feeling she'd do well, it's still lovely when you get confirmation like this from the universe that, yes, occasionally, good things *do* happen to good people. Barbara almost had a heart attack when she heard the news, and even Laura herself is playing it down, but secretly pleased, I think. I always know whenever she does that lop-sided smile thing.

She maintains her kids reacted as if she'd been chosen to go on *Who Wants to be a Millionaire?* and she had about a half-hour of blissful peace while they all ran upstairs to write their lists of what they wanted with their share of the cash she was *going* to win. In vain she tried to point out that if she won, the prize wasn't by any means life-alteringly huge, and in any case would be used towards taking them on a summer of cultural excursions around the city. The National Gallery, the Museum of Natural History, the latest exhibition of da Vinci Codex sketches, that type of thing. Under pressure, though, she did admit that their lists were just too funny.

Emily's was: '1. Yacht. 2. Two weeks in EuroDisney. 3. Lexus jeep for Mom. 4. Remainder to be put in secure bank vault so when I'm sixteen, can get boob job.'

So as not to ruin their fun, though, she did break her hard and fast rule of only healthy organic food at mealtimes and let them order a family bucket of KFC chicken nuggets, fries, coke, the works. Ordinarily, Laura has a strict ban on allowing any of her offspring to eat anything that comes off on the end of a coronary heart-scraper, as she puts it, but that night and for one night only, they were allowed forbidden food to mark this rare and special occasion.

She said that celebration alone was miles better than any magnum of champagne.

Chapter Sixteen

Laura's big day and we're all here for her. *Tattle* magazine are very generously (believe me, I know how much these promos cost), hosting a morning coffee reception in the fabulously posh Merrion Hotel, in a function room they've hired especially to announce the competition results. Kick off is at 11 a.m., perfect timing for Laura, as the kids are at school, and because it's a *very* special occasion, she's splashing out and dispatching baby Julia to a local crèche. This is unheard of. Ordinarily, I'm always trying to encourage her to leave the baby just for a few hours in the mornings to give herself a bit of head space, but she point-blank refuses, on the grounds that: a) the fees are so extortionately expensive, she's always saying you'd swear you were forking out to put a child through Harvard medical school; and b) her children would get 'insufficient stimulation', they learn far, far more at home, under her watchful gaze. Which, given that she's so brainy, and was playing championship chess from the age of six, is probably true.

Anyhoo, just this once, she caves in, and, under great duress, reluctantly drops baby Julia off. I then take full advantage of this and drag her off to my hairdresser's first thing, to get a blowdry and a manicure, my treat. Just to let her know, whatever today's result, how proud I am of her. By the time we're done, she's looking fabulous in a very Laura-like way: neat, scrubbed, immaculately and elegantly turned out in the same, grey 'going to court' good outfit she lent Barbara for our ill-fated lunch a while back.

We jump in a cab to the Merrion Hotel and miracle of miracles, the perennially late Barbara is actually there before us, smoking a fag outside and finishing it in two drags, a Very Bad Sign with her. She's in white jeans and one of those white netting tops that look a bit like see-through curtains, and she looks so tense and stressed that, honestly, your heart would go out to her.

'No news about the show yet, then I take it?' Laura asks her, as we all hug and kiss.

'Oh yes, I got the part and Serena's whisking me off to Broadway to guest star in my own one-woman show,' Barbara snaps, stubbing out her fag. 'I just decided I wouldn't bother telling either of you, that's all.'

'No need to take your nerves out on us,' I calmly intervene.

Now, don't get me wrong, I'm every bit as anxious as she is about the result, maybe even more so, but am trying desperately, desperately to think positive and attract the out-come we want.

Mainly because the alternative is just so unthinkable.

'Sorry,' Barbara mutters as we head inside and make our way to the function room. 'It's just the not knowing that's driving me nuts. Plus Angie says her audition went brilliantly, and is already acting like she's cast, which is driving me slowly up the wall. Last night, just to get away from her, I went out and had pity sex with Nathaniel. Yet again.'

'Who?'

'That barman guy. And by the way, *now* is a very good time to wipe that look off your face. I only did it to take my mind off things. Then it struck me, no wonder my nerves are jangling, I haven't had sex in weeks.'

'Why's that,' Laura asks drily, 'did you pull something?'

'Ha bloody ha.'

'And is that what you wore last night?'

'Yeah, why, what's wrong with it?'

'Dearest, you look like a coffee filter.'

Then my mobile rings, and I'm not kidding, both Barbara and I nearly leap six feet just in case it's The Call . . . just in case . . . just in case . . .

It's not. It's Amanda from Best's confirming a big meeting that's arranged for later in the week to discuss the storyboard for the first Original Sin commercial. Sophie, apparently, is insisting on my being there. I hang up the phone and notice that Barbara is actually clutching at her heart, hyperventilating. And I'm nearly getting as jumpy as she is. Jaysus, how much longer can this go on for?

'Eleven in the morning,' she says. 'Do you think it's too early to order a stiff brandy?'

I don't answer her, but I know exactly how she feels.

The function room is packed to the gills and buzzing when we get there. I'm not kidding, everyone is so chic and glamorous, I'm doubly glad I dragged Laura and myself off to have hair and nails done this morning. I actually know one of the features editors at *Tattle*, Caroline Owens, and am delighted to see her making a bee-line over to where we're standing by the door. She shakes us all warmly by the hand and actually lights up when I proudly introduce Laura as a finalist.

'Oh, you must be Laura Lennox-Coyningham?' she says. 'I absolutely adored your story!' And I know by her enthusiasm that she really, genuinely means it. Mag-hags are great people to know, but sincerity isn't exactly their strong suit.

'I have two pre-teens and I can tell you it really struck a chord with me. The bit about your daughter wanting a spray tan and a belly top because all her friends are now going around dressed like the Pussy Cat Dolls had me howling.'

'All true, I'm sorry to say,' says Laura, doing her lop-sided smile thing.

'Do you know, I read your story and thought: thank God I'm not alone. My ten-year-old wants her navel pierced for her next birthday, and I honestly don't know what to say to her. For God's sake, the child is *ten*. To me, she's still my little baby and I want to dress her in orphan Annie clothes, you know, all long smocks and Victorian boots.'

Laura nods sympathetically. 'You're preaching to the converted,' she smiles. 'And to think, at that age I wasn't even allowed to wear denim jeans. Do you know, for a special treat, I bought my daughter one of those pretty, long, white smock dresses from Zara, which was adorable on her, but the little madam fought with me and said she wanted to go out with a pillowcase wrapped around her waist instead.'

'Because it's "hot", I'll bet,' Caroline grimaces. 'Sweet love of God, if I hear that word once more, I'll scream.'

'Oh, you really must introduce a swear box system,' Laura says encouragingly, 'It's a terrific deterrent and phrases count, too, you know. Particularly: "You've ruined my life."'

'Or, here's another one,' Caroline chips in, smiling wryly. 'How about: "I never asked to be born anyway?" That gets a lot of airtime in my house. Hmm. Good suggestion, I might very well give it a try.'

I think it's a conversation that only another mother could really understand.

Pretty soon, we're all being ushered into our seats, and I'm delighted to say Laura, Barbara and I are all put in the very front row. This I interpret as a Very Good Sign. You know, kind of like at the Academy Awards, if you're a nominee and you're allocated a seat beside the toilets, chances are things aren't looking too good. Barbara is fidgeting away beside me, starting to drive me a bit nuts, if I'm being brutally honest.

'Are you switching off your phone?' she hisses at me, through gritted teeth.

'Course I am, why?'

'Suppose The Call comes during this? What'll Serena think if she can't get hold of either of us?'

'Then she'll leave a message, like normal, sane people do and we'll call her back when we're done and dusted here. Honey, you need to calm down. I'm every bit as antsy as you are, but short of sending my mother out to do one of her magic, fail-safe novenas, there's not much we can do but wait. Anyway, this morning's all about Laura, remember?'

'You're right. Sorry. How long do you think this'll go on for?'

'*WHAT?*'

'What I'm asking is, do you think they'd notice if I slipped out to the loo and slapped a nicotine patch on? Just so I'll last the morning? Sitting still isn't exactly my forte these days.'

'Barbara, if you don't chill out and start behaving, I'm off to get a tranquillizer gun to use on you. For your own good, you understand.'

'OK, OK, OK. I'll just twitch away here, with my phone switched off, and think of all the karmic reward points I'll get for being a supportive friend.'

'Good girl.'

'Just one more thing and then I'll shut up.'

'What?' I hiss.

'Your mother *is* doing her magic novena, isn't she?'

I roll my eyes to heaven and say a silent prayer.

Please, dear God, let Serena Stroheim cast this bloody show ASAP. Because I honestly don't know how much more of this I can take. Bloody hell, being an actor must just be the worst job imaginable. All that waiting around on phone calls that might or might not change your life would have me on double whiskeys every day. With tequila chasers. Washed down with vodka.

Next thing, there's a polite ripple of applause as Caroline takes to the podium right in front of us and makes a very funny speech about being a busy working mum and all that it entails. The constant exhaustion, the guilt at leaving your kids with a minder while you go to an office, weighed up against the overwhelming need for adult company and a healthy bank balance. She even coins a phrase that I've never come across before (and in my line of work, you pretty much get to hear everything, but this is a new one on me), a phenomenon called 'placenta-brain'. Seemingly, this is when you're so ga-ga in the few months just before and after childbirth that you start finding your car keys in the fridge and thinking it perfectly normal. Or when you wonder where the post is, then you realize you've put it in the washing machine along with a load of babygros, and now everything is on a rinse cycle.

'All ahead of us,' I whisper to Barbara beside me.

'Are you kidding me? These genes end here, thanks very much.'

Anyway, apart from the cynical touchstone on my left, I notice there're a lot of heads nodding like Buddhas in the audience, Laura's included, and suddenly I'm filled with an overwhelming rush of admiration for these women. I mean, for God's sake, I can barely organize myself and a Useless Builder, let alone get up in the middle of the night, do a feed, then drive kids to school, then put in a full day's work, then go home and do it all again. Every single day without any let-up until they're, like, eighteen. Oh, and you're supposed to function on no more than about four hours' sleep. AND try to keep a marriage going at the same time, which everyone knows is a full-time occupation in itself. At least if shows like *Desperate Housewives* have taught me anything.

God almighty, these women don't deserve cash prizes, they deserve medals.

Anyway, in no time Caroline is introducing the magazine's owner to announce the results. Up steps a Mr Desmond Lawlor, who I've never actually met before, but I know of by name, as he owns several very diverse publications: from financial magazines to movie guides to one or two of the more gossipy glossies, which are the ones I usually end up poring over. Just to check who's Botoxed and who isn't, who's going out with who, and who's newly-dumped and single again. All work-related, natch.

Anyway, Desmond Lawlor is maybe in his sixties, in good shape for his age, slightly greying, sprightly and so distinguished-looking that if central casting were looking for an 'honourable elder statesman' type, he'd be the very man. There's no beating about the bush, he just goes straight to the results, in reverse order, a bit like on *Miss World*.

Third place goes to a Polish woman with three kids, who Desmond tells us wrote very movingly about her experiences as an immigrant here, and the challenges of living in a new country and having to learn English from scratch, all the while dealing with a young family, far away from her own home. She gets a thunderous round of applause and heads up to the podium to accept a warm handshake and a cheque from Desmond.

I squeeze Laura's arm encouragingly.

'Now all of you ladies in the audience I'm sure are familiar with the legendary comedienne Joan Rivers, and I can tell you, our runner-up's wit, humour and wry take on motherhood reminded me very much of that great lady's style . . .'

I swear, I knew before he even said it. I just *knew*.

'. . . in second place, with her hilarious story entitled "Checkout Time is at Eighteen Years", is Laura Lennox-Coyningham!'

Barbara and I are on our feet in a nano-second, and I'm not joking, there are tears in my eyes as I watch my girl take her well-earned prize. You should just see her, she looks as cool and unflappable as ever, but the lop-sided smile is set in place so I know she's chuffed. Bloody hell, two grand she's just won . . .

The winner is equally popular: a young, fresh-faced teenage mum who, amazingly, found herself pregnant at seventeen and, against everyone's advice, still went ahead and sat her Leaving Cert. And got straight honours in all her subjects, winning a place to college into the bargain. She makes a touching, short speech about how she's coming up to her first-year exams and how much support she got from all her tutors and lecturers. 'Don't get me wrong,' she says into the mike that Desmond holds out for her. 'I wouldn't change anything for the world, but there are times when I'm collecting my son from the babysitter, and I'm telling you, I'd only KILL to go out drinking Red Bull with the rest of my classmates.' A huge roar of laughter, a novelty-sized cheque is handed over, a flash of cameras and it's all over.

We're straight over to squeeze our gal to death and make those 'dolphins mating in a nature documentary' squealing noises that women do when over-excited, as we all are now. Even Barbara waits a good four to five minutes before switching her phone back on to check for messages.

'Two thousand euro,' I say to a glowing Laura. 'So what'll you do with it? A well-earned holiday maybe?'

'Every red cent is going towards the kids' cultural improvement summer programme,' she beams at us.

'They'll go bananas!' says Barbara, 'You're going to have to throw a few playstations in at the very least, to sweeten the deal.'

'I'm fully aware I won't be courting popularity with this decision, but you know what? This morning I overheard George Junior calling his brother 'gibbon spawn' and I thought, that's *it*. A summer educational programme is precisely what my family need.'

'May I say, I'm terribly pleased to hear it,' says a plummy-toned voice from behind. The three of us turn around to see Desmond Lawlor himself, coming to shake Laura's hand. 'Money well spent, if you ask me.' He smiles in this benign, kindly way he has that reminds me of my dad. No, scrap that. Now that I see him up close, he's actually more like my granddad.

Laura politely introduces Barbara and me, and Barbara, I'm pleased to say, manages to de-clamp her mobile from her ear for long enough to say hi.

'May I ask you a question, my dear?' Desmond says to Laura. Trust me, he's one of those men who can call you 'my dear' and it kind of makes you feel like a Victorian lady in a hoop skirt clutching a phial of smelling-salts.

'Of course,' she smiles.

'Are you one of *the* Lennox-Coyninghams?'

'Guilty as charged,' she says lightly. 'Although normally, if I tell people I'm a lawyer I usually tack on to the end of my sentence, "but don't worry, I'm getting all the help I need".'

'I've met your parents several times,' he goes on, smiling kindly. 'Socially, I'm pleased to say, never in a court-room scenario. Do you plan to return to the Bar?'

'I have the days counted,' she smiles. 'Literally.'

'But I trust you'll keep writing until then? No false modesty, my dear, but you do have a unique voice. Sharp as a razor and smart as a whip.'

'Well, I . . .'

'It's just that, if you were interested, I think we might be able to offer you some freelance work. Something along the lines of a column, perhaps?'

Barbara steers me away on the pretext of getting coffees for all of us, leaving the two of them chatting away goodo.

'I think we're just big blurry shapes to Laura now,' she says sagely.

'He's offering her a gig! This is incredible!'

'Oh you poor deluded eejit,' she says, shaking her head. 'Have I taught you nothing? Don't you understand body language? Can't you tell when a guy is trying to get into someone's knickers without my having to use glove puppets and semaphore to hammer the point home to you?'

'Laura and . . . *Desmond*? No, you can't be serious. For God's sake, he's an old man.'

'In some cultures, mid-sixties is considered the prime of life.'

'There's listed buildings out there that are younger than him.'

'Plenty of women find age a turn-on. Our Laura, for one.'

And then it hits me. Sweet Jesus, she's right. I mean, when George Hastings came along all those years ago, we wrote him off as an old, old man who she'd be wheeling to his bridge club and feeding through a straw in no time. Desmond is exactly her type.

Her identikit type, to be exact.

'But he seems like a nice guy, doesn't he?' I say to Barbara, a bit worriedly, if I'm being honest.

At that moment, we both look over to where Laura's standing, deep in conversation with Desmond. And then she dust-flecks him. Right in front of our very eyes.

'Done deal, if you ask me,' says Barbara.

One sneaky snipe of champagne in the hotel bar later and finally we get to quiz the still-glowing Laura.

'He offered me a bit of freelance work,' Laura says primly. '*C'est tout*. End of subject. Absolutely no need for further discussion, and I do NOT want this to become a subject of gossip amongst you pair. Yes, phone numbers were exchanged, but just so I can pitch some ideas at him, for a possible monthly column. And, come to think of it, I do actually have an idea. What do you think of this? "Motherhood: the ties that bind . . . and gag".'

'So, I didn't notice him wearing a wedding ring,' says Barbara, ignoring her and cutting straight to the chase, as ever.

'Your point being?'

'For a man his age, that can only mean one of two things. Gay or divorced.'

'Neither as a matter of fact,' Laura replies, cool and unflappable as ever. 'Widowed.'

Chapter Seventeen

Brilliant news. I mean fantastically, unbelievably amazing news and all it took was:

1. Three back-to-back 'magic' novenas to whatever saint up there my mother happens to have a hotline to.
2. Me spending the last, agonizing few days reading all Barbara's horoscopes in just about every glossy we have in the office, and picking the most favourable one. ('Good news! A time for celebration is here, so crack out the champagne and get partying.') Then reading it down the phone to her, only embellishing it slightly to make it sound like a miracle was imminent. (OK, so maybe I made up the bit about the champagne.) Now, admittedly, the 'good news' that particular horoscope refers to is pretty generic and not necessarily career-related; I mean, there's days I find discounted Woolford tights in the House of Fraser and that's a cause for minor celebration, but it was the best one I came across for our Barbara, a Capricorn. And I only cheated by throwing in a line from the Aquarius horoscope in the box below, as it was far more positive and even said 'dreams do come true, just believe in yourself'. Ordinarily, she thinks all of this is complete rubbish, but did later admit it helped her get through yet

another nail-bitingly anxious morning.

3. Me sending her daily affirmations and quotes from my dog-eared law of attraction book ('Giving thanks for what you want in advance inevitably sends a far more powerful signal out into the universe.') According to the book, some people even go around with 'attitude is gratitude' note-books in their pockets; the idea being that every time you think of something you're grateful for, even if it's only getting a decent parking space, you make a note of it and keep saying thank you, to keep 'em coming, so to speak.

The universe, it would seem, a bit like my Auntie Maisie, appreciates good manners. Anyway, Barbara gave it a lash and said she only thought she'd gone a tad too far when Evil Angie found her in front of the bathroom mirror, clutching a tube of Colgate and thanking the world and its sick dog for her best actress Oscar, her Tony Award for best Broadway newcomer and her Irish Theatre Award for: 'best, hottest and generally all-around most amazing actress to have been employed by Serena Stroheim, ever in history, ever.'

Laugh all you like, but these little things are what get us through times of great stress.

Anyway, at the close of business on Friday, the long-awaited miracle came to be. I was holed up in yet another meeting at the Best agency (still no sign of Daniel coming back from the States, ho-hum), and had my phone off for most of the day. I figured I'd be done and dusted by seven-ish, but Sophie insisted on going through the first-draft scripts for all of the commercials with a fine toothcomb. Best's have also selected a director for our first shoot, someone called Tom Howard, who I haven't heard of but who apparently shot a highly successful beer commercial for them some time ago. 'Wait till you see him,' Amanda whispers to me. 'V v v cutie. Hot hot hottie. We like.'

Anyway, hours after the others have all deserted the place, Amanda and I eventually crawl out of the boardroom, both of us so wrecked and mentally exhausted from a full day's brainstorming that we can't even face the freebie Choca-Mocha kisses that are just lying there for the taking. We'd no choice, we had to work later than the others, as she and I are hatching an idea that's, well, just a bit 'out there'. And we're not quite ready to announce it just now, as chances are the whole concept could get shot down before it even leaves the ground. Our strategy is to make this product skyrocket with a bang so loud you'd think the Space Shuttle Challenger had just been launched, but what we're planning is risky and we need approval from the top. Which means Daniel. Who's still in the bloody States. Which means conference calls most of next week, probably.

'So what's he up to, anyway?' I ask Amanda, who's great for dishing out info, as we both pack up our briefcases and call it a night.

'Your guess is as good as mine. There's two rumours doing the rounds about him, so take your pick. The smart money says he wants to expand the company and is looking at opening up in New York. Wouldn't it be soooo amazing? Madison Avenue, if you don't mind, in which case there'll be a near riot to get posted over there, even just for a few months. Do you realize that they have sample sales over there where you can get Prada dresses WITH shoes AND bags for, like, two hundred bucks? If that rumour is true, then I'll harass him day and night to be moved there. Could you just imagine the money I'd save in those discount stores? For God's sake, Vicky, if you work in advertising or PR, they practically throw designer goods at you, for free. In fact, I'd say *they* pay *you* just to take stuff off them.'

'So . . . Daniel's most likely there on business,' I say, fauxcasual, fishing a bit.

'Depends on who you talk to. Course the other rumour doing the rounds is far more interesting.'

'Yeah?' I say, thinking, shit, did that sound breezy enough?

'Patti from accounts said she heard it from Megan in sales that Louisa in marketing definitely heard him say he has some girlfriend on the go over there. A buyer at Bergdorf Goodman's, apparently. Apart from that, we don't know much more, but it does make sense. I read that single women in New York go on, like, five dates PER WEEK, so can you just imagine how a guy like Daniel would go down over there? He'd be like—'

'Like a Mars bar at fat camp,' I say, finishing the sentence for her and trying not to sound too morose about it. I mean, for God's sake, I tell myself sternly, how could he NOT be dating over there? The guy is the whole package: single, good-looking, a laugh, oh and lest we forget, a squillionaire . . . I'd hazard a guess that Manhattan minxes are, at this moment, impaling each other with their Manolo Blahnik stilettos just to get a crack at him.

Anyway, it's not like I'm the least bit put out about this or anything. I mean, tomorrow is my big night out with Peter, the PR dinner. Lovely, handsome, intelligent Peter, who I'm nursing high hopes for. He's been calling and texting regularly, and basically is making all the right noises that he and I could really be on our way to couple-town. And while we're on the subject of tomorrow night, may I add, ahem, ahem, watch this space. I have a whole day ahead of me of spray tanning, hair straightening, French manicures, the works. I'll be so match-fit, the guy won't know what hit him. *And* Barbara will be at the PR dinner with the friend who looks the image of Edward Norton. (Note to self: his real name is Charlie. Do NOT drunkenly refer to the guy as Edward Norton, or, worse, Barbara's name for him . . . Baldie.) The point being, I'll have on-site back-up. And I cannot wait.

The building is weirdly quiet and echoey and kind of spooky as Amanda and I clickety-clack down the glass brick staircase. She switches her phone back on and I do the same, all of a sudden realizing that it's been off for most of the bloody afternoon. Oh shit. Eight missed calls and eleven texts.

Immediately I figure at least two have to be from Eager Eddie, who I've been studiously ignoring, but seems to be one of those guys that becomes keener and keener the less interested you are. As if you'll be so worn down by their persistence that eventually you'll fall into their arms, probably out of sheer exhaustion from giving them the run-around, as much as anything else. At present, he's averaging one call and several texts a day, and is living proof that the whole notion of 'The Rules' actually does work. On a certain type of fella anyway. Eejits, some people might call them.

To my surprise, though, the first six messages are all from Barbara, escalating in tone from 'mild hysteria', to 'I think I might be having a coronary, call an ambulance', to 'you're only audible to dogs right now'.

They went something along these lines . . .

3 p.m.
'Vick, oh Jesus, Vicky answer your phone. Quick, for the love of God, you won't believe what's happened . . .' Beep . . .
3.05 p.m.
'VICKY!!!! Where the f**k are you anyway? And why is your bloody phone switched off!! This is a grade one emergency and I have to talk to you urgently . . . IMMEDIATELY!!' beep . . .

She's shouting so loudly down my message minder that even Amanda can hear her loud and clear as we make our way past the dark, deserted office reception area.

'Is your friend OK?' Amanda asks, really concerned. 'She doesn't sound the best, if you don't mind me saying.'

'Not too sure, it's a toss up,' I say, a bit worried myself now, fearing the worst and skipping through message after message till I find one that actually has some hard info. No kidding, Barbara's sounding so panic-stricken and out of control, I still can't discern whether the news is unbelievably good or horrendously awful.

And then I hear it. The message I've been waiting for. It came through at 5 p.m. and was from a very cool, crisp Serena Stroheim.

'Vicky, Serena here, just to let you know I've finalized the casting on the show. Perhaps you'd like to ring me to discuss it further. Let me also set your mind at rest that your friend did a wonderful audition and I've offered her a role. I'm not certain whether she'll accept it or not; there was a lot of squealing on the phone when I called her earlier, but I think that usually qualifies as a yes. Chat soon.' Beep . . .

I slump against a wall, suddenly exhausted as the tidal wave of relief sweeps over me. Thank you God, thank you universe, thank you law of attraction, thank you any divine force that made this miracle happen . . .

'Good news, I hope?' says Amanda, not too sure if I'm having an anxiety stroke or not.

'Mmmm,' is all I can nod.

'Come on, you need a drink. You know, it's Friday night Salsa night here, and all the gang are going dancing. A few tequilas and the sight of sexy men swaying and gyrating is just what you need right now.'

I smile at her. God, Best's is just the coolest place. I'm only surprised the entire creative team didn't do a conga line out the door the minute they all finished work, led by Sophie.

'I'd love to, Amanda, but I really have to meet up with this friend, wherever she may be . . .'

'Ok . . . well . . . you don't mind if I go, do you? I mean, I didn't get these blonde tips put in my hair for nothing.'

'Of course not, and you look fabulous,' I say as we step into the cool night air and start looking for taxis. 'Go. Score. Enjoy. Have loads of gossip for me next week.'

She and I hug goodbye, jump into our separate cabs, and I call Barbara. It's really hard to hear her as she's obviously in some packed, noisy bar somewhere, so I have to shout a bit.

'IT'S BRILLIANT NEWS . . . CONGRATULATIONS!!!' I nearly have to shriek at her. 'WHERE ARE YOU? I'M ON MY WAY.'

'Vicky!!! My heroine!!!! The woman who's turning my life around!!!' She screams back so loud the taxi driver winces a bit. 'The two of us are in the Dakota bar celebrating, so get your gorgeous ass in here RIGHT NOW!!!'

'The *two* of us?' I shout back, thinking, could she be with Laura? Unlikely so late on a Friday night . . . Nathaniel, the barman guy she has flings with from time to time? Maybe someone new that I don't know about yet?

'Yeah. Me and Angie. She got cast as one of the leads, too!!! Isn't it fabulous?'

Perfectly valid reasons why I can't stand the bloody sight of Evil Angie.

1. If user-ism were an Olympic sport, she'd represent the country and probably take home gold. It's as though she's ingratiatingly sweet to you in direct proportion to how useful she perceives you to be. Viz. when I meet her and Barbara a bit later in the Dakota bar, she's so all over me, it's actually embarrassing. Now that she sees me with a

'producer' hat on, I honestly think the girl will have to be surgically removed from up my bum.

2. Barbara, high as a kite on champagne, lets it slip that I'm involved in casting for not one, but seven different commercials, and I'm not kidding, Evil Angie actually asks me who the casting agent is and if she can get seen? For God's sake, even Barbara was only messing when she asked me that, and she's miles more modelly-looking *and* she's my best friend. Bad enough that all my hard work in getting *A Midsummer Night's Dream* up and running could now actually benefit this self-serving cow, but now she wants to muscle in on the Original Sin ads too? Unbelievable, just unbelievable . . .

3. A bit like the Queen, she never carries cash and is one of those people that'll sit in a bar, order drink after drink, and let whoever she's sitting with foot the bill. Without even a twinge of embarrassment, nothing. Even in the taxi the three of us share on the way home, she says to Barbara, 'Babsie, darling, can you get this? I'll sort you out when my next voiceover cheque comes in.'

4. She lies about little things, and my theory is if you can carry off a lie about a little thing, then a larger one will be no bother to you. Oh and by 'little things' I'm referring to her ludicrous claim to be a natural blonde (when we all know perfectly well that there's no such thing), a size eight (if she's a size eight then I'm Caroline of Monaco), and that she just missed out on getting cast in the Keira Knightley role in *Pirates of the Caribbean*. Honestly, what does she take us for? The girl is an out-and-out *fantasist*.

5. She's one of those women who always, always have a boyfriend, and just seem to effortlessly flit from long-term relationship to long-term relationship. And for some bizarre reason, this annoys me more than anything else listed above.

Barbara officially has the patience of a saint. If Evil Angie was my flatmate, there would be a bloodbath. Anyway, this is Barbara's night and I don't want to ruin it for her, so I'm forced to do a major attitude re-adjustment and focus on the fact that my girl attracted what she wanted into her life and, like the good book says, this is a major cause for celebration and saying 'attitude is gratitude' etc., etc.

The only time I actually want to slap Evil Angie is when Barbara leaves us to go up and buy a round. The malevolent cow waits till Barbara's well out of earshot, then turns to me and says, 'So I hear you girls have this sort of club going, where you all project-manage each other. You know, so everyone helps each other to get what they all want out of life.'

'Mmmm,' is all I can mutter, momentarily furious with Barbara for telling her.

'And you're looking for a man, aren't you?'

Jesus, I hate her. I make a big show of pretending I hear my phone ringing and checking to see if there's a message, just so I don't have to answer the evil cow.

'Cos you've been single, like just for *ever*, haven't you?'

I just sip my drink, willing Barbara to hurry back.

'Although Barbara did mention that you're taking some guy to a PR do tomorrow night, and she's going with his friend, just to keep an eye on you. Must be a scream, having a chaperone . . . I mean, at your age!'

I do my best to tune her out, and am half-wondering how unethical it would be for me to ring Serena Stroheim and ask/beg on bended knee for her to reconsider her decision to cast this evil, bloody cow.

'Don't get me wrong, Vicky, if I'd been single for as long as you, I'd definitely consider pursuing a dating open-door policy, like you're doing.'

OK, now I'm actually wondering if it's insensitivity or just plain stupidity that has her interpreting my sullen silence as: 'Oh, you're just so interesting, Angie. Please, please continue humiliating me. I'm loving it and I just can't get enough.'

'Anyway, Vicky, as regards this all-girls freemason's thing you have going on,' she prattles on, with me staring furiously into space. 'Well, the thing is, I'm doing a lot of work on myself right now, I'm becoming an awful lot more self-aware and focused. I mean, I even went out and bought a book by Deepak Chopra and . . . well, I was kind of wondering, could I come along to your next meeting?'

I have to physically bite my tongue from snapping, 'No, you cannot, you evil cow. *Gandhi* was self-aware and focused; you just want to use other people as stepping stones to get what you want.'

Note to self: strangle Barbara and make it look like an accident.

My last and final word on the subject is that if Evil Angie gets better reviews than Barbara, lands a better agent out of this, or, God forbid, upstages her in any way (which I wouldn't put past her), then she'll have me to answer to.

Right then. End of rant. For now.

Chapter Eighteen

Saturday night and we're all systems go for the big PR dinner. I'm actually starting to feel like Peter and I are well on our way to dating exclusively, and am loving every single wonderfully romantic minute of it. This is it. Finally the relationship gods have smiled down on me, and, let's face it, not before time. Peter called not once but *twice* today to arrange for him and his friend Baldie . . . sorry, Charlie, to meet Barbara and me in his local, conveniently close to the Radisson Hotel, where the do is to be held. He seems keen, keeps saying 'we' a lot, and seems to be looking forward to the night as much as I am. So, in a nutshell, all the signs are good that tonight could be the night when we 'seal the deal' if you're with me. I'm excited and buzzy, brimming with confidence that this is it; this really could be The One.

The only teeny fly in the ointment is, all going well, then where exactly do I lure him afterwards? Useless Builder started sanding my wooden floors upstairs, then did his usual trick of half-finishing the job and buggering off for the weekend, leaving the top of my poor little house looking like a desert sandstorm just hit it. Laura sensibly suggested that I just treat it all like a big joke and, should Peter agree to come back to my place, just make sure I have champagne chilling in the fridge (check), fabulous underwear on (check), and crisp new bed linen (check). I'm a great believer in bed karma, i.e., unmade and messy is not the way to get a result, if you're with me. So, one flying trip to the homeware department of House of Fraser later, and I'm ready to rock and roll and my bed is now a field of dreams. ('Build it and he will come, is that your cunning plan?' as Barbara quipped, har, har, har.)

Well, except there's been one glitch. I forgot to shut the bedroom door before Useless Builder got at the sanding machine, so now my ferociously expensive, fab new Frette sheets resemble something Lawrence of Arabia would have slept on. In a tent. With a camel parked outside. In the Sahara.

Anyway, I have come to the mature decision that if anyone judges me on the state of my living space, then it's a sad reflection on them, not me. So in a way, it's a test of character, and if Peter has a problem with sitting on my mother's patio furniture drinking champagne out of plastic cups, that's his problem and not mine. Not that he would, she sez, brimming with the pre-date confidence of someone who got *two* calls from him so far today, not even counting texts. He's just too much of a gentleman. Don't ask me how I *know*, I just do. Woman's instinct and all that.

Six thirty p.m. and I'm ready for action. I'm wearing my 'serial result' good Karen Millen LBD, plastered in fake tan to hopefully take the glare off my natural skin tone (which is a pasty blue), nails done and with my hair straightened from here to France. Just as I'm rushing out the door to my taxi waiting outside, I stop and pick up the law of attraction book, sitting on top of a handbag in the hallway. It's become almost like a lucky charm with me at this stage. When I'm nervous and jittery before a big occasion like this, my little routine is to flip open a page at random and see what message the universe has to send me. Something life-affirmingly positive that'll act like a fantastic omen for the night ahead. With a bit of luck.

Negative feelings will inevitably attract yet more people and situations which will continue to draw you into a spiral of negativity. Just like a vicious circle.

Eh, no, not quite what I was hoping for. I try again as the taxi beeps the car horn impatiently. Oooh, here we go, this is a bit more like it.

If your wish is to attract a relationship, first make certain your thoughts, words, actions and surroundings don't contradict those desires.

Perfect. Well, apart from the bit about my surroundings, that is, but I can just cross that bridge when I come to it, can't I?

Oh shit, no, tonight's too important to me, I need one more go, just for luck.

Expectation is a powerful attractive force. You must school yourself to expect the things you want and conversely, not to expect the things you don't want.

Far more like it. Expect good results and they'll manifest. I mean just look at the progress the girls are all making, I think, as I grab my purse and lock the hall door. (Although why, I don't know, any burglar walking in would swear by the state of the place that I'd already been hit.) Laura's got a column now that'll pay her regular money. OK, not huge amounts, but it's work she loves and can do from home and, until she gets back to the Four Courts, this is a start, isn't it? And Barbara's on the verge of getting the huge showbiz break that she so richly deserves. Very slowly, shifts are happening and the others are starting to get what they want. So whatever way you look at this, there can only be one conclusion about tonight.

It's *my* turn.

First not-so-great sign about the night ahead.

So, the four of us are in the bar, sitting around a table, warming up for the festivities ahead. Barbara's looking effortlessly stunning in a silky black trouser suit borrowed from Evil Angie, still sky-high from yesterday's wondrous news. Peter's friend Charlie is there, too, looking, well, the kind thing to say is that he's made a big effort. I mean, yeah, I may have forgotten that the baldie head is in fact a shaved head which tonight is shining and polished like Daddy Warbucks's, and yes, OK maybe the tux is way too small for him, but on the plus side, he only has eyes for Barbara, to the exclusion of anyone else, and given that she always says sex is better than champagne for celebrating good news, I think the guy might possibly even be on to a winner here this evening. Anyway, the champagne is flowing, and everyone's getting into high old form. Well, everyone except Peter, that is. I can't quite put my finger on it, it's not that he's being moody or boring, just a bit quiet, that's all. And every time there's a lull in the chat, he keeps scanning the room to see who's just come in.

7.00 p.m.

Mystery solved. Out of nowhere, Peter suddenly gets all animated, joining in the conversation with gusto and laughing just that bit too hard at Barbara's wisecracks. It's only when I see a very attractive brunette newly arrived at the bar with a very dishy-looking guy in a rugby shirt, looking steadily over in our direction, that I suddenly know exactly what's going on.

'Isn't that Clare?' Baldie says, spotting her too.

Knew it. Knew it without even being told.

7.10 p.m.

Weird and a bit ick, if I'm being honest. Clare comes over with her date, who she very pointedly introduces to all of us as

James, but then she keeps referring to him in an irritating, cutesy-cutesy way as Jamie. Then Peter introduces all of us, slipping his arm around my waist as he says, 'And *this* is Vicky.' Nothing in his tone would suggest there's anything up, nothing untoward in the gesture itself. It's just that he's never laid a finger on me before, not once. Now Clare's getting all touchy feely with James and Peter's upping the ante on me, holding my hand and making a big show of really looking into my eyes, while I smile awkwardly back up at him. He and Clare lock eyes and make small talk but the undercurrent is something a lot different. In fact, by now I'm actually starting to feel like an incidental character in a Chekhov play, while the principals make a huge show of acting out 'who's more over who, and who's having a far better time with their new partner'.

All I want is to get out of here, drag Barbara to a loo and dissect the whole thing apart, forensically, bone by bone.

8.00 p.m.

'Oh for f★★k's sake,' she says, when we finally get to the Radisson and I finally get her alone in the Ladies. 'OK, so maybe we ran into his ex and you felt you were being paraded a bit, but it's all over now, you've met her, she's met you and everyone can move on. No more of the *Rebecca* factor, with you obsessing about what his ex is like, Mrs De Winter. I mean, yeah, she's pretty and everything, but I'd swear I saw acne scarring under all of that concealer. And she was definitely trying it on a bit too hard with that rugby dude she was hanging out of. All I can say to you is, if Clare was a garden plant, she'd be clinging ivy.'

'Bless you for that very charitable thought,' I say. 'Although there's just one teeny niggling worry formulating at the back of my head.'

'Shoot.'

'He must have known that she'd be there. Which is why he picked that bar for us to meet up at in the first place.'

'YPB?'

'Speak in bloody English, will you? I'm too addled to read your subtitles.'

'Your point being?'

'Nothing, I'm just trying to figure out whether or not tonight's being a total waste of a blow-dry and make-up, that's all.'

'Vicky, get a grip, will you? He chose that bar because it's his local and it's near the hotel. He's moving on, Clare's moving on and the only one who's making a total game show out of them casually bumping into each other is you. He's a sweet guy, who seems to like you as much as you like him, he ticks all your boxes and you're going to have a great time with him tonight, even if I have to ram margaritas into your bloodstream for the duration.'

'Yeah, yeah, I suppose so,' I say, still a bit off-kilter, if I'm being honest. 'It was just a bit of initial awkwardness, that's all, wasn't it? And it's all behind us now. Isn't it?'

'There's the Dunkirk spirit. Of course it is. Peter's hot-looking and the fact is, if he hadn't moved on with you, it would have been someone else. Apart from her, you're the first woman he's dated in seven years, so of course it's understand-able that he's a bit antsy about the whole Clare thing. Be patient. Slow down. Give the guy a break, that's all I'm saying.'

I look at her, a bit taken aback. Since when did Barbara get so tolerant of guys in general? Normally, if they do the slightest little thing to piss her off, she's written them off and is out of there and straight on to the next one, dragging me in her wake, usually.

'For Christ's sake, Vicky, take a look at my date if you want to cheer yourself up. A baldie I can handle, but a shaved head by choice is a bit neo-Nazi for me.'

And, just like that, the old Barbara is back in the room again.

'You're not supposed to come out with stuff like that!' I hiss at her, hoping no one overhead.

'Well, excuse me for being honest. The guy is basically an oven mitt with a pulse.'

'Barbara!'

'Only the truth. Your guy looks like James Bond in a tux. Mine looks like the best man at Wayne Rooney's wedding.'

'I really am grateful, you know that,' I say, suddenly overcome with the enormity of what she's putting herself through for me. And on a Saturday night too, when I'm sure she has a string of miles more interesting fellas to be out on the town scoring with.

'Hey, I'm only paying the favour forward, that's all. I mean, up until yesterday, my career was twitching on a slab in a mortuary. Now, and entirely thanks to you, I have a big fat job!'

Second not-so-great sign about the night ahead.

There must be about five hundred people here, and the ballroom is packed to the gills. I find the table that we're at, and the four of us head inside, taking our seats. It's doubly thorny for me as: a) I'm the only one who actually knows anyone else here and I don't want to get lost in the crowd catching up with people while leaving my guests stranded on their own with no one bar each other to talk to; b) Baldie, sorry, I mean *Charlie's* making absolutely no effort to do anything other than chat up Barbara; and worst of all c) Peter, my lovely fab Peter, doesn't seem to give a shit about anyone or anything other than his mobile phone. All my best leaning-into-him moves, a great way to create the illusion of intimacy in a packed place, are totally wasted. Now, of course I accept that in every relationship, there comes a time when romance has to give way to reality. It's just that I never even got to have any romance with this guy, not even a whiff of it.

I'm not kidding, from the minute we're seated at the table he whips the bloody phone out of his jacket and proceeds to engage in what I can only describe as a texting marathon.

'Something important? Maybe an emergency at your school?' I eventually say, wishing I could adopt at will a tone that would cut through crystal, like Laura can. And if it sounds a bit on the snotty side, bear in mind that our starter course has arrived, been eaten and cleared and he's *still* at it.

'No. I just wanted to make sure that Clare was OK, that's all. Look, I really am sorry about this, but Vicky, do you think I could talk to you? There's something I really need to get off my chest.'

Well, about bloody time, I think, finally, this is starting to sound positive. Not to mention the fact that it's the first time since we sat down that he's actually looked directly at me. Right then, I may not be psychic, but I think I can guess what's coming. Yes, this is it. I can practically *feel* it. He's going to tell me now that ever since they broke up, Clare's being over-clingy and that she probably stalked him into that bar, determined not to let him move on and be happy with someone else. Specifically, me. Which will be my cue to be supportive and understanding, and never, ever to fall into the trap of slagging off his ex. No, aloof and dignified will win the day. Until we're well-established as a couple, that is; then in a few months' time, I can start weaning him off answering her texts and going to pubs where he'll know she'll be. Until then, I'll play it bright and breezy, like I'm absolutely fine with all this shit-ology. He's a good guy, I remind myself, and God knows, they're thin on the ground from where I'm standing, so isn't he worth playing a long game for?

'Yes, Peter, of course.' I smile in what I hope is a compassionate yet non-clinging way. So he'll see me as the anti-Clare in time.

'What did you think of that guy that Clare was with?

Because I thought he was a total jock-strap and I honestly don't know what she's doing with him. I'm actually kind of worried about the whole thing. Maybe I should call her. Just to make sure she's OK. What do you think? Do you think I should call?'

Third not-so-great sign about the night ahead.

OK, now I actually don't know which was worse: Peter texting Clare the whole time, or him talking about her incessantly. First one, now the other. In fact, I think I nearly preferred it when he was ignoring me and focusing all his attention on his shagging mobile. Right the way through dinner, it was nothing but Clare this and Clare that. I got her life story in such fine, forensic detail, I could probably write the girl's autobiography for her. By the time dinner's over, I could almost do a police re-enactment of the last seven years of her life: how she and Peter met, set up the school, moved in together, how he whisked her off to Barbados to celebrate their three-year anniversary, how she wanted a cat and he didn't, and then he surprised her with one on Christmas Eve which she christened 'Muffy'. (No, really.) Then we had a minute account of the deterioration of the relationship, taking in her 'let's see other people' speech, right up until they 'accidentally' ran into one another this evening. With a few drinks on him, he even gets that 'puppy dog' gooey look in his eyes whenever he mentions her name. Believe me, I know.

It's only happened about two hundred times so far.

I don't think I've uttered two words for the whole meal, in fact half the time I'm wondering if Peter even realizes that I'm around. I've just sat there umming and aahing and doing the sympathetic hear nod, but all the time, I'm busy thinking, 'Hmmm. Should I use this cloak of invisibility I seem to be wearing for evil or to fight crime?' The final blow is when he drifts off and stares into the middle distance for ages then turns back, looking like . . . like he's a Siamese twin and I'm a revolving door.

'Vicky?'

'Yes?' I answer curtly, patience at a very low ebb by now.

'What time do you think this do will be finished at?'

'It's a black-tie do, Peter, what exactly do you mean?'

'It's just that I might call on Clare on my way home. Just to check that's she's all right. You don't have a problem with that, do you?'

Somehow, he misinterprets the icy glare I give him as being full of loving warmth and consideration, because, next thing, he comes out with, 'No, of course you don't. You're really something, you know that, Vicky? You're so cool about all this. You're probably the only person I can really talk to about the whole thing, and you're such a great, great listener.'

It's well after the main course has been cleared before I can drag Barbara off to the Ladies again for yet another emergency de-briefing session.

'Right then,' she says firmly. 'So, OK, he's not over his ex . . .'

'Not OVER her? That's an understatement on a par with saying that . . . that . . . oh shit, I can't even think of something smart-alecky to back that up with. What am I going to do, Barbara? I went to so much bother over tonight, I had such high hopes, and it was all shaping up so well, and now the best I can possibly hope for is that I end up as his rebound person.'

I'm doing my best to sound cool and rational but what I actually want to do is slump down in front of the Ladies dressing table, right here, right now and bawl my eyes out. But of course I can't, because there's people here I know, so I have to cover over the cracks with lip-gloss and go back out there, and smile and get through the rest of this miserable, huge disappointment of a night. Somehow.

It's almost becoming like a pattern with me, the more I like a guy, the worse they seem to treat me. 'You're a great girl, Vicky, and you're such a good listener,' is all I seem to get and I'm sick of it. Enough is enough. Tonight was supposed to be my turn to get lucky, and here I am, dressed up like a right dog's dinner, sitting beside a guy who's confusing me with a hotline to the Samaritans – and not having the first clue where it all went so wrong. Barbara, thank God, knows me well enough to know when I'm close to break point, so she stands behind me in the mirror and starts massaging my shoulders, like I'm a heavyweight boxer and she's my trainer.

'OK, here's what I suggest,' she says very decisively. 'Plan A, we leave now. Just run out the door and leave Baldie and Ex-Files to cop on that they've been dumped.'

'Can't,' I say dully, although I'm sorely tempted. It would be unbelievably rude, granted, but then my date's total and utter lack of interest in me affords me some wriggle room. Oh, who am I kidding? I'm stuck here and that's all there is to it. 'Too many people would see us go.' I sigh so deeply it physically hurts. 'Plus there's a charity auction on after the meal, and it would look terrible if we just upped and left right now.'

'OK then, plan B, we stay for the auction, then I'll come up with an ingenious cast-iron excuse, like my feet are killing me, or my chicken fillets are about to fall out, or I want to get home to see *Newsnight*. You know, something brilliant that no one can argue with. Like diarrhoea for instance. As I always say, you can do a lot of things but you can't negotiate with diarrhoea. Best excuse ever dreamt up by mankind.'

'Thanks, hon, but it was kind of long-term plans that I was thinking of. I think we need to be brutally honest here and accept that while "project Barbara" and "project Laura" are shaping up very nicely, "project Vicky" has been a total loser. And I can't figure it. I just wish I knew what I was doing wrong. I feel like I've been on this fifteen-year losing streak and here

I am, doing my utmost to turn it around and I bloody well can't.'

I'm a bit choked now, and in spite of my best efforts, fat, wobbly tears are starting to well up.

'Come on, stop *expecting* failure . . .'

'But that's the thing, I wasn't! Not tonight! I had a great attitude altogether, I even went out and spent a fortune on all new bed linen . . .'

'Vicky, you want to attract the right guy and you will. OK, so maybe we revise our strategy. I think we need to accept that the dating-one-guy-at-a-time pattern isn't working for you, and go back to the drawing board.'

'What do you mean, the drawing board?' I ask dully, feeling like I might as well have a big F for Failure stamped across my forehead.

'Another Thursday night on the town, babe. What else?'

She's right, of course she is. It's just the sheer effort required in picking myself back up off the floor yet again and doing the whole clubby/pubby scene with her right now just sounds so bloody exhausting. Oh for God's sake, I think, catching a glimpse of my defeated expression in the mirror, just look at the effect that hope has on me. This is what happens when I send all my longing for love and romance out into the world. I end up a nervous wreck, on a date with a fella who barely realizes I'm even here.

'Or,' I say, turning back to Barbara as I get up to go, 'maybe I'll just stop fighting fate and become one of those single spinsters who drink a half bottle of wine alone every night, and keep cats, and complain when the neighbours have late-night parties. Maybe I struggled with my destiny for long enough and now it's time to wise up to the inevitable. My name is Vicky Harper and I repel men. Born to live out the rest of my days alone.'

'You certainly didn't repel Eager Eddie,' she says as we

head back outside where the auction's just about to begin.

'I won't even dignify that with a wisecrack.'

'Oh now, come on,' she says, kindly, squeezing my arm. 'At the risk of sounding like a kids' TV show presenter, what have we learned from the past few months?'

'I give in. Stop asking me hard questions.'

'Focus on what you want and not what you don't want. If it can work for me, then it can work for anyone, babe.'

By the time we get back to the table, Peter has now abandoned all pretext that he's on a date with me, and is actually on the phone to Clare. Chatting away goodo. And he doesn't even have the grace to hang up when he sees me coming back, just keeps on talking. One of those excruciating 'no, no, you were right and I was wrong', type conversations that, frankly, is making me want to vomit.

'I'll rip the phone out of his hand and dance on it if you want,' Barbara thoughtfully offers when she sees what he's at. 'Cos, you know me, I'm like that.'

'No need,' I say, smiling a bit over-brightly, aware that people, even, maybe, clients could be looking over. 'The minute the auction's over, we're so out of here.'

'Suits me. Baldie on my left here is seriously starting to drive me nuts.'

'Shhh! He'll hear you!'

'Sorry, Charlie the razor-happy geek on my left is driving me nuts. That any better?'

With that, the auctioneer launches into his mile-a-minute patter and I sit very still, half-afraid to move in case by inadvertently scratching my head or something, I'll have bought a painting worth five grand. And you should see some of the items: holiday cruises, a full pamper day at Powerscourt Springs (only the poshest health spa in the whole country), a role as a film extra in a movie that Gabriel Byrne is shooting here, a Graham Knuttel painting, some really unbelievable stuff. Whoever did the PR for this gig must have had some serious connections.

One cursory glance down the list of items to be auctioned off tells me they're all waaaay over my humble budget, so I opt for sitting mutely, hands locked at my side to avoid financial embarrassment, and amuse myself by properly scanning the room, the first time all night I've really had a decent look around at who's here and who isn't. No one I know in the immediate vicinity, apart from a competitor of mine at the table behind me, who blanks me as I look over. Which in the mood I'm in, actually suits me just fine.

Ooh, then I see a friend of Paris and Nicole's sitting at the table beside us, dressed like an extra from a Jane Austen adaptation, in a pretty empire-line dress with her hair swept up and ringlets framing her face. She's got her own social diary, very handy for free press, so I make a mental note to self to be really nice to her afterwards.

'Sold to the gentleman at the back!' says the auctioneer, and the room applauds politely. 'For four and a half thousand euro!' and now the applause strengthens.

Unbelievably, Peter is still chatting away on the phone, jacket off and finger in one ear like a stockbroker, oblivious to how rude he's being. At one point Baldie, sorry, I mean Charlie, asks him if he'd like to order a drink, and Peter actually waves him to shut up, like we're all in a public library or something and we're daring to shatter his concentration. Bastard. Rude bloody bastard.

'And now lot number four, a three-day holiday in Paris, the city of love, flights and five-star accommodation in the Hôtel de Crillon, do I hear six thousand euro?'

Without even being aware of it, I must have drifted off, because the bidding is racing on, getting furiously higher and higher all the time, while I'm sitting here staring into space.

'Eight and a half thousand euro, do I hear nine?'

I look over to Peter, who is smiling, actually smiling, down the phone, and I take one long, last look at him. Cos after tonight, he's banished to the land of 'never to be seen again'. And he just looks so handsome, it almost breaks my heart.

'Yes, I have nine thousand euro, to you sir, the gentleman at the back, do I have nine and a half thousand euro? Do I hear the magic ten?'

. . . so what lies ahead for me? Oh God . . . it's nothing I'm looking forward to. I have to somehow readjust my attitude, pick myself back up off the ground again and get back out there with Barbara yet again to see what I can dreg up some Thursday night . . . and then, who knows? Go through all of this shite all over again, most likely . . .

'Sold to the gentleman at the back for ten thousand, euro!'

More mad clapping, and a lot of feet thumping now, and all the while I'm desperately trying to come out of this awful slump I'm in and be all positive and focused . . . law of attraction book . . . I'm racking my brains to remember what it says is the key to relationships, or in my case, the total and utter lack of them . . .

'Our next item is a luxury spa day at Powerscourt Springs, for a very lucky lady. The package includes unlimited treatments, lunch and a bottle of champagne to really chill out over . . . perfect for the busy working girl who needs a little "me" time, do I hear five hundred euro? Yes, sir, five hundred to you *again*, sir.'

. . . there's something in the book about filling yourself up with love like a magnet, so that you'll attract it to you . . .

'Eight hundred euro! Do I hear a thousand? Thank you, sir!'

. . . but the trouble is, I've spent my whole life attracting emotionally unavailable cretins, and the fact is, whatever I've been doing wrong all this time, guess what? I'm *still* doing it . . .

'Two thousand five hundred euro, sir, thank you! Do I hear three thousand? Come on, gentlemen, time to spoil the lucky lady in your life!'

. . . I glance over at Barbara, who's looking, well, a bit bored actually, but Baldie actually has this liquid-eyed expression as he's chatting her up. She has about as much interest in him as she has in the price of J-Cloths, and yet there he is, looking at her adoringly, hers for the taking, should she so choose . . .

Oh for f★★k's sake, I think, suddenly furious, where did I go so wrong tonight? My luck with guys is so unbelievably bad that I'm actually starting to think that I'm paying off some huge karmic debt from a past life. Hmmm, maybe that's the answer, maybe I should give up on the Butterfly Club and start doing past-life regression therapy instead . . .

'Sold! Yet again, to the gentleman at the back! Sir, may I say, you are single-handedly keeping this auction going!'

'Is that the same guy who's buying everything?' Barbara whispers hopefully to me.

'Whoever he is, he must have spent well over sixteen grand by now,' says Baldie, and I turn to look at him in utter astonishment. Well, in my defence, it's the first words he's uttered to anyone other than Barbara all evening.

'Well, I wonder who he's with tonight?' Barbara says, giving me a significant look. This may sound innocuous enough, but is in actual fact girl-code for: 'Because if by some miracle someone that filthy wealthy also happens to be single and straight, we're so in there.' It seems that a lot of the single women here have the same idea, as out of nowhere there's a lot of elegant, bejewelled necks and bare, fake-tanned shoulders craning to see who this mysterious guy with cash to burn is; all of a sudden there's suddenly a lot of compact mirrors out and lip-gloss being hastily re-applied. You can almost feel feathers being preened and peacock tails being paraded out for show.

'And who is the lucky lady you'll be giving this beautiful spa voucher to?' the auctioneer calls down to whoever mystery man is, a bit cheekily.

'She's here, actually,' comes a distant voice from the very back of the ballroom. Now there's a wave of Chinese whispers circulating all around us, 'She's here, he bought it for someone who's *here*.'

I join in the general neck-craning, to try to make out who he is, but it's too dark, and whatever table he's sitting at is just too far away from ours. Barbara and I meet in an eye-lock and simultaneously shrug. Well, it was too good to be true really, that the mystery millionaire guy could be free and single. Besides, I tell myself, he's probably ninety-five with a colostomy bag and a Zimmer frame. And he bought the spa day as a gift for his nurse to thank her for feeding him through a tube. Probably.

'And the lucky lady's name?' says the auctioneer, into the mike.

'She's a Miss Vicky Harper.'

'Sorry sir, what was that name again?'

'The gift is for Miss Vicky Harper. She's sitting right over there at table nine.'

Sweet baby Jesus and the orphans. I do not believe this. It's Daniel Best. For definite. I'd know the voice anywhere. Not only that, but the minute the auctioneer moves on to the next item, he's on his way over to me from the back of the room. I don't even have time to collect my thoughts, barely even get an emergency conference with Barbara. Before I'm even aware of what's going on, he's standing right beside me, with the cheeky grin, looking as divine as ever, in a sexy, scruffy, yes-I-may-have-put-on-a-tux-but-just-look-at-how-dishevelled-the-rest-of-me-is way.

'Surprise!' he twinkles down at me, in that half-teasing way he has. 'I saw you across the room earlier and, well, I just thought you deserved a treat.'

'I . . . that is, I thought . . . you're . . . supposed to be . . . aren't you in America?' is all I can stammer, I'm that stunned.

'Got back this morning. So right now, I've been awake for about thirty hours non-stop, and my body thinks it's tomorrow fortnight. In other words, I'm just about ready for a mortuary.'

'How was your trip?' I smile, trying my best to sound cool and you know, normal.

'Fantastic, very productive. I've perfected my Robert de Niro impression AND my Clint Eastwood. Just in case there's rumours going around that I was skiving over there. "*Go ahead, punk, make my day.*" What do you think?'

'Did de Niro really say that?' I'm aware of the silence around our table as everyone's taking in this bizarre conversation, but you know what? For the first time tonight, I don't care.

'No, no, that was Clint Eastwood. My de Niro is: "*You talking to me? Cos, I don't see anyone else here?*"'

'Bravo, Robert de Niro to the life, I'd have sworn Raging Bull himself was here talking to me.' I give him a handclap.

'Ehhh . . . except that was from *Taxi Driver*. Now, of course, I could do my *Raging Bull* impression for you, but I'm not properly attired. I need the aul boxer shorts on for that. And of course to put on twenty stone.'

I laugh, and for a minute it's like we're the only two people there, and then from out of the corner of my eye, I realize . . . Barbara and Baldie are both staring at him, waiting to be introduced.

'Sorry, Daniel, this is my best friend, Barbara Fox.'

'I've heard a lot about you,' she says, and you can practically see her assessing him, weighing him up, taking everything in, deciding whether she likes him or not.

'And this is . . .' *Shit, shit, shit, what's his real name?* Oh yeah . . . 'Charlie.'

They all shake hands, then Barbara throws in. 'Nice gift. Wish I worked for someone like you.'

'It's by way of a thank you, actually,' Daniel smiles, turning back to me. 'You have no idea the fantastic work this lovely lady has been putting in for Best's over the past while, and I just thought, when all seven of the Original Sin commercials are in the can, you might fancy unwinding in style. That's all.'

'I'm really touched.' I'm about to gush on a bit more, still a bit overwhelmed, when . . . Oh for God's sake, I do not believe this. For the first time all bloody night, Peter decides to put his phone down and actually take notice of me. Arm on my shoulder, the works. Suddenly, out of the blue, he's decided to act like a date again.

No way out, I'll just have to introduce him. Rats anyway.

Then it strikes me, this is the second time I've met Daniel out socially and each time I've been with a different guy. He must think I'm Mata Hari, and the irony is, if he only knew the sad, awful, lonely truth.

'And this is Peter,' I eventually say, a bit unenthusiastically.

They shake hands and Daniel just nods and smiles pleasantly, taking it all in.

'Well, great to see you, Vicky, but I'd really better get going,' he eventually says.

'You're leaving now?'

'I'm that jet-lagged that if I don't go voluntarily, there's a fair chance they may have to wheel me out of here if I stay any longer. So you take care and I'll see you soon. OK?'

'OK.'

And just as quickly, he's gone.

Chapter Nineteen

The Butterfly's next meeting. July.

Right. Our progress to date, in order of who's doing the best and who's, ahem, shall we say, lagging behind the class a little, and maybe in need of some remedial project-management. Or a kick up the bum, or whichever way you choose to put it.

LAURA. In a flashback to our schooldays, she's easily and effortlessly the gold star, top-of-the-class girl. Item one on the agenda, discussed at great length among the three of us, is a certain Mr Desmond Lawlor, proprietor of *Tattle* magazine, who true to his word gave Laura a weekly column to write, which is already in print (well, OK, maybe only two columns so far, but as a proud friend, I'm allowed to brag), and proving hugely popular.

Last week's was called 'Why No Self-Respecting Mother Should Ever Run Out of Threats on the Eve of a Bank Holiday Weekend,' and it was all very funny and very Laura, involving a (true) story about how she caught Jake and George Junior having a major, blow-up row. Nothing unusual there, except that George Junior was actually taking a tiny drop of blood from his brother, with a rusty safety-pin. When interrogated separately by Laura, always best, she claims, if you want the hard, cold facts (it's a tactic she read that they use on terror suspects in

Guantánamo Bay), George Junior claimed he needed the blood for a medical experiment he was doing, for which he'd promised his brother in return six Jaffa Cakes and a Cornetto. His defence was: 'Oh come on, Mom, using a rat is just too cruel.'

In her column, Laura then segued into a hilarious diatribe about how all she has to look forward to is their teenage years, and ended up describing in detail a vivid dream she had had, flashing forward to five years hence, where she came home from a late session in King's Inns to find a trashed house, toilet flooded, broken grandfather clock, smashed window-panes and the family dog drunk. Only to have her kids try to convince her that all of this happened while they were innocently out doing the Stations of the Cross.

I loved reading it, because it felt just like having a conversation with Laura, and nearly burst with pride when I saw her photo at the top of a page in *Tattle*, with her hair tied back, in the grey woollen 'court' outfit, neatly and sensibly dressed as always. But I hadn't quite realized the effect she was slowly starting to have on the world at large till I was in a supermarket queue one day and overheard two harassed-looking mums talking about her column and actually *quoting* from it. Her lines that ran: 'My all-time favourite household chore is ironing. My second favourite chore being banging my head on the bedpost until I'm unconscious.' For a split second, I almost felt like I was friends with Carrie Bradshaw from *Sex and the City*.

Course the main item Barbara and I want to know concerns the same Mr Desmond Lawlor (it feels peculiar referring to him by his first name, trust me, he's just one of those patrician, older and wiser types that have the effect of making me feel like I'm ten years old again), and his interest in our Laura. We both have a strong intuition that it may well go beyond the professional, but trying to get hard information out of her is like getting blood from a turnip. Every time there's a bit of teasing or mild slagging when his name comes up, she clams up and goes all 'politiciany' on me. I'm not messing, at one point she even used the phrase: 'I couldn't possibly comment.'

So case closed. For the moment at least.

Anyway, whatever Mr Desmond Lawlor's intentions are towards her, and whatever is or isn't going on, it's had one noticeable side effect. With that unerring sixth sense that men seem to be born with when it comes to a woman moving on with her life, George Hastings, ex-husband from hell, can practically smell that there's something in the air. I can't put my finger on it, the only signs I have to go on are that: a) he's being an awful lot nicer to Laura, and even took the three older kids to see the new Harry Potter movie last week. Now, just to give you a rough idea of just how unheard-of that is, Jake apparently said: 'Dad's bringing us to the movies? *DAD?* Do you mean *OUR* dad?' Point b) he's referring to Miss Human Botox an awful lot less, but did let it slip that she's going off to Ibiza with her pals for the summer break. So maybe the age gap is beginning to show, or maybe it's just plain old-fashioned loneliness that has him behaving an awful lot more responsibly towards his ex-wife and children, but whatever the outcome, Barbara and I have made a non-negotiable pact.

If he as much as *attempts* to inveigle his wormy way back to her, we'll club together and get that hit-man we promised Laura after him. And not a jury in the land would convict us.

BARBARA. Again, nothing but gold stars hanging out of her. Rehearsals have begun in earnest for *A Midsummer Night's Dream* at the dance studios in town, so, to be honest, I haven't seen nearly as much of her as I'd like. We still haven't got around to organizing yet another Thursday night trawl around the town, but that's as much my fault as hers.

Between finalizing a list of sponsors for the show, getting

invitation lists together, not to mention publicizing its three-night run, myself, Paris and Nicole have barely seen the light of day. And that's on top of the work I'm doing with Best's about the upcoming commercial shoot, and all the press that's involved, which . . . well, more anon.

Anyway, I do manage to snatch a quick brunch with Barbara for a lightning update session. It seems that she's building herself up to play the part of Hermia (one of the 'star-crossed lovers', not that I'd know, but for those who care, the fact is it's a leading role), with the same scary discipline and dedication that you'd normally associate with Russian teenage gymnasts training for the Olympics. Not only is she up at six a.m. every day doing voice warm-ups, but then she goes to the gym on her way into rehearsals, so she can be in peak condition to face the mighty Serena Stroheim.

Then absolutely no falling into the trap of 'ah sure, let's just go for the one drink after work' with the rest of the cast. No, she's straight home for a strict session of line-learning followed by a sensible early night. As she herself puts it, there's no such thing as 'just the one drink' with actors. Many's the time on occasions past she'd be dragged into the pub, full of noble intentions to have one margarita and then head home, only to find herself falling out the door at closing time, then being dragged off to a nightclub. Those days, she assures me, are now gone. This is the new, improved, ultra-professional, model of puritanical virtue and sobriety Barbara.

'My God,' I said, looking at her in awe. 'I've never seen you working so hard.'

'You've never seen me working, full stop.'

I really couldn't be happier about the whole, wonderful way that 'project Barbara' is shaping up, and the only teeny fly in the ointment which is detracting from her coming top of the class is . . . you've guessed it: Evil Angie.

The stupid cow is cast as Helena directly opposite Barbara, so they're kind of a Tweedledum and Tweedledee pairing as far as the show goes. Now I can't be 100 per cent sure, as I'm only going on the few tit-bits Barbara has let slip, but it seems that there's a lot of old ham-actor tricks going on behind the scenes here. Again, hard for me to gauge as I haven't had nearly the amount of gossip-time I'd normally get with Barbara, but she did mention that Evil Angie has taken to coming home early after rehearsals, too. And 'running lines' with Barbara. And asking had she any ideas about how the scene should be played? And then going into rehearsals the following day and passing off Barbara's brilliant ideas as her own. This on top of her slavishly copying any interesting new character quirks and traits that Barbara starts introducing.

I haven't sat in on a full rehearsal yet mainly because, with everything else that's going on, I barely even get a chance to fight with Useless Builder these days. Plus Serena was far too polite to discourage me, but did mention that she'd be far happier if I stayed away until the cast were in a position to do a full, off-book run-through, in a few weeks' time. Barbara rowed in here, too, and said she'd never be able to concentrate if I was sitting on a stool watching her. Four hundred people in the Iveagh Gardens looking at her doesn't faze her but me on my own, apparently, does.

Anyway, I haven't time to argue, so for now at least, I agree.

My progress to date. Well, there's always one sent to the back of the class with a 'must do better' report to bring home, and guess what? As usual, it's me. Needless to say, I've heard nothing from Peter since the infamous night of the PR dinner; he skedaddled out of there as soon as he reasonably could, presumably back into the arms of Clare, where I'm taking a wild guess he still is. Running their bloody language school together like some kind of TEFL Brangelina, good luck to them. Nor could Barbara and I even get in a decent on-the-spot post-mortem after he'd gone, on account of Charlie/Baldie still hanging out of her. And I was bursting to talk to her about Daniel, too, but had to wait until I could get her alone at brunch the next morning to really pick things through with a fine toothcomb.

So she went home with a guy and, typically, Cinders here went home alone. To the brand-new sheets that I had such high hopes were going to see a bit of action. Feeling very down in the dumps and despondent about the whole Peter situation, I blew the dust off my bed (you should have seen it, even Miss Havisham would have been mortified at the general manki-ness), and snuggled under, with a copy of Laura's *Tattle* magazine for company. A very different ending to what I'd thought the night promised.

Anyway, I flicked the magazine open at random and there was a feature on the new dating craze that's sweeping through the States like wildfire, wait for it: eye gazing dating. Apparently, it's the same principle as speed dating except that you don't actually speak to the guy opposite you. The rules are, you just gaze into each other's eyes and see if there's a 'non-verbal chemistry'. The theory is that by eliminating boring small talk of the 'seen-any-good-movies-lately' variety, you're far more likely to find a guy you genuinely connect with on a physical level. Then there's 'read dating', which is the same thing all over again except you are allowed to talk, hurrah for that, and it all happens in a bookshop. Except knowing me, some cute guy would catch me in the self-help section reading books with titles like *10 Reasons Why Single Women in Their Thirties End up Going Completely Batty*, *Why Singletons Die Alone and Unloved* or suchlike.

Then I found a quiz on the back page called 'Are You a Hopeless Romantic?' You know, questions along the lines of:

Q: Do you know the lines from Four Weddings and a Funeral *off by heart?*
(Check.)
Q: Do you believe in love at first sight?
(Check, absolutely. It just hasn't happened to me yet, that's all.)
Q: Do you and your partner have a 'special' song?
(Not really, unless you count 'Black Betty' by Ram Jam, which my teenage boyfriend used to love moshing to. Eughhhh . . . even all these years on, I still shudder.)
Q: Have you given thought to what your wedding day will be like, even though you're single?
(Are you kidding me? I even know what caterers I'll use. And it'll be in a marquee in my mum's back lawn. With a proper mariachi band. And orchids everywhere. The poor groom, you'd almost have to feel a bit sorry for him, there won't be a single decision left for him to make.)
Q: Ditto, how he'll propose to you, even though you're more likely to get selected for a random VAT audit/jury service than get a marriage proposal any time soon?
(I'm ashamed to say the answer is yes. Barefoot on a beach in Cancun, which he'll just have whisked me off to on a surprise trip, to mark it being exactly six months between our last anniversary and our next anniversary.)

Oh for f**k's sake, I thought, tossing the magazine aside and slumping back on to the pillows. Who am I kidding? Eye gazing dating and bloody read dating. Or else trawling through match.com trying to find a guy that's under ninety-five, straight and still has both his kidneys.

That's what I have to look forward to.

Chapter Twenty

A few days after the infamous PR dinner, and I'm in a taxi on my way to the Best agency to sit in on a casting session with Amanda. Not that there's a huge amount of actual casting involved. As with all commercials, we've gone through an agency that screens the models, whittles the list from dozens down to maybe fifteen or twenty, and puts them all on tape for us. So, technically, all we have to do is sit in Best's editing suite (no, really, they even have an editing *suite*), narrow the field down still further, make our own notes and comments on what we've seen, then wait for Sophie's ultimate seal of approval when she joins us for an afternoon meeting. It may sound doddley enough on paper, but believe me, if we get the mix wrong and somehow match the wrong model to the product, we're done for.

And all of this, presumably, has to be approved by Daniel, too. Now that he's back in town, so to speak.

Anyhoo, over that snatched brunch the day after the PR do, I did, however, finally get to dissect the whole night over with Barbara. In between her running to the gym and rushing home to study the text of *A Midsummer Night's Dream*, that is. Her thoughts on the subject can be summarized as follows.

Any single men I might have a vague flicker of interest in have to be cleared through her. Butterfly Club non-negotiable rules. On this point, she's rock-solid and as immovable as ever. In response, I pointed out that so far, so rubbish. Of the two potentials who did pass the Barbara Fox stringent quality-control tests, one turned out to be a virtual stalker: yes, Eager Eddie himself, who, unbelievably, is still calling and texting me, wanting me to go to another pipe band festival, this time on some remote island somewhere. He has to be the only man in living history that's taking my completely and utterly ignoring him as a sign of deep interest. Honestly, I'd change my phone number, only the sheer amount of hassle involved is too much for me.

Then of course, there's her second attempt at matching me up: Peter. Ex-Files himself. The less said the better. Although when I do raise this point to her she just says: 'Don't sigh and don't do the head shake. At least you're making progress. Slow progress, yeah, but then you can't put a time-frame on finding a life-partner, can you? Look, Eager Eddie may have turned out to be a bit of an oddball, but in my defence, technically, on paper he seemed OK.'

'How do you mean, on paper?'

'Say you'd met him in an internet chat room, you'd have rung me, all buzzed, going: 'Oh, I met this guy and he has a proper job, is straight and single and ticks all the right boxes.' Hindsight is twenty-twenty. So now we know that he likely has a kid's room in his house for his non-existent children, and that his idea of seducing a woman is to love-bombard her into sub-mission, but you can't hold me responsible for not being able to read his mind, now, can you? Then, with Ex-Files, you would have ended up like Princess Di, claiming that there were three of you in this relationship so it was a bit crowded. At least now you know that's *not* what you want. And you were saved all the bother of having to go on *Panorama*.'

She's right, of course. I *am* getting a helluva lot clearer with the universe about what I don't want, although I probably could have had a wild guess at the outset that a guy still obsessed with his ex was a non-starter. It certainly would have saved us all a lot of bother, and don't get me started on the small fortune I forked out on hair, nails, dress, shoes, new underwear, waxing, Frette sheets, tickets for the do . . . etc., etc. I could have had a weekend in Paris for far, far less.

'I know,' I say dully, sipping a latte that's stone cold by now. 'And in the cold light of day, of course, I don't want to end up just sharing a suite of rooms in someone's heart. Last night was such a disappointment, that's all . . .'

'That's the girl. Diana herself couldn't have put it better,' she says, gathering up her bag and, I get the impression, only half-listening to me. 'Right then, gotta go. Me and Angie are doing line-runs for the rest of the afternoon and I want to do a voice warm-up first. Vicky, remember my words. Dating is nothing more than a numbers game and we're going to pump up the volume a bit here.'

'Oh, right, OK then,' I say, figuring this is my cue to just shut up and look forward to our next night of trawling yet more watering holes. I'm reluctant to pin her to a date, as she's so busy with the show, but she did promise me that we'd go a-hunting in the not-too-distant future.

'So, emm . . . we'll hit the town again, soon?' I ask hopefully as we both head outside.

'Oh yeah, about that. Could we leave it until a night when I don't have an early rehearsal call the next morning? It's just I'd hate to turn up for work minging of alcohol and hungover as a dog. It would just be soooo unprofessional. That OK with you, hon?'

'Oh, eh . . . yeah. Sure, no problem.'

'Thanks, babe. I knew you'd understand.'

I have to say, this new über-career-focused Barbara takes

quite a bit of getting used to. Time was, nothing, absolutely nothing came between her and a bar stool. And on the subject of Daniel Best, she's an awful lot less positive than I'd hoped for, which puts me, if possible, into even worse humour.

'Yeah, cute. Ish. I mean, if he were a seventies footballer, he'd be Kevin Keegan.'

'That's it? That's all you have to say?'

'I spoke to the guy for all of eleven seconds. What am I now, his biographer?'

'Well, what about him buying me the spa voucher? Don't you think that was a lovely gesture?'

'Yeah, but then isn't his whole company ethos to treat any- one who works for him like gods and goddesses so they'll work even harder?'

'Well, yeah, I suppose . . .'

'I'm no farmer, but I can smell manure a mile off. You've been working your arse off for him and he's keeping you on- side. Get over it.'

It's at this point I decide that I actually miss the old Barbara. She was far less bossy and pontificating.

'Vicky,' she goes on, persisting in torturing me with what I *don't* want to hear. 'He talked to you for a few minutes, then he buggered off home.'

'I know, but then, he did say that he was jet-lagged, and he did see me out on a date with someone else, for the *second* time, too . . .'

'So? In theory, that should make any guy keener. I'm sorry, hon, I'm sure Daniel Best is great fun and everything, and in a perfect world we'd all love to see a squillionaire sweep you off your feet and take you into the sunset. Believe me, I hate to be the one to give you an emotional colonic, but the hard cold fact is . . . I just don't think he's interested.'

Which is why, when I do bounce into the reception of Best's

a few days later, I'm not fazed when the receptionist (oh soooo cute in a young Brad Pitt way, blond-tipped hair and biceps you could grate cheese on) says to me, 'Oh, Miss Harper? If you have a moment before your meeting, could you pop up to Daniel's office on the top floor? He asked me to send you up as soon as you came in.'

Right then, this is OK, I think, as I make my way across the marble floor to the lift, very glad I'm wearing my good Carolina Herrera black suit, and doubly grateful it's been safely at the cleaners for the past few weeks. In a million years it wouldn't have survived being next or near Useless Builder wielding his sanding machine like a lethal weapon and covering every stitch of clothing I possess with a layer of dust about an inch thick.

As I lash on a bit of lip-gloss the minute the lift doors glide shut after me, my mind races. Daniel can only want to see me because of the commercial, that's all, I decide as the lift zooms skyward. I mean, what else can it be? Chances are Amanda and probably Sophie are both up here already, and we'll have our regular meeting, same as always, just in Daniel's office instead of the conference room, where we'd normally sit, stuffing our faces with all the free chocolate that's always lying around. He's been out of town for ages and now wants to be fully in the loop of what we've been working on. Yeah, that is by far the most likely scenario. Course it is.

But there's absolutely no sign of anyone else at all when I do get up to the penthouse level. There's just me and yet another ludicrously good-looking receptionist with shoes to die for, who ushers me into Daniel's office with a toothy smile and a bright 'Hi Vicky, he's expecting you.' I knock a bit tentatively and in I go.

And am almost blown away by the sheer, overwhelming size and scale of the room I'm in. No kidding, you could comfortably hold a party for fifty people here and it wouldn't even seem crowded. There's a huge heavy oak table with what seems like a dozen chairs neatly dotted around it, and a giant floor-to-ceiling window directly behind, with a large desk – so big you could probably sleep on it. And standing behind it, phone in hand, is Daniel. As cute/scruffy as always, in a comfy, fleecy tracksuit and trainers, looking, well, totally out of context with the magnificent opulence of the rest of the room. In a million years, you'd never think this man owned not only the company but the entire building as well. I overhear him saying brusquely down the phone, 'Hey! Those are details! You're the details person, *you* handle it.' And it's only then that I get a sneaky glimpse at a whole other facet to his character. The alpha male side. The side of him that built up all of this and is now most likely on the verge of going global. Apart from that, based on appearances alone, if someone told you he'd come to do the windows you'd almost believe them.

He grins at me in that cheeky way he has, and mimes at me to take a seat while he wraps up his phone call. Then, in one athletic movement, he comes round the giant desk and slides down on it right beside where I'm sitting. At least, it looked like an athletic movement, but then that could just be the tracksuit throwing me off. He's almost in my body space, but not quite.

'Sorry about that, just had to do a bit of troubleshooting.' He smiles, then waves all around him. 'So, whaddya think?'

'Wow,' is all I can say. 'In fact, I'll see that wow and raise it to a wowee. Daniel, I'm not messing, it's like Monty Burns's office in *The Simpsons*.'

'Excellent,' he says, launching straight into a perfect Mr Burns impression. '"Smithers, release the hounds."'

I giggle, then remember I still haven't the first clue why he wanted to see me.

'So . . . emm . . . did you enjoy Saturday night?' I ask tentatively.

Half-wondering who he was with. A girlfriend, maybe?

'Oh, yeah, I wanted to say sorry for rushing off so early, but there was a very good chance I'd have fallen over with the tiredness if I'd stayed any longer. The gang of lads who dragged me along keep telling me I was no crack at all.'

Not with a girlfriend, then.

At least not that night.

'Then there was the small matter of that crappy wine they were serving. I wouldn't shampoo a dog with it. So as soon as my mates started ordering more of it, I figured it was time to go. Besides I must have been punch drunk with tiredness, when I woke up the next morning I realized I'd only spent about ten grand on a romantic holiday in some posh hotel somewhere.'

Now that sounds like a single-man statement if ever I heard one, I think, getting more and more hopeful by the minute. I mean, if he had a GF, wouldn't he just say something like: 'Oh, Mary-Lou's delighted with the fab, luxury mini-break I bought for her.' He would, wouldn't he?

Then he produces an envelope from the top of his desk and slides it over to me.

'I left without giving you this, by the way,' he smiles. 'Enjoy every minute of it.'

Oh my God, it's the spa voucher. Suddenly I remember my manners.

'You know, I can't thank you enough for buying this, Daniel. It was such a ridiculously expensive gift . . .' I begin. But he cuts me off in the midst of all my 'you shouldn't have's and 'there was no need's.

'Hey, I've been in touch with Sophie Boyd and she's really thrilled with you, and with everything you're doing. And so's everyone else here, too. So, just my small way of saying thank you, that's all.'

'But you spent a fortune . . .'

'Now don't belittle this moment with your pricetaggery,' he says, waving at me to shut up. 'I want you to enjoy yourself when the contract's up and what better way? I thought all girls loved being dressed up like Egyptian mummies and then submerged in mud with cucumbers on their faces. Unless I've been misinformed.'

'You're spoiling me.' I smile back at him. 'Keep it up.'

There's a split second where we're just looking at each other, and no one says anything, and I'm just wondering whether or not I thanked him enough, and should I gush a bit more, when his internal phone goes.

'On the way,' he says to whoever it is. 'That's Amanda,' he says turning back to me. 'She's waiting for us in the editing suite.'

'Oh, you're sitting in on this with us?'

'Course I am. If I'm going to be an extra in one of these commercials, the least I can do is find out what the competition's like.'

Definite sign he's interested:

As we walk together to the lift, he presses the button and there's another comfortable silence. Then he turns to me and says, in a very offhand manner, 'So, that guy you were with the other night. Your boyfriend?'

'Ehh . . . no,' I say a bit too insistently, but then I can't believe he just asked me that. 'Just a date,' I smile. Did that sound OK? Casual enough?

'Just a date,' he repeats as we step into the lift together. 'Then, what about that other guy I met you with a while back? Scottish accent, reddish hair? You introduced me and I forget his name.'

'Oh, you mean Eager . . . sorry, Eddie, it was Eddie,' I say, hating that I'm blushing a bit now.

'So then is *he* your boyfriend?'

Bugger, half of me thinks there's no way to answer that without sounding like I'm some kind of multi-dating tart that's out with a different bloke every night of the week, while the other, more rational half of me (which, let's face it, I don't hear from all that often), thinks, so what? Yes, I'm single, yes I'm actively looking for someone, and yes, I go on dates. Get over it.

'No, just another date.' Then I back-pedal a bit. 'But one that didn't really work out.'

Sign he's not:

Nonchalant as ever, he just shrugs indifferently and says, 'Atta girl. Sure, you're only young once.' Arms folded, body language as good as saying, 'Yeah, right, whatever.'

Definite sign he's interested:

As soon as we're out of the lift and striding towards the editing suite, he turns to me again. 'Vicky, do you have plans for the weekend?'

'Well, as a matter of fact . . .' I begin, and then realize, oh f★★k it, the preamble's no good, I'll have to tell him the whole story. So I do. It all comes out. Everything. All about Serena Stroheim and how Barbara and I are producing a show, and it's Shakespeare in the park and how, miraculously, it all seems to be coming together, but most of all, how *exciting* it all is.

'Nice sidestep, but you still didn't answer my question,' he grins. 'What are you doing for the weekend?'

'Oh, did I not? Well, that was all a big build-up to my saying, meeting up with our costume and lighting designer and final-izing seating for the opening night. Plus working out guest lists, and you know what a nightmare that can be . . .'

Shit. Then I realize, I've fallen into the trap of coming off far too busy to squeeze in a date. That's if he *was* indirectly asking me out. Which I'm actually not too sure of. Was he? Bloody hell, it's really hard to tell with this guy. So I gamely plump for the damage-limitation option.

'So I'll be working most of Satur*day* and Sun*day* . . .' I say, putting particular emphasis on the 'day' bit so he'll miraculously cop on that my *evening* plan is to sit on patio furniture gossiping down the phone to Laura or Barbara if she's not too busy making vowel sounds and fending off competition from Evil Angie. And all the while eating a de-luxe single-gal-size tub of Ben & Jerry's. So in other words, come nightfall, I am the most available girl he could meet.

Sign he's not:

In spite of my looking at him hopefully with a 'why do you ask?' faux-innocent expression, he totally sidesteps the whole thing and just says: 'Fantastic about the show. Fair play to you. And if you're looking for sponsorship, look no further.'

Oh. No invite out, then. Oh well. But I will most definitely take him up on the sponsorship offer. So, at least that's something, isn't it?

Yeah, of course it is. I just can't help feeling a bit deflated. And like I f**ked up without even being too sure of what exactly I did wrong.

Anyway, on the plus side, all goes brilliantly in our casting session, and within the space of an hour, having sat through screening after screening, we've selected a shortlist of models for Sophie's ultimate approval. All very exotic, leggy, glamorous creatures, 100 per cent in keeping with the femme fatale image we're looking for. Then, Amanda (who's appearing as a redhead today, by the way) and I get brave and decide to throw in the one idea we've cooked up between us that we never in a million years think Daniel will go for.

'Look, there's something we both need to talk to you about,

while we have your undivided attention,' is her opener, throwing a 'back me up here' glance my way.

'Shoot, but allow for my short attention-span,' he says, looking at both of us evenly.

Oh yeah, with his feet up on the seats. Suddenly I can't help smiling at the instant flash I get of what he must have been like in school. The class messer. Always at the back of the bus. Most likely always in trouble. Most likely with loads of girls chasing after him.

'We advertise the ads,' Amanda pitches to him bravely. 'In the print media. The time, date and channel that each commercial will be broadcast at.'

'When Baz Luhrmann made the famous Chanel commercial,' I chip in, taking up the baton, 'the advertising agency took out ads in the trade press. Everyone sneered and said it was money down the drain, but their sales went up by *400* per cent. And that's the kind of huge splash we're aiming for here. Remember, our Original Sin commercials will be just like mini-movies.'

'Ladies,' he says, sitting back, arms behind his head and grinning, looking like he has all the time in the world. 'You've convinced me. Loving everything you've both done so far, the *Casablanca* theme, the black-and-white smoke-filled bar, the whole femme fatale thing, the works. You've my full permission to pitch it to Sophie and tell her I think it's a gem of an idea.'

Amanda and I lock eyes and glow simultaneously.

'Just one suggestion,' he goes on, now looking into the middle distance, like a brainwave is just coming to him. 'The first commercial we're shooting: Thou Shalt Not Covet . . .'

'. . . Thy Best Friend's Eyes,' we both chime in perfect unison.

'She's getting ready to go on a first date,' he says slowly, like he's formulating his thoughts. 'Think . . . perfect first dates. Think the excitement of . . . really liking someone, and that special first night out with them. That adrenalin rush you get when you walk into a bar and there they are waiting for you. They've gone to a huge effort for you and you for them. That's the kind of vibe that would work brilliantly here.'

He's right, it's an incredible idea, and suddenly it's like the missing piece of the jigsaw has slotted in. That's it, of course, that's why our model is coveting her friend's make-up, she's going on a first date and wants to be . . . fabulous.

'So, in other words . . .' I say, trying to see it in my mind's eye. 'The anti-hero becomes the hero. The one who's envious is the one whose story we're following. On her date.'

'Now you've got it.' He grins at me.

Second time today I've seen a slightly different side to Daniel: this time it's the guy who, for all his messing, is shit hot at his job and didn't get to be where he is today without sheer talent and ideas. In fact, I'm strongly starting to suspect that the whole laid-back image is just one big front to lull people into a false sense of security.

Anyway, while Amanda's waxing lyrical about what her ideal first date would be I go back to my storyboards and start scribbling his idea down straight away. Before I forget.

'What about you then, Vicky?' he says, looking straight at me. 'You've gone very quiet. What's your ideal first date?'

Shit. I don't know is the answer. And I'm the one who's supposed to be a hopeless romantic?

'Emm . . . well . . . it would definitely involve margaritas . . .' I begin.

'Right, margaritas, Mexican vibe, I'm with you. Go on.'

He's looking at me, arms folded, with that slightly teasing look he gets in his eyes sometimes, so I'm left wondering, is he messing or not?

Now Amanda's looking at me expectantly, too, so I better come up with something.

Quick.

I rack my brains and something strikes me.

'He'd tell me to meet him in a cocktail bar,' I say slowly. 'Hence the margaritas. And the only thing that I'd find a bit odd is that he'd ask me to bring my passport.'

'Oooh, I love where this is going!' Amanda squeals.

'Then,' I say, warming up, 'we'll jump in a cab and I'll wonder why he won't tell me where we're going . . .'

'Yeah, yeah?' says Amanda, eyes sparkly.

'. . . but I'll notice signs for the airport and slowly begin to cop on. Then we'll go to check in but he still won't tell me where we're off to, he'll make me swear not to look at the destination on the computer screen . . .'

'. . . but you'll cheat,' says Amanda, really getting into this little fantasy. 'You won't be able to resist and you'll peek up and it'll say . . .'

'Paris!' the two of us chime together, then burst out laughing.

'Where else?' I say. 'City of lovers.'

'And he'll take you to a fabulous hotel,' Amanda goes on. 'And he'll have pre-arranged to have a bottle of champagne waiting for you when you arrive . . .'

'. . . and your favourite meal pre-ordered. And then a show afterwards, maybe even an opera . . .'

'Ohh, I love it!' Amanda squeals. 'So the lesson for you, Vicky, is to have all your waxing done before a first date. Oh, and of course the good matching underwear. Like the Girl Guides say, always be prepared.'

'Right then, if we're done here, I better go,' says Daniel, abruptly getting out of his seat.

'Oh, sorry, was it us talking about waxing? And underwear?' says Amanda, puzzled.

'Nope, gotta another meeting. Ladies, thanks so much and keep up the good work.'

And in a split second, he's gone.

I continue scribbling away on my storyboards and it's only after a few seconds I notice Amanda studying me.

'What?' I say, feeling her gaze on me.

'You know, if you were to ask me,' she says, slowly, very slowly, 'I'd say Daniel likes you. Trust me, Vicky, I can smell a crush a mile off.'

'What makes you think that?' I say, my face the colour of Heinz tomato soup.

'Oh . . . just, you know, woman's intuition. Too bad he's off the market though.'

'Is he?'

'All over the office this morning, honey. Why do you think he was in New York for so long, when we're mad busy here? There were loads of rumours doing the rounds, but it turns out he's moving in with the girlfriend he's been seeing and apparently the trip was to go apartment hunting with her. Cathy from marketing heard it directly from Jason in accounts who got it straight from Lynda in personnel, which everyone knows is as good as the horse's mouth, cos she's like, really friendly with Daniel. He's gone and bought some flashy penthouse on the Upper East Side and it only cost about, like, five million. Can you believe it?'

Chapter Twenty-One

Good news and bad news to report, so I'll start with the good. But before I do I'll just say this much: bloody hell, I wish this law of attraction came with an instruction manual, because all around me everyone's getting what they want out of life . . . excepting yours truly. Which brings me first to the good news, concerning Laura, who continues to shine as our resident golden girl.

A couple of days later, and I've been at my desk since seven a.m. (No choice, I just have too much to do.) In fairness to Paris and Nicole, I don't think either of them have left the office any night this week before eight in the evening and so, inspired by Daniel and his 'keep employees happy by lavishing expensive gifts on them' policy, I'm seriously racking my brains to come up with some kind of suitably glamorous reward for the pair of them, by way of a thank you. I'd go a long, long way before I'd find girls as well-connected as they are, prepared to work the hours we're all having to. The girls have been taking care of the guest list for the upcoming opening night of *A Midsummer Night's Dream*, and have been majorly pulling out all the stops to make it as A-list as is humanly possible. 'We're going after *glitterati*, not *glutterati*,' as Nicole says, and to be honest, Lynne Franks herself probably couldn't have put it better. At my end, I'm up to my tonsils with the first Original Eyes campaign; so for all three of us, it's twelve, thirteen, fourteen hour days all the way . . . we've no choice.

For the moment, at least.

Anyway, it's during yet another one of these crazy, hectic mornings in the office when we're all trying to juggle about ninety things at once that Laura calls.

'I know you're busy, dearest,' is her opener. 'So I won't labour this with a preamble. Fantastic news, which I HAD to tell you right away, oh . . . hold on . . . sorry about this . . . just cover your ears for a moment. JAKE AND EMILY, WHATEVER THE PAIR OF YOU ARE DOING, YOU CAN STOP IT RIGHT NOW . . . oh for goodness' sake, sorry about this Vicky. CAN'T THIS FAMILY GO ONE DAY WITHOUT A RIOT?'

The yelling is so loud that I actually have to hold the phone at arm's length for that bit, and even Paris winces over at me from where she's standing by the photocopier.

'I really do apologize, dearest, God above, I must sound like Sharon Osbourne. Are you still there?'

'Ehh . . . just about.'

'There's usually only a two-minute delay between my having to holler like that and them ripping each other apart again, so I'll be quick. I have the most wonderful news and I had to share it with you right away.'

Then, clear as crystal, I can hear Emily shouting downstairs to Laura: 'MOM, YOU DON'T GIVE ME THE RESPECT I DESERVE.'

Then Laura hollers back up to her, 'YOU KNOW WHAT? YOU'RE ABSOLUTELY RIGHT! I GIVE YOU TOO MUCH.'

Anyway, while this little one-act radio play is going on, my mind races. Oh my God, it's to do with Desmond Lawlor. Has to be. That's it, he's asked her out, to some piano recital or similar, I bet ... don't get me wrong, I'm thrilled for her, of course I am, but a tiny part of me is feeling ... well, a bit deflated, to be brutally honest.

I mean, I'm the one who wanted to attract romance into my life, so what's Laura doing right that I'm getting so hopelessly wrong? And am continuing to get hopelessly wrong.

And why does Daniel have to buy a bloody *penthouse* anyway?

Sorry, that just slipped out.

'REMEMBER WE TALKED ABOUT NOT USING OUR HORRIBLE VOICE?' Laura pulls me back to our phone call, screaming upstairs to Emily, then she's back to me again.

'Wow, way to guilt her,' I say.

'Thanks, it's what I do. So sorry, dearest, I really can't apologize enough for that outburst. It's just that if I don't implement a zero tolerance with the little madam, there's always a price to pay.'

'So, tell me the news,' I say, trying to sound bright, and half-wondering what Desmond asked her to, although my money's on a cello recital somewhere. Or else an obscure one-act play in German by some writer I never even heard of maybe ... you know, something classical, cultured and very, very posh.

'I've been asked to take a case!' Laura squeals in a voice so ecstatic, so utterly and totally over the moon that now I feel like a complete heel for my, ahem, little flash of jealousy. 'Can you believe it?' she goes on, barely pausing for breath. 'After all this time, a friend of my father's who's a solicitor just called me now and offered me the brief.'

'Oh, sweetheart, I really am thrilled for you ...'

'... now, it's no great shakes, it's just a minor offence, only district court, so we're not exactly in *The Winslow Boy* territory here, but ...'

'That is so fabulous! So what's the case?'

'Absolutely black and white. A clear violation of paragraph two, subsection four, of the 1961 Road Traffic Act . . .'

'Give it to me in layman's terms.'

'Idiot client forgot to pay his parking fines.'

'Oh. Right. Well, honey, who cares about what the case *is?* The fact is, it's court! You're back!'

There's just one tiny question that's burning at the back of my mind . . . but, typical Laura, she beats me to it.

'And of course, I'll have to donate pretty much every penny of my fee to buying a huge gift for my mother who, astonishingly, has agreed to child-mind, may God have mercy on her.'

'Wow, fair play to her,' I say, a bit stunned, to put it mildly.

Laura's mother is all right for doing the odd Saturday night, probably out of guilt more than anything else, but always adamantly refused to take care of the kids so Laura could go to court, claiming that daytime babysitting, school runs etc., would interfere with her tennis/bridge/searching in forests for eyes of newts to put in her potions/broomstick practice/ whatever the hell it is she *does* get up to in her spare time.

Oh well, maybe the old she-witch is mellowing with Botox.

'Well, I for one couldn't be prouder of you,' I gush, still feeling a bit guilty for jumping to conclusions about her love life. 'I know you'll get that wig and gown on you, stride into that courtroom like you were never out of it, and shear the defence like Delilah.'

'Let's hope not, dearest, I *am* the defence. But, for the moment at least, I almost feel like a character in a sitcom. You know, where they say, 'This is so wonderful and, for once, *nothing* can possibly go wrong!'

So that's the good news and now to the bad. Much later in the afternoon, I had to run over to Iveagh Gardens to meet with Serena Stroheim's lighting designer, a sweet guy, absolutely lovely, tanned, toned and with a sensational body, which as we all know is girl code for . . . gay. He's called Stephan, is brilliant fun and keeps making me swear to introduce him to the city's gay bars, like I'm not having enough trouble at the moment among the straight community. Anyway, he's so thorough about his job and makes me inspect the lighting rig so many times that the upshot is, it's well after seven in the evening before I crawl back to the office, exhausted, but still with yet more work to do.

I wearily let myself in and am almost knocked over by Paris and Nicole, both with their coats on, like they were only just waiting on me to get back so they could skedaddle. And not that I blame either of them, really.

'Girls, I'm so sorry, my meeting ran way over . . .'

The first warning sign I get is when Paris yanks me out into the office corridor and closes the door firmly shut behind us.

'What's up?' I ask, suddenly worried. The office is flooded? A random VAT audit? Some kind of rodent problem? 'Give me the last sentence first.'

'Vicky, I'm really sorry about this, but while you were out, this guy called and he insisted on waiting for you. I didn't know what to do, I tried calling your mobile but it was switched off, so, well, the thing is . . . he's in your office right now . . .'

'Was he carrying chocolate?' I say hopefully, thinking, please let it be Daniel, please let it be . . . but then the right lobe of my brain, the sensible side I'm so rarely troubled by, kicks in. Even if it were, what difference would it make? He's off the market, so to speak, so the fat lady's officially sung on that one. Not that there ever was anything to speak of really . . . sorry, I don't know why his name just keeps slipping out.

'He doesn't have chocolates, no, but he's got the biggest bunch of flowers. And he asked so many questions about you, quite personal stuff too, that . . . well, I just got a bit freaked, that's all.'

I soothe her and reassure her she did the right thing, but all the time I'm thinking . . . who'd be buying me flowers? Not to mention sitting in the office waiting for me? The girls, God love them, can't get out of the place quick enough. We say our goodbyes and in I go.

Oh shit. I really do *NOT* believe this.

Eager Eddie, carrying a bouquet so huge, it almost dwarfs him.

One of those 'bird of paradise' arrangements. Which is a large piece of floral irony if ever I saw it.

'Vicky . . . this has gone on long enough,' is his opener while I just stare at him, knocked for six. 'You've been ignoring my calls and texts . . .'

'How did you find out where I worked?' I say hoarsely, eventually managing to interrupt him, when I'm over the initial shock, that is. You should just see my stance: arms folded, 'don't mess with me' body language. At this precise moment, I'm even intimidating *myself*.

'Phone directory.'

Bugger. Oh well done, Sherlock, how else could he have found out? By hiring a private detective to trail me? Mind you, I don't think for one minute I'd actually put that past him.

Anyway, he thrusts the flowers at me with this stoic, 'you've wounded me deeply but I'm bravely trying to rise above it' expression, and all of a sudden it's as if there's two little angel voices in my head, one good, one evil. Like in a cartoon. On and on Eager Eddie goes about how I'd been the one who wanted to take things slowly . . . so he backed off, as I asked him to . . . but now enough time has passed, and he wants us to move forward . . . as a couple (my teeth actually gnash a bit when he comes out with that) . . . And what's my problem anyway? . . . And why does this always happen to him with women? . . . I was all over him in the beginning and now, here I am . . . giving him mixed signals . . .

EVIL ANGEL VOICE IN MY HEAD: 'Ah, sure God love him. In his good suit, with flowers for you and all. Makes a change from Peter/Ex-Files, now doesn't it? And it's not like they're exactly battering your door down for dates with you these days, now is it? Give him another chance . . . go on . . . you can do it . . .'

GOOD/SANE ANGEL VOICE IN MY HEAD: 'You've two choices. Call the doorman right now and get him thrown out of here, or else turn on your heel and walk out. Obsessives tend to adhere, and this kind of OTT behaviour must be nipped in the bud right NOW. Go on, show him you mean business. Once and for all. Go on . . . you can do it . . .'

It's a see-saw. I'm just about to cut him off in the middle of a speech he's delivering, which is actually sounding suspiciously rehearsed to me, about how he has a table booked at a bistro down the road and can't we just discuss this over a bottle of wine? For a split second I waver. But at the next thing he comes out with, good/sane angel wins.

'You know, Vicky, you can play at this hard-to-get crap all you like, I've dated women like you before. The ones who want to test some poor sap by giving him the perpetual run-around. Game-players, that's what you all are.'

He's smiling, but the tone is cold. Cutting. Nasty.

Right, that's it. Enough. Good/sane angel wins this round. After all, I'm not a psychiatrist, and I'm just not qualified to deal with all of this shite.

'Eag . . . Eddie, you need to leave. Now, please. We're not in a relationship, I don't know where you got the idea that we ever were, and right now, I'd like you to go.'

He looks at me like I've just slapped him across the face.

'You know something, Vicky? Before you came back, your assistant told me you hadn't had a serious boyfriend in years, and that you'd probably be pleased to see me, so you needn't come off all hoity-toity like you're not actually delighted I'm here.'

'Eddie, you're not hearing me. Please just GO.'

'Single women in their thirties. Desperate bitches the lot of you. You should be down on your hands and knees thanking me for showing the slightest bit of interest in you . . .'

He's very close to me now, and is starting to shout. I'm cornered, he's physically blocked the door, my phone is on my desk just out of reach, and now I'm starting to get a bit panicky. Shit, shit, shit, why didn't I ask Paris and Nicole to hold on for a bit?

'I mean, how old are you anyway, Vicky? Thirty-four, thirty-five? You're doing really well to have someone like me ask you out. Face it: I'm the best offer you're going to get. I'm the one in the buyer's market, remember. I could go into any club tonight and pick up a girl half your age and far better-looking than you. Easy.'

Yeah, as long as she's in a strait-jacket, I'm thinking, really frightened now. The guy is deluded, and I haven't the first clue how I'm going to get him out of here . . .

Then my phone rings. He looks around but I make a dart for it and grab it.

'Hello, oh hi, that's perfect timing,' I say, my voice shaky. 'Look, how far are you from my office? That close? Fantastic. Quick as you can, then . . . yes. Oh, just I'm having a bit of a problem with an unwanted visitor and I know you'll sort it out for me. No, I'll stay on the line till you get here.'

Then I turn back to Eager Eddie, who's looking at me, pole-axed.

'It's my brother on the phone,' I say, as coolly as I can, and I'm only hoping he hasn't clocked that my hands are trembling. 'On his way to . . . emm . . . rugby training. He'll be here in no time, so if I were you, I'd take this opportunity to leave. Now.'

I look as him as evenly as I can, and after staring him down for what seems like an age, he eventually nods and makes to go.

Thank God, I'm thinking, thank God, thank God . . .

He's just at the door, and I still have the phone clutched to my chest, when he turns back again. 'You know something, Vicky? I think you really have a problem, you know that? You're a pathetic person, and if you ask me, you really need help.'

I don't answer, let him get the last word in if he wants, I really don't care, I just want him gone. And a second later, he is. I take the precaution of locking the door before I go back to the call.

'Mother of Divine Mercy, are you OK? What was all that about?'

'Sorry about that, Laura. I just . . . I came back to the office and . . .' I tell her, in glorious Technicolor. And she's amazing and, typical her, starts listing off all these legal test-cases and precedents about harassment that show how the law is there to protect me from headers like this one. And about how I could easily take action if I wanted, and that barring orders were practically invented for the Eager Eddies of this world.

'You know what, hon?' I say, wearily slumping down at my desk. 'I'm just glad he's gone. Sorry for casting you as a rugby-playing brother, best I could think of under pressure.'

'All right, dearest. Although I did smirk at the thought of either of your beloved brothers wearing rugby kits on their way to training.'

I don't blame her one bit for that either: my middle brother's idea of exercise is to pick up a snooker cue, while the youngest one's idea of an intensive workout is prising the lid off a tin of Carlsberg. And the thought of either of them coming to my rescue almost makes me smile a bit, too, the joke in our house used to be that, if anything happened to me, they'd step over my rotting corpse just to get at my car keys.

'Sure you're all right? You're very welcome to come over here, you know.'

Oh dear God, spare me. No offence, but after a shaky experience like this, a pleasant soirée chez Laura with all the kids there would have me reaching for the horse tranquillizers.

'Thanks so much, but I've a bit more to do here, and then I really just fancy an early night. Another time, maybe?'

'Like when they're all at college? Don't worry, dearest, I understand.' And I can almost hear the lop-sided smile. 'Actually I was ringing you with some other news, which I couldn't tell you earlier, because of little ears. But I think it's safe to speak now as the baby's gone down and the others are probably all out rioting on street corners, most likely.'

'Laura!'

'Summer months, what else can I do? Call social services, I'm a crap mom. So, anyway, to cut to the chase . . .'

'The case?'

'No. Desmond Lawlor.'

Oh.

'Dearest, I am aware that I haven't spoken these words to you in over fifteen years, but . . . I think I might like him. Really like him.'

'Oh, hon, that's wonderful.' And I *do* mean it. Honestly.

'He's been calling quite regularly,' she says, her voice dropping several notches, as if the baby will suddenly wake up and miraculously understand this conversation. 'And I thought nothing of it. Mostly it's been work-related, about the column

and such, but then it did strike me that he did seem to be showing an excessive amount of interest in it. Then earlier, he rang
and asked me to . . . now, promise you won't laugh?'

'I promise, but as I have just dealt with a deranged stalker, the
laugh would probably do me good.'

'I'm meeting him this Saturday . . .'

'Yes?' To go to some Brahms concerto in the national
concert hall, I'll put money on it. Isn't that where all . . . emm
. . . suitors who are, shall we say, a bit advanced in years, would
take someone like our Laura?

'. . . to have afternoon tea with his mother.'

And I'm so shocked, not at Desmond asking her out, but at
the fact that his mother is *still alive* . . . for the first time today,
I can't think of a single thing to say.

Hours later, and I decide to walk home, glad I left my car
there and badly needing to clear my head. Fresh air and a bit of
healthy exercise, that's just what I need right now. This virtuous
state of mind only lasts for about two blocks, and then I think,
oh bugger this walking lark, I'll ring Barbara and see if I can
talk things over with her instead. Yeah, miles better idea. She'll
put the whole rotten Eager Eddie fiasco into perspective for me
and who knows? Maybe even get me laughing again.

'KA, KA, KA, MUM, MUM, MUMMMMMM, BA, BA,
BA, BA, MMMM . . .' Honest to God, is all I hear as she
answers.

'Barbara? Please tell me that you haven't been sucked into
some kind of mind-controlling cult?'

'Hi babes, sorry. Voice exercises. Look, I know I haven't been
in touch, but it's just all been mental here. How are things with
you? On the man front, I mean?'

And so I fill her in. Everything. The works. I've been dying
to tell her, and I don't leave a single thing out. And then, I don't
know why, but out of nowhere I start to get a bit teary.

Exhaustion, disappointment, the fright I got earlier, everything just seems to come on top of me at once. And going home, alone, to an empty house, yet again, doesn't help matters much either.

'Vicky, are you OK?'

'No. Yes. I dunno, tired. Fed up . . .'

'Look, why don't you call over for a drink? A nice bottle of wine and you won't give a shite about being lonely. Trust me.'

I waver for a bit, then decide, yeah, that's just what I need right now. Not to be alone is a very good idea.

'Well, do you mind? I know you've your big dress rehearsal coming up and I don't want to disturb you if you're . . . emm . . . doing voice stuff, or anything.'

'Not at all. Get your gorgeous ass around here right now. I was just saying to Angie, we need to take a breather, too. Hang on, ANGIE? WILL YOU NIP DOWN THE OFF-LICENCE FOR SOME VINO?'

Oh bugger. In the whole of my health, I'm still not able for Evil Angie, but the way I'm feeling tonight, there's a good chance I might just knife her if she starts her 'so what have you done for my career lately' crap on me.

'Ehh . . . actually, Barbara, on second thoughts, I think I might just call it a night.'

'Oh. Are you sure?'

'Sure. You and Angie enjoy your wine and I'll chat to you tomorrow.'

'Well, if you're sure,' she says, a bit worriedly. 'Call you after rehearsals tomorrow, OK?'

'OK,' I sigh, wearily clicking off the phone and walking on, past the summer evening revellers, sitting at pavement cafés, all enjoying the long, balmy evening.

Couples everywhere, that's all I seem to see. Hand in hand, laughing, enjoying life. Like you're supposed to.

And I get to thinking . . . there's Laura, moving on with life, back in court with a man asking her out. I mean, OK, he might not necessarily be my type, but she seems to like him and that's all that matters. Then there's Barbara, slaving away, on the verge of what I really believe will be the big break she truly deserves. And then there's me. On my way home to face yet another long, lonely night. And it's not like I haven't tried, put my heart on the line, really made an effort. God knows I've done the groundwork, and where has it got me? Being threatened by a lunatic obsessive in my own office who then has the gall to tell me that *I* need professional help, that's where.

Maybe there's just something I need to face up to.

A little amendment that needs to be made to the law of attraction book.

Yes, anyone can get anything they want through sheer force of will, is what it *should* say . . . except for love. Because how do you make someone love you?

I mean, a *penthouse* for f**k's sake.

Chapter Twenty-Two

Believe me, it wasn't my intention to guilt-trip Barbara when I got a bit teary on the phone that time, honestly, but I think it must have had that effect on her because right after work, the next Thursday, she calls me and tells me we're going out. No arguments, no discussion, we're just doing it.

'But what about your big dress rehearsal this weekend? Don't you want to stay home and, I dunno, run lines and make those weird howling noises all the time?'

'I promised you a Thursday night on the trawl and I'm not taking no for an answer. You've worked so hard on this show for me that it's the very least I can do. As your project manager, I'm officially telling you it's time to put past disappointments behind you and move on. Like I always say, if you want to get over someone . . . get under someone. Over and under. Simple as that.'

Which is how I find myself in Major Tom's bar and lounge, sipping a glass of white wine that frankly could double up as acid for a car battery. Not that I'm ungrateful to Barbara for taking time out to hook me up (she sez hopefully), but, for about the tenth time tonight, I find myself asking her, 'Why *here*?'

I have to shout, mind you, because there's a match on and wouldn't you know it, the only seats we could get are right under the giant plasma TV screen.

'Look around you, dopey,' she says, drinking beer from the bottle and looking effortlessly sexy, even though she's come straight from work and is in leggings and a baggy sweatshirt. I, on the other hand, am in the good Karen Millen work suit and might almost pass for her financial adviser. And I don't mean that in a good way, I mean it in an older, prissy, spinsterish-looking way. Oh Christ, all I need is Dame Edna glasses and a blue rinse to complete the effect.

'It's a well-known sports bar, therefore, for our purposes, a target-rich environment. If this place was a TV show, it would be . . . you know, something presented by Jeremy Clarkson and Richard Hammond.'

'Don't get it.'

'A guy magnet. Trust me, within another round, someone will have chatted you up.'

She's right, someone does, but it's a woman called Dixie (no, really, that *is* her name), who's wearing flat shoes and no make-up or bra. She's chatting away, only pausing to holler and thump on the table whenever her team scores, almost sending our drinks flying. Not even Barbara is being approached, which is highly unusual, but then just about every pair of male eyes here is glued to the match. I'm presuming things will pick up once it's over, but Barbara doesn't give my theory much of a chance.

'Come on, Vicky, drink up, you've that *big meeting* tomorrow morning, remember?' she eventually says, invoking our pre-agreed dating code-phrase that means we're outta here.

I don't put up any arguments till we're outside, then, as we're hailing down a cab I say, 'I don't get it. Shouldn't we have done another half-hour in there? Whatever match was on couldn't have lasted much longer, and there were some serious cuties gathered around that big screen. Without wedding rings. I checked. You know me, I've X-ray vision for that type of thing.'

'Honey, the only person hitting on you in there was a dyke.

And you're too naïve to have even spotted it. So now, they probably think we're a pair of beards who only go to sports bars so we can hang out with butch-looking women. Right. Next stop, the Bailey.'

On and on we go, bar after bar, and honestly, by closing time I have absolutely no good news to report. Nada, not a single thing. Or should I rephrase, *I've* no good news to report, Barbara, naturally, was hit on right, left and centre, so nothing unusual there. As she and I were deep in conversation, though, her standard response to any poor unfortunate who dared interrupt her was, after a cursory glance of assessment: 'We are TRYING to have a private conversation here, do you mind?'

'Barbara, do you think maybe we're losing sight of our end goal here? Maybe? Just a bit?' I tentatively asked, when we'd moved on to our *fourth* bar and still no joy.

'I'm saving you from arseholes. I mean, did you see the state of that last one? Looks like his mother picked out that suit for him. Fifteen years ago when he was making his confirmation.'

On the plus side, though, I haven't seen her in so long that we do get an awful lot of catching-up done. Rehearsals, it seems are going brilliantly, and everyone is blown away by Serena's boundless energy and amazing ideas for the production, which is kind of music to my ears. Plus it's beyond fab to hear Barbara, the same girl who most likely knocked about two years off her life-expectancy through sheer nerves and blind terror when she first met the mighty Ms Stroheim, now chat away about her like they're bestest pals. You should hear her: it's all Serena this, Serena that. The big dress rehearsal is coming up in the Iveagh Gardens, so they're all getting psyched up for that.

The only other major update she has is that Evil Angie has split up from her make-up artist boyfriend and is now dating Oberon, King of the Fairies.

'What?' I splutter when she divulges this particular nugget of info.

'That's his character in the show. And he's straight, you eejit. Anyway, he's been hanging around our flat twenty-four seven and the only thing is . . .'

He fancies Barbara, I think, secretly delighted to see her getting one up on Evil Angie. Finally.

'. . . I'm not 100 per cent, Vicky, but I'm pretty sure he has an eye in my direction and . . . well, he's fun, he's a cutie, hot bod, me like. But he's dating my friend, so that's the end of that, really. Come on, drink up, no joy here either. We'll go to Krystal.'

'Just a thought,' I say, as we gather up our stuff to go. 'OK, so this guy is seeing Ev . . . sorry, Angie at the moment. But who's to say what'll happen in the future? My point is, yes it's very noble of you to automatically reject a guy because he's dating a friend, but what you have to ask yourself is this. Would she do the same for you?'

'Course she would,' Barbara snaps, a bit too quickly, though.

Midnight.

We're both sober, amazingly in my case as I'm normally rubbish with drink and my hit-rate is an embarrassing total of . . . one. And she was female. Plus, at this stage, I'm almost nauseous with tiredness and am practically fantasizing about getting home to bed. Alone, that is, to sleep. Oh, just listen to me, I'm officially sounding like a granny. I'll be saying novenas and making gooseberry jam next.

'I just don't get it,' Barbara is saying as we hop out of a cab outside Krystal nightclub, her favourite late-night haunt. 'Where are they all tonight, anyway? It's like the *Village of the Damned*.' Not that matters are vastly improved when she does haul me up to the members' bar upstairs. Slim pickings, we silently nod at each other, dragging ourselves up on two bar stools.

'Oh, here comes my f**k buddy,' she hisses at me, as Nathaniel the barman, her on-again, off-again love interest, zooms over to ask her what she's having. She orders a margarita; I completely lose the run of myself and go for a fizzy water, although if the truth be told, what I'd actually, *really* love is a cuppa tea, a Hobnob, home, and bed.

In that order.

Anyway, Barbara and Nathaniel are soon deep in conversation, and I'm just on the point of reaching for my handbag and slinking off home when a slightly familiar-looking guy slides up on to the bar stool beside me. Older, maybe fifties, soulful expression . . . or maybe then again, that's just me romanticizing him. Wouldn't be the first time, either.

'Hey, pretty lady, don't tell me you're leaving?' he says, in a gravelly, cigars and cognac voice.

Oh shite, this is driving me mental, I *know* I've met him before . . .

'At the risk of jogging a lady's memory, in answer to your bewildered expression, yes, we have met before. And no, I can't remember your name either, my dear. Although I have a vivid recollection of your scribbling your phone number in biro on my cuff.'

Oh for f**k's sake. *Now* I remember. The last time I was here with Barbara, I was so trolleyed drunk that what he's saying is seriously beginning to ring a bell. Did I really write my phone number on his shirt cuff? Christ alive, I must have been plastered . . .

'So should we re-introduce ourselves? I'm Tom, by the way. Pleasure to become, emm, re-acquainted with you. I don't actually recall how long it is since we last met, but then time is irrelevant here in the seventh circle of hell.'

'Vicky,' I smile, shaking his hand and trying to weigh up whether I fancy him or not. No wedding ring, which is a good start. And it's a bonus to find out his actual, correct name: I have this vague idea that the last time we met, I kept drunkenly calling him Tom, no Tim, no Tom.

'May I get you a proper drink? I assume that glass of water in front of you is some sort of joke.'

'Oh, well, go on then, a glass of white wine.'

'Glass of white for my friend Vicky here, and I'll have my usual,' he calls over to Nathaniel, who's still deep in chat with Barbara.

Barbara's here, brilliant, I think, as I introduce them. She'll do her twenty-questions lark on him and screen him for me, won't she? Course she will. So the three of us chat for a bit, and I swear I can physically *see* Barbara trying to get the measure of him. Our drinks arrive and I can't help noticing that his is a double whiskey, on the rocks. Which he pretty much gulps back in one, then shakes the empty glass at Nathaniel as if to say, same again. And there's just something about the smooth, practised way he does it, that half makes me think this is a regular occurrence.

On the plus side, though, he's full of funny stories and anecdotes about the club, where it seems he's such a regular they might as well have his name carved on the back of one of the bar stools there. Barbara starts quizzing him about what he does, which I take as my cue to nip to the Ladies. She joins me a few minutes later, shaking her head and giving a thumbs-down sign.

'Attractive, if you're into those middle-aged Frank Sinatra types, and I think he does like you, but take my advice and stay away, Vicky,' is her verdict.

'Give me one good reason,' I say, suddenly all defensive. I mean, come on, the first bloke who's shown a flicker of interest in me all night, and all of a sudden I'm in a position to be picky?

'He's a boozer. Look at him, alone, in a late-night drinking hole, knocking back doubles. Big trouble. Avoid, avoid, avoid.'

'Barbara, no offence, but look at where your screening has got me so far. Nowhere.'

'You know, I asked him what he did for a living and he said he's a director 'in-between gigs'. You know what that's code for? It means he hasn't worked in . . . like, for ever, because no producer worth their salt will touch him with a bargepole. Makes you wonder why, doesn't it?'

'It's not that I don't appreciate your advice, but on this occasion – now maybe it's the loneliness talking but, just for tonight, I'm choosing to go my own sweet way. And he's only had two drinks, what the big deal? I've seen you knock back five times that amount and you've seen me . . .'

'Nathaniel says he's in here alone, most nights, always the last to leave and always stocious by closing time. I'm telling you, Vicky, guys like that are fine, but only if you happen to love dating a project.'

As if to back up her point, she shoots me a loaded 'told you so' look when we rejoin him. It's nowhere near closing time and yet he's already lined *three* more doubles up in front of him. Which is unusual. Normally at closing time in this country, the rattle of the bar shutters coming down is a bit like the bull run in Pamplona; guys just seem to crawl out of the woodwork to get a last order in. But up until then, no one really panics and . . . you know, *lines them up* like this . . . at least, no one that I've ever seen outside of a Western movie.

'OK, so he likes a drink,' I mutter to her as we head back to our seats. 'And, yes, maybe he likes to sit in clubs on his own. No man is perfect and, after all, it's nothing that the right woman couldn't work on and sand down, you know, gradually. Over time.'

'Oh yeah, sure. Because men always change.'

Well you know what? Right now, I don't care if Barbara doesn't approve. Because, where has her seal of approval landed me? It's OK for her, she's doing her dream gig and there's Nathaniel with his tongue practically hanging out of his mouth every time he looks at her. She doesn't have to go home alone tonight, if she doesn't want to. If Tim, no Tom, no Tim makes a move on me, I decide, slipping back up on to my bar stool, it's game on. I just wish I could get his name straight in my head once and for all . . . TOM. That's it, definitely Tom.

He doesn't. Four a.m., and I'm actually yawning into his face, I'm that exhausted. Nathaniel's closing up for the night, and even the indefatigable Barbara is starting to worry that she has to be up in a few hours' time.

And I've lost count of how many drinks Tim, sorry TOM's had, but the funny thing is, he's not falling over, or in a coma, as I would be. No, he's as cool and articulate as ever. It's only as Barbara and I are putting coats on, grabbing bags and really, really, *really* going home this time that he makes a move.

He grabs my hand and pulls me to him, kinda roughly, but I like it.

'So how about meeting up this weekend?' he asks in the deep, gravelly voice.

I don't even have to think about it. Not for a second. Decision made.

'Love to.' And no need for phone numbers scribbled on shirts this time, I think, a bit smugly. 'Here, let me give you my card.'

Chapter Twenty-Three

I should have guessed that something was seriously amiss when the scariest woman on the planet, aka Laura's mother, calls me in work the next day.

'Vicky, is that you?' she says imperiously. Even though I answer the office phone clearly saying, 'Hello, Vicky Harper speaking.' Contrary old cow.

'Mrs Lennox-Coyningham speaking. I'm afraid there's a slight problem here and I'm going to have to ask for your help. No choice in the matter, I'm afraid.'

Shit, I think, racking my brains, what's the old battleaxe on about? Today's Laura's big day in court, well, traffic court, but who cares, it's still court and Mrs L-C is supposed to be babysitting . . . oh no, I think as a slow, sickening feeling creeps from the pit of my stomach . . . oh no, *please*, please don't let this be happening . . . please . . . not today . . .

'You see, Laura left me in charge of the children while she went off to the district court this morning,' and I'm not kidding, even the way she emphasizes the word 'district' court makes it sound like an insult. 'Leaving me here at her house for the day. Alone. With the children. All of them. No play dates arranged for the older ones, nothing.'

'Yes, Mrs Lennox-Coyningham?' I say in a dear-Jaysus-

294

please-don't-let-this-call-be-about-what-I-think-it's-going-to-be-about tone.

'But the thing is, with all the screaming and general hysteria in this house, I've come down with one of my dreadful migraines, and I really have to go home now and lie in a nice dark room. So if you could possibly help out, Vicky, and get over here right away, I'd be most grateful.'

She says this in a tone that's not expecting any argument, and I nearly drop the phone in pure disbelief.

'But . . . Mrs Lennox-Coyningham, I'm in work! I mean, I can't . . . I'd love to help out, of course, but the thing is, we're snowed under here and it just isn't possible for me to drop everything and . . .'

'Vicky, I really wouldn't ask, only this is an emergency. I tried your chum Barbara, who seems to be at a perpetual loose end to me, but for the first time I can remember in decades, she actually has some sort of job, and is in rehearsals it seems, or at least so she tells me.'

'But, no offence or anything, but I'm the world's most useless babysitter, isn't there someone, anyone else you could ask? An agency? *Any*one?'

'Believe me, if Laura only had a reputable child-minder I shouldn't dream of having to trouble you, but this is an emergency. And my migraines can take *days* to recover from.'

Just as she hangs up, my mobile goes. Laura, sounding about fifty times more stressed than normal, which God love her, is really saying something.

'Vicky? Oh thank God, what am I going to do? I'm on my way into court with my client and Mum just called to say she can't babysit for me . . . I think I'm actually having palpitations . . . my chest is constricted and I can't breathe . . .'

'Shhh, shhh, calm down, hon, I'm a step ahead of you, your mum just phoned here and explained. It's OK, I can go over.'

Out of the corner of my eye, I can see Paris and Nicole look-ing at me as if to say, 'Eh, no you can't, we've our backs to the wall here.' But I hold firm. What else can I do? I've no choice.

'Oh Vicky, I really hate imposing on you, when you're so busy, but I really don't know who else to turn to . . .' She breaks off here, and I'm almost sure I can hear her getting a bit choked. 'I'm literally on my way into the courtroom now and there's no turning back. And if you know how much it broke my heart to leave the kids this morning. Oh shit, what the hell is *wrong* with me? For the last few years, all I've dreamt about, all that's sustained me is going back to the Bar and now here I am . . . and I just want to be with my babies. Julia was up coughing half the night and it nearly killed me to leave her . . . bloody hell, will you just listen to me? I've just turned into one of those pathetic clinging mums . . .'

'Honey, it's absolutely fine and there's no need to panic,' I interrupt her, doing a fair impression of someone who sounds calm, although I'm far, very far, from feeling it. 'I'm on my way over to your house now and don't worry, of course I'll stay there till your case is finished.'

'Vicky Harper, I'll be indebted to you until the day I die and that's a promise. OK. I've left enough food in the fridge for the whole day, and there's veggie burgers in the freezer if Emily gets stroppy about not eating. Now Julia seemed all right when I left her this morning, but there's a thermometer in the medicine cabinet if you want to take her temperature. And the Calpol is there, too, just in case. OK, I need to switch my phone off in court, but I'll call when we get a recess . . .'

'Laura, stop panicking, I can cope. Now relax, go in there and win.'

It's absolutely fine, I think, driving over to Laura's, still a bit shell-shocked, but then, you gotta do what you gotta do. Don't you? Course you do. A couple of deep, soothing breaths later and I'm almost calm. I mean, come on, it's only babysitting, not rocket science. If I'm able to run a successful company, not to mention get an outdoor show off the ground without any prior experience whatsoever, then taking care of four kids for one day should be a doddle, comparatively speaking. Yes, OK, so I had to postpone two meetings till tomorrow, but I did take my laptop with me and can easily get loads done from Laura's front room while the kids are all engaged in healthy outdoor activities and while the baby peacefully slumbers.

In fact, I'd say I might even get *more* than normal done, given that I won't have to deal with the office phone ringing every two minutes. Paris and Nicole were absolutely brilliant, practically shoving me out the door with reassurances that they'd take care of everything, and that if there was the slightest problem, they'd call me. Today in court is a huge deal for Laura and I have to be there for her, simple as that.

Besides, wait till you see, the kids will probably just play happily in the garden with their . . . emm . . . swingballs or emm . . . spacehoppers . . . or whatever the latest fad in toys is, then come in knackered, then crash out in front of the TV.

To be honest, I really don't see what all the big fuss about child-minding is, really. Yes, OK, I have to be there to supervise, but apart from that, what else can there possibly be to it?

11.00 a.m.
The minute the hall door is opened, Mrs L–C is out of there like hot snot, practically leaving a trail of dust in her wake. Not even a thank you, nothing. She just calls after me, 'They've all had breakfast, Vicky, but I've no idea what you can do about lunch. I can't think straight with one of my heads.' Into her Mercedes and gone.

It's a lovely hot summer's day, so I'm vaguely surprised to see George Junior and Jake glued to the TV, but then I figure as long as they're being quiet, who am I to argue? Emily is up in her room with some pal of hers who's wearing a belly top and who has a pierced navel. She's introduced to me as Tiffany-Amber and as the pair of them seem happy enough in their own company, I leave them to it. Baby Julia's dozing away in her little Moses basket up in Laura's room, so all quiet on the Western Front, then. I make myself a coffee, plonk the baby walkie-talkie monitor yoke, or whatever you call it, down beside me and switch on my laptop, feeling very Mary Poppins altogether.

11.05 a.m.
Oh dear God, I'm so stressed I'd ring my own mother to beg her to give me a dig-out, only she and my dad are in the bloody Algarve golfing with their pals. Baby Julia is in my arms screaming so loudly that I'm afraid the neighbours will actually call social services. I thump on Emily's door to see if she'll help me, but it's locked, and the little madam just shouts back, 'Either feed her or change her and then she'll shut up.' Brilliant.

Then just as I'm trying to figure out how to take off a nappy (there are these ridiculous sticky labels on the side, for God's sake, so I'm rooting around Laura's dressing table for nail scissors to cut the bloody thing off), the Third Gulf War erupts from the TV room downstairs, with Jake and George Junior fighting each other over what programme to watch next. I snip the nappy off Baby Julia, miraculously managing to avoid puncturing the poor child with the nail scissors, then leave her lying on Laura's immaculately made bed and screech downstairs, something along the lines of: 'George? Do not call your brother a puke-hole! Now find a TV show you can both agree on or else I'm unplugging it and you can both play outside in the sunshine and fresh air!'

No effect on the row whatsoever. In fact, if anything, the

fighting gets worse, and I'd swear I can hear the kind of language you only get on football terraces as they continue to tear lumps out of each other.

11.10 a.m.
Oh no, I don't believe this. In the space of thirty seconds while I was out of the room, Baby Julia's gone and weed all over Laura's crisp, clean sheets. I can hear my mobile ringing and ringing downstairs, and it could be work and I can't get near it. Meanwhile the screaming match downstairs continues unabated, and this time, my repeated threat of kicking them both outside to play elicits sneering laughter.

11.30 a.m.
I think I might actually have the clean nappy on.

11.31 a.m.
No, I don't. It just fell off her, and now she's wailing again. Maybe she's hungry, maybe that's what's wrong. I thump on Emily's locked door and ask when she had her last feed?

'How do I know?' is the muffled answer. 'Now go away, what we're doing takes privacy.'

She must be on some Bebo-type internet chat room, I fume, making about my fortieth attempt to get the nappy to actually stay on the baby, while she's wriggling and squealing around the bed like I'm torturing her.

11.45 a.m.
Success. Apparently the sticky bit on the nappy goes at the back, not the front. Don't ask me who invented these things. For God's sake, the Pampers box doesn't have any kind of instruction manual with it; I mean, you'd think they'd make it simple for non-parents.

299

Had to strip Laura's bed, too, and put the weed-on sheets in the wash. And trying to get Baby Julia back into a clean baby-gro is a bit like trying to dress a wriggling eel.

11.50 a.m.
As I'm checking on the messages on my phone (three missed calls, all from the office), the TV-room row gets so vicious that I burst in, baby still screaming in my arms, and demand that they both go outside. Or else, I dunno, read books or something. Anything, just to shut the pair of them up. George Junior and Jake only stop bickering to laugh at me, then go back to the far more interesting business of tearing each other apart.

'Hard work and discipline! That's what you pair need!' I snarl at them, trying to do my best Laura impression whenever she's giving them one of her icy dressing-downs. But it only makes them piss themselves laughing at me even more.

'Hard work and discipline?' sneers Jake. 'What is that, anyway? Some kind of theme park?'

12.00 noon
The baby is still screeching, and I'm trying to copy that thing I've seen Laura do, where she microwaves the bottle, then tests the temperature of it against her wrist before a feed. I've watched her do it a thousand times, and no kidding, she's actually able to achieve it in one fluid, skilful movement. When I try it, though, the bloody thing nearly scalds my arm so badly that I drop it on the floor, letting out a string of curses, then apologizing to the baby just in case 'f★★ketty-f★★k' ends up being her first coherent phrase. She can't quite talk yet, but does come out with the odd word or two, and knowing my luck will do a perfect impression of what she just heard me saying in front of Mrs Lennox-Up-Your-Arse-Coyningham.

Shit, shit, shit . . .

I rinse the bottle under the tap, figuring, ah sure it'll be grand, then just as I'm about to feed the poor starving, screaming child, my phone goes again.

Daniel Best.

Bugger, I'll have to take it. It must be important.

'Hello?' I almost have to shout to compensate for the blaring TV and the blazing row which is still ongoing inside.

'Vicky? Is that you? Are you OK?'

'Oh absolutely grand!' I lie through my teeth. 'Just . . . emm . . . well, a friend of mine had a bit of a childcare emergency here, and emm . . .'

Baby Julia has now thrown the bottle back on to the floor and vomited all over my good Karen Millen *black* suit. 'Don't worry a bit!' I almost sing with hysteria into the phone. 'Everything's all set for the shoot next week, the press is totally under control, and I've my laptop with me in case there's an emergency, which, of course there won't be . . . !' Cue the most blood-curdling yelling ever heard this side of a Hammer House of Horror film, coming from the upstairs bedroom.

'Vicky!' I can hear Tiffany-Amber, Emily's friend, screaming from behind the locked door in blind panic. 'Jaysus, quick, get an ambulance, will you!'

'Oh shit, Daniel, hang on a minute will you?' I leg it upstairs, phone in one hand, screeching baby in the other, and bang on Emily's bedroom door. A very shame-faced-looking Tiffany-Amber opens it, holding a needle and a blood-stained wad of cotton wool. Emily is lying on the bed, writhing in agony, blood all over her white T-shirt. For a second I think they've been at some weird satanic ritual, but then Tiffany-Amber says, 'It wasn't even my fault anyway, I mean, she asked me to pierce her belly button for her, and then just as I was sticking the needle in, she went and moved. It was an accident. Honest.'

'Vicky?' I hear Daniel's voice on my phone as I stand rooted to the scene, which, honestly, looks like something from a Tarantino movie. 'Vicky, are you still there?'

'Sorry, Daniel, there's . . . emm . . . there's a bit of an emergency here and . . .'

'Look, where are you?'

'What?'

'Give me the address and I'll be there as soon as I can.'

12.30 p.m.

I do not believe this. I really don't. I'm just trying to change Baby Julia out of yet another babygro after she puked up for a second time over the one I had her in. She's still screeching, the row is still going on downstairs and Emily and Tiffany-Amber are in the bathroom using the good lacy towels to soak up blood. Dear God, I must have aged about six years in the past hour and a half, I'm thinking, as suddenly there's an authoritative thump at the front door.

I run downstairs, Baby Julia in what already smells dangerously like a very dirty nappy in my arms, and fling open the hall door.

It's Daniel. Grinning, in his Gap chinos and a white T-shirt. Oh my God, I could hug him. Just for turning up. Just for being here.

'Now tell me the truth,' he says, arms folded, looking at me in that cute side-on way that he has. 'I'm taking a wild guess that you don't actually have any experience with kids, do you?'

'How on earth did you know?' I practically have to wail over the ongoing row in the living room. 'I can't believe you're here. I mean, don't you have emm . . . you know, like . . . a huge corporation to run, and all that?'

'Vicky,' he says, gently taking Baby Julia from my arms and lifting her up. 'I'm one of seven kids, and at the last count had eleven nieces and four nephews, with two more on the way. If there's one thing I can do, it's take care of kids. Lesson one, here's how you hold her. She's a baby, not a football. Hi there, sweetie pie!' He coos at Baby Julia, who's miraculously stopped wailing and is just staring at him, completely mesmerized.

'Hey, is that the unmistakable whiff of a dirty nappy I'm smelling?'

12.45 p.m.
The guy is unbelievable. Just incredible. Within two minutes flat, he's sorted out the row between the boys in the living room, with the promise that if they shut up and behave, they can come with him to a Harley-Davidson bike show this afternoon. Apparently H-D are huge clients of Best's (wouldn't you know it, only the coolest people for Best's), plus Daniel insists he has to go anyway, and has tickets to spare.

It works like a charm. That on top of the fact that the boys copped on they'd be getting there in Daniel's brand-new, showroom-condition Aston Martin, parked in the drive, which pretty much sealed the deal. They hopped into the back of his sports car like a pair of obedient choirboys, like there'd never been a cross word spoken between them all morning. Meanwhile, as I manage to get the still-screeching Emily, and a sobbing Tiffany-Amber into my car on our way to the hospital, a neighbour who I vaguely recognize sticks her head through the front door and worriedly asks if everything's OK?

'Fine, not a bother,' Daniel calls back cheerily. 'Just a routine trip to the emergency room!' You should hear him, his tone is so relaxed and confident, you'd almost swear this was our idea of a fun-filled family day out.

'Would you like me to take the baby for you, while you're gone?'

She's looking at me with such concern that I might as well

be handing out business cards that say: 'Nanny Choke-Child, now out of prison and accepting play dates.'

'We'd really appreciate that, wouldn't we, Vicky?' Daniel says, shooting an encouraging glance at me. 'Sure you don't mind?'

'No, not at all,' says concerned neighbour. 'Although maybe we shouldn't mention it to Laura. Last time my kids went near little Julia here, the poor child ended up getting head lice from my youngest, and I still haven't heard the last of it.'

Off they go, and Daniel walks me to my car, where Emily is now genuinely writhing in agony. 'Oh God,' I say, panicking. 'Are you sure it was OK for us to hand over the baby like that? I mean, suppose . . . suppose . . .'

'Well now, I could hardly bring her to a bike expo with me, and, no offence, but, based on what I've seen, I wouldn't trust you with her for a full afternoon, never mind what she might catch in the hospital.' He's grinning at me in that crinkly-eyed way he has that, in the middle of all this mayhem and screaming kids, I'm actually starting to find quite sexy. 'Believe me, Vicky, we'd no choice, and your friend will understand.'

No, make that *irresistibly* sexy. You should just see him, all tall and calm. And I just feel tiny beside him. Tiny and useless and incapable of looking after kids for longer than five minutes.

'My friend's going to go mad,' I say to him. Laura suddenly comes to mind, and I'm trembling even at the thought of having to tell her what's happened. 'What'll I say when she calls? One of her kids is in the emergency room, one's with a vermin-infested neighbour, and I've sent the other two off with a man they've never met before?'

'Hey, come on, we'll think of something,' he says, grinning, the eyes all crinkly. 'You keep in touch and let me know how you get on at the hospital.'

'Who's your man?' asks Tiffany-Amber, as I clamber into the car and wallop the door shut behind me.

I have to pause for a second before I can even think straight. It just sounds so bizarre that I have to say it aloud – almost so I'll believe it myself, as much as anything else.

'His name is Daniel, he's the head of a huge company, he's like, a self-made gazzillionaire, I'm doing some freelance contract work for him, and today . . . today . . . he's babysitting Emily's brothers.'

'Gorgeous-looking though, isn't he?'

4.30 p.m.

I needn't have worried about a thing. It's all fine, crisis averted.

Emily needed two stitches, a tetanus shot and a very stern lecture from a junior doctor who, God love him, looks as if he hasn't slept in about a fortnight. She's calmed down now, the screaming has mercifully stopped, and Tiffany-Amber managed to keep us both entertained during the interminable wait on a hospital trolley by showing us her routine for an audition she has coming up to be in a girl band.

'That's my number-one goal in life,' she explains to me. 'And my dad says it doesn't even matter that I can't sing or dance, cos girl bands are all shite anyway. And if I don't get into the band, then I'm going on *The X Factor*. The quicker I get famous, the quicker I can become a WAG.'

And I don't think the child has even turned thirteen.

5.15 p.m.

I thought Laura would totally flip, but, astonishingly, she doesn't. When she gets home she just hugs Baby Julia tight, and Emily even lets her give her a peck on the cheek, which normally is unheard-of.

'I am so glad to be home,' Laura keeps saying over and over. And she doesn't even bat an eyelid when I tell her that I've let the boys go off with Daniel for the afternoon.

'I can't do it again, Vicky,' she says, slumping down at the kitchen table, totally worn-out. 'I thought all I wanted was to go back to work, but it turns out . . . I didn't after all.'

'I'm not with you. What do you mean, you didn't? All you've talked about since the baby was born was getting back to work. It's all you've dreamed about. You're the girl who has the days counted, remember? I'm surprised you don't have pie charts stuck to the fridge with the number of days you have left till the baby's in school.'

'I know, I know,' she says, looking a bit distant and slowly stirring the cup of tea I've made her. 'But did you ever find your-self in a situation where the one thing that you thought you wanted most out of life turned out, well, not to be what you were chasing after all? There I was in my wig and gown, and I should have been the happiest barrister in the Four Courts, but I wasn't. All I wanted was to be here. Home. With my family. On the plus side, though, I will get a terrific column out of this.'

God only knows what happened to Laura in that courtroom, but it's had the weirdest effect on her.

6.45 p.m.
Daniel's flashy car pulls into the driveway, and out get the two boys, now clad in Harley-Davidson T-shirts, baseball caps and sweatshirts; the full works. Daniel, it seems, is officially their new best friend. And, after today, mine.

I bring him into the kitchen to meet Laura, and I can practically see her sizing him up, this guy she's heard so much about, billionaire-turned-babysitter.

Like so much in my life, you couldn't make it up, you really couldn't.

'I really can't thank you enough,' she says politely, although he refuses to join us for a (I'm guessing, badly needed) glass of wine.

'Love to stay, but I'd better get back to the office,' he says, grinning. 'I've some calls coming in from the States that I need to be there for.'

Oh shit, yeah, of course, the girlfriend. Or maybe something to do with the bleeding . . . *penthouse* he's buying her. Lucky, jammy cow, whoever she is.

'I really, really owe you,' is all I can say as we show him back out again.

'Pleasure,' he says, playing it all down and doing his sideways look at me. 'So, I'll see you soon, yeah?'

'Definitely. Sure, we have the big shoot next week.'

'Eh, yeah, yeah, the shoot, of course. Well, we'll talk.'

The minute he's out of sight, Laura closes the hall door behind us and we move back inside.

She doesn't say anything for ages, but is doing her lop-sided smile, so I get in ahead of her.

'OK, OK, I know what you're thinking, but I can officially tell you he's spoken-for.'

'Did I as much as open my mouth?'

Chapter Twenty-Four

I honestly don't think I've ever be able to understand any man, as long as I'm alive. And at my age, that is a seriously pathetic admission. That night, sitting at her kitchen table, Laura and I comb over it again and again, and, with her lawyer-like brain and my tendency to fantasize anything and everything, here's what we've come up with.

Laura's theory:

The fact that Daniel may or may not have a girlfriend/life-partner/fiancée/whatever the hell she is in New York is purely based on hearsay and nothing else.

My theory:

Yeah, and she could be in a wheelchair after a horrific car crash in which he was driving, so therefore, while being incredibly sweet and attentive to other women, feels a deep moral obligation to remain with Miss X or whatever her name is, for the rest of his life.

Laura's theory:

Even if the rumour about him being 'off the market' is true, which in true lawyer fashion, she's not prepared to acknow-ledge, the fact is that she's over there and he's over here.

Seriously putting himself out for me, viz., today. Men do absolutely nothing unless there's something in it for them, ergo, he likes me. (Don't get me wrong, I love this theory, but can't help feeling that if something sounds too good to be true, it usually is.)

She then makes me text him, out of manners and nothing else, to say a huge thank you for the dig-out today. Which I do. Well, that is, I have to do about three practice drafts first, to make sure they hit the right light and breezy, casual tone, but I eventually send it off.

Mainly because Laura reminds me it's only a bloody text message after all, and not St Paul's first letter to the Romans, and to just get over myself.

My theory:

Yeah, but if my learned friend is right, and if Daniel does somehow, miraculously, fancy me, then how come he's never asked me out, on a one-to-one? If Laura's on the money, then he's not exactly doing anything about it, now, is he? Maybe he's just this incredibly nice guy, who's always bending over backwards for people who work for him, all fully traceable back to guilt over the wheelchair-bound girlfriend, see my previous theory listed above. And he never replies to my text, either.

Laura's theory:

She now reckons I've had one glass of vino too many and need to take a taxi home and sleep it off. On this point, at least, we agree.

A few days later, it's Sunday, but still a mad busy day, as this evening marks the official dress rehearsal for *A Midsummer Night's Dream*, and Barbara, God love her, is almost on the verge of a nervous breakdown. She's too uptight to talk, eat, drink, sleep, you name it, with the result that her nervousness has all transferred to me, and now I'm hopping around the place like *I'm* the one who has to perform tonight.

There'll be no audience there, I do my best to reassure her, in a snatched phone call as I'm hopping out of the shower. Only crew and . . . well, me. I'm not helping her, though; in fact I think I'm only making her worse.

Anyway, sad and all as I feel having to go into my office on a Sunday, I've no choice. I jump into my car, making a mental note of everything I have to do for tonight. Programme has to be proof-read before going to the printers tomorrow . . . check. Opening-night guest list has to be confirmed . . . check. Dressing-room allocations have to be OK'd with Serena's assistant . . . check. It might sound like a mammoth amount of work, but between Paris, Nicole and myself, we're pretty much on top of things.

If nothing goes wrong, that is.

And as if all of this wasn't enough to be getting on with, the first Original Sin commercial is also scheduled to be shot at eight a.m. tomorrow morning . . .

I can't think about that now, though, I just can't. There's a good chance I'll have a full-blown anxiety-attack.

One thing at a time. That's the time-honoured way to handle all stressful situations.

Yes, of course it is. Deep breath and remind myself that the law of attraction doesn't come with a pause button.

I am now attracting great success for Barbara, and love and romance for me, thank you universe, if it's no bother . . .

Anyway, I'm just about to reverse my car into a space outside my office when my mobile goes. I assume it's either Paris or Nicole, both of whom said they'd meet me at the Iveagh Gardens for the dress rehearsal later on tonight, but surprisingly, it's not.

A man's voice, deep and gravelly, which it takes me a second to place . . .

Oh bugger, I do not believe this. Today of all days. This of all weeks. After all this time, after all my waiting and wondering, Tim, no Tom, no Tim finally decides to ring me.

'Hey beautiful,' he growls into the phone, and I'm not messing, he sounds like he was out half the night, which, knowing him, he probably was. 'Just wondered if I could persuade you to have brunch with me. If you're around, that is.'

What is it about guys? I silently fume, shaking my head in disbelief. I mean, all the time I wasted, practically willing various guys to call me, and then at probably the single busiest time I've had in the whole year, here's this one, all relaxed and casual, wanting to meet for brunch. Half of me is saying, politely refuse, explain that you've far too much on. If he has a gram of interest in you, he'll reschedule something else. And everyone knows, saying no to fellas only makes them keener, doesn't it?

But then . . . the chronically single half of me is saying: Sure, right, off you go, put bloody work ahead of all else, and spend the day slaving alone in your office, instead of taking one lousy hour off to meet a very sexy, attractive man for a quick bite . . . And I have the cheek to wonder why I'm still alone? I mean, even *The Law of Attraction* says something about when opportunity comes a-knocking, only a right gobshite would say: 'Yeah, I'm really sorry, but I have to work, can you come back later?'

Or words to that effect.

Oh no, now I have it. It says: 'Opportunity dances with those who are already on the dance floor.' Right then, decision made, and to be honest, it's a no-brainer.

Half an hour later, I find myself in the Espresso Bar, an achingly trendy restaurant, sitting at an outdoor table, waiting for Tom, no Tim, no Tom. Definitely *TOM*.

Note to self: on pain of death do not accidentally let the

wrong name slip out. Anyway, as ever on these occasions, my mind's gone into overdrive, split neatly down the middle like a computer screen thus.

Con.

He's bloody well late. And I don't have time for this. Feeling impatient and annoyed with myself for just dropping every-thing on such a crazy day to meet some guy who doesn't even have the decency to arrive on time, I'm just about to pay for my cappuccino and exit stage left, when in he saunters.

Pro.

Oooh, the hormones are starting to get the better of me. I completely forgot just how attractive he is. And this is my first time seeing him in daylight. He's in a crumpled linen suit, and is wearing shades, but it's the George Clooney voice that really gets me going. He sits opposite me, asks for the wine list and whips off the sunglasses to study it.

Con.

Oh dear God, the eyes are not just red, they're crimson. In fact he doesn't just look like he's been on the batter last night, he looks like he's been on a non-stop bender for about the last five months. No, scrap that. The last five years, more like.

Pro.

He has that older man thing going, where he seems genuinely interested in me nervously prattling on about the show tonight. And, because he's a director, he seems suitably impressed that we managed to nab THE Serena Stroheim. It flashes through my mind . . . should I invite him to the open-ing night next week? But the trouble is, although we counted on a twenty per cent refusal rate, we haven't had nearly as many as we'd allowed for, hence, seating is going to be a problem to the extent that I think even my own family will be doing well to get in. And it looks like myself, Paris and

Nicole will end up sitting on upside-down orange crates backstage.

Con.

I ask him about his work, and he gets very vague and elusive, saying something about a gig he has coming up, but that for the past year, he's mostly just been doing the odd freelance day's work here and there to support, wait for it . . . *both* of his ex-wives. With a child by each of them. I mean, OK, fair enough, but it is quite a container-load of baggage. And I should know, I saw that movie *Stepmom* about three times. And let me tell you, the stepmom is always, always, the baddie, even if she happens to be played by Julia Roberts.

Another con.

It's still relatively early and, without hesitation, he orders a bottle of wine. I vaguely protest, half-afraid I might come across as a boring pain in the arse, but I know if I have more than a sip, I'll probably keel over and fall asleep. And today of all days, I cannot afford to do that.

'So who says it's all for you, my dear?' is his husky, red-eyed response.

Yet another con.

Oh dear God, I have never, ever in all my days seen anyone put a bottle of wine away so fast. Not even Barbara with her famed hollow legs could keep up with this guy. And his stories are all about how he drank the proceeds from the sale of two houses in-between divorces. At one stage he actually says that if he had to choose between sex and a round of drinks, the drinks would win out every time. Suddenly I start to feel a bit like one of those pioneer pin-wearing, temperance-movement types, amazed how such an attractive, and I'm sure talented, man could be so blasé about throwing his life away over booze. But I don't get a chance to say anything, because next minute he's ordered a double whiskey on the rocks.

'After midday now,' he growls at me from behind the shades. 'Socially acceptable to move on to the hard stuff.'

Right then, that's my cue to leave, I think, gathering up my stuff. I make my excuses and he stays on, impatiently looking over his shoulder for the waitress to hurry up with his drink. 'So, I'll call you,' he says. 'I think I'd feel a little more comfortable seeing you under cover of darkness. Whaddya say, my dear?'

I just mumble something about really, really needing to go (the God's honest truth), and leave. Don't get me wrong, he's devilishly attractive, and if we'd been on a night-time date, it mightn't have highlighted the boozing so much. I might have fallen for him, probably might even have dragged him home with me out of feeling sorry for him – and just wanting contact with another human being. Just wanting to feel anything other than unremitting loneliness for a change. But right now, I'm just not in the mood to be someone's enabler. Or boozing buddy. Not being rude or anything, but I haven't the time.

Another thought strikes me as I head back to my office. Barbara was right about him. One hundred per cent on the money. Oh shit, I can't resist. I know she's probably got her head down the loo throwing up with nerves about tonight, but I need to speak to her too badly. I call her mobile, and from the sounds of it she's already at the Iveagh Gardens, warming up or whatever it is actors do before a big show. I know she must be in absolute ribbons based solely on how narky she is with me on the phone.

The conversation goes along these lines:

ME: 'I had brunch with Tim no Tom no Tim and I'm just ringing to tell you that you were right and I was wrong. A total and utter waste of my time, and at the rate he's drinking, he'll probably end up on a waiting list for a new liver in a few years' time. I'm not messing, the guy would have put George Best to shame.'

HER: (*Snapping the face off me, real grade one narkiness.*) 'What are you telling me for? Don't you have a diary? Or a blog?'

Note to self: I totally understand that her general rattiness is down to nerves and nothing else, but do not, under any circumstances, attempt to hold any kind of normal, adult conversation with Barbara until well after the opening night. Like, about a week after. I'd say she'll be back to herself by then.

The dress rehearsal is scheduled for eight p.m., but I need to be there a bit earlier to run through a few programme notes with Serena, and also finalize the opening night seating plan with Paris and Nicole. Anyway, I'm just getting back into my car, laden down with files and yet more colouredy folders when my mobile goes.

And it's Daniel.

'Hey,' he says, sounding as relaxed and laid-back as ever. 'Just wanted to say sorry for not getting back to you, it's been . . . well, things are kind of hotting up here, so I've spent most of my weekend in the office, tied to a desk, pathetic and all as that sounds.'

'Snap,' I smile.

'So all set for tomorrow morning? The big day?'

'Ehh . . . I kind of have tonight to get out of the way, first.'

'Tonight? Don't tell me, another date? So how many guys is that you're seeing right now? Or is it hard to keep track?'

'Ha, ha, you're hilarious. No, it's the dress rehearsal for the show I was telling you about in the Iveagh Gardens . . .'

'The one I promised to invest in, and then you never came back to me about?'

'Oh, don't worry, you're on my target list all right. There's a

315

sponsorship pack on its way to you, and it is all for a really good cause . . .' He cuts me off in full pitch-mode.

'Well, if I'm putting good money into this, do you think there's any chance I can see the dress rehearsal? If you're not taking someone else, that is?'

Oh my God, I can't quite believe this. I'm not even sure how it happened, but about half an hour later, in he strolls to the Iveagh Gardens, cool as a breeze and looking like he just came back from a fortnight in Tenerife, and not at all like someone who's been chained to a desk for the weekend. I'm chatting to Serena and her assistant when I see him saunter in from a distance, jacket thrown over his shoulder, while Paris and Nicole are busy with seating plans and generally being runners for the cast, bless them.

Oh my God, it's a full-blown Mr Darcy moment. Just like in the *Pride and Prejudice* TV series when Lizzie sees him coming towards her with that wet shirt stuck to his manly chest . . . all of a sudden, the force of attraction I'm feeling for him is making me weak-kneed.

I introduce Daniel to everyone and, I swear, I can practically see thought-balloons coming out of people's heads: 'So who is this cutie that Vicky's been keeping under wraps all this while?' Or maybe that's just my paranoia going into overdrive. Miraculously, neither Paris or Nicole seem to know him socially, and what's even more amazing, he doesn't ogle either of them when they shake hands, which is kind of unheard-of. Most guys take one look at their twenty-something pertness, lack of wrinkles, dewy skin etc., etc., and they're goners.

But not Daniel. I might be imagining it, I mean, I *must* be imagining it, but it really does seem like I'm his focus of attention. He's chatty, friendly, and . . . almost flirtatious with me . . . ?

Oh shit, I must have that wrong. He's seeing someone else, I tell myself sternly as we sit down for Act One. He's *involved*.

This is not a date . . . repeat, this is NOT a date . . .

Which is kind of a shame, actually, because if it were, it would be just perfect. He and I are sitting right at the back, on our own, and the place just looks magical. The lighting designer has worked miracles, and just as the sun is slowly setting, he's bringing up twinkly fairy lights, creating this magical, mystical effect, perfect for *A Midsummer Night's Dream*. The weather's held up, it's been a hot day, and the evening is cool and clear . . . perfect, I couldn't have stage-managed it better.

The show starts, and I'm on the edge of my seat till Barbara comes out. And then . . . there she is. Looking like a goddess in her long, Shakespearian costume, the wild red hair tousled and rolling down her back. And she's *brilliant*. Absolutely jaw-droppingly, scene-stealingly amazing. Just like I knew she would be. And I'm not just saying it, nor am I imagining it. At one stage Daniel whispers to me, 'Wow, your friend is incredible, how come I've never seen her in anything before?'

He leans in close to say it, and no kidding, I actually do get goose bumps.

This is not a date . . . this is not a date . . .

We're sitting closer, far closer to each other than we need to, and as Act Two begins, and it gets a little chillier, he slips his jacket off and puts it around my shoulders.

'Your hands are like ice,' he whispers, slipping his warm hand over mine and holding on. And I don't let go.

He's just being friendly. This is not a date . . . repeat ad nauseam . . .

The show is a wow, an absolute wow, and even though there's only about eight of us in the audience, we're all spontaneously on our feet by the final, hilarious scene. And Barbara is the undisputed star. No question, no one to touch her. I'm on an absolute high, floating on air as we all meet backstage, everyone hugging each other, everyone euphoric, unable to believe that it all went so well. I even find it in myself to congratulate Evil Angie, who was . . . well, better than OK . . . but then comparing her to Barbara's electrifying performance is just not comparing like with like. She's all over Daniel when I introduce them, but he's his usual laid-back self, congratulates her and then goes back to telling Barbara how stunning she was.

'It's only the truth,' I say, hugging her for about the tenth time. 'If you were a dame of the British Empire you'd be . . . Helen Mirren. No question.'

I'm feeling so euphoric that I even find myself hugging Serena and telling her that if the opening night goes half as well, we're on to a winner. She's probably the only person in the backstage, makeshift dressing rooms not dancing around the place, though. She just looks at me with her scary glasses on and calmly says, 'Beware of a good dress rehearsal, my dear.'

There's a cosy, quiet pub around the corner which everyone adjourns to and Daniel and I stroll there together, arm in arm. In a friendly, casual way, of course. This is not a date . . .

The actor who plays Oberon, King of the Fairies, is chatting up Barbara big-time, so I don't actually get to do what I normally would: i.e., drag her off to the Ladies and dissect the whole behind-the-scenes sub-plot that's unfolding romance-wise.

'So, you must have been surprised to see Daniel here tonight?' she asks me, in very pointed girl-code for: 'Because I certainly was. What exactly is going on and what's the story?'

'Yes, he's offered to invest in the show,' is my deflective answer. Girl-code, for: 'Don't ask, not too sure myself what's going on, but believe me, you'll be the first to know.'

Oberon is too busy yakking away at her for us to get any more chance to talk, and Daniel and I . . .

It's the weirdest thing. I think, possibly because I know this isn't a date, I can really relax and chat and be myself with him.

He's completely mad about the show, raves about it and is insisting on coming to the opening night with me next week, and all the time we're sitting closer and closer to each other. He's right in my body space now and I'm NOT imagining it. At one stage, his fingers just lightly brush off mine as he's picking up a drink, and it's like . . . electricity. I don't think I've ever felt such an overwhelming physical attraction to any guy like this before. It's like every time he as much as runs his hands through the big mop of curls, all I can do is wonder what he looks like with the shirt off . . .

I only had two drinks, I swear, but when he offers to drive me home, I don't put up any resistance. We say our goodbyes, slip out of the pub, and before I know it, I'm plonked in the passenger seat of his posh Aston Martin, unable to take my eyes off him. He's focused on the road ahead, but every now and then turns to me to see if I'm OK . . . I am . . . absolutely . . . I just can't help wondering what would happen if I was to slip my hand inside his shirt, that's all . . .

This is not a date, Vicky, this is not a date . . .

Too soon, way too soon for my liking, we're outside my house, and for once I'm not even embarrassed that there's a skip sitting outside it. He turns off the engine and I know, I just know he's waiting to be asked in, so I go for it.

'Daniel, there's something I have to ask you . . .'

'Mmmm . . .' He's moved in close to me, and we both know exactly what's going to happen. But I have to ask him first, it's burning me up.

'Is it true . . . now you can tell me to mind my own business . . . but is it true that you've . . . you've . . . and, you know, now that I'm about to ask you I'm fully aware of how nosey this sounds . . . but . . . is it true that you're seeing someone in the States?'

'Who told you that?' He's looking at me sideways now, and

for the first time in the whole, magical night, that teasing twinkle is gone from his eyes.

'Emm . . . well . . . I heard it at the office, when you were over there . . . I'm sorry, I was . . . emm . . . just curious, that's all.'

'Vicky, the last time I listened to office gossip, I think they had me married off about three different times, divorced then re-married with kids all over the place. What can I tell you? It's all total bollocks.'

'But you were in the States for so long, everyone said . . .'

'What exactly did they say?'

'Well, that there was a penthouse involved. And that you were moving in with . . . emm . . .'

Now he starts to laugh, the eyes crinkle up at the edges and I know he's back to himself again.

'Vicky, yes, I was in the US for a long time, and I can't tell you why, just trust me on that, OK?'

'OK.'

'Besides,' he says, turning slowly to me. 'If I were involved with someone else, would I be sitting here with you? Would I even attempt this?'

He puts both his hands on my face and we kiss. Slowly, gently, almost dreamily.

For a second he pulls away and I move with him.

'What, what's the matter?' Don't stop, not now . . .

'Now there's something I want to ask you.'

'Sure,' I say, wanting, desperately wanting to feel him kissing me again.

'Vicky, I know you date your fair share, and why shouldn't you, you're a beautiful woman, but . . . I'm not just some other guy to you, am I? You're not seeing anyone else?'

'Come back here,' is my answer, as I drag him over to me, kissing him hard now, intensely, like this has been building between us for the longest time.

Next thing, wordlessly, we're both getting out of the car and going inside. I don't even have time to explain or apologize for the state of my house/building site, we're in my tiny hallway, undressing each other, me slowly unbuttoning his shirt and trousers, him peeling my underwear off, almost in slow motion, like he has all the time in the world. Then, we're going upstairs, strewing a trail of clothes behind us, and at one stage, one of us, I'm not even sure who, kicks over a pile of tiles, sending them crashing to the hard, granite floor.

'I'll replace them in the morning,' he says thickly, in-between kissing, which is so intense and hungry now I can hardly bear it. Finally, this is it. Me and Daniel, naked and alone in my room, filthy unmade bed and all. Oh my God, now it's happening so quick.

We're going so fast, I can barely take in what's happening . . . then out of nowhere, in-between his furious kisses I suddenly open my big mouth and say, 'Daniel, you're like a gazzillionaire and you've probably had sex with supermodels and gymnasts . . .'

'Shhh,' he whispers, kissing my earlobe, then my neck, then down further still, making me groan with pleasure . . .

Oh my God, that's it.

I, Vicky Harper, think I'm in love.

Chapter Twenty-Five

Definitely in love. Stop the presses. It's official. We did it so many times last night that neither of us slept a wink, but you know what? I don't care. Dawn is slowly creeping through the shutters, we're cuddled up together, and I honestly think I could die and go to heaven, right here, right now.

Daniel, being Daniel, however, starts messing.

'So this is where you live,' he muses, staring at the plastered, unpainted walls, the raw, unvarnished bare floorboards and, oh yeah, let's not forget the industrial-sized bag of cavity wall insulation lying in the corner. 'Now, OK, it's not exactly the Ritz Carlton . . .'

'Enough out of you!' I say, wide awake now, playfully throwing a pillow at him.

'You're supposed to say, "It'll be lovely when it's finished. And I hope that I'm still alive in the year two thousand and fifty to see the end result." '

He roars laughing, then leans over to my bedside table.

'So what's this then?'

Oh shit, now he's picking up the battered, well-thumbed law of attraction book. OK, I say, reasoning quickly to myself, it could be worse, he could have found far more embarrassing books than that. *How to Make Any Man Fall in Love With You*, for one. Or *Seven Secrets of Highly*

Seductive Women. Or, God forbid, *How Camilla Did It.*

'It's actually . . . emm . . . a kind of philosophy book,' I say primly, or as primly as I can sound given that I'm stark naked with only a sheet covering me. 'Myself and Laura and Barbara are all . . . emm . . . sort of . . . reading it at the moment . . . we're all very interested in . . . emm, you know, mind-expanding . . . stuff. Metaphysics and the like. What can I say? I have very brainy friends.'

He flicks open a page randomly and starts reading aloud.

The law of attraction is obedient and will always deliver whatever you wish. But beware, as with every genie in the bottle scenario, there's a caveat. Focus on whatever you don't want and it's a proven fact that the law of attraction will manifest what it is you're thinking of. Put simply: dread something and you'll summon it towards you with the speed of light.

He tosses it aside and snuggles into me again, warm and cuddly, and next thing we're kissing again and he's murmuring into my ear, 'So if I keep saying "I don't want sex with Vicky" then this'll keep happening?'

'Now you're getting the hang of it,' I whisper, sliding underneath him this time. 'Clever boy.'

Oh my God, I'd forgotten how bloody amazing being in love is. I've all the symptoms: the inane grin on my face, the glow in my cheeks from a sensational night with my lover, lack of appetite for anything other than sex and more of it. It's like I've been so starved of any kind of romance, love, affection you name it, for so long that now I'm making up for lost time and savouring every fabulous minute of it.

At six a.m., we're both in the shower together and it's just so amazing. He watches me dressing and the fact that we both have to turn up on the set of the Original Eyes commercial is the only thing stopping me from hopping back into bed with him and happily spending the rest of the day there. We leap into his car, and although he offers to drive me straight to Ardmore Studios, where the shoot is to take place, for once, I'm finally able to think straight and ask him to drop me off where I abandoned my car last night.

'Wouldn't it look a bit suspicious if we both arrived together?' I say, not letting go of his hand.

'Do we care?' is his teasing answer as we kiss goodbye.

'Hey, you're the one who says there's enough gossip about you in the office!'

I'm just about to clamber out of his car and get into my own when he pulls me back.

'You know, Vicky, I want us to go on a first date. A proper first date. Last night doesn't count.'

'Doesn't count?'

'Introductory sex, that's all. Only a warm-up act, baby. No, I want you and me to . . . well, I'm keeping it a surprise, but will you keep next weekend free?'

'Mmmm, you talked me into it.' My hand is on his thigh now, and I'm not messing, I could leap on him in the car right this minute and risk arrest for indecent exposure. And I wouldn't care.

'Sure you're not dating any other guys? No other boyfriends you want to tell me about?'

'Eh . . . lemme think,' I say teasing, pretending to be ticking guys off my fingers. 'No, he's not around, emm, no . . . he's having electric-shock therapy . . . ehh . . . no, he didn't make parole this week, nope, you're in luck . . . this weekend is clear.'

'And you have the cheek to call me a messer?'

I just laugh and look at him adoringly, in all of his gorgeousness, still unable to believe my sheer good luck.

'No, Daniel, there's no other man in my life. Hand on heart; I'm not involved with anyone else. Believe me.'

'Not to put too fine a point on it, or anything, but any time I bump into you socially, you are with someone else.'

His tone is light and breezy, but . . . for some reason, he's not smiling now.

'Hey, can I help it if I'm like . . . this irresistible sex goddess that men go bananas over?' I tease. Jaysus, if he only knew the irony of that statement.

'Vicky . . .' he's turned to me now, and is focusing on me in that dark, intense way he has. 'I'm serious. Believe me, I've been down this road before and it's . . . well, it's not something I'm prepared to do again.'

A hint of an ex-girlfriend in the air, one who cheated on him, maybe? Not that it matters, not now that we're together. As if I'd ever treat him like that, *ever* . . .

'There's no one else. I swear.'

'Final answer?'

'Final answer.'

I remember reading somewhere that the first signs of a couple having a hot office romance are: a) they arrive in separate cars; b) they studiously ignore each other in front of other people; and then c) they leave within a few minutes of each other.

Not me and Daniel though.

I'm as happy as a sand boy, really, nauseatingly Broadway happy, singing away in the car as I drive to the studio, absolutely bursting to have a full de-briefing session with the girls about this latest, miraculous, unbelievable twist. Memories of last night keep flooding back to me in wonderful, glowing waves. No, there's no doubt about it. I'm in love. Funny, I think, pulling my car through, the things that life can throw up at you. One day I'm tearing my hair out over Ex-Files, sorry I mean Peter, then Dipso Man turns up just to shatter any romantic illusions I might have had about him, and then . . .

Daniel. They were like the warm-up act to The Real Thing.

I glance at the clock on the dashboard. Seven a.m. Well, there is one person I know who'll be up and about at this hour who I can share this unbelievable news with . . . Laura. I ring her from my mobile and she answers straight away.

'Vicky! I didn't expect to hear from you today, isn't your first big shoot for the commercial this morning?'

'On the way there now. I just had to tell you . . . oh Laura, last night I had the most fantastic, mind-blowing sex I have EVER had in my entire life!'

'Oh really? Because I cleaned up baby vomit and unblocked a toilet. But please, continue.'

'With . . . now are you ready for this? Daniel Best!'

'Oh my God! Full story, please. And omit nothing, however trivial.'

'I'll have to fill you in later, I'm almost at the studio now. I'll call in after work and go through it forensically with you. All I'll say for now is, prepare to be truly astonished at just how miraculous the law of attraction can be.'

'Yes, and on that very subject, I have a news bulletin for you, too. I had tea with Desmond and his mother and he's asked me out again. To a black-tie charity do at the Four Seasons, no less. Can you believe it?'

'Oh my God, you just up-sexed me! I'll call in to you tonight for the full truth and nothing but!'

I'm thrilled, 100 per cent ecstatic for Laura that everything's finally turning around for her, and Barbara and me . . . but very quickly go back to daydreaming about Daniel again. Oh God, I feel all warm inside just thinking about him. This really, really is it, I think, this is him, this is The One.

All I have to do is not mess it up. That's all.

With perfect synchronicity, his car arrives at the same time as mine, we jump out together and hug like we haven't just parted company twenty minutes ago. I know, all a bit syrupy/gooey, especially at this hour of the morning, but then that's just what LURVE does to me.

Don't mess it up, don't mess it up . . .

Something vaguely comes back to me about the bit he read from the law of attraction book this morning, the part about whatever you dread you attract, but I shove it to the back of my mind where it belongs. No, life at the moment is like in a sit-com, where the lead character says, 'What can possibly go wrong?'

Turns out I don't have to wait too long to find out.

Daniel and I head into the studio, which is looking just *amazing*, far more impressive even than the designer's sketches, a girlie boudoir come to life, all in black and white, with a huge, Victorian gilded mirror dominating the set.

'What do you think?' I ask Daniel, proudly.

'Talk about the wow factor,' he says, squeezing my hand.

To be honest, when Sophie approved the preliminary sketches, I was kind of afraid it would end up looking like an amateur production of *Gigi*, but it works, even beyond my wildest dreams. Our two models – the one who's going on a first date, and the one whose Original Sin products she's busy coveting – are in the make-up trailer and I'm just about to call Amanda to see where she is when Sophie strides over to us, in top form.

'Daniel, sweetie,' she coos. 'And Vicky, doesn't this look fantastic?'

And I'm not joking, the bobbed hair is so perfectly executed, she must have been up since about four a.m. getting it to sit so obediently.

'Always good to see a happy client,' Daniel smiles, shaking her hand.

'I didn't expect to see you here this morning.'

'Actually, I just came to support my girl here,' Daniel says, cool as a fish's fart, and as if to further highlight our 'new couple' status, the dote even slips his arm around my waist. I glow, then blush as Sophie gives a knowing, woman-of-the-world-type nod.

'I see. Well, our director's here too, come and say hi. He's just over here, setting up.'

'Oh yeah,' says Daniel as the three of us walk over towards a vast lighting rig, where there's a few guys with their backs to us. 'Somebody . . . Howard, isn't that who we normally use?'

'Yes. Tom? Come and meet Daniel Best. And Vicky Harper too, of course.'

Oh f★★k.

No. No, this cannot be happening.

It's him. Tom, no Tim, no Tom. Dipso Man himself.

He turns around, spots me and is straight over, planting a stale boozy kiss on my cheek.

'Vicky! Yes, you could say that I certainly met Vicky,' he says in the gravelly voice.

Please don't say any more: I'm looking at him, willing him to shut up with the panic in my eyes . . . please just go back to your rig now, and I'll somehow get Daniel out of here and everything will be OK . . . please . . .

But Daniel picks up on something. Don't ask me how, but before I know what's going on, he says to Tom, 'So have you two worked together before, or something?'

Please, Tom or whatever your bloody name is, just say yes and leave it at that, please, this man is too important to me . . .

But he doesn't.

'As a matter of fact, Vicky and I are dating. Hey, yesterday does count as a date, doesn't it, my dear?'

Chapter Twenty-Six

The chances are I might, just might have been able to get away with that. That's if I'd been lucky enough to drag Daniel out of the studio, sit him down and explain.

The whole truth, everything. I had brunch with the guy and that was it. And OK so maybe I did end up with Daniel that night, but it was all unplanned and . . . and maybe we'll even end up having a laugh about it. I mean, it is kind of funny when you think about it really, I wonder weakly. You know, what are the odds and all that . . .

But it's mayhem on the set, completely hectic, I'm being dragged in about twenty different directions and I'm not even sure where Daniel is. Then just as we're going for a lighting rehearsal, I spot him, over by a monitor, arms crossed, standing alone and looking deep in thought. But as I move over to him, smiling hopefully, shrugging, wanting to talk to him, desperately needing to explain, he moves off.

'Everything OK?' is all I get to say to him.

'Not now, Vicky.'

'Look, I know this looks terrible, but you have to let me explain . . .'

'Nothing to explain. You went straight from one guy to another. On the same day, for Christ's sake. And what's worse is that you lied to me.'

'It wasn't like that! You have to listen to me, Daniel . . .'

'You looked me in the eye and you lied.'

'I didn't! You have to hear me out . . .'

'Time and a place, Vicky.'

And he strides off, ostensibly to look at the set but really to get away from me.

None of this is helped by Tom in an embarrassingly loud voice clapping me on the back and saying: 'So we must have that night-time date we talked about soon, my dear. Day-time socializing isn't really me, somehow. Maybe dinner after the shoot tonight?'

I glance around, hoping, praying that Daniel is too far away to have heard, but he's actually a lot closer than I'd have thought.

'Tom, please stop this, you're mortifying me,' I hiss, not wanting my private business to become some kind of side-show.

'I'm afraid I don't understand, Vicky. You were all on for it yesterday. Not twenty-four hours ago.'

Then I turn back to where Daniel was standing a second ago, but now he's gone. Oh God, this is such a nightmare. Then, just as I think things can't get much worse, guess what? They do. Amanda's over, asking if the on-set rumour is true; that I'm simultaneously dating the director *and* Daniel Best? And doesn't he have a girlfriend in the States anyway? Now I feel sick. I'm an 'on-set rumour', and am suddenly too weak and shaky to even care.

'I . . . just can't get into that right now,' I say to her, in a tiny, weak voice. Because if I do, there's a good chance I'll burst into tears. Bad enough that the crew must think I'm some kind of tart-for-hire, but now I can't get near Daniel, can't even see him.

By lunchtime, hours later, we've three shots in the can, three more to do and there's still no sign of him. He's not in the canteen with everyone else, and when I try calling his mobile, he doesn't answer.

I actually don't know how much more of this I can take, so I slip outside for a breath of air. Kind-hearted old Amanda is straight on my heels, asking me if I'm all right, and offering me a cigarette, even though I don't smoke.

'You OK?' she asks, genuinely concerned, bless her.

'Mmmm,' is all I can nod, by way of an answer. Mainly because if I elaborate further, the hard rock of pain and sheer disbelief inside me will dissolve in a big flood of tears. And I've too much to do today. Amanda and I have worked too hard, and there's just too much at stake here. I have to put a brave face on things, suffer it out here today, somehow get through the day, then sort out my private life when I get home.

'Emm, Vicky, it's none of my business or anything, but just to let you know that Daniel said something about going back to the office. Anyway, he's left and said he won't be back.'

Right then. Message received, loud and clear.

We wrap on the dot of five, the first commercial successfully in the can, and everyone on the set is in high old form at how well the day's shoot has gone, and dying to get to the nearest pub for a drink. Everyone except me, that is. Somehow, I managed to get through the awful, miserable day, but as soon as we're wrapped, I can't get out of there fast enough.

'Are you sure you won't come for a drink?' Amanda asks, as we walk towards our cars. 'I hope you don't mind me saying, but you really look like you could do with one.'

'I'm fine,' I lie. 'Just tired. I need to swing by my office and then just go home and collapse.'

'OK. But, well, it's none of my business, but . . . well, you know I'm here for you if you ever need to chat. And whatever is or isn't going on between you and Daniel, well . . . I'm sure you can sort it out. He's a nice guy, Vicky, he's one of the good 'uns. I promise.'

I'm too touched to even answer her, so I settle for a big teary hug instead. Then when I'm finally, finally alone in my car I do what I've wanted to do all day . . . dissolve into a flood of hot, stinging tears. By far the worst kind, and I should know.

I can put up with bloody Tom and his boozy breath and all the lewd, suggestive shite he's been coming out with all day. I can even put up with being the gossipy talk of the sound stage.

But I can't put up with Daniel having the wrong idea about me, I just can't.

I try calling him again from the car, but it's his voicemail, yet again, so I leave a teary message in a weak, wobbly voice just asking him to call. Which he doesn't. So then I call Barbara, forgetting the time, and that she has a tech rehearsal tonight, so I've absolutely no chance of getting to comb things through with her either. Shit.

Force of habit more than anything drags me back to the office on my way home, just to check up on emails, and make sure everything's on track for the big opening night of *A Midsummer Night's Dream* this Friday. The sheer bloody bad luck and unfairness of what happened this morning has now slowly begun to fade a bit, and now I've moved on to the second stage of getting a shock: anger.

For God's sake, I'm now starting to think, in a sudden flash of irritation, if Daniel is going to flounce off in a snot without even listening to my perfectly innocent explanation, then sure what hope is there for us? I mean, yes, OK, in his shoes, if I discovered in front of a whole studio full of colleagues that he'd been with someone else the same day as me . . . OK, yes, I might be a bit miffed, but I'd at least listen to an explanation, wouldn't I? Course I bloody would. And when I'd heard the full story, I'd laugh and then forgive, in that order.

Feeling a little bit stronger, I park the car, and just as I'm heading into the main door downstairs that leads to my office, James, our lovely, elderly doorman, stops me in my tracks.

'Eh, Vicky love? Just to let you know you've a visitor upstairs. The two young ones you have working for you have left, and I wasn't sure what to do, but your man seemed happy enough to hang on for you.'

'Oh, thanks, James, thanks so much,' I say, my mood suddenly gone from irritated despair to euphoric elation in a nano-second.

It's him, it just has to be, I think, pressing the lift-call button. Of course it is! Come on, come on . . . No, the lift's too slow, so I race up the stairs instead. How could I even have thought Daniel, my lovely wonderful Daniel, would ever stay in a snot with me over such a stupid misunderstanding? I think, racing faster. Wait till you see, I'll fall into his arms now, we'll end up having a great old laugh about the whole situation, and it'll be just like putting the clock back to last night, when everything was wonderful between us. I finally get to the top of the stairs, out of breath and cursing my unfitness and . . . there he is.

Except it's not Daniel at all.

Eager Eddie is sitting outside the office, carrying a bunch of roses so big it's like he might fall over.

'Vicky . . .' he says, rising as soon as he sees me. 'I just wanted to say that . . .'

'You need to leave.' I cut him off, all of my anger and irritation now flooding back to me. 'Now. No discussion, no explanation, I want you gone.'

'I just had to tell you that I felt really bad about the way we left things between us . . .'

'Did you just say between *us*? Eddie, how can I stress this to you, there is no *us*. Never was, never will be. I'm giving you five seconds to get out of here, and then I'm calling security.'

My voice is hoarse and cracked with anger and impatience and sheer exhaustion. And I know I'm pushing it a bit when I refer to poor dothery James downstairs as 'security', but it's the best I can come up with off the top of my head.

Eddie just looks at me, nodding and weighing up whether I'm for real or not, so I glare right back at him, not budging. After what feels like an eternity, but is probably only a few seconds, I eventually say, 'Right then, that's it, I'm getting help.' I stride purposefully off towards the stairwell, but he's hot on my heels, grabbing my arm roughly and twisting me towards him. OK, now I'm actually starting to get intimidated, and am trying to wrench myself from his grip when the lift door suddenly glides open.

And out steps Daniel.

'What's going on?' he asks, taking in the scene in a glance.

I really do not believe this.

Suddenly, it's like everything's happening in a sickening slow motion.

'Vicky, really I need to speak to you,' Eddie splutters at me, with a face like an outraged sprout. 'I didn't come all this way to be thrown out.'

'I asked a question,' Daniel repeats, slowly, his voice cutting like ice. 'What's going on?'

'I need you to leave right now,' I snarl at Eddie, out of nowhere finding the strength to wrench my arm back from him.

'Better ask this bitch here,' head case Eddie practically roars at me, threateningly, intimidatingly, almost violently, as he flings the flowers on the floor and marches off down the stairs. 'You're nothing but a bitch, do you hear me? Stupid pathetic bitch! And you have the nerve to call yourself my girlfriend?' And he's gone. Finally.

I can't hold the tears back any more, I'm just so relieved to see Daniel. There's a long, awkward silence as we just look at each other, him taking in the whole scene. Red roses strewn all over the floor, me standing there trembling, on the verge of tears.

'I'm so glad you're here . . .' I eventually begin, realizing I'd better be the first to talk.

But there's something wrong. He's just looking at me, with such a weird, hurt expression that it's breaking my heart.

'I don't get it,' is all he says, simply. 'You're still seeing that guy, too? So how many of us do you have on the go, Vicky? Do I have to take a number and wait in line?'

'Daniel, you have to listen to me . . .'

'Why couldn't you just have been honest with me and said you're seeing other guys? Lies and deceit, two things I just can't handle.'

'Daniel, please, you're not even giving me a *chance* . . .!'

'You know, I can take anything as long as people are straight with me, and you couldn't even do that much.'

'Daniel!'

If he'd been furiously angry about it, I probably could have handled it, but he isn't. He's cool and controlled, and is just looking at me, shaking his head in sad disappointment. And that's what's worse than anything.

A split second later he's gone.

Still numb from the whole miserable day, I somehow make my way to Laura's for tea, sympathy and a shoulder to cry on. The kids are all with George Hastings for the night; unbelievable I know, but out of nowhere he's suddenly decided to start acting like father of the year. Laura answers the door, looking jaw-droppingly stunning in a . . . wait for it . . . brand new outfit.

'Bought it with my column money,' she says, incorrectly interpreting my face-like-a-beaten-tambourine expression. But then Laura's famous for never spending a bean on herself, ever; whenever there's spare cash it invariably goes on the kids. 'Well, aren't I allowed a treat once in a while?'

'Ehh . . . yeah . . . yeah, of course,' I say, automatically following her into her spotless kitchen, where she pours me a very welcome glass of white wine.

'You look like you could use this, dearest. Now, sit down there and spill,' she says, gently, bless her. And out it all comes tumbling, with the same play-by-play of emotions normally reserved for world cup finals. Laura, as ever, is cool, unflappable and, typical lawyer, plays devil's advocate.

'You've got to put yourself into Daniel's shoes,' she says, taking a demure sip from her glass of vino. 'Imagine how you'd feel if the boot was on the other foot. Suppose you were the one to have this fabulous romantic night with him, then, a few hours later, accidentally discover that he was out with someone else on the same day? Then when you go to his office to clear it all up, there's some other bird there, causing a hysterical scene with him and flinging flowers all over the place? How would you like it?'

'Not a bit,' is all I can mutter, numbly. 'It's just killing me that I never even got a chance to explain. Every time I try to call, he doesn't answer. And now he's out there, thinking the worst of me, and . . .'

I'm interrupted by the doorbell ringing, and I look at Laura in surprise. Up she gets to answer it, and a second later is leading Desmond Lawlor into the kitchen.

Oh dear God, she's going on a date. Tonight's her date, and I've been so caught up in my own emotional mini-drama that I forgot, and now here I am playing gooseberry and generally ruining the mood for her with my whingey moroseness.

I am such a crap friend.

I do my best to sound upbeat, chirpy and bright as we

chit-chat with Desmond about the charity do they're off to tonight.

As soon as I've stayed long enough to be polite, but not so long as to outstay my welcome, nor to taint the place with the overwhelming whiff of 'loser' which must be practically reeking from my pores at this stage, I'm out of there.

And about a half-hour later, I'm back. Back in the freezing, dark, empty, lonely building-site that I call home. The scene of the crime. Remembering last night, as if it was a dream. Like I could forget.

I try his phone one last time. He doesn't answer, so I collapse on to one of my mother's patio seats, flinging the phone as far away from me as I can.

So how long did that happiness last, I wonder? Barely twelve hours, by my calculation.

Serves me right for dreaming.

Chapter Twenty-Seven

But the show must go on. Somehow Wednesday, the big open-ing night, comes around. I'm not quite sure how I managed to drag myself through the last couple of days, but now here we are, in the Iveagh Gardens, ready to rock and roll.

Numbness and hard work to the exclusion of all else, there you go, that's the Vicky Harper remedy for dealing with heartache. And with every day, whaddya know, it does actually fade a bit. Or at least, that is, it will. I have to go back into Best's next week to view the edited commercial, which Sophie's insisting I sit in on. I'm looking forward to it about as much as I would to root-canal work, but I made this mess, attracted it even, and now, somehow, I'm just going to have to deal with the consequences, aren't I? Besides, given the way this awful, never-ending week has played out, chances are Daniel will be avoiding me just as much as he has been since Monday. Oh God, I still wince at the memory. And what have I got to look forward to? SIX more commercials to be shot over the next few weeks, all of which are to be directed by bloody Tom and his useless, big, alcoholicky mouth.

Barbara reckons I over-attracted. 'Huh?' was my bewildered answer. Tried too hard, she explained, focused on too many guys at the same time with . . . disastrous consequences. In her defence, she did take full responsibility for being the architect

338

of the multi-dating strategy, and has kindly said we'll rethink, revise and re-launch me back on the singles scene the minute the show is over, behind her, and she gets her life back again. After the show, after this weekend.

Which bring me to my next question: and then what? Back to trawling clubs, pubs and bars again? So I can be fixed up with: a) more obsessive head cases; b) guys obsessed with their exes; or c) alcoholics? And all the while ruining any chance I might have had with the one that I really, genuinely did fall for?

Not a tempting proposition, really, when you think about it. And what are the odds that I'll walk into some night spot, meet someone remotely acceptable, who'll be single and available and not a mental case or a booze hound, who'll call when he actually says he will, whose light will be 'on', who everyone will like, and who I'll eventually, years down the line, end up happily married to?

Oh for f**k's sake. I've more chance of all six of my numbers coming up in Saturday night's Lotto draw.

And no word from Daniel. Not a single thing. Nothing.

It's almost showtime and Paris, Nicole and I have been here at the Iveagh Gardens pretty much since sunrise this morning, with the usual list of stuff that can't be tackled till the last minute. The weather just couldn't be more perfect, mild and still after a fabulously rare sunny day, and more of the same forecast for our next two shows. But tonight's the night, tonight's the big one. I've invited five of the hottest agents in town, along with just about every casting director you can name. And what's more *they all show*. It's just gone seven thirty now, thirty minutes till curtain up, and the seats are almost full to bulging. I've never seen anything like it; the atmosphere is just electric. Paris had this inspired brainwave of enclosing coloured fairy wings with the invitations, the kind you buy for kids in Marks & Spencer, and some fashionistas here are actually wearing them, adding to the whole, wonderful, festive party atmosphere.

I spend the last half-hour to curtain frantically nipping out front then backstage, although everything seems to be running even more smoothly than I could ever have hoped for. I even get to give Barbara a good-luck hug backstage, where I find her near the outdoor loos, sucking on a cigarette, and paler than I've ever seen her looking in her life. I think she's too nervous even to be narky, so I leave her to it, and run back to front of house, where Laura is just arriving with the three older kids and . . . Desmond.

'How's our girl holding up?' she asks me, as we all hug and air-kiss.

'Grade one rattiness,' I say, far from calm myself. 'Which means she's probably on the verge of throwing up, but if she gives half the performance she turned in at the dress rehearsal, I reckon we're home and dry.'

'That's wonderful, dearest, but I was, in fact, asking about you.'

'Oh . . . me? Oh, sure, I'm absolutely fine!' I over-compensate in front of all the others. 'Nervous about the show, you know, of course, obviously, but . . . so far so good!'

She looks at me keenly and nods curtly, girl-code for: 'I'll speak to you later, in private, when we've time to chat properly.'

'Now all of you thank Vicky for the tickets,' she says sternly to the kids.

'Yeah . . . ehhh . . . thanks very much,' they all mutter in unison, but then chances are they'd all far rather be at *Pirates of the Caribbean* or whatever blockbuster is showing at the multiplex.

'Yes, you are kind,' says Desmond in that kindly fatherly way he has. 'A cultural excursion for the whole family is just the ticket, really.'

Oh my God, this must be getting serious. He just said 'the whole family' without batting an eyelid.

My own family are here too, in force, messer brothers, smug married sisters-in-law, even my Auntie Maisie, who, judging by the flushed look of her, I think might just have had a gin and tonic too many before they all got here.

'Why have you not got us sitting beside celebrities, Vicky love?' she hisses at me. 'I'd only kill to meet your man that reads the *Nine O'Clock News*. Look, he's sitting over there all on his own, ah go on, why can't you introduce me?'

I make my excuses and get the hell out of there to run around backstage. Five to eight.

'Ready or not, here we go,' says Serena, as I wish her luck.

'Whatever tonight's outcome,' she says, in that cool, even way she has, 'I want you to know it's been a pleasure working with you, Vicky. You deliver on your promises, nothing is a problem for you, and you keep well out of my hair. You can count on me to come work with you any time. And believe me, there aren't too many producers I'd say that to.' Now I know she's most likely only being polite, but it's possibly the nicest thing anyone's said to me all day. All week, in fact.

Paris and Nicole excitedly whisper to me that they're going to slip out front and watch the show from behind the back row, but I decide to stay behind-the-scenes instead. It's been such a full-on, hectic day that it's actually just what I need, to be alone, for the next few hours at least, right at the very side of the stage so I can see what's going on, but so well back from the action that no one can see me. There's a few bushes behind, which kind of shelter me, and a lovely, peaceful spot for me to gratefully plonk down on, which I do.

One quick prayer that nothing goes wrong and we're off.

Oh my God, it's going even more magically than I could have hoped for. Barbara's just made her grand entrance, and was a magnet to the eye. Real star quality in action. Now we're off to the forest, Puck and Titania are doing their thing, there are actual roars of laughter coming from the audience, and so many spontaneous rounds of applause, I've lost count. I hug my knees with sheer relief at how well it's going, and now that we're on the rollercoaster, so to speak, there's really nothing to do but sit back and enjoy the show.

And what a show. For the first time, me, the uncultured, the one who barely knows the difference between a bona fide posh play and a kiddies' panto, can really see what all the fuss and hype surrounding Serena Stroheim is all about. And well-deserved too: she's woven magic out of a fairly nondescript park setting, and is really giving people a night to remember for a long, long time to come.

Next thing it's the interval and, no kidding, the thunderous round of applause goes on for about five minutes. I head back out front, back into the throng, back to find Paris and Nicole and to check that all's OK. I'm just about to make my way through the crowd to the front entrance, when a director from the Children's Hospital, an elderly, brisk doctor called Muriel Stanford, grabs my arm, stopping me to chat about the show. She's raving away, saying it's just the best thing she's seen in the longest time, and is just asking me why this couldn't become an annual event when . . . no, no . . . I must be seeing things. I *must* be.

I do my best to focus on Muriel and gratefully accept all the sweet things she's saying about the show, but it's very hard to concentrate because, in the thick of the crowd, coming towards me, I'd swear I can see Daniel.

I don't even have time to react. Muriel pulls me back into the conversation, and I'm aware that I'm being rude by glancing over her shoulder, but there's no mistaking it. It *is* Daniel.

He's been grabbed aside now by a gang of impossibly

well-dressed women, all of whom seem to know him really well, and who are trying to get him to sit beside them for the second half. I can't hear what he's saying to them, it's too packed and noisy and crowded, and I can't even tell whether he's seen me or not. And I'm nervous and jumpy now, and I don't know why. I mean, why would he come here?

There's no reason for him to be here, unless . . .

No, the sensible thing for me to do is to not even attempt to finish that sentence. If he had come here to see me, then why doesn't he just come over? Instead he's laughing away with those girls; I can even hear him loud and clear doing what sounds like his Jack Nicholson impression. Or maybe it was his Schwarzenegger, it's hard to tell the difference with all this noise and racket going on.

On cue, the sound boys ring a loud bell, just like at a proper theatre, to let everyone know it's almost time for Act Two to kick off, sorry, I mean Part Two. I'm still deep in chat with Doctor Muriel, who's invited me to come out to the hospital to visit the kids, an invitation I'm only too delighted to take her up on. The Part Two bell goes off again, more furiously this time as the interval's gone way over time; a good sign that everyone's enjoying themselves. I can't linger any longer, I make my excuses and slip back to my quiet, secluded little backstage hiding place, unnoticed by anyone, I think.

I'm wrong. Totally wrong. Just as the lights come up on the second half, there's a rustle in the hedgerow and bushes behind me. I turn around, startled, and there he is. Really.

Daniel squeezes in beside me and because the space is so enclosed and cramped, we're now sitting side-by-side, practically on top of each other.

It's the weirdest thing. We look at each other and though neither of us says anything, you can hear the odd Shakespearian line wafting through from the stage.

Lord, what fools these mortals be . . .

OK, so we both smirk at bit at that, then the smiling stops, and now he's looking at me in that really intent, focused way that he has.

'I came to say sorry,' he eventually says.

'I never lied to you,' I whisper, terrified we'll put off the actors with this play-within-a-play that's going on under their noses. 'You have to believe me. I had one lousy brunch with Tom . . . whatever his name is, decided he was a raving alcoholic and that was it.'

'It doesn't matter,' he says softly, moving in closer.

'And that other Scottish guy? Eager Eddie we all call him. The guy is a complete obsessive, he was just waiting for me outside the office, I had nothing to do with him being there . . .'

'It's OK, shhhhhhh . . .'

'And . . .and . . .' I'm glad we're whispering now, because if we were on our own, there's a good chance I might start shouting. Can't help it, it's just days of pent-up rage and annoyance all spilling out in one messy go. 'You never even gave me a chance to explain. You just jumped to conclusions and ran.'

'Vicky, I'm sorry. I just didn't know what to think. I hadn't a clue what was going on. And I didn't want to be made an eejit of. But I just wanted you to know that I've really regretted the way I carried on. I thought the best thing for me to do was back off for a bit, but then . . .'

'But then . . . what?' I'm looking at him, hardly daring to hope. No kidding, but the entire success or failure of the whole up-till-now-disastrous 'project Vicky' depends on what comes out of his mouth next.

'Well, I knew tonight was a big night for you . . .'

He trails off, looking into the middle distance, and I think, oh OK then. He just wanted to wish me luck and, well, I suppose we do have to work together, so he wanted things nice and tied up between us. He's a nice guy that doesn't like awkwardness, particularly with anyone he has to work with.

I'm just a loose end that needed tying up.

'Vicky,' he eventually says, softly this time. More like the Daniel I knew from the other wonderful night. 'What do you say to . . .'

'To . . .?'

'To, well, us dating exclusively. You know, just you and me. And that's it. And no drunk directors or mental Scotsmen or that other guy I met you with at the PR dinner . . .'

'Ex-Files. That's his nickname. Obsessed with his ex, who he then got back with. That very night, if I'm not much mistaken.'

'So,' he says, looking at me in that cute sideways-on way. 'Do you want to think about it?'

Oh my God. This must be . . . well, religious people must feel like this when unbelievable miracles happen, out of nowhere. I feel like I should be at a Lourdes grotto and not a city-centre public park.

I pull him by his shirt, in closer to me. 'I don't need to think about it. The answer is a big, huge yes. Yes please, in fact.'

His lips are a fraction away from mine now, almost touching but not quite.

'There's nothing I wouldn't do,' he says, smiling now, 'to get you to come on that proper first date with me. Like we talked about . . .'

'Did you just say there's nothing you wouldn't do?'

'Yeah, of course.'

'You might just regret that . . .'

'Why would I regret that?'

'Because all my family are here tonight and . . . well, now you can say no if you want . . .'

'Say no to what?'

'Braver men have run a mile from situations like this . . .'

'Vicky!'

'Well, the thing is . . . do you think you'd be ready to meet them?'

Epilogue

The Butterfly's A.G.M. One Year Later.

Yes, an annual general meeting sounds a tad dramatic, I know, but then we just had so much to celebrate, it's unbelievable. Our progress in the last twelve months has been so staggering, that if you saw it in a movie, you'd say things like that never happened in real life. To illustrate, let me start with our Barbara.

Oh my God, the reviews for *A Midsummer Night's Dream* were so stupendously amazing that I probably could have written them myself. Barbara was pretty much unanimously hailed as the official Next Big Thing. ('Charisma you could surf on,' is one review that still makes me so proud of her.) She really, truly did steal the show, and deservedly went on to land herself an award for 'Best Newcomer'. ('Best newcomer?' she quipped at the time. 'So now I'm an overnight sensation after fifteen years?') Don't get me wrong, though, she was beside herself, particularly when she managed to nab probably the hottest, hippest actors' agent in town into the bargain. And she hasn't looked back since: one thing has seamlessly led on to another, and right now she's shooting a period drama about Henry VIII where she plays a very sexy, earthy, scene-stealing Anne Boleyn. Then after that, she's back to the theatre again, in an Oscar Wilde show, and best of all, after that she's off to Broadway to work with . . . wait for it, Serena Stroheim, who asked for her especially for a new show she's directing!

In all the years I've known Barbara, I've honestly never seen her so happy and fulfilled, still bowling fellas over like ninepins, but with work lined up until well into next year. Quite a change from twelve short months ago . . .

Sneakily, Laura and I did, to our shame, rejoice a bit at the reviews that Evil Angie got for *A Midsummer Night's Dream*. Or rather, the lack of them. Apparently for any actor, the worst kind of review is one in which you're completely and utterly ignored, as she was. If this was the show that effectively was a launching pad for Barbara, then it also spelt the end for that awful, minging cow. Evil Angie, however, isn't one of those people who can be happy for a more successful friend, so shortly after this she moved out of the flat she shared with Barbara, much to the jubilation of all concerned.

Laura probably had the single biggest U-turn of all of us. She is still happily writing away for *Tattle* magazine, making quite a name for herself, but most unbelievably of all, she has actually turned down briefs so she can continue writing, working from home, and doing what she really loves best: being with her family. Money is flowing in regularly now, so the days of going cap in hand to her mother are long gone AND Desmond is still on the scene. All very discreet, very demure, and very Laura.

There's never a question of him staying overnight when the kids are there, but they have snuck off for the odd weekend to cultural events all over the place, Glyndebourne for one, and there's talk of the Edinburgh Festival soon. In public, though, the only evidence that she and Desmond are a couple is when she dust-flecks him, which she does so regularly that Barbara and I reckon this can only be love.

And then there's me. Twelve months on and . . . yes, I'm single again. Daniel dumped me there a while back, said we were going nowhere and that he wanted to move on, so heigh ho, it's back to the singles scene for me . . .

I'm JOKING . . . ! Had you there for a second, though . . .

No, all messing aside, we're still together and I can summarize the last, fabulous year thus:

Number of fabulous weekends away: twelve. (Well, everyone knows the mini-break is the true definition of how you know you're really in a couple.)

Number of times Daniel, bless him, has braved my family with particular regard to messer brothers: an astonishing fifteen. Elder messer brother even went as far as to tell me that he can't find a single thing to slag Daniel about, which mightn't sound like it, but is actually praise from Caesar, and his ham-fisted way of saying, 'Yep, he's all right. One of us.' In fact, with the family, poor patient Daniel tends to get hijacked by messer brothers and is regularly dragged off to soccer matches/car shows/golf tournaments. The measure of the man is that I've yet to hear a complaint slip his lips. When pressed, all he'll say is, 'I like them, they're good crack.' And ever since they were all booked to see Ireland play in a friendly, then missed their flight because they were all in the airport bar and claimed never to have heard the final boarding calls, only for my fab wonderful Daniel, one quick phone call later, to arrange for a helicopter to take them, well, that sealed the deal as far as my siblings were concerned.

Length of our proper first date: seventy-two hours, which must be some kind of record, I reckon. It was just like I'd always dreamed, or as Barbara would say, visualized. The day after *A Midsummer Night's Dream* Daniel asked me to be ready and waiting at my house, and the only clue I had was that he said to bring my passport.

Oh, who am I kidding? The minute he said that, I knew exactly where we were going and where we'd be staying, and I was right. Yes. The very same trip that Daniel paid seriously over the odds for that night of the charity auction . . . Paris.

The Crillon hotel on Place de la Concorde, to be exact, in the most fabulous, romantic city in the world. Except, well, we didn't exactly see too much of it. In fact we spent so much time in our room/suite big enough to have a party in, that one of the chambermaids asked us, in broken English, if we were enjoying our honeymoon?

Most romantic gesture of all in the last year: And the award goes to . . . no, not the time he sent roses to the office for no reason, not even the time he whisked me off to New York to see . . . wait for it . . . the office space that Best's are setting up their US branch in. (Sample sales, here I come.) By the way, it's only on Madison Avenue, and that was the reason for his pro-longed stay away; and yes, he is buying a penthouse, but just for himself to stay in for when he's over there. (Ahem . . . and me and Laura and Barbara when the three of us skited over with empty suitcases for a shopping trip just before Christmas.)

No, amid a lot of dense competition for the title, the single most romantic gesture of the year happened just after Daniel and I got back, arm-in-arm and still all dewy-eyed, from our Paris first-date trip. It was lunchtime when we got home and, ever the gentleman, he dropped me back to my house and helped me carry luggage inside. (I've never been much of a one for travelling light.) Useless Builder was there, lunch roll in hand, feet up, reading the *Daily Star*. Well, I only wished I'd had a camcorder to record it: Daniel lit into him, demanding to know exactly what had been done since I'd been away, what was left to do, and an exact, wait for it, breakdown of what was left to do, including an estimated finish date? And this was the alpha male side of Daniel in action, not the messer side of him I know so well. Well, Useless Builder's jaw actually dropped, as I have to say, did mine. The upshot was that, one heated exchange/blazing row later, Daniel fired him, and organized the builders Best's use to finish the gig. Which they did, within about eight weeks and with minimum fuss.

Some mornings when I wake up in my picture-pretty little doll's house, and pad across my carpeted bedroom to my stunning, under-floor heated state-of-the-art bathroom, I often think back to that happy day.

It wasn't the roses, the champagne, the trips, the full-on romance that sealed the deal for me and Daniel.

It was the day he kicked Useless Builder's arse for me.

Because that's when I knew. Just *knew*.